INTO
THE
FIRE

Also by M.J. Arlidge

DI HELEN GRACE

Eeny Meeny
Pop Goes the Weasel
The Doll's House
Liar Liar
Little Boy Blue
No Way Back (an eBook novella)
Hide and Seek
Running Blind (an eBook novella)
Love Me Not
Down to the Woods
All Fall Down
Truth or Dare
Cat & Mouse
Forget Me Not

OTHER NOVELS

A Gift For Dying
Eye for an Eye
The Wrong Child

M.J. Arlidge has worked in television for the last twenty years, specialising in high-end drama production, including prime-time crime serials, *Silent Witness*, *Torn* and *Innocent*. In 2015 his audiobook exclusive, *Six Degrees of Assassination*, was a number-one bestseller. His debut thriller, *Eeny Meeny*, was the UK's bestselling crime debut of 2014 and has been followed by fourteen more DI Helen Grace thrillers.

X @mjarlidge
f /MJArlidge
@m_j_arlidge

INTO THE FIRE

M.J. ARLIDGE

ORION

First published in Great Britain in 2025 by Orion Fiction,
an imprint of The Orion Publishing Group Ltd.
Carmelite House, 50 Victoria Embankment
London EC4Y 0DZ

An Hachette UK Company

The authorised representative in the EEA is Hachette Ireland,
8 Castlecourt Centre, Dublin 15, D15 XTP3,
Ireland (email: info@hbgi.ie)

1 3 5 7 9 10 8 6 4 2

A CIP catalogue record for this book is
available from the British Library.

ISBN (Hardback) 978 1 3987 0828 0
ISBN (Export Trade Paperback) 978 1 3987 0829 7
ISBN (Audio) 978 1 3987 0832 7
ISBN (eBook) 978 1 3987 0831 0

Typeset at The Spartan Press Ltd,
Lymington, Hants

Printed and bound in Great Britain by Clays Ltd,
Elcograf S.p.A.

MIX
Paper | Supporting
responsible forestry
FSC® C104740

www.orionbooks.co.uk

Day One

Chapter 1

It was now or never. If she didn't act, if she didn't *seize* this unexpected opportunity, she might never get another chance.

Selima kept her head down, shuffling along at the back of the line of silent workers, looking for all the world as broken and listless as them. But inside her heart was racing. She'd long given up hope of freeing herself from her torment, the soul-crushing routine of back-breaking labour and casual violence, but fate had thrown her a lifeline, one last chance to gain her freedom.

She wasn't sure what the injured woman's name was – she was a new addition to their ranks and didn't speak much English – but whoever she was, she had Selima's undying gratitude. Their team of a dozen workers, clad in a uniform of drab joggers and tatty face masks, had been trudging back to their transport when the new recruit had suddenly collapsed. Her legs had gone from underneath her and she must have hit the ground hard, for she appeared to be unconscious, her mouth slack, her eyes rolled back. It was shocking, unexpected ... and it jolted Selima from her torpor. She'd been following her co-workers in a daze, stumbling towards the open mouth of the van, but the poor woman's collapse had roused her. Selima looked at the stricken woman, then up at the awaiting van, a shiver running down her spine. She'd sat mute and hopeless in the blacked-out interior many times before, but tonight the mouth of the van seemed even more menacing than usual. Selima had the strong feeling that if she stepped inside again, she might be swallowed up completely, disappearing from the earth as surely as if she had never existed. The thought stung her, bringing tears to her eyes, the horror of never seeing her children, her beloved husband again, too much to bear. Somehow she had to resist, somehow she had to find the will to *survive*.

Now she had her chance. Naz, their chief minder, a pitiless thug with heavy scarring around his unmoving, prosthetic eye, was stooped over the young Syrian, slapping her face with his rough palm. His charge failed to respond, however, prompting an anxious look at his accomplice, who remained by the van doors, counting the workers in. Aggravated, but concerned, the associate now hurried over, keen to be away before they were spotted by someone. This was highly unlikely of course – they were in a scruffy back-alley in the dead of night – but his anxiety persuaded him to drop his guard. For a moment, the eleven queuing women were unattended, the injured worker occupying both guards' attention. The others seemed clueless as to how to respond, their lengthy imprisonment robbing them of all agency, but Selima was not going to let this golden opportunity pass.

She took one step to the left, heading away from the line of human statues. Then another, moving obviously out of formation now. She half expected to be yanked back into line, a snub-nosed revolver shoved in her face, but darting an anxious glance in her captors' direction, Selima saw that the two men were still crouched over their charge. Speeding up, she padded away, the mouth of a nearby alleyway beckoning. She had no idea where it led, but she assumed it would spit her out into a street where there would be people, life, perhaps a police officer.

Anything – arrest, incarceration, even deportation – would be better than this.

'What do you think you're doing?'

Selima kept walking, breaking into a half-jog, praying that this snarled question was aimed at the ailing woman. But as she heard her minders scramble to their feet, she knew she'd been spotted. A quick glance over her shoulder confirmed this, Naz now tearing towards her, his face contorted with murderous rage. Already he was reaching into his jacket, to pull out what? An iron bar? A gun? It was too late to slip back in line. Too late to pretend she'd made a mistake. A rebellion like this would not be tolerated, her life forfeited, which meant Selima had no choice.

She had to run.

Chapter 2

She ran her index finger down his face, gliding gently over his nose to his mouth, before deftly plucking the joint from his lips. Startled, Helen's companion looked up at her, an expression of amused outrage on his handsome face.

'I was enjoying that ...' Christopher protested, reaching out a strong arm to try and reclaim his prize, even as Helen leaned back, keeping it out of reach.

'You know the rules, you can't smoke in here,' she teased, nodding towards the opulent interior of the penthouse hotel room.

'Don't be such a killjoy. The smoke detectors never work in these places.'

'And besides,' Helen added, continuing to evade his playful lunges, 'smoking marijuana is illegal. Didn't they teach you that at the National Crime Agency?'

This provoked a laugh from her date, who leaned back into the plump pillows, clasping his hands behind his head to reveal his broad chest.

'So, what are you going to do, Helen? Arrest me?'

His eyes sparkled mischievously for a moment, before he added:

'Oh no, wait, you can't, can you ...?'

Helen's expression narrowed. She'd only been seeing Christopher for a couple of months, but during that time he'd taken great delight in teasing her about her self-imposed exile from the world of law enforcement. He was an experienced forensic accountant, shedding light on the financial misdeeds of gangsters and fraudsters, whilst she had walked away from a highly decorated career as the head of the Major Incident Team at Southampton Central. She'd quit on a point of a principle, and didn't regret her decision for a minute, but his good-humoured barbs still landed, tapping into an uncertainty about her identity, her role in life. She was no longer Detective Inspector Helen Grace. She was just ... Helen.

As if reading her mind, her bedfellow continued:

'Tell you what. Instead of hectoring me like an angry school ma'am ...'

Helen frowned, but Christopher persisted, unabashed:

'... why don't you take a puff yourself? It won't kill you. It might even do you some good. You've been very tense of late.'

He reacted too slowly, Helen snatching up a pillow with her free hand and slamming it into his cheek. Laughing, he fended off her attack, continuing his provocation.

'Go on, I dare you. Just one tiny little puff ...'

Helen glared at him, the smoldering cigarette still clutched in her fingers. She had always been a smoker, so it wasn't a great leap, but she'd never been a fan of drugs. Still, a challenge was a challenge.

'Have it your way ...'

Placing the joint to her lips, she inhaled deeply, rolling the smoke around her mouth, before letting it slide from her nostrils, gentle plumes drifting up into the air.

'Happy now?' she enquired, handing the cigarette back to her date.

'Delirious,' he replied, gazing affectionately at her, as his hand came to rest on her hip, his thumb running gently over the silky sheen of her nightshirt. 'You?'

Surprised by the question, Helen hesitated before answering. It was not something she had ever had time to ponder before, her hectic work-life affording her no time for introspection. But now, freed from her obligations, the possibilities seemed boundless. She could smoke drugs, she could spend long evenings making love in expensive hotel rooms, she could be happy. She could even fall for someone, a luxury she'd never afforded herself.

'I'm doing pretty good,' Helen responded, shrugging casually. 'Nothing special, but good enough...'

It was a blatant tease and Christopher responded immediately, a frown creasing his features, as he stubbed the joint out into an empty glass.

'And what would it take to make you truly happy, Helen Grace?' he asked, as his hand slid up her side, brushing against her breast.

Helen said nothing, as his thumb strayed to her nipple. A shiver of pleasure rippled through her and she leaned into him, her lips seeking out his, enjoying his hot, smoky breath. She could sense his desire, his lust enveloping them both and, without warning, he reared up, flipping Helen onto her back. Now it was his turn to bear down on her, kissing her fiercely, but Helen had been expecting this move and used his downward momentum to her advantage, rolling hard to the left to divert him onto *his* back. Surprised, Christopher tried to protest, but he knew it was hopeless, that he was beaten. Helen wanted him, another wave of pleasure pulsing through her as she descended upon her lover, but it had to be on her terms. Her world was changing, her life in flux, but she still liked to be in control.

Some habits die hard.

Chapter 3

She sprinted down the darkened street as if her life depended upon it.

Bursting out of the shabby alleyway moments earlier, Selima had been horrified to find that the quiet residential street was deserted, not a soul around at this late hour. For a moment, she was flummoxed – she'd been so sure she'd find salvation here – but there was no time for delay, with her pursuers so close behind. Instinctively she darted left down the street, tearing along the pavement. Selima was young, fit and desperate – surely this combination would propel her to freedom, away from the awful nightmare that had consumed her for the past two years? Yet the remorseless footsteps behind reminded her that danger was close at hand, that her tormentors would not give up until they had her in their clutches once more.

Adrenaline coursing through her, Selima upped her speed, straining every sinew to put some distance between herself and her pursuers. Up ahead, she could see traffic lights, a crossroads, cars speeding by. It was a hundred feet away, maybe a little more, but it would take her less than a minute to reach it. Once there, she could throw herself in front of a car, risking all to get someone's attention. It would be desperate, dangerous, but presumably her captors would think twice before attacking her in front of dozens of witnesses? Surely she could rely on the good hearts of the passing motorists? True, she'd received no kindness, no generosity since she set foot in this blighted country, but the ordinary people of Southampton were surely as decent and caring as anyone else? For her sake, she hoped so.

From nowhere, a hand snatched at her trailing arm. Yelping in fear, Selima realized that Naz was nearly on top of her, his breathless curses echoing in her ear. Terrified, she darted to her right, leaving the pavement and slipping between two cars into the road. Surprised by this move, Naz hesitated, earning Selima precious breathing space as she tore towards the crossroads ahead. She was now only fifty yards away and if she could maintain her speed, she was sure she'd get there first.

To her immense relief, a vehicle now swung into the road ahead, dazzling her with its headlights. It was coming directly towards her and she waved her hands wildly above her head, desperately trying to attract the driver's attention.

'Help me! Please *stop*...'

Her voice was shrill and cracked, but it seemed to have an effect, the vehicle screeching to a halt just in front of her. Relieved, Selima slowed down, thanking the heavens for her good fortune. But as the headlights flicked off and the shape of the vehicle became clear, Selima's hopes turned to ashes. It wasn't a passing car, or even a police vehicle. It was the white van. Naz's partner in crime had cut off her escape route. Even now, he was climbing out of the cab, as his ally closed in from behind.

'*Min xilas bike, Xudan...*'

Selima whispered the prayer to herself as she scanned the street for any means of escape. And to her surprise her desperate plea appeared to be answered, the terrified fugitive spotting a cut-through directly to her right, leading away from the street. Selima didn't hesitate, peeling off to the right, even as Naz lunged at her once more. This time his fingers gained purchase, grasping the soft fabric of her top, but wrenching her arm free, Selima sprinted on, seeking the sanctuary of the alleyway.

She stumbled, bouncing off the walls in her desperation to escape. She could hear two sets of footsteps behind her now and laboured to stay ahead of their rage. The alleyway was littered with rubbish, but hurdling the detritus, she made it to the end, spilling out into the night air once more. A new vista opened up in front of her, but it was scarcely more appealing. In her desperation to escape, Selima had left the city streets behind, only to run straight into a shopping parade. During the daytime, this place would have been bustling, but at this late hour, the shops were closed, the metal security grilles down. She was trapped. Moreover, she was alone.

Or was she? As she pushed deeper into the lonely precinct, she spotted something up ahead. Something that made her heart soar. It was a light. No, more than that – it was a shop! As Selima broke into a sprint, her eyes fixed on the kebab sign glowing in the darkness, beckoning late-night revellers. She wasn't sure if it was still open, or if she'd be welcome there, but Selima sensed that if she could just make it to the sanctuary of this late-night eatery, she would be safe.

Swallowing her fear, Selima raced towards the light.

Chapter 4

Helen looked out over the city, entranced by the twinkling lights below. The hotel had been Christopher's choice and she approved. The Mayflower was a new boutique hotel on the fringes of Watts Park, whose penthouse suites commanded magnificent views over Southampton. The vista was particularly beguiling at night when the cityscape came alive, a mass of sparkling whites, yellows and reds. Helen could have stood for hours watching the cars, the late-night revellers, wondering where they were going, who they were with, what pleasures awaited them.

Tugging the fluffy bathrobe around her, Helen couldn't deny that she *was* content. Happiness had always been a relative concept for her. It wasn't something she'd had much experience of, nor was it something she expected. But despite the questions about her future that continued to trouble her and the guilt she felt about abandoning Charlie and her colleagues at Southampton Central, she couldn't deny that there *were* elements of her new life that she enjoyed. The time to be herself, to explore new things, to make a stab at having a proper, functioning relationship. Her liaison with Christopher was still in its early days, but the dating app algorithm that had paired them seemed to know its stuff. They were of similar age, had a background in law enforcement and both enjoyed the occasional retreat from the world, usually in an upmarket hotel. Helen knew her funds wouldn't last forever, that at some point she would have to think about future employment, but for now at least she was content to savour the moment.

Pressing her head to the glass, Helen allowed her gaze to wander over Southampton, seeking out new diversions. Christopher was in the shower, meaning she had a moment's solitude to savour. Smiling, her eyes moved back and forth, like a prison search light, seeking signs of life.

Then she spotted something that immediately set her nerves on edge. Maybe a hundred feet below, in a gloomy shopping parade, a young woman was sprinting at full pelt, casting frequent looks behind her. Instinctively, Helen pressed closer to the glass. What on earth was this woman doing in that deserted spot so late at night? And who was she running away from?

Moments later, Helen had her answer, two burly figures coming into view, racing after the fleeing woman. Helen's body tensed, a host of unwelcome questions pulsing through her mind. Why were they chasing her? And what did they intend to do if they caught her? Helen found herself whispering encouragement to the fugitive, urging the young woman to stay ahead of her pursuers and now, to her enormous relief, she saw the woman reach a kebab takeaway, the only establishment still open. Helen watched intently as the woman disappeared inside. Her luck was out, however, her two pursuers following her in, before dragging her out onto the concourse. As she fought to free herself from their clutches, a man appeared in the shop doorway, wearing a chef's apron over a bright pink t-shirt, but he made no move to intervene, remaining frozen to the spot.

Helen's heart was hammering in her chest. Surely the takeaway owner would get involved? Or at least call the police? But to her horror, he did nothing, watching on impassively as the two thugs threw the poor woman to the ground. Immediately, their victim scrambled to her knees, clasping her hands together, imploring them for mercy. But they were clearly not the forgiving type, Helen gasping as one of them pulled what looked like a bicycle chain from his jacket pocket. Was Helen imagining she heard a cry, the woman shrieking out in fear and desperation? Either way, her terror did not save her, the man bringing the chain down on her with all his might.

Helen was already on the move, sprinting towards the door as Christopher emerged from the bathroom, towelling his hair.

'Hey! Where's the fire?' he cried, as she surged past him.

Helen didn't respond, flinging the door open and racing down the corridor. Behind her, she could hear Christopher calling out, but she powered on, reaching the emergency exit and pushing into the stairwell. Perhaps it would be more sensible to take the lift, but Helen couldn't risk any delays, convinced that every second counted.

She flew down the steps, jumping them four at a time, myriad questions rattling round her brain. What had this woman done to provoke their anger? Why was their attack so violent? And how come they were so blatant about it, apparently heedless of possible witnesses to their crime? Consumed with a desire to understand, to intervene, Helen burst into the lobby, causing the night manager to look up sharply. Breathless and sweaty, she raced on, her robe flapping wildly behind her as she ran towards the exit. Frustrated, she discarded it, sprinting across the lobby in her satin nightdress. Seconds later she was on the street, pausing momentarily, before spotting a dimly lit cut through to the shopping precinct. Sprinting across the road, her bare feet pounding the tarmac, Helen pushed away all thoughts of danger, disappearing inside the shabby passage.

Suddenly plunged into a gloomy darkness, Helen tore on, barely pausing as her leading foot hit something sharp. Shrugging off her discomfort, she kept going, convinced the punishment being meted out to the anonymous woman would be far worse. The corridor seemed endless, but now finally Helen burst out into the desultory parade, casting wildly around her. Immediately she spotted them, a shadowy group not fifty feet away. She'd been hoping for cries, a struggle, signs of life, but to her horror, the woman lay motionless on the ground, her breathless attacker looming over her.

Helen didn't hesitate, tearing towards the clutch of figures, her speed increasing with each stride. Athletic, lithe and light on her feet, she made little sound and it was only at the last second, as the vile thug raised his arm for yet another blow, that he seemed to clock her approach. The expression on his face changed suddenly, alarm at an approaching intruder morphing to shock as he struggled to process the image of a striking woman in a nightdress bearing down on him. But before he could respond, Helen took off, flying through the air, and planting a solid foot squarely in the middle of his chest. The man fell backwards, landing heavily on his back and gasping in shock. Surprise was now Helen's ally and she stepped forward decisively, crunching the heel of her foot into the prone thug's exposed cheek, slamming his head into the floor. Dazed, in pain, he blinked stupidly at the night sky for a moment, before turning away to groan and whimper. Helen paid him no heed, for she could hear footsteps behind her. Turning, she saw the other thug bearing down on her. He was clearly a street warrior, with heavy scarring around his prosthetic left eye, and intent on doing her some serious damage.

'I don't know who you think you are, lady, but—'

He didn't get any further, Helen's powerful right foot snapping up sharply into his groin. Her assailant groaned, his face contorted in agony. Helen was not minded to show him any mercy, however, driving her fist into his stomach, prompting him to double up sharply, before bringing her elbow down on the back of his neck. With a pitiful groan, he collapsed to the concrete, out cold.

Turning, Helen hurried over to their victim, who lay motionless on the ground. Kneeling down next to her, Helen gently raised the injured woman from the floor, cradling her in her arms. The young woman's face was bloodied and bruised, her body quivering with agony, but she was alive, which was a relief given the sustained brutality of the attack. Desperately worried, Helen shouted out to the takeaway owner to call an ambulance, only to discover that the shop was now swathed in darkness, the 'closed' sign clearly visible.

'What the f—'

Helen was about to launch a volley of abuse in his direction, but now the woman in her arms coughed violently, a mist of blood drifting from her lips.

'It's OK, love, you're going to be OK,' Helen intoned, trying to sound as friendly and positive as she could. 'We're going to get you help. You're going to be fine.'

The woman's eyes swivelled in her head, before finally coming to rest on Helen, her expression a mixture of pain and confusion.

'I'm a friend,' Helen reassured her. 'And I'm going to get you out of here. But I'm going to need you to stand. Do you think you could do that for me?'

Helen regretted now coming out without a phone or any means of summoning help. They would have to make it back to the road, or the hotel just beyond, and they would need to do so fast, before her attackers rallied. But the woman in her arms made no move to respond, barely registering Helen's presence.

'Can you tell me your name?' Helen asked, remembering her basic training. 'What are you called?'

And now Helen did see a reaction, the woman raising her head, trying to find the words, even through a clutter of broken teeth.

'Selima,' she whispered, before sinking back into her arms.

Helen nodded, smiling warmly at her. The injured woman seemed to be in her twenties and of Central Asian or Mediterranean appearance, with ebony hair and rich brown eyes. Intriguingly, she had small tattoos on both her chin and forehead – a cross and a gazelle – though an explanation of their significance would have to wait. The important thing now was to get away.

'OK, Selima. My name's Helen and I'm going to help you, but we do need to get you on your feet. I know you're in pain, but we've got to *try*. Do you think that you can do that for me?'

Selima raised her head again. She looked as if she wanted to say something, but in the end this proved beyond her, so instead she simply nodded, trying to raise her head a little higher.

'That's it, slow and steady...'

Helen slipped her hand behind Selima's back, trying to lever her off the ground. For a moment, Selima seemed to respond, a brave smile tugging at her lips. Then suddenly her expression changed markedly, her face clouding over, panic etched in her features. Helen stared at her for a moment, confused, before realizing the magnitude of her mistake. Convinced that one of Selima's attackers had roused themselves, Helen turned to look behind her, but she'd barely moved before she received a savage blow to the back of her head. Her whole body lurched sideways, her head spinning, but now a second blow came, sending her crashing to the ground. Her face hit the concrete hard, tearing the skin on her cheek, even as her arms relinquished their grip on her injured companion. Gasping, choking, Helen half-raised her head, but the world was spinning around her, darkness threatening to consume her, and she fell back down to earth with a crash.

She lay there on the dusty concrete, breathing heavily. She felt nauseous and disoriented, yet even through her confusion, she heard Selima cry out once more. Summoning what remained of her strength, Helen attempted to rise again, struggling first up onto her knees and then, falteringly, onto her feet. The precinct floor seemed to sway in front of her, and Helen staggered sideways as if on the deck of a pitching ship. Vomit was rising in her throat, she couldn't see properly and, as she clamped her hand to the back of her head, her fingers found hot, sticky blood. For a moment, Helen felt sure she would faint, but in spite of this, she was now moving forwards again, following the sounds of Selima's distress.

Everything was a blur, she could only see outlines, colour and shapes, but even through her confusion, Helen knew that Selima was being dragged away. Now a new sound cut through, an engine roaring, the sound of a vehicle screeching to a halt. Desperately trying to focus, Helen made out the blurred shape of a white van, its one working brake light pulsing red at her. She heard doors open, a cry, then the doors slam shut again. Helen knew exactly what was happening and tried to focus on the vehicle, but the number plate was too far away, too indistinct, for her to make out. Worse still, the van itself was now receding in her fractured vision, driving away at speed. Forlornly, Helen cried out, raising a hopeless arm as if to stop it, only succeeding in unbalancing herself in the process. Startled, Helen was now pitching forward, powerless to stop herself as first her torso, then her head, connected sharply with the ground.

Then everything went black.

Chapter 5

She lay on the floor, consumed by darkness. Selima's body was racked with pain, her face swollen and bloody, but nevertheless she forced her eyes open. She wanted to convince herself that she *was* still alive, but more than that, she wanted someone to reach out to her, to ease her suffering. She'd been confined in the gloom of this van many times, the lack of windows rendering the interior virtually pitch black, but over the weeks and months she'd trained herself to penetrate the darkness, to pick out individuals amidst the crew of workers who were her constant companions in suffering.

Sobbing gently, Selima sought them out, her tired eyes raking their faces for a sympathetic gaze, a consoling word. But there was no movement, no reaction from her fellow captives, just eleven pairs of hostile eyes surrounding her, their anger, their condemnation clear. For a moment, Selima thought she was imagining it, but then a hissed voice made the collective mood plain.

'What have you done?'

The rest of the journey passed in utter desolation. Selima had dreamed of liberation, had dared to imagine that she might bring this hideous nightmare to an end, but she had gambled and lost. Now she would pay the price.

Selima clamped her eyes shut, hoping against hope that if she did so, then the awful reality, the crushing sense of doom, would dissipate. Perhaps when she opened them again, she'd be back in the freezing accommodation block, the terrible events of tonight just a bad dream, a cautionary tale reminding her to stay in line. But the burning agony in her cheeks, her chest, her legs gave the lie to that hopeless fantasy.

The van slowed now, before speeding up again, bumping over rough ground. With each jolt and jar, Selima's fear rose. What was she going to do? What was she going to say? How could she successfully plead for her life? Normally she would invoke her children, appealing for clemency, but she knew that would cut no ice. Should she offer to work for free? Or debase herself in other ways to ensure her survival? But these ideas withered as soon as they were born. There would be no reprieve, no salvation, tonight.

The van shuddered to an abrupt halt, the engine dying. A moment's silence, the tension thick in the van, then the rear doors were flung open. The security lights that flanked the perimeter of the site flooded the interior, revealing the hostile expressions of those around her, but Selima's attention was not focused on them. Instead, her gaze came to rest on the statuesque presence that now filled the doorway. The woman who housed them, controlled them, degraded them. A few months back, Selima had heard one of the guards let slip her real name – Leyla – but in the camp everyone called her "Boss".

'Everybody out,' Leyla barked, gesturing angrily at the van's inhabitants.

Immediately, the other workers sprang into action, hurrying to obey. Hoping her tormentor hadn't yet heard about her failed escape attempt, Selima complied, labouring to raise herself from the floor.

'Not you,' her captor hissed.

'Please ... please ... I not mean any harm,' Selima garbled. 'I ... I am ... lost, confused.'

But she received no reply, Leyla leaning in and grabbing her by the hair. Selima cried out in pain, but her attacker barely responded, grunting angrily as she hauled her from the van. For a moment, the cool air was a relief, but Selima had no time to enjoy it, as she was now being force-marched across the dusty yard.

'The rest of you, follow me,' Leyla barked, picking up the pace.

Selima couldn't see anything, her face pointed to the floor in an agonizing headlock, but she knew the others would obey. This woman, this cruel, savage woman was the Goddess of their world, the architect of the numerous indignities they endured and the few crumbs of comfort they enjoyed.

'Please, I'm sorry ... I'm sorry ...'

Selima knew she had to say something, to beg for her life.

'I do anything ... anything you want.'

'It's too late.'

'Forgive me ...'

They came to a sudden halt. Now her tormentor raised Selima up, clasping her ponytail with an iron fist as she held her face to hers, their noses just inches apart.

'You ungrateful bitch,' Leyla snarled. 'You could have done well here, could have earned some money for your mongrel family, but you blew it. I offered you a home, a wage, a future, but you threw it back in my face. Now you must pay the price.'

Leyla broke into a wicked smile, prompting Selima to cast an anxious glance over her shoulder, taking in the bulky machine directly behind them. Immediately, terror arrowed through her, whole being consumed by fear.

'Please, I beg you ...'

Shoving her head down angrily, Leyla was on the move once more. Now Selima was screaming, twisting violently in her vice-like grip, but it was no good. She was powerless to resist, her fate all but sealed. She saw Leyla reach out, pulling down the lock lever, before wrenching the battered metal door open.

'No, no...'

Selima was digging her feet into the earth, determined to save herself from a fate worse than death. But a savage stamp on the back of her calf loosened her grip and she now found herself being bundled inside the hulking metal contraption. Stumbling on the lip of the doorway, Selima pitched forward, landing with a thud on the filthy floor inside. Aware of her terrible predicament, she struggled to her feet clumsily, turning to try and escape through the open doorway. But before she could move, the heavy door slammed shut, the lock lever descending sharply, trapping her inside.

This time the darkness was total.

Chapter 6

'You've got to let me out of here.'

The paramedics looked up at Helen, incredulous.

'Do you *understand*?' Helen persisted fiercely, trying hard to stop the interior of the ambulance spinning. 'There's a . . . a situation I need to deal with. Something that can't wait.'

'The only situation you need to deal with is yourself,' the older paramedic replied, a kindly twinkle in his eyes. 'Let's focus on that shall we, my love?'

In truth, Helen was finding it hard to focus on anything. She knew she was concussed and had lost blood, though beyond that, the details of her ordeal remained vague. She couldn't recall how many times she'd been hit, only that her attackess' metal chain had struck hard and true.

'Forget me,' Helen choked, dismissing the paramedic's intervention. 'There's a young woman in real danger. She's just been brutally attacked and bundled into a van. We *need* to find her.'

She just about managed to gasp the words, before running out of breath. Once again, however, her pleas were met by a mixture of surprise and alarm.

'Where was this? You say there was an attack of some kind?' the younger female paramedic chipped in.

'It was at the parade of shops. Where you found me.'

'We didn't see anyone,' she replied quizzically. 'Apart from the two nice ladies who found you of course ...'

'No, no, they'd gone by then ...' Helen said weakly, suddenly aware of how mad she must sound.

Looking quizzically at her, the older paramedic took up the baton.

'Can I ask, Helen, have you been drinking tonight?'

She shook her head violently, immediately wishing she hadn't.

'I haven't drunk in over thirty years,' she replied angrily.

'Drugs then?' he persisted. 'Have you taken anything?'

'Why on earth would I do that?'

'Lots of people do,' he said, without judgement. 'And you've obviously had a bit of an evening, so ...'

Perplexed, Helen stared hard at him, then lowered her gaze to look at herself. She was battered and bruised, shoeless and dishevelled, with only a skimpy nightdress preserving her modesty. Sweaty, tousled, with smudged make-up and eyes that refused to focus, Helen suddenly realized what a state she must look.

'You think I've been partying?' she countered angrily. 'Is that why you think I look like this?'

'I don't know what you've been up to,' he replied cautiously, clearly alarmed by her growing anger. 'None of my business really. I just assumed—'

'Well, I haven't been,' Helen interrupted, her frustration bubbling over. 'I was staying at the Mayflower and I spotted a woman being attacked. I went to her aid and this is the result.'

She gestured to her head wound, feeling nauseous and giddy once more.

'Right ... OK ... it's just that you look like you'd maybe lost your balance and hit your head. Are you absolutely sure that's not what happened? Because if that was case, there's no shame in it. We see it all the time, don't we, Sheila?'

His companion nodded tersely, clearly less sympathetic to late-night drunks than her more mature counterpart.

'Let me be very clear,' Helen hissed, trying to control her fury. 'I saw a violent attack, no, actually an abduction...'

This slight change in Helen's story prompted a brief, pointed look between the paramedics, but she pressed on.

'So I intervened. I'm a police officer, right. It's what I'm trained to do, so would you please stop treating me like some raving drunk and let me go. You've got no right to keep me here, trussed up like a turkey. I've done nothing wrong.'

'We *know* that. And you're only secured to stop you falling off the stretcher and injuring yourself further. We're nearly at the hospital. Why don't we get you checked out and then see where we are, eh?'

Agonized, Helen tugged hopelessly at her restraints, bellowing out her frustration. Even as the cries died away, she clocked the female paramedic looking at her shrewdly.

'You're a police officer, you say?'

Her tone was even, but her scepticism was clear. Obviously it was not common to find police officers in a state of undress lying face down in the gutter.

'Yes. Well, I was until recently anyway. A detective inspector in the Major Incident Team at Southampton Central.'

'But you're not anymore?'

'No, I resigned six months ago, but that's not the point. The point is I know what I'm saying and it's God's own truth, so will you please stop this vehicle and let me out. I've *got* to find her...'

A long silence followed, broken only by the shriek of the siren above. Both paramedics looked at each other, the more senior officer clearly trying to find the right words in response. But in the event, his female colleague got in first.

'Look, Helen, you've had a nasty knock to the head, so what say we get you checked out and then we can talk about this missing girl, eh?'

Her condescension was crushing, her decision final.

Helen was trapped.

Chapter 7

She hammered her fists against the metal door, desperate to escape.

'Let. Me. Out.'

Selima's voice was still strong, in contrast to her battered body, her assault on the door growing weaker with each pitiful blow. There was no way out of this tomb, the metal door barred shut.

'Stay calm, stay calm...'

Selima moved away from the door, cradling her throbbing fists, praying that things might still work out OK. It was fine, everything would be fine. Yes, Leyla was cruel, but she wasn't mad. She didn't really intend to go through with it. This whole thing was being done for show – to terrify her and warn the others against future rebellion. If Selima could get through the night, she would be released tomorrow, having paid her dues. She just had to stay strong.

Seating herself on the ash-strewn floor, Selima started to hum to herself, reassuring melodies from her childhood. Immediately, her mind was drawn back to her hometown, to sun-kissed Sirnak, images of her family filling her thoughts. Mischievous Azwer, loving Rojan and determined Yezda. She was blessed to have children who were such a credit to her. They would grow up to be strong, ambitious, prosperous – all the things she'd never been. If she'd helped them in some small way by making these sacrifices, by leaving her beloved Turkey to seek work, then maybe, just maybe, it had been worth it.

Yes, this was what she must do. She must focus on hopeful things, positive things, that would get her through the night. Then once morning had come, once she had been released from this awful...

Selima froze, all thoughts of her children suddenly evaporating. Was her mind playing tricks on her, or had she really heard an ominous creaking sound? Her body was rigid, her senses alert and now, to her horror, she heard it again. A long, laboured metallic moan as the machine cranked into life.

Instantly, Selima was on her feet, blundering blindly towards the door once more. She connected sharply with the metal surface, cannoning backwards, before righting herself and searching for the outline of the door. Where the hell was it? She thought she'd re-traced her steps but must have become disoriented. Quickly, she felt her way along the wall, desperately clawing at the metal, as the pitch-black interior began to echo with an insistent banging. Was it Selima's imagination or was the temperature already starting to rise?

Panicked, she maintained her progress around the cylindrical contraption, her leading hand now jarring nastily against the frame of the door. Cursing, she sucked her hand, the iron tang of blood bitter on her tongue, but a superficial wound was the least of her worries. She *had* to get out of here.

The clanking sound had now morphed into a slow, insidious hum, the whole incinerator seeming to throb with deadly purpose. Finding some purchase at the top of the door, Selima pulled hard at the metal, straining with all her might to bend the lip in her direction. Even the slightest movement could be enough to shut down the machine, perhaps even to afford her a chance of escape, if she could work on the fissure. But the hard steel refused to budge, stubbornly resisting her assault. Sweating profusely now, Selima re-doubled her efforts, the air thick and warm around her.

Screaming out her exhaustion and terror, Selima let go, defeated. Running her fingers down the side of the door, she found a new handhold, and pressing her foot on the adjacent wall for more leverage, tugged with all her might. Ten seconds, twenty seconds, thirty seconds and more she kept up her desperate struggle, but yet again her efforts proved fruitless and she sank to her knees, tears filling her eyes. This couldn't be it, could it? Her grand adventure ending in the most barbaric way possible?

The sweat was pouring down her face now, mingling with her tears. She could barely see, her senses felt muffled and blurred, but she had to make one last attempt to escape, for those who loved her, as much as for herself.

'Please, help me. Someone. Anyone. I don't want to die...'

She hammered on the door, using her last remaining vestiges of energy to make a noise fit to wake the dead.

'Save me, please save me. You will be next...'

Still she pounded the metal. In her mind's eye, she could see the lever lock suddenly rising, the door being thrown open, cool air flooding in... but there was no response from outside, no cavalry riding to her rescue.

'I have children. They need me. Please help...'

Selima petered out, knowing that all was lost. She would never see her husband again, never lay eyes on her beloved children. Worse still, they would never know what became of their loving, naive mother, her fate a mystery for the rest of time. She had hoped to help them, to lift her family from dire poverty, but had achieved nothing save for her own destruction.

It was so hot now that she could scarcely breathe. Her hair was stuck fast to her scalp and she swayed unsteadily on her knees as the savage waves of heat assaulted her relentlessly. Any second now she would pass out, be consumed by raging fire, but she would not die cursing her killers, rather imploring the mercy of her children.

'Yezda, Rojan, Azwer...'

Outside, her desperate cries echoed across the desolate yard, before slowly drifting away into nothingness.

Day Two

Chapter 8

They sat in silence, their eyes glued to the scene in front of them. There was a sense of expectancy within the team, but also a marked tension. Everyone knew that there was a lot riding on this.

Detective Inspector Charlie Brooks stole a look at her watch, then picked up her binoculars, running an eye over the dockside below. From their vantage point in a derelict warehouse, the assembled members of the Major Incident Team had a bird's-eye view of Southampton's main port, a bustling collage of articulated lorries, cargo containers and cranes. There was much to distract the eye, but one key element was missing.

'He's late,' Charlie hissed, checking her watch again. 'Where *is* he?'

She angled a glance at her colleagues, but they looked equally mystified.

'The boat docked two hours ago. He must have disembarked by now,' she insisted.

'I checked in with the team down there a couple of minutes ago,' DC Malik replied. 'They've counted out twenty-five other lorries, but so far there's no sign of him ...'

The young officer's sentence petered out, summing up the general sense of frustration. Charlie could feel sweat prickling on the back of her neck, her anxiety rising. Their intelligence had been crystal clear. A lorry would be arriving from Rotterdam on the 7.15 a.m. boat, transporting a dozen illegal immigrants, hidden within crates marked as machine parts. They had the name of the driver, the registration plate of his truck, even the rendezvous point he was to drive to after leaving the docks. Charlie had a team stationed there of course, but wanted to end things here, swooping on the trafficker before he had a chance to leave the port area. This was part of the deal she'd made with Border Force, as the tip-off had come from their helpline and they wanted to share in the glory.

'Do you want me to go down to the ship? Take a look?'

The offer came from DC James Roberts, one of three new officers they'd had to recruit following the dismissal of several MIT colleagues six months ago. That had been a dark day for the team – the three male officers were some of the worst examples of corruption, misogyny and incompetence they'd ever come across – but it had been crowned for Charlie by the resignation of her friend and colleague, Helen Grace. Now it fell to Charlie to lead the team, but six months on it still felt profoundly odd, the lack of her mentor an uncomfortable reality.

'Not yet,' Charlie replied, trying to sound purposeful. 'Not until we're sure all vehicles have left the ship. If he is down there, I don't want to spook him. He's an experienced operator, who'll know the scene, know the faces. Anything, or anyone, that's not familiar might rattle him. And with the greatest of respect, you don't look much like a docker...'

It was meant kindly, Roberts was a fresh-faced fast tracker, but Charlie's joke elicited only an awkward smile, as though she'd offended him. Her immediate reaction was to want to say more, to rescue the situation, but she held her tongue. No point making things worse by appearing overly concerned about a junior officer. They were here to do a job, not engage in team bonding ... and yet how Charlie would have loved to find some common ground with her new colleagues. Her eyes drifted from DC Roberts to fellow recruit DC Shona Williams, who immediately dropped her gaze, as if underlining the lack of connection with their new boss. Turning back to the docks, Charlie swallowed her discomfort, raising her binoculars once more, but the knot in her stomach refused to budge. In truth it had been there since the day Helen Grace resigned.

Her mentor's sudden departure was more than just a personal blow for Charlie, it had been a seismic event for Hampshire Police. Enraged by what she perceived to be a culture of complacency and cover-up, Helen had not spared her former employers, lambasting Chief Superintendent Rebecca Holmes and other senior figures in the local press, accusing them of conspiring to shield an offender in their own ranks. Helen's principal target had been the top brass, but every officer in the station had felt the sting of her attack, leaving those that remained feeling unsettled and angry. Morale was low, resentment high and there was no question that the new recruits to the team had been unnerved by Helen's damning indictment of the Force. It was Charlie's job to make them feel settled, valued, inspired even, but so far her efforts had been a total failure.

'DC Williams, would you check in with the team at the rendezvous site at Portswood? Make sure there's no signs of life there? Just in case he's slipped through somehow ...'

Shona Williams nodded obediently, picking up her radio and moving away. But it was action for action's sake, a way to break the silence and fill the time, as their prize continued to elude them. With each passing second, Charlie's anxiety grew, aware that it wasn't just the eyes of her fellow team members that were on her today. Her boss, Chief Superintendent Rebecca

Holmes, had made it clear that she expected swift results in their fight against human trafficking and modern slavery. With so many resources being diverted to Dover to deal with the small boats, new opportunities had opened up for the traffickers at other ports along the South Coast, Southampton proving a particularly popular entry point. Charities estimated that dozens of illegal migrants slipped through the port every week, flooding the local economy with cheap, forced labour and enriching crime bosses across Europe. According to local politicians and the police commissioner, the situation was becoming intolerable, meaning the hottest of hot potatoes had landed in Charlie's lap. She needed a result and she needed one fast.

'Perhaps you *should* take a quick look, DC Roberts? This doesn't feel right to me...'

The young officer looked surprised, Charlie contradicting her earlier order, but rose quickly nevertheless. Charlie knew she risked looking foolish and indecisive, but the truth was that she *had* to know. If this was a bust, if they'd been sold a pup by Border Force, better not to prolong the agony. Still the thought made her sick to her stomach, the idea of all their preparations, all their efforts, being for nothing. Charlie had made a big play of this operation, demanding extra resources and manpower from Holmes, promising major results, determined to establish her authority as the new head of the MIT by making her first significant arrest. But as the minutes ticked by with no sign of their prize, Charlie had the sickening feeling that it had all been for nothing, that she'd once more be left empty-handed and embarrassed.

The shadow of Helen Grace had never felt as long as it did today.

Chapter 9

Helen took a deep breath, then pushed through the heavy glass doors.

The atrium of Southampton Central was as chaotic as ever, assorted members of the public mingling with police officers, their conversations a mixture of alarm, antagonism and frustration. Weaving through the melee, Helen made her way quickly to the front desk, suddenly feeling self-conscious and exposed. Clocking her approach, the cheery smile on the face of custody sergeant PC Mark Drayton faded, clearly shocked to see Helen back at her old stomping ground.

'Do my eyes deceive me or has Elvis just *entered* the building?'

He chuckled to himself, his tone knowing and sarcastic, his obvious enjoyment of Helen's discomfort checked only briefly, as he noticed the cuts and bruising on her left cheek, a souvenir of last night's encounter that make-up couldn't fully conceal. In truth, the impact of that violent struggle had been profound, Helen feeling dizzy, nauseous and lethargic, despite her discharge from South Hants hospital in the early hours of the morning. She'd returned home to shower and change, but felt little the better for it.

'Good to see nothing changes, Mark. Still making yourself laugh.'

'If I didn't, I'd probably cry,' he replied evenly, appraising her with naked curiosity. 'So, to what do we owe the pleasure?'

'Well, I'd ...'

Helen hesitated, profoundly aware of the strangeness of the situation, then pressed on:

'I'd like to report a crime.'

This time PC Drayton's reaction was one of surprise, his consternation clear. Slowly he reached for his keyboard, his eyes still glued to Helen.

'And was this a crime you were the victim of?' he asked cautiously.

'In a way,' Helen replied carefully. 'I took a nasty knock to the head and I'm feeling pretty sick as a result, but the real victim was a young woman. She was attacked and abducted right in front of me.'

'I see,' PC Drayton continued, his brow furrowing. 'And when was this exactly?'

'Just after midnight at the Bedford Place shopping parade. I saw her being attacked, so I intervened. But I was outnumbered, so ...'

Helen kept her expression neutral, concealing her white lie. She had no desire to reveal her stupidity at having taken her eye off her assailants, an oversight that had proved disastrous. Where was Selima now? Was she even still alive?

'So your involvement was purely coincidental then?'

'Exactly. But anyone would have done the same.'

The custody sergeant's reaction suggested that he very much doubted it and for a moment Helen feared he might accuse her of being a have-a-go hero, of deliberately seeking out the encounter. Fortunately, he did no such thing, continuing with his note taking.

'I'm assuming you had no prior acquaintance with this lady?'

'Not at all. I don't know why she was being attacked, what her connection to her assailants might have been, but I do know that she was savagely beaten with a bicycle chain before being bundled into the back of a white transit van.'

'Did you get the registration number by any chance?'

Helen shook her head weakly, as another wave of nausea swept over her.

'Make and model then?'

'No, sorry. I'd been hit on the head, I couldn't see anything clearly.'

Drayton nodded slowly, looking ever more doubtful, as he added:

'I take it then that you can't accurately describe her attackers?'

'Not especially, it was pretty dark, though one of them definitely had facial injuries and a prosthetic eye, I think.'

'What about the victim then? Do you know her name?' Drayton persisted.

'Only her first name – Selima. She's mid-twenties, black hair, brown eyes, with distinctive facial tattoos. I'm guessing she's from central Asia, though I can't be sure...'

'And were there any witnesses to the attack? Other than yourself, I mean?'

Now there was no disguising the suspicion in his voice. Immediately anger flared in Helen, aggravated at the merest suggestion that she was mistaken or, even more outrageously, making the whole thing up.

'Well, yes, actually. There's a guy who runs a kebab shop in the parade. He was there, he certainly saw the initial attack, maybe her abduction too.'

'Name?'

'No idea,' Helen replied, her tone laced with irritation. 'We didn't exchange details. I was concussed, lying on the floor...'

In her peripheral vision, Helen noticed a couple of heads turn. She was aware she was making a scene, but that had never stopped her in the past, so she persevered:

'…but there's only one kebab shop on that parade. If you send someone down there now, I'm sure he'll talk to you, confirm what I've said. If there's CCTV or traffic cams, it would obviously be great to get that footage too. Should give you a clear sight of the van, perhaps even the driver too.'

Drayton paused in his typing, looking up at his former colleague with a look that was half amusement, half irritation.

'Well, I'll certainly write up the report and see where we go from there—'

'I'm sorry, PC Drayton, have you listened to anything I've said?'

Helen knew that she was overstepping the mark here, but she couldn't help herself.

'I've reported the brutal assault and abduction of a vulnerable young woman. Someone who even now could be in grave danger. What part of that don't you understand?'

The custody sergeant looked at her curiously for a second, a wave of anger clouding his features, before he straightened himself up to his full height.

'The part I don't understand, Helen,' he replied, stressing the last word, 'is the bit where you get to come in here, as a civilian, and tell the police how to conduct their affairs—'

'Look, that's not what this is abo—'

'Ordering them to investigate a "crime",' Drayton continued tersely, 'of which there appears to be very little evidence. That's not how it works.'

'I do understand that,' Helen replied, backtracking. 'And I'm sorry if I offended you. It's just that the situation is urgent and we need to act.'

As soon as she said it, she regretted it, her former colleague pouncing on her slip.

'We? There is no "we" anymore. You left us, remember?'

And there it was, plain as day. Beneath the polite attention lay a simmering resentment, a quiet fury at her decision to call out her own police force, to resign on a point of principle, criticizing her former employers publicly. Her betrayal of the tribe had been neither forgotten, nor forgiven.

'Now, was there anything else, because there are others waiting?'

Turning, Helen pushed through the crowds, hurrying across the atrium and out through the swing doors. She was angry, embarrassed and bitterly disappointed. She had come here on an urgent mission, seeking help and assistance, hoping that her past endeavours might at least win her a hearing with a senior officer. But she was leaving empty-handed, her presence at Southampton Central neither beneficial nor welcome. Clutching the rail, she staggered back down the steps in the spring sunshine, a fresh wave of nausea assailing her. Swaying momentarily in front of the glass and limestone building, which for so many years had been her sanctuary, Helen turned to look back at her old HQ, before promptly vomiting on the floor.

Chapter 10

She felt sick to her stomach, her innards knotted. Emilia Garanita had walked these corridors numerous times before, her role as a local crime reporter affording her frequent access to Winchester prison. Her previous visits had all been in a professional capacity, however, and had often been illuminating, even enjoyable. Today was different. This time it was personal.

Following the straggling line of mothers and children into the visitors' centre, Emilia sought out the nearest table, smoothing down her collar and flicking out her hair. This was not done for her father's benefit, but for hers. She wanted the old bastard to see what an impressive, successful woman she'd become. Keeping her chin high, she tried to project strength and defiance, even though her stomach was turning somersaults. Once more Emilia felt the urge to turn and run, but she stayed where she was, refusing to show any weakness.

And then suddenly there he was. Emilia was catapulted back years as a small, hunched man in his early sixties shuffled towards her, looking plaintively in her direction. Time seemed to stand still as he covered the final few yards, Ernesto Garanita's eyes projecting a humility and tenderness she'd never seen before. Moments later, he was seated in front of her, smiling warmly at his daughter.

Emilia exhaled slowly, her face rigid, determined to resist his overtures. Ten seconds passed, then another ten, the elderly man continuing to beam at his estranged daughter, before finally her patience snapped.

'Why am I here, Dad?'

Ernesto Garanita stared at his daughter in surprise, running a hand over his greying moustache, before replying:

'Is it so odd that a father wants to spend a little time with his daughter? Hell, nobody else comes to visit me here.'

'You've been here for over fifteen years. And *now* you decide to play the doting father?'

Her scorn was clear, but the prisoner seemed barely to notice, his expression remaining penitent and remorseful.

'Please, Emilia, I know I've been a bad parent, I know I've let you down...'

'That's the understatement of the year,' the journalist fired back quickly. 'You prostituted your own children, turned them into drug mules and then when we resisted, you let your pay-masters do *this*.'

Emilia gestured angrily to the heavy scarring on her left cheek, the emotion suddenly bubbling up within her. Her refusal to carry on the family's trafficking business had cost her dear, memories of the acid attack she'd suffered as a teenager pulsing vividly in her mind now, fury suddenly assailing her. Where was this all coming from? As far as she was concerned, she'd dealt with her trauma, her anger years ago. But perhaps it had just lain dormant, waiting for an outlet.

'Please, please,' Ernesto protested, looking pained. 'That of all things I reproach myself for. I didn't ask for that to happen, I didn't want it to happen, but I couldn't stop those guys. Once you work for them, you work for them, no exceptions.'

'Then you should have chosen your "friends" more carefully, shouldn't you? Because it was me who paid the price for your stupidity.'

There was a long silence, father and daughter eyeballing each other unhappily, before the former broke into a nasty coughing fit that racked his whole body. When he finally managed to gather himself, he looked up at his daughter once more, his eyes rheumy and sad.

'Look, I know I messed up, that I let you down badly,' he said eventually. 'That's why I wanted to see you. I wanted to say sorry...'

'Too little, too late, Dad.'

Annoyed with herself for wasting her time, Emilia rose abruptly.

'Please, Emilia,' her father pleaded, reaching out to her, as another coughing fit threatened. 'Listen to me. I was weak, I know that. I was greedy, I was selfish. Yes, I was doing what I felt I had to do to put food on the table...'

'Oh, spare me, please!'

'...but I know now that my choices were *wrong*. That every decision I made, every step I took was *wrong*. Because of what it meant for you, for us. Do you think I wanted to spend most of my life behind bars, separated from everyone and everything I loved?'

'That was your choice. You're not here by accident.'

'Which is why it hurts so much,' he continued, as if keen to get everything out. 'All the suffering I caused to you, to your brothers and sisters, it's all my fault.'

'Well, at least that we can agree on.'

Emilia towered over him, if not satisfied, then at least victorious. Her heartless, absent father had finally owned his immorality, his cruelty. Not that he would gain anything from it. Her wounds might be old, but they were still raw.

'But it doesn't change anything and much as I'd love to stay here chatting, I've got work to do. So, if you've said your piece...?'

'No, not yet.'

This time there was frustration, even anger, in his voice. Slapping his chest harshly to still his barking cough, he gestured urgently at Emilia to resume her seat. And such was his sincerity, his passion, that to her surprise Emilia found herself complying. Something told her that she was about to learn the real reason for her surprising summons.

'Emilia, my love,' he eventually continued, his emotion evident. 'I didn't ask you here to fight. Or for absolution. I know it's too late for that. But I do want to ask for your help.'

Emilia said nothing, suddenly wrong-footed and suspicious. Her father had never asked for her assistance before. Had not tried to contact her once in all the years he'd been behind bars. What could he possibly want from her now?

'Well, if you're hoping that I can get you out of here, you'd best think again,' she replied caustically. 'I'm no lawyer and to be honest, I'm not much of a baker either, so we might have to forgo the chisel in the cake.'

'For God's sake, Emilia, can you not be serious for one minute?' he said, slapping the table, silencing her and causing several heads to turn. 'I know I'm never getting out of here, I'm not an idiot.'

Aware that he'd caused a commotion, her father leaned forwards, lowering his voice as he continued:

'I just... I just want you to help me end things the *right* way...'

This time Emilia had no comeback, the import of his words slowly taking hold, as he added:

'I'm dying, Emilia.'

Chapter 11

They sat in hushed silence, their eyes glued to the snake of foreign lorries, bringing in vegetables, flowers, electric cars, televisions and more, but there was no sign of Adam Peeters, the Belgian haulier who they'd been assured was smuggling a dozen desperate souls into the UK.

Breathing out heavily, Charlie pondered her options. She still hadn't heard from DC Roberts, who'd hot-footed it down to the embarkation zone, nor from DC Shona Williams, who must by now have reached the rendezvous site in Portswood. So what to do? She could pull the operation, saving valuable money and resources, trying to salvage what she could from another missed opportunity, or she could persist with the operation, potentially making the situation worse if they *were* wasting their time here with no genuine prospect of an arrest. Charlie's authority was already in question, her reputation on the line, so the choices she made now mattered.

'Five more minutes,' she muttered to DC Malik, who nodded soberly. 'We'll give it five more minutes.'

But she'd barely finished when her radio crackled into life.

'DC Roberts to DI Brooks.'

Charlie snatched up her radio.

'This is DI Brooks. Go ahead.'

'We have eyes on the prize,' Roberts breathed excitedly.

Hope surged within Charlie. Raising her binoculars, she scanned the busy dock.

'Right, where are you ...?'

And now she saw it. Just as their tip-off predicted. An Iveco lorry with a Belgian plate – 1 AYB 209 – driven by a lone male. He was behind schedule, a good couple of hours past his disembarkation time, but he was here at last.

'Alert Border Force,' Charlie demanded, turning to DC Malik. 'Tell them to seal the exits and stand by. I want him in cuffs before he gets anywhere near the gates.'

Charlie was on the move, heading fast towards the stairs, as she raised her radio again.

'DC Roberts? Where are you now?'

'I'm staying with him. Proceeding on foot, maybe thirty feet behind.'

'Keep it steady, don't do anything to spook him.'

'Roger that.'

Charlie had now reached the ground floor, teasing open the door.

'Team A, are you in position?'

A crackle of static, then her officers answered in the affirmative.

'Team B?'

'Ready and raring to go.'

DC McAndrew's Scottish burr rang through loud and clear, energized and professional as always. Pushing the door a little further open, Charlie strained to pick up the progress of their prize once more. The truck was a hundred yards away, lumbering towards the turn that Charlie had earmarked as the best spot for their ambush. Peeters would have to reduce his speed then, hopefully allowing them to make their intervention without any danger of injury or escape.

'Come on, come on...'

After all the tension, frustration and delay, now Charlie just wanted to get on with it. But there was no question of going too early, of alerting their mark to their presence. Rocking back and forth on her heels, she implored him not to dawdle, the passing seconds seeming like hours, but now finally he approached the turn.

'Right, this is it. All teams standing by.'

Deftly, Charlie strapped on her identification armband, whilst plucking her warrant card from her pocket. She had a clear view of Peeters, a burly, unshaven man in a dark blue polo shirt, watching him intently as he began to turn the heavy steering wheel.

'Go, go, go,' Charlie shouted, as she sprang from her hiding place, tearing towards the cab. Even as he turned the heavy vehicle, Peeters seemed to hesitate, pivoting to take in the onrushing officer. Charlie saw his expression change from surprise to confusion. Now his attention was diverted by another alarming sight – uniformed officers hurling a stinger across the road in front of him, half a dozen plain clothes CID appearing from nowhere, bearing down on his vehicle. Charlie took full advantage of his distraction, leaping onto the side of the cab and wrenching the passenger door open.

'Hey? What are you doing?' the trucker protested, shocked.

'Police!' Charlie responded, flashing her warrant card. 'Kill the engine and put your hands on your head.'

But the trucker made no move to comply, staring at Charlie in horror.

'Have it your way,' she hissed, leaning over and wrenching up the handbrake.

Immediately the lorry ground to a halt, Charlie thrown against the dashboard, as the driver hit his head on the sun visor. But Charlie had been expecting this and was quicker to respond, reaching across him and turning off the ignition, before whipping out the keys. As she did so, the driver's door was flung open and a breathless DC Roberts appeared, reaching towards their captive.

'Right, mate, let's do this nice and slow, shall we? No sudden movements ...'

Peeters was too stunned to resist, allowing DC Roberts to haul him from the cab. Charlie didn't dawdle to watch the show, instead descending swiftly and tossing the keys to DC McAndrew.

'Right, let's open this up and get those poor folk out ...'

Charlie was marching towards the back, nodding purposefully at the approaching Border Force officers. One of them, an athletic young woman, now mounted the back of the vehicle, tugging fiercely at the bolts that secured Peeter's precious cargo. What would each of these poor souls have paid for their transit here? £5k? More? It was easy money, if only you could keep them quiet and calm. Not an easy task when the journey was arduous and the air supply scarce. Border Force had already had two fatal incidents in the last six months, desperate immigrants suffocating to death in the most appalling circumstances, but Charlie pushed those thoughts from her mind, dearly hoping they wouldn't be facing anything so hideous today.

With a soft metallic moan, the heavy doors swung open. Charlie was first to react, climbing up into the truck, relieved to see it stacked with tall crates marked 'machine parts'.

'Let's get these open.'

Her colleagues swarmed past her, setting to work. As they did so, a triumphant-looking DC Roberts came into view, pushing his defeated charge in front of him. These were the days that made Charlie feel good, when she realized she was actually giving something back. Turning, she took in the officers' feverish work as they used crowbars to break the crates open.

'Quick as you can, please ...'

Charlie cracked her knuckles, rolling her neck to relieve the tension. She had no idea what state the concealed immigrants would be in and she wanted them out and on their way to a hospital or police station as fast as possible.

'Nothing in this one,' the nearest officer declared. 'Just machine parts.'

'OK, let's keep going. They are probably in the crates further back. We're only looking for a handful of people, remember?

But despite her confident tone, Charlie felt the first shiver of alarm. All the details were right – Peeters had turned up as predicted, the crates were marked as machine parts – the tip-off had to be correct, didn't it?

'Nothing in this, either,' DC Williams offered, shaking her head dolefully.

'Keep looking,' Charlie urged.

But one after another the crates were opened and passed clear. Still Charlie clung to hope that their prize lay in wait deep in the bowels of the vehicle. But as the final crate was opened, the full extent of her error became clear: there was nothing in the truck apart from agricultural machine parts. Turning once more, she took in the unfortunate driver, Peeters' expression – one of indignation and outrage – and behind him DC Roberts, whose reaction was even worse. Anger, frustration, but deep embarrassment too.

Charlie had staked a lot on this operation, putting her reputation with Holmes, with the team, on the line. And she had lost.

Chapter 12

Emilia continued to stare at her father in disbelief, scarcely taking in his words. He had tried to explain his situation, to flesh out the details of his condition, but Emilia could only think about *why* he was telling her this. What he might stand to gain from this sudden confession.

'Look, back up a bit, will you?' she demanded. 'Have you got any proof that this is actually *real*?'

'You think I'm bullshitting you?' her father fired back. 'Of course I've got *proof*. You can check with the prison medical staff. I've ... I've got stage four lung cancer. It's my own stupid fault, of course, but there it is. They say I've got three months left, six tops.'

Emilia stared at him. She didn't know what she'd been expecting from today's meeting, but it wasn't *this*.

'Look, I haven't asked you here to perform miracles, Emilia. I've got several years left on my sentence. Even if I tried to get that commuted because of my illness, I'd be dead before anyone got near considering my case. I'm going to die in this place and there's nothing I can do about it.'

Despite herself, Emilia felt a pang of compassion. Her father deserved to suffer for what he'd done to her, but even so, dying in this crumbling dump was a pitiful way to go.

'I don't want your sympathy, nor do I expect your love,' he continued. 'But I would like to do what I can to make up for the past. I ... I want to die with a clear conscience.'

'And you think you can do that by offering me an apology?' Emilia scoffed. 'There's nothing you can possibly say that could make up for the way you exploited us, the way you *abandoned* us. Your arrest killed Mum, you do know that, don't you? And who was left to pick up the pieces? To bring up *your* children?'

Ernesto dropped his gaze to his feet, his shame clear. As he did so, the prison bell rang loudly in the background, signalling the end of visiting time, but Emilia wasn't finished yet.

'So, forgive me if I don't go all gooey when you offer up a mea culpa. Words are cheap, Dad, it's actions that count. And throughout your life you've not done a single thing – not *one* thing – that's helped us. All you did was hurt us and that's something you'll have to live – *and die* – with.'

Had she been expecting those words to crush her father? That her damning verdict would render him speechless and tearful? If so, she was to be disappointed, her father nodding thoughtfully, as he replied:

'I couldn't agree with you more, Emilia. You are a chip off the old block.'

Emilia shook her head angrily, dismissing the notion.

'But I *do* think there is a way I can help you. That's why I asked you here. But it *must* remain between you and me for now. You cannot under any circumstances tell your brothers and sisters. It's our secret, OK?'

He angled a glance at the prison officers, who were now starting to move the visitors on. Leaning in closer, Ernesto lowered his voice as he continued:

'Come back again tomorrow and I'll tell you how I intend to help you. Trust me, it'll be worth your while ...'

Emilia looked at her father, confused and unsettled, fighting the curiosity that was bubbling inside her.

'What do you mean, Dad? What are you talk—'

But Ernesto had already risen, turning back briefly to place a meaningful finger to his lips, before taking his place amongst the departing throng.

Chapter 13

Fortune favours the brave. It was a maxim Helen had always believed in, refusing to be downcast or diverted when she knew she had a job to do. So, despite her rejection at the hands of a former colleague, despite the nausea that still gripped her, she strode purposefully through the busy shopping precinct, zeroing in on her target.

The takeaway sign was illuminated, the shop door open, a group of sixth-formers idling nearby with freshly fried chips. And though the smell of a slow-cooking doner kebab was the last thing Helen felt she could stomach right now, she made swiftly for the takeaway. The clock was ticking and every second counted.

'Morning, my darling, what can I get for...'

The owner's jaunty welcome petered out as soon as he realized who'd entered.

'Look, I don't want any trouble, OK?' he said, holding up his hands, as if afraid of her.

'Well, you won't get any from me,' Helen countered. 'But I do need your help.'

The owner said nothing, eyeing her with unease. He was a muscular, powerful-looking man in his late thirties, with a handsome face and kind eyes. Normally, Helen imagined he would have been a cheery, friendly presence. But as at her old HQ earlier, her welcome here was cautious, bordering on frosty.

'I urgently need to find the young woman who was attacked last night. Did you happen to spot the van's registration or what direction it drove off in?'

'Van?'

'Yes, the van that she was taken away in. You witnessed the attack, you must have seen her dragged off to the van. We need to find it ASAP.'

'I didn't see any van.'

Helen eyed him, surprised. It was possible he'd retreated inside the shop by that point and thus hadn't seen anything. But Helen wasn't convinced. If you'd just witnessed a vicious attack, surely you'd peek out the window to see what happened next?

'We can come back to that. What about the two guys who attacked her? Did you get a good look at them? Could you describe them to me, to the police?'

But already the owner was shaking his head.

'I'm not sure what you mean...' he replied, falteringly.

'Come on, man, I saw what happened. You were standing in the doorway when the attack started. They were no more than ten, maybe fifteen feet from you.'

Her words hung in the air, urgent and terse. For a moment, Helen thought he was going to respond, the uncomfortable takeaway owner staring at his feet, as if trying to find the words to describe those vicious thugs. But when he looked up again, his expression betrayed only mystification and concern.

'What men? What young woman?'

'No, no, no, don't try and pull that one. I saw you last night, you were wearing the same bloody shirt for God's sake...'

She gestured at his pink Inter Miami top, her frustration boiling over.

'You saw it all. Their vicious attack, that poor girl lying on the ground, whilst you did nothing. I intervened, I tried to save her and got a nasty wound for my troubles...'

She turned slightly, lifting her long hair to reveal the bandage stuck to the base of her skull.

'So don't tell me you saw nothing, because I don't believe it. I *won't* believe it.'

Still he stared at her, stupefied, before shrugging dolefully.

'I don't know what to tell you, lady. I didn't see any attack, any men. Maybe it happened somewhere else, maybe you're confused. I saw *nothing*.'

He clearly wanted to shut the conversation down, but Helen wasn't done yet.

'What about CCTV then?'

Immediately, she clocked his reaction, the owner suddenly looking alarmed, as his glance slid to the camera on the back wall.

'The camera's pointing at the doorway, it must have picked up something. Let me check that. If what you're saying is true...'

'It's not working. Sorry.'

Helen stared at him in disbelief.

'I can see the bloody red light, man. Of course, it's working. It's recording now, just as I'm sure it was last night...'

'It's not working, OK? So please leave, I have work to do...'

He started to turn away, but Helen was too quick, grasping his arm over the counter.

'Please,' she implored. 'There's a vulnerable young woman out there who desperately needs your help. Don't turn your back on her.'

And now she saw him hesitate, concern clouding his certainty. For a moment, Helen dared to hope that he might relent, but then he deftly removed her hand, concluding:

'I don't know what you're talking about. I don't know you, or this girl, so please leave my restaurant or I'll have to call the police.'

The irony was not lost on Helen. Six months ago, she'd have been able to *demand* his cooperation, force him to hand over the CCTV footage, but now she was powerless. As if to ram home the point, the disgruntled owner yanked open the door for her, ushering her out with the final insult:

'You need to see a doctor, lady. There was no crime here.'

Chapter 14

It was cruel, barbarous, inhumane. No, it was *pure evil*.

Viyan Bashur stood in the claustrophobic space, staring down at the thick layer of ash beneath her feet. She longed to be out of here, partly because of the terrible danger you put yourself in, standing inside this lethal contraption, but mostly because of the hideous scene in front of her. This mottled sea of grey, punctuated with the odd flash of dull silver, an earring or ring that had survived the intense heat, was all that was left of Selima. The thought made Viyan's head spin, even as her heart burst with grief.

She had known Selima for over two years, encountering the young mother on the very first day of her own imprisonment. Viyan, then fresh off the boat and exhausted from her arduous journey across Europe, had been reeling, shocked that the trust she'd put in the traffickers had been so cruelly betrayed. Selima, more experienced than her, with a canny eye for how life worked in this awful camp, had taken Viyan under her wing, keeping her out of harm's way. Perhaps it was because they were both Kurdish, perhaps it was because she recognized a fellow mother, either way Viyan had been profoundly grateful for her protection and support at one of the most distressing points of her life. The rules of the camp were strict, the imprisoned workers forbidden from talking to each other, from forming any sort of friendship, so Selima had taken a great risk in protecting Viyan, the latter regretting now that she'd never sufficiently expressed her heartfelt gratitude for Selima's covert acts of kindness.

Selima was not made of stone, of course. She too had found life in this camp intolerable. And in the end, she had snapped, making a sudden, desperate bid to escape. Viyan hadn't witnessed it, she'd been detailed to work at the abortion clinic last night, but she'd seen the aftermath, watching in horror as her poor friend was dragged to the incinerator. The threat of a fiery death had often been invoked by their captors, but Viyan had thought it was just a stunt, borne of a desire to provoke and humiliate them. Now she knew different – the frantic, agonized screams of her friend still ringing in her ears.

Pushing the hideous pile of ash towards the door, Viyan was suddenly gripped by a terrible sense of foreboding. Would this scene be repeated in the future, with *her* as the unfortunate victim? Was Viyan staring at her own future right now? The thought made her shiver, tears pricking her eyes. The notion that she would never see Defne, Aasmah and Salman again was unthinkable and yet this had been Selima's fate, her family consigned to a lifetime of wondering what had become of their beloved mother, so why not her?

Leaning heavily on her broom, Viyan felt breathless and dizzy. The dire transformation in her fortunes was too disorienting to process. For many years, she'd had a good life. A nice home, a loving husband, three healthy children, even the makings of a career, having trained to be a primary school teacher. Then the great earthquake had struck, devastating her entire region. Overnight, she had lost everything. Mercifully, her children had been pulled from the wreckage, but her husband had not been so lucky. There had been no time to bury him, no time to grieve however, Viyan desperately tried to keep her baby, her daughters and her ailing mother safe, as they were transported to a refugee camp on the border with Syria.

Perhaps it was because they were far from Istanbul and thus out of sight of the national government. Or perhaps it was because they were Kurds. Either way, aid had been painfully slow in arriving, other regions seemingly favoured instead. Slowly their situation had grown intolerable, Viyan having to beg, steal and borrow just to put rice in her family's mouths. The change in their situation had been calamitous and threatened to cost them their lives, disease rife within the overcrowded refugee camp. With no hope of their house being rebuilt and no means to support her family, Viyan had made the fateful decision to risk all by attempting to make it to Europe, paying the traffickers the last of her paltry savings to smuggle her into the UK, leaving her children in the care of her elderly mother. They had promised her a job, prosperity, opportunities. The reality had been very different, Viyan and the other workers becoming little better than slaves. Would her captors ever honour their agreement to release her when she'd paid off her 'debts'? Or would they work her until she was broken in mind and spirit? Was it even possible she would end up in this incinerator, screaming for mercy as the temperature soared and her skin crackled and blistered?

Swallowing down her horror, Viyan re-doubled her efforts, desperate now to be out of the grim metal cylinder. Gathering the ashes of her friend neatly into a pile, she swept it briskly into a large grey bin bag. She was careful, considerate, but still flecks of ash crept into her eyes, her nose, the young mother wiping her face angrily with her grubby arm. Desolate, hurting, Viyan nevertheless persisted, eventually sealing Selima's feathery remains in the bag, before hurrying from the appalling machine. Outside the fresh air was invigorating, Viyan pausing for a moment to drink in the strong sunshine, something she'd seen too little of since her fateful decision to leave Turkey. But then she spotted one of the guards looking at her with naked hostility, his hand resting on the butt of his handgun, so she hurried on her way, crossing to the huge metal waste containers at the rear of the site.

Carefully mounting the rickety staircase, Viyan eventually made it to the lip of the container. She'd already secured her mask over her mouth and nose, but it made no difference, the stench making her gag. The container was nearly full, weeks of medical waste and human tissue lying bagged and dumped inside, creating an aroma that could only be described as unholy. It was no place for her friend, or any human being to end up in, but fearful of being disciplined for idleness, Viyan uttered the shortest of farewells:

'Goodbye, sweet Selima. You will live on in my thoughts and prayers.'

Gently she lowered the bag into the container, before wiping away a tear. Would this be *her* final resting place too? Raising a shaking hand to her face, Viyan rested her index finger on the small, turquoise moon tattoo on her chin. She'd had it inked shortly after the birth of her eldest, the traditional Deq marking signifying hope and optimism for the future, and she pressed her finger hard on it, praying feverishly for redemption, for salvation, for deliverance. But her prayers died on her lips almost as soon as they were uttered.

There was no hope here.

Chapter 15

'To be honest, I'm just delighted you're alive.'

It was said with a laugh, but looking up from her laptop, Helen realized that there was real concern in Christopher's expression.

'More or less,' she replied ruefully, trying to focus on the images on the screen, which seemed to dance in front of her. 'And, look, I'm sorry for running out on you like that. I should have said something, but there wasn't time. She was in real danger...'

'I know and I understand,' he replied, smiling warmly at her. 'Though I wish you'd taken me with you. I hate to think what could have happened to you if things had turned out differently.'

Helen nodded soberly, painfully aware now of how reckless her intervention had been, but grateful that someone at least believed her version of events. Christopher accepted her story without question, clearly trusting her, which moved her more than she could say. Few people seemed to have faith in her, or put any stock in her opinion, anymore.

'So, what now?' he asked, sliding her overnight bag across the floor to her. 'I've got your clothes here, your phone's in the side pocket by the way, but now that I've satisfied myself that you're still in the land of the living, I really ought to be getting back to the office. Unless I can help in any way?'

Nodding her thanks, Helen dropped her eyes back to her screen, on which were numerous images of female faces, all of them decorated with elaborate, lightly inked tattoos.

'I think the woman I saw last night had tattoos like this...' Helen replied, turning the screen to face her lover. 'It says here that they're called Deq tattoos. Young mothers mix their own breast milk with dye pigments to signal a change in their status, their hopes for their children, for the future...'

Christopher pulled a face, surprised by this revelation, but Helen ignored him.

'It's common practice amongst traditional Kurdish communities. A kind of rite of passage thing...'

'So you think the woman you saw has kids, is married perhaps...'

'Probably, and given what I know about her ethnicity, her name, those tattoos, I'm guessing she's probably from a Kurdish community in Turkey or Syria. But that's as much as I've got really.'

'None of the other shopkeepers in the parade had any CCTV footage that can help?'

'No. That place is pretty rundown, the security basic, plus they wouldn't give it to me anyway.'

Helen sat back in her chair, a heavy sigh escaping her lips.

'Well, Rome wasn't built in a day,' Christopher responded kindly. 'If you think she's Kurdish, that's a good place to start. If you can find out her full name, perhaps you can begin to work out what's happened here, where she might be.'

He held out an encouraging hand and Helen squeezed it briefly. Simple acts of intimacy weren't really her thing, but she was genuinely grateful for his support when the odds seemed so stacked against her.

'You're right, I'm not going to let it go. I *can't.*'

Christopher smiled at her indulgently, but Helen meant every word. Just because she wasn't a police officer anymore, it didn't mean that she could sit by in the face of blatant criminality and danger. The rest of the world might have chosen to believe that no crime had been committed last night, but she was determined to prove otherwise, to do what she could to shed light on Selima's fate.

She couldn't live with herself if she didn't.

Chapter 16

He pulled on the smoldering cigar, letting the bitter smoke play over his tongue, before expelling it with a satisfied sigh. Matthijs Visser was not a patriotic man by any means, but he generally favoured Royal Dutch cigars, loving their elegant look, their aggressive, peppery taste. He always carried a pack with him, reaching for them whenever he had something to celebrate.

Today's operation had not gone entirely to plan, thanks to an unforeseen hold-up on disembarking the ferry, but this hardly mattered when the outcome had been so pleasing. Another Dutch lorry had suffered engine trouble, meaning the final few cargo vehicles were delayed leaving the ship, but eventually they had departed, pushing into the familiar environs of Southampton docks. This was always the point of maximum danger, when Visser's heart was in his mouth. What if one of his concealed charges had somehow smuggled a mobile on board, dialing 999 in a desperate bid to escape their fate? What if one of them suddenly panicked, hammering on the walls of the lorry, revealing their presence? What if the Border Force officials were employing dogs or, worse, thermal imaging equipment? Everything had appeared normal this morning, but still Visser had gripped the steering wheel tightly as he crawled forward, his eyes fixed on the Belgian lorry forty metres ahead.

He needn't have worried of course. The border officials in the UK were horribly overstretched and, besides, he'd made preparations. Preparations which paid off handsomely as a clutch of plain clothes law enforcement officers sprang up from nowhere, descending on the startled Belgian haulier. A brief hold-up ensued, as the drivers behind were diverted around the incident, but the delay was brief and Visser was soon on his way. He kept a straight face as he glided past the unfortunate Peeters, spread-eagled on the ground with a police officer's knee in his back, but as soon as he was clear of the docks, speeding around Southampton's ring road, Visser allowed himself a small whoop of triumph, tugging a cigar from his breast pocket in celebration.

Sometimes it really did feel like taking candy from a baby, the over-stretched British authorities powerless to stem the flow of human cargo across the channel. Yes, transporting illegal immigrants was complicated and potentially risky, but it was a doddle compared to the drugs game. Visser had spent thirty years of his working life in that business, acting first as a spotter at the docks in Rotterdam, before graduating to transporting the goods himself, and for a time he had enjoyed it. For a boy who'd had nothing as a kid, who'd been a genuine street rat, the money that cocaine smuggling afforded him was dizzying. But the prizes on offer had attracted others too, the drugs scene in the Netherlands transformed by the arrival of the Moroccan gangs. Competition had spiked and with it the violence, the scars on Visser's chest and legs a testament to that. He had come close to losing everything, so in recent years had pivoted, opting for a less hotly contested trade instead. How easy, how calm, his latest incarnation seemed to him, loading up migrants who wanted to follow orders, who were motivated to make it to the UK undetected. Lambs to the slaughter they might be, but as long as they were docile whilst under his care, that wasn't his concern. So long as they were alive when he flung open the doors at the remote Hampshire farm, he would get his money.

Placing his cigar gently in the ashtray, he angled a look at his satnav. Could he make it to the end destination without allowing himself a comfort break? It would be pushing it, as he'd been on the go for hours, but it was tempting to try. Finding somewhere out of the way to stop was a headache and he dare not risk a service station, as he could never be sure that one of his charges wouldn't make a run for it, now that they'd reached the UK. Such a breach in security would result in loss of earnings, or worse, detection by the authorities, a thought which made Visser shudder. He had no desire to spend his middle years behind bars, caught in some nightmarish extradition process, with only the promise of a long prison stretch in the company of former gang members or competitors to look forward to. No, it was too risky, so best press on. There was no point taking unnecessary risks.

Teasing the accelerator, Visser checked his side mirrors. There was always a chance he was being followed, but given the spectacle at the docks today, he doubted it. The road seemed clear, his path ahead set fair, so he snatched up his cigar, smiling at his good fortune. The sun was shining, life was good and he'd soon be rid of his cargo, placing them in the care of their new owner. He had not always been a fan of this itinerant lifestyle – it was fraught with danger and had wrecked his marriage to Suzanne – but all that had changed.

He *loved* his visits to the UK now.

Chapter 17

The woman looked up sharply as Helen entered, surprised by her unexpected appearance. Helen had spent her life walking into unfamiliar environments, where her presence was not always welcome, but in the past she'd had a warrant card to hide behind. Today she had nothing, except good intentions.

'Can I help you?'

Her hostess was a tall woman with long, ebony hair, sparkling eyes and a gentle smile. Abandoning the box she'd been packing, she approached Helen, her hand outstretched.

'Harika Guli. I'm the manager here.'

Helen immediately felt herself relax, accepting Harika's handshake and running her eye over the threadbare, cluttered interior. A few minutes internet research had singled out the Kurdish Welfare Centre in Woolston as her most promising port of call. Set up ten years ago, it was a home from home for the Kurdish community in Southampton, a fount of knowledge about life in the UK. The centre's handful of volunteers gave their time freely to assist Kurdish migrants who were new to the UK, advising on immigration, the law, finances, education and more besides. It was run on a shoestring, kept afloat by a steady stream of modest donations, its handful of volunteers giving up their time three afternoons a week to keep the place going, but its reputation was good and its reach significant. If you lived in Southampton and were of Kurdish heritage, odds on you'd find your way here before long.

'My name's Helen Grace. I'm a former police officer and I was wondering if I could ask for your help?'

'Former police officer?' Harika enquired, her eyebrow raising just slightly. 'So what are you now? A private investigator?'

'Oh no, nothing like that,' Helen replied, quickly. 'I'm here ...'
She hesitated momentarily, trying to find the words.

'...I'm just here as a concerned citizen.'

'I see.'

Harika's smile was still welcoming, but she was evidently confused, so Helen continued quickly.

'I'm looking for a young woman, who I think is Kurdish. I don't know her full name, nor why she's in the UK, but she's in real danger and I need to locate her urgently.'

'Danger from whom?'

'I don't even know that, I'm afraid. But she was attacked last night by two men who bundled her into a van and drove off. I'm desperately trying to find out what's happened to her.'

Instantly, Helen saw her companion react, confusion morphing to concern. Gesturing to Helen to take a seat, Harika replied:

'Can you describe this woman?'

'Late twenties, shoulder-length black hair, brown eyes. She has Deq tattoos on her face, a small cross on her chin, a gazelle on her forehead ...'

Nodding, Harika exchanged a meaningful glance with the pair of middle-aged women at the rear of the shop, who'd ceased packing up donations to take in this exchange, before returning her attention to Helen.

'Plus, she told me her first name was Selima. I'm wondering if you've encountered anyone matching that description? Or know of anyone who might point me in the right direction?'

Helen watched on hopefully as Harika turned from her, slipping into her native tongue as she discussed Helen's urgent enquiry with her fellow volunteers. Helen felt her stomach tighten, suddenly aware of how desperate she was for a lead, some insight into this awful crime. She knew also that the women's response now was crucial, given that Helen had no other obvious resources to exploit in her hunt for the missing woman. When Harika turned back to Helen, however, her face was a picture of disappointment and frustration.

'Selima is a common name, but I'm afraid none of us know anyone who fits your description. The tattoos suggest that she probably *is* Kurdish and it is true that a lot of our countrymen – and women – make the journey here, particularly from Turkey. As you know, the Kurdish community is...'

Harika hesitated, choosing her words carefully as she continued:

'...perhaps one of the least favoured ethnic groups in Turkey, as far as the government is concerned at least. This, plus the problems our people have endured following the great earthquake, mean there are always people on the move, seeking ways to earn money for their families.'

Her tone was angry and defiant, her passion clear.

'Many Kurds have made their way here in the last couple of years, particularly from the south-eastern regions of Turkey where the situation is worst, and it's possible Selima comes from there. But if we haven't seen her, then I'm afraid it's likely that she's either *just* arrived in Southampton or been brought here illegally, possibly both...'

She trailed off with a disappointed shrug, aware this didn't get Helen any further forward.

'Given what happened last night, I'm guessing the latter,' Helen agreed, her heart sinking. 'They treated her ... well, they treated her worse than an animal. It was disgusting.'

Helen's tone was bitter, provoking earnest nods from the three women. The women here knew they were the lucky ones, having the resources, education, connections and luck to relocate without having to run the gauntlet of the criminal gangs.

'It's horrible, I know,' Harika responded. 'But it's only going to get worse. We had many problems in our community *before* the earthquake, but now ...'

She didn't need to elaborate, hundreds, perhaps thousands of rural Kurds seeking sanctuary in Europe and the UK, driven from Turkey by desperation, desolation and in some cases starvation. It was a grim picture, a flood of anguished refugees walking straight into the hands of traffickers and gangsters, intent on capitalizing on their plight. It made Helen's blood boil and, by the looks of things, she wasn't the only one.

'We do what we can to help,' Harika continued earnestly. 'We're working hard to set up safe, legal routes to this country, whilst trying to assist those who've decided to remain in Turkey. Twice a year, we organize a charity drive to ensure that those who are suffering back home get at least the basics.'

Helen ran her eye over the piles of children's pyjamas, football shirts, sanitary products, toys and books that the three women had been diligently packing. It was well-meant and heartening to see that charity was not dead, but in truth it was a meagre response to a dire humanitarian situation. As if reading her mind, Harika added:

'It's not much, but if our efforts can help even a few families ...'

Her companions nodded in earnest, clearly sharing her zeal. Harika was about to elaborate on their sense of mission, but spotting Helen's concern and impatience, she abruptly changed tack.

'Could you not go to the police about this missing woman?' she enquired. 'Or maybe one of the local refugee charities? There's one, Christian Aid, on Bridge Street, whom we often have dealings with.'

'Or maybe the immigration authorities?' another volunteer added.

The women were hitting their stride now, running through a list of local charities and government agencies, but privately Helen knew these were not avenues she could pursue. She was out of the loop now, an exile from the forces of law and order, a woman with zero authority to be demanding cooperation from the police, local charities or council organizations. The urgency of the volunteers' voices, their emotion, compelled her to do something to help Selima, however. And though it was true that she had few resources and a dearth of viable avenues to pursue, all was not quite yet lost.

There was *one* other person she could call on.

Chapter 18

Charlie weaved through the throng, making her way to a discreet table at the back of the pub. The Cross Keys was not a pub favoured by Southampton Central's officers and since it was only a stone's throw from her old HQ, Helen had asked Charlie to meet her here, keen not to advertise her presence in the vicinity of her old stomping ground. She had the feeling it wouldn't serve either of their purposes to be spotted together.

Helen smiled brightly as her old friend approached, but her positivity was not reciprocated. Her former colleague looked pale, drawn and distracted.

'Hey stranger,' Helen said cheerfully. 'Everything OK?'

'Don't,' Charlie replied bluntly. 'I've had the morning from hell and there's little chance of things getting any better before bedtime...'

Helen was shocked by the weariness in Charlie's tone. On many occasions in the past, Charlie had buoyed her up with her vigour and enthusiasm, but today her former colleague looked angry and despairing.

'Problems at home?' Helen asked anxiously, relieved to see Charlie dismiss the idea with a swift shake of the head. 'Is it Holmes, then? Or the team?'

Immediately, she regretted asking, Charlie looking up sharply, as if Helen had just accused her of something.

'Why do you say that?' she demanded.

'No reason,' Helen covered quickly. 'An educated guess, born of long experience, that's all. You know I don't talk to anyone at the firm anymore ...'

Charlie raised an eyebrow, as if suggesting that the truth might in fact be that the firm no longer spoke to *her*, before eventually replying:

'A major cock-up down at the docks, one which made me look extremely foolish.'

Helen desperately wanted to reach out to Charlie, to tell her she was sorry for her plight. But there was no question of her offering any such solace, an awkwardness having infected their friendship since Helen's shock resignation.

'Honestly, I feel like we're just spinning in the wind on this one,' Charlie continued, shaking her head wearily. 'Each time we think we've got a solid lead, it turns out to be either small fry, or a total bust. We can't even seem to get *close* to the problem, let alone get a handle on it ...'

'What are we talking? Drugs? People? Contraband?'

'All of the above. This morning it was a group of illegals hidden in the back of a Belgian lorry. Except they weren't, meaning they probably found some other route into the country. For all I know they're out there right now, in the car washes and nail bars ...'

Helen nodded, but said nothing. It was impossible to contradict her old friend, scores of British towns depending on illegal workers to keep functioning. It was a sorry indictment of modern, convenience culture, a race to the bottom in which shops and small businesses forced exploited employees to work long shifts for meagre pay just to keep their customers happy.

Few shoppers realized that they were helping to fund exploitation and reward criminal gangs and those that did, turned a blind eye.

'Speaking of which...' Charlie carried on briskly. 'I ought to get back to base, so was there anything specific...? Or was this just a social call?'

This time Charlie's tone had a distinct edge. The two women had not seen each other properly since Helen's departure, Charlie's anger and disappointment at what she perceived to be Helen's 'abandonment' of her vocation rendering any such meet-up both problematic and unlikely.

'Actually, I *did* want to ask you a favour,' Helen replied quickly. 'I know it's awful timing, but I've run out of options...'

And now Charlie's expression clouded over, her gaze finally landing on the nasty cuts on Helen's cheeks.

'What's going on? You look like you've been in a scrap?' she enquired.

'Don't worry, I'm fine,' Helen replied, shrugging off her concern. 'Though I did get a couple of nasty lashes with a bicycle chain last night.'

She lifted her hair briefly, to reveal her bandage, provoking an instant reaction.

'Jesus Christ, Helen, what happened?'

'Well, the short version is I witnessed a fight and intervened to help a young woman, but got clobbered for my pains.'

'Have you reported it? That's a serious assault and—'

'I tried, but it's not me I'm concerned about,' Helen responded, glossing over her earlier failure. 'The young woman, who's probably been trafficked from Turkey or Syria, was dragged off by two guys, thrown into a van. They'd already beaten her severely by the time I arrived, so God only knows what happened to her afterwards.'

Charlie's expression betrayed her alarm, but even so it was with a note of caution that she responded:

'So how can I help you?'

'Look, I'm not asking for miracles,' Helen replied swiftly. 'But I've written down the details here – times, locations, a description of Selima – and I was wondering if you could run it through the PNC to see if anything comes up.'

'Shouldn't be a problem, though we are up against it at the moment, so might take a bit of time.'

'The sooner the better,' Helen persisted, aware she was seriously pushing her luck. 'And if you were able to at least *mention* it to uniform, to keep an eye out for her, I'd be very grateful. She was taken by two young men, driving a white transit van with a broken left brake light...'

'Look, Helen, you know I'll do whatever I can to help, but without tangible evidence that a crime's been committed, I can't possibly get uniform involved.'

'I appreciate that, but maybe you can just mention it to some of the more experienced officers? I could really do with their help on this one, because I'm shooting blind right now.'

Charlie nodded sympathetically, but her face said it all. She would never be as rude or blunt as the desk sergeant, but it would be a hard sell to colleagues whom Helen had first abandoned, then flayed in the local press. Harder still for Charlie to waste what meagre political capital she had left fighting battles for her former mentor, especially with Chief Superintendent Holmes breathing down her neck. Helen was clutching at straws and she knew it.

'Really sorry to have to cut and run like this,' Charlie said, rising. 'And I *will* be in touch if I turn anything up, but in the meantime, you take care of yourself, yeah?'

'Sure thing,' Helen promised, swaying slightly as she rose, steadying herself on the table.

'Are you *sure* you don't need to get yourself checked out?' Charlie asked, delaying her departure momentarily. 'I know the wait in A&E is never-ending, but if you're suffering from concussion, it's better to be safe than sorry.'

'It'll pass and, besides, I'm not sure it's really that anyway. I've been feeling terrible for days, to be honest, dizzy, nauseous and so bloody bloated. Who knows, maybe I'm just allergic to civilian life...'

Charlie grimaced at Helen's joke, but her expression now seemed to shift slightly, a shrewd, almost quizzical look in her eyes.

'Let's hope it's just that. Because if I didn't know better, I'd say it sounds like you're pregnant...'

With that, Charlie departed, waving a hand as she went. Helen watched her go, surprised, wrong-footed and, if she was honest, speechless. Of all the punchlines that Charlie could have supplied, she hadn't been expecting *that*.

Chapter 19

Swallowing her distress, Viyan tried to focus on the job in hand. More than anything now, she just wanted to get back to the dormitory, to throw off her clothes and bow her head under the pitiful excuse for a shower. She was desperate to scrub off the residue of the day's grim duties, to feel *clean* again, but there was little chance of being excused yet. There was still work to do.

Work. Her whole existence, this whole place, revolved around the idea of unstinting labour. From the minute you were shaken awake in the morning to the moment you were marched to bed at night, Viyan and her fellow captives were compelled to work their fingers to the bone, whether it was cooking, washing or cleaning in the camp, or disposing of dangerous medical waste in the outside world. Idleness was not tolerated and illness forbidden, despite the fact that many of the workers suffered from fevers and breathing difficulties, thanks to the unsanitary conditions in which they were held. How bitterly ironic it was that Viyan had fled Turkey to escape the privations of a dangerous and unpredictable refugee camp, only to end up in even more unpleasant and threatening conditions in her adopted country.

Cursing angrily, Viyan re-doubled her efforts, feverishly scrubbing the kitchen counter. It was true that loyalty and industry was rewarded to some degree in this vile place, Viyan now allowed to work in the farmhouse after two years of diligent labour. But if anything this made her situation *worse*, Viyan forced to witness first-hand the luxury and comfort her captors enjoyed. Twice a day, she was expected to clean the kitchen, prepare the food and wash the dishes, in silence and without complaint. She was not allowed to rest, not permitted to use the facilities and expressly forbidden from enjoying even a crumb of the copious leftovers that were handed to her, despite the hunger pangs that assailed her night and day. Though she spent most of her life in the company of either her captors or co-workers, it often felt to Viyan that she was invisible, irrelevant, a non-person. It was almost as if, when they'd confiscated her passport and phone on that first night, the old Viyan had ceased to exist. Her captors certainly never used her name, her co-workers were too scared to speak to her and in truth sometimes it was only the excruciating pain of her day-to-day life that convinced Viyan that she *was* still alive. She felt like she was living in a vacuum, robbed of identity, of purpose, of hope, a zombie stumbling through a monotonous, remorseless existence.

Giving the counter one last angry wipe, Viyan was about to turn away when a noise outside startled her. For a moment, she was mystified by the strange screeching and hissing, but peering nervously through the window, she now spotted the articulated lorry coming to a halt in the dusty yard.

For a second, it was like stepping back in time. This battered, old lorry, with its grimy headlights, faded paintwork and dented Dutch plates was the same vehicle *she'd* hidden away in, over two years ago now. It seemed hard to credit that she'd actually been excited as she'd climbed into her hiding place in the container, before they crossed the channel to England. For her it had been the end of a long and arduous journey and, she hoped, the start of a new life. How wrong she'd been. A wave of deep sadness swept over her, as she watched the driver descend from the cab, throwing open the rear doors to release his human cargo. She knew full well the shock, dismay and anguish that awaited the truck's inhabitants tonight. Even now they were starting to emerge, another assortment of the displaced from Asia's varied disaster zones. They'd come seeking sanctuary, but instead had landed in Hell.

Would the flow of desperate souls ever stop? Or would there always be work for that Dutch thug? The dangers of illegal immigration, the casual cruelty of the gangmasters, was well publicized, government infomercials and social media postings warning desperate souls against gambling on thin promises. Yet still they came, risking all, losing all, ending up displaced and forgotten in a faraway land. Would any of them survive? Or would they all end their days here, a shadow of the passionate, hopeful people they had once been?

Viyan felt she knew the answer, realizing now that those who fell by the wayside would always be replaced by fresh arrivals, like the poor souls who'd just emerged blinking into the scruffy yard. In truth, there was only one solution to her current predicament. She had often thought about it, but had pushed the idea away as being impossible, dangerous, futile. But now there seemed no other way, her situation even more urgent following Selima's horrific fate. She *had* to escape. If she ever wanted to see her family, her homeland, again, she would have to find a way out of this camp. The alternative was a slow, painful, agonizing death. No, she would not, could not let that happen. She had to get out of this place.

The only question was *how*?

Chapter 20

Dropping to her knees, she reached underneath the old, iron bedstead, her hands seeking out the handle and tugging the heavy trunk towards her. The weight made Leyla smile, testifying to the healthy state of its contents. Quickly negotiating the code on the padlock, she teased it from its mooring and lifted the lid. The stacked lines of £50 notes inside were a familiar sight, but still she let out a little gasp, bewitched by their beauty.

Picking up a wad of notes, she brushed it across her cheek, loving the smooth feel of it on her skin, before bringing it to rest beneath her nostrils. Slowly, Leyla breathed in the scent of it, closing her eyes in ecstasy. It's a myth that money has no aroma, especially with notes as well-used as these. She loved to imagine the scores of previous owners, the notes thrust from hand to hand in shops, warehouses, car parks and shady alleyways, before ending up here, in *her* hands. All these notes, all this wealth, was now hers to do with as she pleased. As a child she'd had little money and certainly no power, which is why these piles of cash gave her such a charge. Money meant freedom, meant security, meant control. She'd worked hard every day of her life to earn it, but she now fought even harder to protect it. Trafficking was a lucrative but dangerous business, other gangs constantly trying to force their way into the profitable Southampton labour market. So far Leyla and her crew had repelled these clumsy incursions, but their triumph had come at a cost. Blood had been shed, bones broken, her own brother, Naz, losing an eye in the struggle for dominance. The low-life responsible for that particular outrage was now six feet under, but it still rankled Leyla, a blatant attack on her flesh and blood, an affront to both her authority and prestige. This was the price that had to be paid, however, and she knew for certain that she would sacrifice her own life, as well as those of her brothers and the hired muscle, rather than be bested by a rival gang. She would never be second place. She would never be the victim. She was the 'Boss', pure and simple.

Pocketing the wad of notes, Leyla shut the trunk and slid the padlock back in place. Pushing it back under her bed, she rose and crossed the room. Through the window she could see Visser crossing to the farmhouse, whistling loudly. She always looked forward to his visits, heralding not only a break from the monotony of camp life, but also the arrival of fresh merchandise. On this particular occasion, his timing was impeccable. After last night's fun and games, they were one body down.

'Is the lady of the house in?' Visser called up, his pronounced Dutch accent making her smile.

'In the bedroom,' she sang back, giving the heavy trunk another kick to ensure that it was fully out of sight.

Retrieving the wad of notes from her pocket, she gave it one last, tender stroke. It pained her to relinquish so much cash, but she never begrudged the Dutch trafficker his share. Without his regular deliveries, her operation couldn't function. On cue, Visser appeared in the doorway. Crossing swiftly to him, she grasped his shoulders and kissed him three times in the traditional Dutch way. Disengaging, her eye dropped to the tattoo on his forearm, a tribute to the mysterious 'Suzanne', whom she had often wondered about, but never mentioned. Leyla's relationship with Visser was cordial, but transactional. She would never consider asking him about his background, just as he would never dare ask about hers. Smiling warmly, she held out the notes to him, pleased to see the greedy expression in his eyes.

'Your reward for a job well done. How was your crossing?'

'Easy as pie,' he purred, accepting the money.

'Any issues with the authorities? The cargo? Anything I need to know?'

'No, nothing,' he replied, shaking his head. 'It's all as we agreed. Five Turkish, three Syrian, two Afghans and a couple of Albanians. They are all exhausted and hungry, but they are quiet. They'll be ready to start work in the morning.'

'I'm glad to hear it,' Leyla responded. 'But you must be tired too, after your long journey,' she continued, taking the Dutchman by the arm and leading him from the bedroom. 'Viyan is downstairs, probably standing idle. Why don't you get her to fix you something to eat? Afterwards, she can make up a bed for you in the guest house.'

Her companion nodded happily, a wolfish smile tugging at his lips.

'Yes, I saw her on the way in. Pretty one, isn't she?'

'She certainly is, but you know the rules, Visser. We don't touch the merchandise, do we?'

It was said with a smile, but Leyla's steely gaze belied her bonhomie. She was in deadly earnest, happy to dispense with – or dispose of – anyone who didn't understand the value of her cargo.

'Of course, Leyla. I'm a perfect gentleman, as you know.'

It was said breezily, but Visser was backtracking fast, which pleased her. The Dutchman was useful, but at the end of the day, he was just a mule, a cog in the machine. Leyla knew he had money problems, she knew he had emotional entanglements, all of which could be used against him if necessary. Avoiding her eye, the haulier departed, hurrying back down the stairs. Turning, Leyla returned to the window. In the yard below, all was activity, her well-drilled crew marshalling the new arrivals towards the accommodation block. Looking down on them from her first-floor vantage point, Leyla felt that familiar surge of power. She was in control here. Everyone in this camp, from the workers, to their guards, to Visser himself, were in thrall to her success, her strength of character, her will to win.

And they would do well to remember that.

Chapter 21

Had she been too harsh? Too aggressive? Since leaving the pub, Charlie had been replaying her conversation with Helen, wondering if she'd pushed back too firmly on her request for help, even though she'd tried her best to be polite in doing so. It felt odd to be gainsaying Helen, stranger still to be the one with the power, telling her former mentor what could and could not be done. She had been right to refuse, she felt sure of that, as there was no question of her deploying police resources on a half-baked quest for justice. Charlie couldn't get the sign-off for it, even if she wanted to, and if she was honest, she wasn't sure she *did*. Though she hesitated to say it to her old friend, a strong sense of resentment, of disappointment, lingered following Helen's decision to quit. In the days after her rash resignation, Charlie had worked tirelessly to try to persuade her old friend to stay in post, but her words had cut no ice, a failure which still rankled.

Wrenching her thoughts back to the present, Charlie chided herself for allowing Helen to distract her from the matter in hand. Today's operation had been an embarrassing failure and Charlie was sure the reckoning would be swift. She wanted to have something to show for their efforts before the inevitable showdown with Chief Superintendent Rebecca Holmes.

'Right, everyone present?' she asked, casting around the incident room.

On cue, the final stragglers joined the rest of the team at DC Roberts' desk.

'Then let's begin. DC Roberts, would you mind playing the audio recording of the Border Force tip-off?'

The young officer responded, clicking the 'Play' symbol on his screen. Immediately the audio file sprang to life, filling the incident room with a jarring, mechanical noise. Then, seconds later, a male voice cut through:

'Got a shipment incoming,' the man growled breathlessly, fighting to be heard above the background noise. 'Human cargo, twelve bodies. Arriving on the 17th on the 7.15 a.m. boat from Rotterdam. The driver's name is Luc Peeters and he's driving a Belgian truck, registration plate 1 AYB 209. The end location is the Maslen industrial estate in South Portswood.'

Then the line went dead, the audio file coming to an abrupt end.

'Again, please,' Charlie requested.

DC Roberts obliged, the team standing in silence as they listened intently to the anonymous tip-off. As it came to an end, it was DC Shona Williams who spoke first:

'It's a young male, definitely local I'd say, maybe late twenties, early thirties.'

Several of the team nodded in agreement.

'Sounds to me like a working man,' DC Williams continued. 'Maybe he works on the dockside, or for one of the suppliers who cater to the workforce there.'

'Could just as easily be a rival gang member, someone who thought they were putting one over the competition.'

'Not very effectively,' DC Malik offered, though her joke raised few smiles.

'Or it could just as easily be a hoax,' DC Roberts piped up. 'You get all sorts of weirdos calling these hotlines, for a laugh, for attention…'

'Or it could be some rando who's pissed off with Adam Peeters,' DC Williams offered.

Charlie felt a spike of anger and frustration. Peeters was the last person she wanted to think about, the aggrieved haulier having already filed an official complaint over his arrest, promising to sue Hampshire Police for loss of earnings.

'Let's try to stay positive,' she insisted. 'Let's assume this guy knew what he was doing, that he has some knowledge of the trafficking trade, even if his role was only to muddy the waters or mislead us. If that's so, then it would obviously be good to locate him. What do we think that sound in the background is? Can we place him anywhere specific?'

Roberts hit 'Play' once more, Charlie leaning in closer, but still she couldn't make out what the insistent sound was.

'Is that music? Or machinery?' she queried.

'Or some mode of transport? A train rumbling by…' DC Malik responded.

'It sounds to me like a printer of some kind,' DC Rayson pitched in. 'The way there's two bursts of noise, then a brief pause, then the two bursts again…'

They listened again, everyone crowding in this time.

'Certainly could be a printer,' DC Williams said, although she didn't sound convinced.

'But surely it wouldn't be that loud, unless it's printing advertising posters or something?'

Charlie could feel the energy in the room dropping, so stepped in quickly.

'Let's not get distracted going down rabbit holes. We'll mull on it tonight, have another listen tomorrow. What about the number the call was made from?'

'A mobile number via a Lenovo pay-as-you-go SIM,' DC Roberts answered, showing Charlie the digits.

'So it wasn't withheld?' she responded, surprised.

'No, it wasn't, but according to Lenovo, this was one of only two calls that's been made from that number, despite the fact that the SIM was bought months ago.'

'By whom?'

'A Mr John Smith,' DC Roberts replied, pulling a face. 'Given that the SIM was sent to an Amazon locker for collection and the home address given doesn't actually exist, I think we can assume it's not his real name.'

'So he's obviously taking great pains to protect himself, which would suggest there *is* some method here. That he's not a random hoaxer,' Charlie countered, seizing on this new information.

'Even so, unless he uses the phone again, we've got no way of finding him. Odds on the SIM's already in the bin.'

Charlie tried not to let her anger show, though she wasn't entirely sure she succeeded. Was it her imagination or did the team *want* this operation to fail? Swallowing down her frustration, she responded curtly:

'Maybe, but if we feel this guy is relevant, then we have to pursue him. It's possible this man may have rung in with other tip-offs, even if he used a different number to conceal his identity. Thanks to Border Force, we now have voice recordings of all the tip-offs made to the hotline, so our first task is to go through these, see if the same guy crops up again. If we can get dates, times, perhaps divine a pattern of some sort, then we may be able to find him.'

DC Roberts was looking at her with ill-concealed alarm, the

idea of doggedly listening to a mountain of audio messages clearly horrifying him.

'There are scores of them,' he protested.

'Then you'd best make a start straight away. Who wants to assist DC Roberts?'

There was a long pause, before DC Williams reluctantly raised her hand, followed shortly afterwards by DC Malik.

'Excellent, quick as you can, please…'

Turning, Charlie marched off to her office, feeling several sets of eyes following her. She could feel the mood in the room, sense their disquiet, and though she longed to tear a strip off them for their lack of belief, she understood their hesitation. Yes, they had a lead, a slim avenue of investigation to keep them busy, but would it actually yield anything?

Or were they simply clutching at straws?

Day Three

Chapter 22

Helen roared through the city streets, enjoying the buffeting winds that assaulted her body and cleared her mind. Last night, she had been in a strange place, her sleep disrupted by nagging fears and vivid nightmares, but she'd risen this morning determined to be positive and purposeful. Despite all that life had thrown at her, the many cruelties, injuries and indignities she'd endured, she'd always found a way to get back on her feet and rejoin the battle. Today would be no different. Today she would make a difference.

Swinging left onto Marsham Street, she reduced her speed, before bringing her Kawasaki to an abrupt halt at the junction with Balfour Road. Killing the engine, she dismounted, parking up in a bay littered with electric scooters, which lay on their sides like so many fallen dominoes. Shaking her head, Helen stepped over them, annoyed that the world had grown so careless and selfish, even as a discarded burger wrapper danced past, blown down the street by the gusting wind. Pulling off her helmet, Helen scanned the quiet street, her eyes fixing on the down-at-heel money exchange outlet opposite. This was her first port of call today, one of many such establishments she intended to visit.

Her plan was simple. It would be a laborious and probably

fruitless task to engage with local refugee charities or action groups committed to tackling human trafficking. They had few resources, she had no right to demand their assistance, and it was unlikely they would be able to shed much light on the army of illegal, unseen workers who permeated every sector of society. Prostitution, domestic work, car washes, nail bars, hospitality, industrial cleaning – there was no end to the number of different roles these poor souls performed, so trying to seek out Selima by trawling the mean streets of Southampton would be a hopeless task. There was, however, another potential route to seeking her out.

Some of the desperate workers who came to the UK illegally were kept in conditions of absolute slavery, with no pay, no freedom, no agency at all. The majority, however, were given some form of remuneration, however meagre and unfair that pittance might be. This was not done out of kindness, it was purely a business decision. If those who journeyed to Europe with the help of the gangs were able to send money home, then this would encourage others to follow, mistakenly assuming that things had worked out well for the pioneers who went before. A few pounds wired from Southampton to Turkey, Syria or Afghanistan might make a huge difference to those left behind in war zones or beset by natural disasters. During her many years spent pounding the streets of Southampton, Helen had visited dozens of the small, independent money transfer outlets that littered the city. Visiting them all would take several days, so she had decided to prioritize those outlets that had Turkish owners or strong links to that part of central Asia. This list was much smaller and Money Transfer Fast was first up.

As Helen stepped inside, the elderly owner looked up, his expression shifting from hope to hostility as she approached the glass. Clearly he recognized her and, judging from his reaction, was not well-disposed towards the former detective inspector.

'Morning, Emre. I trust you're keeping well?'

'Fine. And you? Enjoying your career break?'

'Absolutely. Should have done it years ago.'

Helen beamed at the seventy-year-old, determined not to react to his jibe.

'I'm pleased for you, but if you've come looking for a job, I'm afraid I'll have to disappoint you. Business is not what it was, as you can see...'

He gestured dolefully to his empty establishment, but his eyes twinkled with mischief.

'You're alright,' Helen replied, maintaining her smile. 'I'm keeping my head above the water for now, but I do need your help with something.'

'Helen Grace asking for my help? Well, that is a first...'

'I'm looking for someone, a young Kurdish woman called Selima. She's new to the country, possibly brought here illegally, and she needs our help.'

Emre looked puzzled, but not hostile, his loyalty to his country and community as strong as ever, despite his many years' residence in Southampton. Seizing on this, Helen described the missing woman, focusing on her distinctive tattoos, and underlining the danger she was in.

'And why are you looking for her?' her companion replied, having digested the details.

'I would have thought that was obvious,' Helen replied briskly. 'I think she's being held against her will, that she's being subjected to violence and intimidation.'

'But why *you*? You are not a police officer anymore.'

'Should that make a difference? I saw what I saw.'

'It makes all the difference,' the proprietor said coolly. 'How do I know your interest in this poor woman is genuine? That you mean well?'

'Oh, come off it, Emre...'

'I feel for this woman, of course I do, if she's in the hands of thugs and thieves. I haven't seen her, but if I did, you can be sure I would do something to help her. But I would not contact you, Helen Grace. I would dial 999.'

It was as plain a push back as you could wish to see, revenge perhaps for a past clash in which Helen had come away the victor.

'You just make sure you do,' she replied, her voice laced with steel.

There was nothing for her here, apart from further obstruction and humiliation, so thanking the owner for his time, Helen took her leave, keen to press on to the next address on her list. Marching back to her bike, she was suddenly catapulted back in time, to her very first case as a WPC. A fatal road traffic accident had led to her discovery of an illegal trafficking ring, young men enslaved on a local Hampshire farm, forced to work in disgusting conditions without remuneration just to put cut-price turkeys on people's plates at Christmas. Progress had been hard, as no one believed that a lowly, female traffic officer could have uncovered such a significant and far-reaching crime, but at least Helen had had her uniform back then, her warrant card, to command respect and compel people to play ball. Now she had nothing but her determination to set against those who'd take great delight in refusing to help. It was going to be an uphill battle, a potentially futile crusade, but she was determined to see it through.

She would not be weak today.

Chapter 23

'Problems at home, DI Brooks?'

Chief Superintendent Rebecca Holmes smiled at her subordinate, but it did not reach her eyes. On the wall behind her, the office clock ticked loudly and Charlie could not resist glancing at it, annoyed to discover that she was twenty minutes late for her regular Friday morning meet with the station chief. Punctuality was something Holmes prided herself on and Charlie's tardiness had clearly not gone unnoticed.

'Nothing out of the ordinary,' Charlie replied with forced cheerfulness. 'Just a last-minute homework crisis.'

This was a lie. In fact, Charlie had had to drag her youngest to school, kicking and screaming, for the third time in as many weeks. Charlie was sure something was up, though Orla flatly denied this, and in the end she'd had to leave her at the school gates quietly sobbing to herself. It was a sight that broke Charlie's heart, a sorry indictment of her skills as a mother.

'I trust it's all resolved now?' Holmes enquired.

This was at best forced politeness, at worst a way of twisting the knife, so Charlie moved the conversation on quickly.

'Absolutely. Anyway, I'll need to be brief, as I have to check in with the team. Was there anything specific you wanted us to discuss?'

'Well, I've digested your report on yesterday's episode.' Her choice of words could hardly have been more damning, 'episode' a euphemism for 'farce'. 'And it doesn't make for pretty reading. Do we have *anything* to show for your considerable outlay of time and resources?'

'Nothing concrete yet,' Charlie conceded, 'but we do have a lead which I think is promising, a possible link to the smuggling operation.'

'Who is it? An end user? A contact at the docks?'

'Probably the latter,' Charlie replied swiftly. 'A local man, possibly connected to the docks, who may be the active accomplice of a major trafficker. We're hoping that if we can find him, he will lead us to the people smugglers. That's what the team are working on right now. They know how important it is that we make tangible progress in this area.'

Charlie knew she was over-egging it, that this might come back to bite her, but was nevertheless pleased with the cloak of management speak she'd managed to throw over their abject failure. Perhaps she *was* getting better at this.

'I'm glad to hear it. Things can't go on as they are.'

She was staring at Charlie intently, the latter shifting uncomfortably under her gaze. Was this a damning verdict on their fight against trafficking? Or a withering assessment of her tenure as leader of the MIT? It was hard to tell.

'Couldn't agree more, so if we're done ...' Charlie replied, making to leave.

'There was one more thing.'

Charlie paused, turning back to face her boss, a thin sheen of sweat forming on her brow. She suddenly felt nervous, as though the real reason for her presence in Holmes' office was about to be revealed.

'I just wanted to give you a friendly piece of advice,' the station chief continued, sounding anything but amicable.

'Ma'am?' Charlie responded, standing a little straighter.

'I think it might be wise if you chose your drinking buddies a little more carefully in future.'

Charlie's spirits sank. Clearly, she and Helen had been spotted in the Cross Keys, the spy promptly reporting their encounter back to the station chief.

'I appreciate Helen is an old friend of yours, but I'm not sure that continued exposure to her is in your best interests.'

Charlie bristled – she made Helen sound like some kind of toxic substance – but held her tongue.

'She might have been an effective, if wilful, officer once, but she is yesterday's news. She turned her back on our community, betraying her colleagues and her vocation in the process. As such, I'm surprised that you would have any desire to meet with her, or indeed anything to gain from such an association, especially as you're still trying to make your mark with the new team.'

The word 'trying' was all-important here, Holmes' inference clear.

'I know you're pressed for time, so let me just say this,' the station chief continued briskly. 'Helen Grace is history. This is your team now, your responsibility. So whatever personal loyalty you might feel to Helen, I would strongly suggest that you cut her adrift. She has already detonated her career. I'd hate for her to do the same to yours.'

Charlie remained silent, aware that her views were not required.

'Does that sound sensible?'

Charlie stared at Holmes, trying to quell her surging emotion. She was annoyed with Helen for putting her in this position, furious with Holmes for talking to her like a child and angry with herself for once more handing her boss an excuse to undermine her. When Superintendent Holmes had first suggested Charlie step up to the role of detective inspector, Charlie had been shocked, even a little uncomfortable about the idea of stepping into Helen's shoes. But she'd also felt buoyed up, pleased that Holmes thought her capable of such an important role. Now, however, it was plain as day that she was on probation, both her competence *and* her loyalty under constant review. Holmes had been apoplectic at the negative headlines in the *Southampton Evening News*, Holmes' competence and honesty questioned on more than one occasion. The station chief had ridden out the storm, hanging on grimly to her post, and was determined to clean out the stables, ridding Southampton Central of Helen's influence once and for all. Charlie's elevation, her continued leadership of the team, depended on her total loyalty to Holmes and a definitive split from her former mentor. In years gone by, Charlie would have dismissed this notion out of hand, as a grotesque affront to common sense and decency.

Today, however, she wondered if it *might* be a price worth paying.

Chapter 24

'Keep smiling at all times, as if we're having a nice chat. I don't want Big Brother spotting that we're talking about anything important.'

Ernesto Garanita nodded discreetly at the prison officer standing by the door.

'I'm all ears,' Emilia responded cautiously. 'Though I'm still not sure what you could possibly offer me, given your current circumstances.'

Her father took a breath, then dived in.

'I told you I wanted to make amends before I died. And I meant it. Which is why I need you to do something for me.'

Emilia's expression clouded over and she leaned back in her chair, instinctively retreating from the man who'd abused her good nature so often before.

'It's nothing like that, believe me,' her father blustered.

'Well, what is it then?'

'So, you probably know that when I was convicted, I was made to hand over everything,' he continued quickly. 'The money, the cars, the drugs...'

'How could I get forget? We were penniless, homeless, remember?'

'Well, the truth is,' her father replied, faltering, 'that I didn't give them absolutely everything. I kept a little something back for myself, in case I ever got out of this hole.'

'I might have known,' Emilia spat back, outraged. 'We were living off handouts, begging for food, and you had a stash tucked away all the time?'

'I couldn't let them take it all away, could I? Anyway, the point is that the police never found it, they never even knew about it, which means you can have it now, all of it.'

'So what are we talking?' Emilia said dryly, gathering her composure. 'What is this little nest egg?'

'£100,000 in gold,' came his earnest response.

Emilia snorted with laughter, the image too preposterous for words.

'What do you think this is?' she replied, smirking. '*The Italian Job*?'

'Laugh if you want to,' Ernesto replied, coughing away his irritation. 'But it's the truth.'

'And where is this crock of gold?' Emilia said, failing to suppress a smile. 'The end of the rainbow? Or maybe it's in one of the vaults at Gringotts?'

'Nothing so exciting. It's at Louisa's house.'

Immediately, Emilia's smile faded, anger flaring at the name of one of her father's mistresses.

'I see. And how do you know she hasn't spent it already?'

'Because she doesn't know it's there.'

Emilia stared at her father for a moment, wrongfooted.

'What do you mean she—'

'I mean I concealed it in her basement just days before I was arrested,' Ernesto interrupted impatiently. 'There was no way I was going to tell her about it. It would have been gone long ago if I had…'

'No honour amongst thieves, I suppose.'

'The point is, Emilia, that it's still there. And it belongs to us. Or more specifically it belongs to you. I have no need of it now, I can't buy myself out of this one...'

He patted his ribs dolefully, as if revealing his diseased lungs.

'And I know I can trust you to spend it wisely, set the family up for good.'

'You're giving us a hundred grand, just like that?' Emilia replied, disbelieving.

'Every penny of it. Honestly, I wish I'd done it years ago. I was never going to get out of here, whatever the lawyers may have promised. But it won't be easy. Louisa cannot know about this, she would take it from us, from you—'

'Why don't you just wait until she's out the house, then send your "associates" in to get it?' Emilia asked bitterly.

'Because Louisa never bloody *goes* out. She's a recluse, a hoarder, an alcoholic—'

'I can see now why you were attracted to her,' Emilia replied wryly, but her father seemed not to hear.

'She lives in a rough part of town, hardly steps foot outside her bloody fortress and even if she did, I couldn't risk getting the old crew involved. If anything went wrong, if she surprised them or something, well, I don't know what they'd do to her...'

For once, Emilia had no comeback. *She* didn't need to be told how callous, how sadistic her father's associates could be.

'I want you to have the money, but it can't be at Louisa's expense. I owe her that at least.'

'So what am *I* supposed to do?' Emilia demanded, troubled. 'Burgle her house? Sneak inside in the dead of night?'

'You're supposed to use your initiative, Emilia. Isn't that what you're good at?'

It was true she'd pulled off much more elaborate stunts than this before, but still she hesitated, fearful that he was tricking her, getting her hopes up only to dash them once more. The whole thing sounded crazy and yet what possible motive could he have for spinning such a fanciful story, unless it *was* true?

'Please, Emilia, you have to trust me on this one,' her father continued, as if reading her mind. 'I'm not trying to trick you, this is *real*. I've stuck instructions detailing how to find the gold to the underside of this table.'

He nodded gently towards the battered slab of chipboard between them.

'When I leave, retrieve the piece of paper, go to her house, find the gold. This is all I can offer you, my last act, your inheritance. Please, my girl…'

His eyes locked on to hers, intense, pleading.

'…let me do this one last thing for you.'

Chapter 25

'Are we sure it's the same guy?'

DC Roberts nodded cautiously at Charlie, not wishing to betray his evident excitement, lest his lead proved to be another false dawn.

'As sure as we can be. Same intonation, always keeping the message short and sweet, and in the earliest one, you can hear that same rhythmic, mechanical sound. I think the same guy has made a number of fake tip-offs to the Border Force helpline over the past few months...'

Moving the mouse to a different audio clip, DC Roberts clicked 'Play'.

'So there's a shipment incoming,' the voice growled. 'Ten illegals from Syria. Arriving on the 5th on the 1.45 p.m. boat from Rotterdam. The driver's name is Geert van Biezen and he's driving a Dutch truck, registration plate 29 KTV 7.'

The line went dead, but the team came alive, exchanging glances. They were crowded around DC Roberts' desk, which was littered with coffee cups and biscuit wrappers after a hard night's trawling, but no one present noticed the mess, their attention squarely on this surprising development. Charlie was quick to pick up on their energy, responding to Roberts with enthusiasm.

'So this tip-off was from...?'

'October the third last year.'

'And the other one?'

'January this year.'

Charlie digested the dates, nodding to herself. Suddenly all thoughts of Helen, of Holmes, were forgotten, the prospect of a solid lead consuming her.

'So the same guy calls three times in the last seven months, always with a tip-off about human trafficking, all of which turn out to be a bust.'

'That's about the size of it.'

'So he's either a serial hoaxer...' DC Malik suggested.

'Or he's deliberately misleading us, drawing attention away from other trucks coming through perhaps,' DC Shona Williams added, concluding her colleague's thought.

'We're certain all of these tip-offs came to nothing?' Charlie queried earnestly.

'Two of them were complete busts,' DC McAndrew responded quickly. 'The third had a moderate supply of hashish on board, but nothing to write home about.'

'And the port of origin for all three of these trucks was Rotterdam?' Charlie asked eagerly.

'Correct.'

'Which might suggest,' she continued, 'that our caller is working with a trafficking outfit operating out of the Netherlands, drawing our eye away from the good stuff to make sure it gets through safely.'

'Can't see why else he'd be doing it. This guy made three calls in seven months, so he's not exactly an obsessive hoaxer and it doesn't sound like he's doing it for fun. He's very efficient, delivering his info swiftly and sharply before ringing off.'

'Are all the calls made from the same phone number?' DC McAndrew asked, pipping Charlie to the post.

'No, three different numbers. But they are all Lenovo pay-as-you-go SIMs and all are used for a couple of days then, presumably, binned.'

'So he makes a few calls using the same SIM card, before getting rid of it?' Charlie asked.

'That's right. Not sure if the other calls are linked, or whether he's just being lazy, getting his money's worth from the SIM card. Too early to say really, we've got no idea how much of a pro this guy is.'

'Any UK numbers that he calls repeatedly? Anything that might suggest he's ringing a regular contact?'

But DC Roberts was already shaking his head.

'Not that I can see. A couple of numbers were called twice, but that's it.'

'Have we run the rule over those numbers to see if they're linked to any known offenders? Traffickers, dealers, associates?'

'Not yet,' DC Roberts replied cautiously, 'but they're mostly pay-as-you-go too, so it'll be hard to track the owners down...'

'We should definitely try though,' Charlie intervened quickly. 'In the meantime, how many calls has our man made with his current SIM, the one he used to call in the latest tip-off?'

'Only a couple. The original tip-off, then one more to a payphone in Freemantle.'

'So it's possible, probable even, that he might make more calls with it?' Charlie said, leaning forward, her expression alive.

'If he follows his usual pattern, then I suppose so...' DC Roberts replied cautiously.

'OK then, so whilst we run the rule over his call history, let's alert the team that we want to triangulate his latest SIM as soon as it becomes active again...'

'Already on it,' DC McAndrew said, rising and hurrying away.

Charlie watched her go, her senses alert. After months of false starts and embarrassing failure, finally they had a potential lead in the case. Having been ill at ease and despondent this morning, suddenly Charlie felt hopeful, even excited. They had a suspect in their sights, someone who'd been running rings round them for months.

Now they just had to wait for him to reveal himself.

Chapter 26

Clint Davies fiddled nervously with his phone, keeping a wary eye on the door. He was running to a tight schedule today, with little time in which to make his various transactions before he was due on shift. If he was five minutes late to work, ten even, it probably wouldn't matter, but a significant delay would prompt questions, and the last thing he needed was his supervisor sniffing around. Given his history, his record, there was bound to be suspicion, something he could ill afford.

The door banged open, but to his disappointment, it was just the cleaner, lugging her mop and bucket into the pub. Honestly, he didn't know why she bothered, the floor in this dive was so marinated in beer that it was surely impossible to return it to its original state, the punters who flocked here on Friday and Saturday nights resigned to their boots sticking doggedly to the floorboards. This morning, however, the pub was deserted, save for the manager who stood behind the bar, scrolling listlessly on his phone. This was how Clint wanted it – the fewer witnesses to this transaction, the better.

'You buying?' a heavily Dutch-accented voice breathed. 'If so, I'll have a Famous Grouse.'

Startled, Clint looked up to see Visser standing over him, smiling genially.

'I do so love your English whiskies...' his companion purred.

'Actually, they're Scottish and help yourself. Mick'll sort you out...'

Clint nodded to the bar. Shrugging, Visser crossed the floor, leaning over the wooden counter and as he muttered his order, waiting patiently as the manager obliged him with a generous measure of Famous Grouse. His demeanour was casual, his body language relaxed, but Clint couldn't help but notice how the burly trafficker carried himself. Body hunched, head down, cap pulled tight to conceal his thick curly hair, as if constantly shielding his face, his identity, from view. Only when his companion sat down directly opposite him, could Clint see his features clearly.

'Everything go OK, yesterday?' Clint enquired genially.

'It was a pleasant journey,' Visser replied carefully, shooting a quick look around the bar to double-check that they were alone.

'When are you heading back?'

'Soon enough. You have any problems?' the Dutchman responded.

Clint shook his head.

'You're sure you're not being watched? Followed?'

'Nothing like that,' Clint responded confidently, shaking his head.

'Any issues at work?'

'Not if I get there on time, so...'

His Dutch paymaster broke into a smile, a flash of gold winking at his companion.

'Direct as ever, Clint,' he chuckled.

'Time is money,' Clint replied. 'And it doesn't pay to take unnecessary risks.'

'My thoughts exactly.'

Visser opened his jacket, delving into the inside pocket. As he did so, Clint caught sight of a vicious-looking knife clamped to the Dutchman's belt, a reminder that this guy was no amateur. Silently, Clint watched on as Visser retrieved an envelope, sliding it under the table and pressing it into his hands. Accepting the package, the docker rolled his neck extravagantly, then darted a quick glance at the contents. He wouldn't count it here, not with other people in the building, but running his finger over the tightly packed notes, he felt assured that the Dutchman had paid in full. He'd never let him down yet.

'Is our business concluded?' Visser asked genially, draining his glass.

'For now. You'll be in touch though, when you need me again?'

His companion chuckled at the urgency, the greed, in his voice.

'I'll get a message to you. Just make sure you're standing by.'

Breaking into a grin, Clint rose to his feet, saluting his comrade.

'You can be sure of it. See you later, mate.'

With a cursory fist bump, Clint was on his way, his rubber soles protesting as he scurried them across the sticky floor. Pushing through the heavy oak doors, he moved fast away from the pub. Now that this business with Visser was over, it was time to move on to the next phase of his operation and he hurried away down the street. The sooner this cash was out of his hands, his wealth laundered to conceal its origin, the better. Tugging his phone from his pocket, he dialled the number quickly. Moments later, the call was answered.

'Yeah?'

'It's me,' Clint responded breathlessly. 'We're on.'

Chapter 27

'Get out of my shop.'

The angry owner barked the words at Helen, his anger rising.

'I have customers waiting, you're wasting my time...'

Helen stood her ground, her expression steely and determined. This was the fourth money transfer outlet she'd visited this morning and the reaction to her arrival had been the same each time. Suspicion, followed by either indifference or outright hostility.

'Look, it'll only take a couple of minutes and it's vitally important,' Helen stressed, trying to placate her middle-aged combatant.

'A girl is in trouble, so what? Girls are *always* in trouble. Trust me, I know...'

Helen's eyes drifted to his wedding ring, then to the framed photo that nestled at an angle next to his monitor.

'You're a father?'

'Many times over, which is why the bills are high and money is short. So please, move along...'

'How would you feel if one of your daughters had been attacked then? Beaten with a chain? Bundled into a van?'

He paused, momentarily caught off-guard by these terrible images, before responding brusquely:

'It would never happen. I would never let it happen!'

'Still, you can't keep your eyes on them all the time. And there are a lot of bad guys out there...'

Helen was hamming it up, but it seemed to be working, the doting father's fear of rising crime keeping the conversation going.

'This young woman is probably a similar age to one of your daughters and she desperately needs your help.'

'Even if I wanted to help, I haven't got time,' he responded, waving his hand in the air.

'She's late twenties, long dark hair. She has a cross tattoo on her chin and a gazelle on her forehead. Her name is Selima...'

And now Helen saw it – a flash of recognition.

'Have you seen her?' she demanded, leaning closer to the glass.

For a moment, the owner seemed lost for words, then he mumbled:

'We get a lot of people in here, a lot of different faces...'

'But she's fairly distinct I'd imagine, given the tattoos, and you seemed to recognize the description. So, please, if you know anything...'

To Helen's intense disappointment, the man's face now hardened, his eyes drifting to the queueing customers loitering impatiently behind her, as he replied:

'If you need to send some money, fine. If not, get out of my shop. I don't know this girl, I've never seen this girl. So, please, just go.'

There was something uneasy, even fearful, in his tone, which intrigued Helen.

'Do you know these people?' she asked, concerned. 'Can they get to you somehow?'

'Get. Out.'

He hissed the words at her – and this time his response

brooked no argument. Helen knew she had to retreat, but she felt certain this was not the end of their conversation. The rattled owner clearly knew something.

The question was what?

Chapter 28

Her eyes were glued to the tall woman at the front of the queue. They had been ever since she started arguing with the owner, intrigued by her desperate tone and his obvious desire to get rid of her. Curiosity turned to surprise and confusion, however, when the woman mentioned the name 'Selima'.

At first, Viyan thought she'd misheard, perhaps even imagined it. She had after all been obsessing on the terrible fate of her friend ever since that awful night. But the strain, the anxiety in the woman's voice convinced Viyan she was on to something, a suspicion confirmed when the athletic woman started gesturing at her own face, indicating the positioning of Selima's tattoos. Any thoughts of this being a coincidence now evaporated, Selima having visited this money transfer outlet many times during the last few years. Despite his angry denials, the owner not only knew Selima well, he'd even had a bit of a soft spot for her, bestowing smiles on her that few others received during their weekly visits.

But why was this strange British woman so concerned about Selima? She clearly wasn't police, otherwise she wouldn't have allowed herself to be dismissed so easily, so who was she? A charity worker? A concerned citizen? Viyan longed to know, but already the woman was on the move, casting only a fleeting look over her shoulder as she headed for the exit. Viyan hesitated, her half-finished transfer form in her hand, wondering what to do next. Here was someone who might help her, someone who perhaps was kind, sympathetic, desperately seeking a vulnerable young mother who, to the wider world at least, must have been completely invisible. How did this well-wisher even know of Selima's existence? And why did she appear so convinced that some harm had befallen her?

Instinctively, Viyan took a step away from the shelf on which she'd been filling out her form. This ally, this potential saviour, was almost out the door. If she didn't act now, she might never see her again. Was this the moment she'd been waiting for? Was this woman's sudden appearance a sign? Viyan had spent a sleepless night at the camp debating how she might escape. Could she evade the nightly patrols and tunnel out under the fence? This plan seemed fraught with peril, especially as she'd heard rumours that there were electronic sensors hidden in the foliage that bordered the fence, designed to pick up the faintest movement. What about smuggling herself out then? Strapping herself to the underside of a departing lorry and hitching a lift to liberty? This she'd also dismissed as being too dangerous, the idea of falling off and being crushed under the truck's heavy wheels too awful to contemplate. By the time dawn eventually broke, Viyan had come to the conclusion that better opportunities to escape could be found in the outside world, during their gruelling work shifts. Had fate already thrown one such opportunity into her path?

Dropping her form on the floor, Viyan cursed loudly and bent down to pick it up, stealing a look at the two minders. Normally bullish and observant, both seemed distracted today. One of them was tapping vigorously on his phone, whilst the other was pawing at Beydaan. Normally, Viyan would have intervened, asking the vicious thug a question to try and pull his attention away from the cowering woman, but today she was happy to entertain his distraction. Today she had to put herself, her children, first.

She took a careful step, then another, quietly padding past the queue of customers. She was now only a few feet from the door. If she could just get outside, catch up with the departing woman, then maybe she could escape. Exhaling slowly, trying to keep her breathing regular, she took another step towards freedom ... then suddenly felt herself tugged violently backwards.

'What the hell do you think you're doing?'

The texting minder had come alive, clocking Viyan's bid for freedom and angrily yanking her back in line.

'That's the end of the queue. Wait your turn like everyone else ...'

His eyes were boring into hers, challenging Viyan to resist, threatening violent retribution at the first hint of disobedience. Desperate, Viyan scanned the room, looking for some opportunity to fight back, even to escape. But the middle-aged owner seemed uninterested in their spat, as did everyone else present. Many of those waiting in line were her fellow captives and those that weren't were immigrants of one kind or another, who generally preferred to keep themselves to themselves. There would be no help from anyone else, so her only hope was to run, but already her captor was on the move, positioning himself between her and the doorway, blocking her path.

Tears filling her eyes, Viyan turned away, angrily clutching her half-filled form. She had come here hoping to send a meagre amount of money home, but instead had been presented with a golden opportunity to escape. But she had been too slow to react and the chance had gone begging. Why hadn't she just sprinted after the strange woman immediately? Why hadn't she called out? Caution had been her undoing today, caution and fear. She had been close to liberating herself, but not close enough.

Something she would regret for the rest of her life.

Chapter 29

She kept the phone clamped to her cheek, even though the device was already hot to the touch. Charlie suspected she was probably frying her brain, but there was no question of hanging up on the control room. She needed the analysts back at Southampton Central to guide her to their prize.

'Come on, come on,' she urged gently. 'I need a fix on him.'

There was a brief silence on the other end, before the operator eventually responded:

'The signal's coming from the junction of Broughton Road and Jennings Avenue. Can't be more precise than that, I'm afraid.'

'That's good enough for now,' Charlie replied, directing Roberts to head in that direction, before adding: 'Stay on the line until we know more. I'm just going to put you on mute, whilst I update the rest of my team.'

Punching the mute button, she snatched up her radio.

'Car one to cars two and three, over...'

After a brief crackle, both DC Rayson and DC McAndrew responded, confirming that they were standing by.

'Proceeding to the junction of Broughton Road and Jennings Avenue,' Charlie continued, keeping her voice crisp and clear. 'Stay back, but stay local, over.'

Once again, both cars responded in the affirmative, so Charlie diverted her attention to the street, stowing the radio once more.

'See anything?'

DC Roberts shook his head, gripping the steering wheel hard as he scanned the street. They were approaching the end of Jennings Avenue, but as yet there was no sign of their quarry. Charlie leaned forward in her seat, as the car slowed to a halt at the T-junction, turning to look down Broughton Road. To her left, the street was empty, so pivoting she looked the other way, taking in the long vista ahead of her. But this was empty too, not a soul around.

Puzzled, annoyed, Charlie unmuted her phone.

'Any update on his whereabouts, control? I can't see hide nor hair of... Hold on a minute.'

Lowering the phone quickly, Charlie peered down the road. A stocky man had just emerged from an alleyway and was walking down the street fast, drawing on a cigarette. He was only thirty feet away and would soon be upon them.

'Turn right and then double back,' Charlie breathed quickly, anxious not to draw attention to themselves.

DC Roberts did as he was bid, the car gliding past their subject. Charlie kept her eyes glued to the mirror, watching with relief as he now turned left into Jennings Avenue, seemingly none the wiser.

'OK, you can turn now...' she said with relief, as she snatched up her radio to update the other teams. 'Suspect now proceeding east on Jennings Road, over.'

Rotating the wheel, DC Roberts carefully turned around, returning to the junction once more.

'Easy now,' Charlie cautioned. 'He may have glimpsed us as he walked past, so let's not get too close.'

Slowly the car rolled to a stop at the junction. The man was now a good fifty feet away, possibly more, so DC Roberts set off once more, easing the car around the corner in pursuit. The subject carried on unawares, tugging his phone from his pocket now to answer a call.

'Is he active now?' Charlie said, her phone still clamped to her cheek.

'Yes, he just received a call.'

'That's our man then,' she replied, satisfied.

'And he's just ended the call.'

'Short and sweet. Thanks for your help, control. We'll take it from here.'

'Right then, DC Roberts, keep your eyes on the prize and ...'

But Charlie now stopped talking, as their suspect had come to a halt. The man, tall and built, wearing a bomber jacket, dirty jeans and docker's boots, loitered outside a set of peeling wooden gates. Pulling a set of keys from his pocket, he cast a cautious look up and down the street, as if expecting to be ambushed.

'Pull in here.'

They couldn't risk driving past him again, so DC Roberts quickly diverted the car into a nearby parking space, killing the engine. For a moment, their quarry seemed distracted by their arrival, but then he turned away, taking one last look up the street, before unlocking the padlock on the gates and slipping inside. Silently, Charlie counted to ten, then nodded to DC Roberts to get out.

Emerging from the vehicle, Charlie signalled to DC Roberts to proceed, whilst she turned her back to the gates, raising her radio to her lips once more.

'Car one to cars two and three. Suspect has entered an industrial estate on Jennings Road. Request car two to park up on Langton Avenue, to cut off an escape from the rear of the property. Car three to remain mobile for possible intercept, over.'

'Car two en route,' came the first reply, swiftly followed by another.

'Car three standing by.'

Clicking off, Charlie re-joined her colleague, who stepped back to allow his superior to take his place. Sidling up next to the gate post, Charlie peered round. A large scruffy court-yard gave onto a handful of outbuildings, the largest being a medium-sized warehouse about a hundred yards away. Charlie watched on, intrigued, as the man entered the warehouse, shut-ting the door behind him. Moments later, she saw him appear in the window, looking out briefly onto the yard, before drop-ping the blind and disappearing from view.

Turning to DC Roberts, she took in his eager, tense expression.

'Right then,' Charlie said quietly, trying to keep a lid on her own excitement.

'Let's do this.'

Chapter 30

Helen leaned on a bollard, tugging a cigarette from the packet, whilst casting a discreet glance back at the money transfer shop. The establishment she'd just left was the fourth on her list and, with four more local outlets under Turkish management to try, she was keen to press on, but something she'd spotted inside the shop gave her pause. As shen had departed, empty-handed and frustrated, she'd glimpsed a line of women queuing to make a transfer. They were all young, hailing perhaps from Turkey or the Middle East, but it was not their look that stood out to Helen so much as their demeanour. The line of women looked cowed, defeated, even scared. The presence of two shaven-headed men, who seemed to have no interest in making a transaction, standing close by only served to pique her curiosity further.

Aware that her lingering presence outside might excite suspicion, she'd feigned a lengthy phone call, before ringing off and pulling up Google Maps, as if searching for some new and unfamiliar destination. Having concluded this dumb show, she'd resorted to her favourite hobby – smoking. But as she turned away from the shop now, sheltering her flickering lighter from the wind, she was startled by a noise behind her. A harsh, barking voice corralling others to move. Glancing over her shoulder, Helen was not surprised to see one of the burly men chivvying the line of women out of the shop.

'Come on, let's go . . .' the impatient thug urged, silently counting the women out as they passed by.

His companions said nothing in response, mutely obeying his command as they filed past her and away down the street. They seemed completely in his thrall, barely daring to communicate with each other, let alone respond to him. Curious, Helen looked closely at the man, but he didn't seem familiar, being markedly taller than the two thugs she'd fought off the other night. Still, his manner, his total authority intrigued her. What sort of hold did this man have over these women? Why did they all look so scared?

The women continued to ghost past her as if she wasn't there. Helen scrutinized them closely, trying to engage them, but they ignored her, moving swiftly on, heads down, eyes forward. Desperate to know what their plight was, Helen wanted to reach out and grab one of them, ask her what was happening, but she resisted, the memory of her recent confrontation fresh, her wounds still raw. Fate now took the matter out of her hands, however, one of the women tripping on the pavement, lurching towards Helen. Helen reacted instinctively, dropping her cigarette lighter and opening her arms to receive the falling woman. The two collided heavily, but Helen had braced herself and soon had the striking, dark-haired woman on her feet once more.

'Sorry, sorry, sorry . . .' the embarrassed woman apologized, staring intently at her.

Helen was about to respond, putting the woman at ease, but the words died in her mouth, as she clocked the young woman's facial tattoo, a simple Deq moon delicately inked on her chin.

Surprised, Helen now felt the woman shove something into her hand, before disengaging and falling back into line without a word. The woman hurried off, her minder close behind, the latter shooting an aggressive, angry look at Helen as he followed his charge down the road. Helen let them go, turning away and crouching down as if to pick up her lighter. Instead, she opened her hand to find a scrunched-up piece of paper. Intrigued, she unfolded it to discover it was one of the transfer forms from the shop. Few of the required details had been filled out, however. Instead, two words in block capitals had been scrawled on the battered piece of paper in black ink:

HELP ME.

Alarmed, Helen spun on her heel, just in time to see the cowed snake of workers leave the tatty street, disappearing down an adjacent alleyway. Retrieving her lighter, Helen jogged down the street, treading quietly but purposefully, until she reached the mouth of the alley. Pausing now, she peered round the brickwork, catching her breath as she saw the women being loaded into a scruffy white transit van. They climbed in without protest, then the tall minder slammed the door shut, locking it from the outside, before casting a wary look back down the alleyway. Helen remained stock-still, praying that he wouldn't see her. For a moment, he hesitated, then moved off, heading away to the passenger door. As he did so, the engine sparked into life, Helen's heart leaping into her mouth as she realized that only the right brake light was working. Her instinct had been right then. This was the same outfit. This was the same van.

Breathless, excited, Helen sprinted back to her Kawasaki, leaping on it and firing up the ignition in one fluid motion. Then she was off, roaring to the top of the street and swinging sharply right, heading fast to where she knew the alleyway opened out at the other end. Sure enough, as she reached the next junction, she saw the van pulling away and moving fast down the road. Helen followed suit, keeping a safe and sensible distance behind her quarry, her eyes glued to the battered van.

They had escaped her once. They would not do so again.

Chapter 31

Charlie was halfway across the cobbled yard when she heard it. The sound of an engine, high-pitched and protesting, growing ever louder. Now she saw the nose of a vehicle pushing through the open gates, as it pulled in off the main road. Horrified, she realized that she and DC Roberts were hopelessly exposed, seconds from being discovered. Acting on instinct, she grabbed her colleague by the collar and pulled him towards her, the pair lurching towards the sanctuary of two large industrial bins that stood proud by the warehouse. Slipping in between the giant metal cylinders, the startled officers pressed themselves to the brickwork as a dark green Luton van sped past. Charlie held her breath, fearing discovery, but the vehicle rounded the warehouse, before disappearing inside.

'You OK?' she asked, receiving a reassuring nod from her startled colleague. 'Alright then, let's go.'

Poking her head out from between the bins, Charlie scanned the yard, making sure no other arrivals were imminent. The coast seemed clear, however, so she emerged, keeping close to the brickwork as she crept along the side of the aged building. Reaching the corner, she peered round, before continuing her progress to the delivery doors at the rear, which had been flung open in expectation of visitors. As she neared the open doorway, Charlie heard voices, soft and friendly, bantering within. Caution was the order of the day now, so she took advantage of a knot in the wooden boards, peering through the tiny hole.

There were two men inside, chatting amiably as they examined the contents of the Luton van, which was packed to the gunnels with electrical items. Their suspect now directed his new companion to unload a number of the boxes onto a nearby pallet. Relaxed, trusting, the seller obliged and before long a towering pile of boxes sat proud on the wooden boards. Satisfied, the new owner now produced a wad of notes from his jacket pocket, thrusting them into the hands of the trader. The latter counted the pile quickly before slipping them into his tracksuit pocket.

'What can you see?' DC Roberts whispered urgently, keen to be in on the action.

'Our man's just bought some electrical goods and as he hasn't asked for a receipt, I think we can assume they're stolen.'

'How much has he bought?'

'Several grands worth,' Charlie replied, keeping her voice low.

'Bit rich for a docker.'

'My thoughts exactly,' Charlie concurred. 'But if he *is* getting paid off by someone, a trafficker or port official, then this would be as good a way as any to launder the cash.'

DC Roberts was about to respond, but Charlie held up her hand to silence him. The dodgy dealer had now said farewell to his companion and climbed back into the cab. Moments later, he was on the move again, the bulky vehicle executing a sharp three-point turn. Pushing her colleague back against the wall, they watched cautiously as the van raced out of the warehouse, before swinging sharply around the corner and away.

Taking a breath, Charlie turned to her colleague.

'Ready?' she whispered, removing her warrant card from her jacket.

He nodded, preparing himself for the arrest. Without another word, Charlie turned and padded quietly into the shadowy interior. Happily, their suspect was still in plain sight, pulling open one of the boxes to inspect the contents. He seemed utterly unaware of their presence, Charlie making it to within five feet of him before she declared:

'Hampshire Police.'

The man froze, his body rigid with tension.

'Turn around slowly, please, hands where I can see them.'

The suspect obliged, turning now to reveal a shrewd, hard-bitten face. He was clearly a working man, muscular and toned, with weather-beaten features which made him look older than he probably was.

'That's it,' Charlie encouraged, taking a small step forward. 'No need for this to be difficult. We just need a word with you at the station, but why don't you start by telling us your name?'

She was virtually on top of him now, removing her cuffs from her belt, ready to claim their prize.

'You want to know my name?' he hissed.

'For starters.'

'Here you go then.'

Charlie reacted, but too late. There were only inches between them and the suspect threw his head forward so violently that she had no time to talk evasive action. His forehead smashed into the bridge of her nose and then she was falling, stars studding her vision. As she hit the ground, she heard a startled groan from DC Roberts, then the sound of footsteps haring away. Shocked, in pain, Charlie stumbled to her feet, to see a winded DC Roberts sprinting after their fugitive. Cursing herself for her stupidity, Charlie did likewise, towards the open doors, hand clutched to her nose, busting a gut to catch up with her attacker.

The chase was on.

Chapter 32

Helen kept her speed steady as she stalked the battered van. She kept a sensible distance, several vehicles in between providing cover, and remained vigilant and cautious at all times, well aware that one false move would compromise her careful pursuit. There could be no sudden moves, no running of the lights, if she wished to remain undetected.

The van continued its swift progress, making its way through the busy city centre and out into the northern suburbs. Though the traffic was thinner here, Helen felt confident she had not yet been seen. The driver would be relying on the limited visibility provided by his side mirrors and, besides, people tended not to notice bikes so much, their eye drawn to bigger vehicles. Many's the time Helen had pursued her prey unnoticed, appearing as if from nowhere at the crucial moment. It had been a long time since she'd been involved in a serious pursuit, however, and as the adrenaline flooded her system, she had to admit to herself that it felt good.

Up ahead, the van slowed, its solitary brake light springing to life. Indicating, it pulled off the main road, moving fast away down a quiet residential street. Aware that the lights were about to change, Helen teased back the throttle, passing them as they blushed amber, before turning the corner. The road ahead was graced with a number of speed bumps, which the driver took at speed, the back of the van hopping into the air. Within her, Helen felt embers of anger stirring. The men clearly had no respect for their charges, barking orders at them and imprisoning them in a windowless van. Was this so they would have no idea where they'd been or where they were going? Or simply to disorient them? It annoyed her to think of those poor women being tossed around in the back of the rusting vehicle with no thought for their safety or well-being. By now they must all be feeling as nauseous as her.

Reaching the end of the road, the van cut right, speeding away once more. Hitting the junction, Helen gave them a couple of seconds, then followed suit, keeping them in sight without appearing too obviously interested. Helen had no powers to pull them over, no jurisdiction to question them, so her plan was simple. She would follow them to their destination, hoping to uncover either their base or a place of employment – be it a brothel, nail bar or factory. Then she could either investigate further or call the police. Either way she hoped soon to be able to liberate the poor women trapped inside the speeding van.

The offending vehicle now cut left down another street, before seeming to double back on itself, heading in the direction it had just come from. Instantly, Helen lowered her speed, concerned by these odd manoeuvres. Had they spotted her? Were they checking to see if she was following them? It was much harder for her to stay concealed on these deserted streets. Was that why the van had pulled off the main drag in the first place?

Helen gripped the handlebars, tension seizing her. This was her one lead, her only shot at finding out what had happened to Selima. She hadn't spotted her outside the money transfer office, but the fact that there was another Kurdish woman in tow, one who had clearly identified Helen as an ally, gave her cause for hope. Perhaps she could shed light on Selima's whereabouts, once those that had exploited and abused these poor women were safely in custody. Only then, Helen suspected, would these terrified women feel free to talk.

Snapping out of her thoughts, Helen realized the van had come to a halt at the junction with the main road. She dropped her speed instantly, then seconds later lowered it again, as the van remained stationary, even though the way was clear. Should she come to a gentle stop behind it, waiting patiently in line? Or would that alert them to her pursuit? Might they even suddenly reverse into her if they *had* clocked her?

She was only thirty yards from the van now, the road empty and open between them, so she once more decreased her speed, slowing to little more than walking pace. Instantly, the van driver seemed to react, pulling out abruptly and swinging left, forcing another car to break sharply. Already the aggrieved driver was honking her horn, outraged by this dangerous manoeuvre, but Helen ignored her, ripping back her throttle and skidding out onto the main road. She had clearly been spotted now, so the race was on.

The fugitives ahead had thrown caution to the wind, breaking the speed limit comfortably as they roared through a zebra crossing and traffic lights. The signs for the ring road ahead made it plain where they were heading. Once they were on the multi-carriage arterial, they could speed off in any direction, even fleeing Southampton if they wanted to. Helen was determined not to let that happen, working hard to match their speed. The wind pounded her, shrieking as it ripped past her helmet, but for her it was a sweet sound. She felt exhilarated, excited, *alive*.

With a squeal of tyres, the van skidded onto the slip road, then raced onto the ring road, provoking another volley of horns from panicking drivers. Helen weaved in and out of the vehicles, barely noticing the angry hand gestures and shouted curses. The van was driving at speed, but there was no hope of them outrunning her Kawasaki Ninja. The question is what the fugitives would do now. Would they try to lead her to some out-of-the-way place where they could confront her? Would they try and shake her off through a series of outlandish, unexpected manoeuvres? Or something more desperate? Helen just prayed that she could bring them in without provoking anything dangerous or disastrous – an accident at this speed might prove catastrophic for the poor souls imprisoned in the back of the speeding vehicle.

Seizing on a gap in the traffic, Helen shot forward, darting into the outside lane, before drawing level with the van. Her move had not gone unnoticed, however, and the driver threw his vehicle to the right, careering directly towards her. A savage impact was just seconds away, so Helen tugged hard on the brakes, riding up and almost over handlebars as the van sailed by, clipping her front tyre hard. She now felt her world spin as the bike executed a vicious 360, before her tyres bit the tarmac and launched her forwards once more. Out of the corner of her eye, Helen noticed the van lurch violently to the left, just missing the central barrier before roaring on its way.

Soon Helen was close behind once more, shaken, but determined, her bike apparently undamaged. The steering on her bike felt heavy and a little uneven, but the engine was roaring and the tyres solid. There was nothing to impede her now, confident of bringing the fugitives in. They had tried to throw her off and failed, she wouldn't let them have another go.

Her speedometer was tipping 100 mph, but Helen didn't relent, aware that the next few minutes could decide the fate of all those trapped inside the vehicle, no doubt terrified and appalled by the ongoing chase. She had to stop the van. She had to flush out those responsible for this awful trade. And now, as she continued to roar forward, she realized that help was at hand. She first noticed the high squeal of the siren, then spotted the blue flashing lights in her mirrors. A police car was bearing down fast on the speeding vehicles, clearly intending to intervene in the dangerous chase. Finally, Helen felt herself relax, confident that the van would not escape. At long last, the cavalry had arrived.

But her optimism soon turned to consternation as the pursuing police car pulled up alongside her, the traffic officer in the passenger seat gesturing at her angrily to pull over. Alarmed, Helen shook her head, jabbing a finger at the speeding van ahead. But the officer responded by shaking *his* head, directing her towards the hard shoulder. Turning away, Helen ignored them, increasing her speed, but the police were ready with their response, racing ahead to block her off from the front, forcing Helen to brake sharply.

Her first instinct was to ease off her speed, circumvent the car and roar on, but now she clocked another police vehicle coming up fast in her mirrors. Cursing, she changed tack, swinging her bike quickly onto the hard shoulder and coming to an abrupt halt. The police car ahead followed suit and Helen marched swiftly towards it, tugging her helmet off.

'Easy now, madam . . .'

The officer in the passenger seat had already emerged and was clearly alarmed by Helen's determined approach. But his anxiety turned to confusion and surprise as he realized who he'd pulled over. Helen took full advantage of this, bearing down on him.

'You idiot, you shouldn't be pulling me over. You should be bringing in that van.'

She gestured angrily in the direction of her quarry, but even as the words left her lips she realized that the speeding vehicle was no longer in sight. Had it darted off a nearby exit? Or just slipped in front of another vehicle, concealing itself from view? Either way it was with a crushing feeling of disappointment and defeat that Helen turned back to the officer in question who stood before her, awkward and uneasy, his pen poised to fill out a Fixed Penalty Charge.

Chapter 33

Blood continued to stream down her face as she tore along the pavement. Charlie had been left shaken and disoriented by their suspect's unexpected attack, but there was no question of letting their fugitive escape. Without him they had *nothing*.

DC Roberts was just ahead of her, keeping pace with the fleeing docker. Having assaulted Charlie, the suspect had raced out of the warehouse and across the yard, careering out onto the street and tearing away down the residential road, determined to evade arrest. Charlie had no idea yet as to the extent of his criminality, but he was certainly guilty of *something*, busting a gut to put some distance between himself and the breathless police officers. Despite the intense pain and disorientation, Charlie managed to keep pace with him, angrily wiping away the blood that crawled over her lips and chin.

At the top of the street, the suspect changed direction, turning right and sprinting off down another street. Charlie pulled her radio from her pocket, rasping breathily into it:

'Car three, come in, please.'

There was a brief silence, then her radio crackled into life:

'Hearing you loud and clear, over.'

'Suspect has fled the yard on Jennings Avenue and is

now proceeding on foot down Broughton Road. Position to intercept, over.'

'Roger that, over.'

Gripping her radio, Charlie charged on. Injured she might be, but she was fit and toned, the recent addition of regular PT sessions finally shifting the last of her baby weight. Though she was a good twenty years older than the man they were pursuing, she was able to keep stride with him. Better still, DC Roberts seemed to be *gaining* on him, just a few yards behind the desperate fugitive. Surely it would not be long now until he was safely in custody.

As if on cue, the familiar blue Renault Megane skidded to a halt at the top of the road, cutting off the man's escape route. DC Shona Williams gripped the wheel, gunning the engine, but DC McAndrew was already getting out, her baton extended. Alarmed, the fugitive now stopped abruptly, DC Roberts barreling into him from behind, surprised by this unexpected move. As DC McAndrew advanced, there was a brief scuffle, then a cry of pain as the suspect rammed his knee into DC Roberts' groin. As the agonized officer collapsed, his attacker pivoted and raced back in Charlie's direction. Slowing her pursuit, she braced herself for his approach, pocketing her radio as she reached for her baton. The assailant was too quick for her, however, and she had only just got her hand on the hilt as he threw himself at her, his shoulder slamming into her cheek. Once more, Charlie felt herself flying backwards, her head hitting the concrete hard. The suspect managed to stay on his feet, continuing on past her. Stricken, Charlie staggered back up, with the help of a convenient wing mirror. Shooting a backward glance, she was stunned to see DC Shona Williams' Renault reversing away.

'What the hell are you doing? He's going that way...'

As she turned to gesture frantically in the direction of the man, she immediately spotted the problem. A rubbish truck was coming up the street, effectively blocking the way ahead for DC Williams. The young DC had done the right thing, reversing quickly and then changing course to try and cut the fugitive off some other way. She would need other officers on hand, however, as the suspect would clearly stop at nothing to escape, so Charlie half staggered, half ran up the road, pursuing the fugitive as best she could. Even now, he cast a concerned look over his shoulder, clearly annoyed that the pursuing officers would not give up. Perhaps if they stuck at it, if luck was on their side, they could still bring him in.

Her vision was blurred, the pavement seeming to rise up in front of her, but Charlie powered on, using every ounce of her determination and energy to keep going. Her feet hammered the pavement, her footsteps echoing round the quiet street. This seemed to alarm the man ahead, who raised his speed once more, pumping his arms violently as he sprinted forwards. He was close to the end of the street and Charlie wondered what trick, what tactics, he would adopt now. His mind must be working overtime, feverishly assessing his options, as he continued his desperate bid to escape.

Hitting the junction, he didn't hesitate, lurching left back down Jennings Avenue. Charlie was half-amused to see him slide over the bonnet of a parked car into the road to speed up his headlong escape, like some action hero in a Hollywood movie, but seconds later her good humour evaporated. To her horror, Charlie heard the anguished squeal of brakes and then the unmistakable thud of a collision. Shocked, she raced forwards, crying out as she spotted their suspect lying face down in the road, blood already seeping from a nasty head wound. Nearby a car idled, stopped dead in its tracks by the accident, but Charlie ignored it, rushing over to the injured man instead. Immediately, her stomach lurched, her heart in her mouth. Their suspect was unconscious, a crimson pool of blood already forming a halo round his head.

Desperate, Charlie punched the call button on her radio.

'This is DI Brooks, requesting urgent assistance. We need an ambulance ASAP and...'

But as she looked up, the words died in her mouth. There was no point calling for her colleagues because they were already here, DC Williams gripping the steering wheel of the offending car, her face a picture of abject horror.

Chapter 34

They cowered in the gloom, disoriented and fearful. Ever since they had been herded back into the battered van, the unnerved workers had been utterly in the dark, confused as to why the driver was going so fast, why they were being thrown around so violently. It made no sense to them – they'd undertaken this journey numerous times and it was usually as uneventful as it was soul-crushing. So why was their minder driving like a madman today? Viyan thought she knew the answer, but kept her counsel, not wishing to provoke the anger of her fellow passengers. What she'd done had been reckless, foolhardy, and might yet rebound on her badly. But she didn't regret it, she knew that she might never get a better chance to liberate herself and was glad she'd seized the opportunity. Indeed, at one point, her hopes had soared as she thought she made out the faint sound of police sirens in the distance, but then that sweet sound had receded and with it, Viyan's chance of freedom.

Had the woman given chase? Pursued them somehow? She'd been wearing biking leathers in the money transfer shop and could easily have kept pace with the rusty van if she'd managed to get to her bike. For Viyan, this could be the only explanation for their captors' desperate, erratic driving. Though the others moaned and wailed as they were thrown from side to side like galley slaves on a raging sea, Viyan loved it, praying for things to get worse still. If the van crashed, then surely they would be found, rescued, liberated? Obviously such an outcome would be risky, with injuries, even death, a possibility, but were they not slowly dying anyway?

To Viyan's dismay, however, after the sound of the sirens faded, their journey resumed in a more sedate manner. She was still not sure where they were, their route unfamiliar, the turns unexpected, the sound of the road underneath strange and confusing. As the minutes passed, however, she realized that they were once more tracing a well-trodden route, leaving the roaring traffic and blaring horns behind to head out into the countryside. Before long they were bumping along rough dirt tracks and shortly afterwards she heard the driver calling out to one of his fellow minders, ordering him curtly to open the main gates as he dropped his speed to a crawl.

Viyan's heart was in her boots, her hopes crushed. Had they simply lost their pursuer? Or had something bad happened to her? Had *she* crashed? Viyan prayed silently for her deliverance, prayed that the woman's resolve would remain, perhaps even strengthen. Whatever suspicions the mysterious woman in the money exchange entertained have only have been strengthened by the pursuit. Had she noted the registration plate of the van? Viyan desperately hoped she had, as a hastily scribbled two-word note would hardly count as evidence. Please God she wouldn't abandon her quest now – in Viyan's mind this benevolent stranger was her only hope.

The van lurched to a halt, throwing the rattled occupants into each other once again. Moments later, the back doors flew open, blinding them all and provoking a chorus of groans. Viyan kept her eyes to the floor, hoping to blend in with the crowd as they exited the van, but immediately her hopes were dashed, the driver's booming voice filling the metal void.

'You, out.'

She kept her eyes to the floor, determined not to react.

'I said move it.'

Her irate minder had climbed into the van and now feel upon her. Viyan's body was rigid, primed to resist, but in truth she stood no chance. A meaty hand gripped her left arm and she was hauled from her seat, striking her head on the low ceiling. This provoked no sympathy from anyone present, her attacker gripping her by the hair as he led her from the van, tossing her onto the rough ground outside. Quickly, Viyan scrabbled to her feet, ignoring the dust that ballooned into her ears, her eyes, her nose, but he was quickly upon her, grabbing her by the hair once more and pulling her face to his.

'What did you give her?'

'What do you mean? I did nothing,' Viyan protested.

'Bullshit,' her interrogator shot back. 'You slipped that woman something. What was it?'

'What woman? What are you talking about?'

Without warning, her attacker pulled his gun from his belt, slamming the butt into her cheek. Instantly, Viyan's knees gave out, but she remained upright, held in position by his fist, as he continued to beat her.

'Get off me, you pig. You're hurting me,' she screamed.

'I'll do more than that, you little slut, unless you tell me what you gave her.'

'I don't know anything about any woman. I wanted to send money home, that's all.'

'Have it your way,' he replied, suddenly releasing his grip on her.

Surprised, Viyan righted herself, confused as to why her

attacker had given up so easily. But her relief was short-lived, the thug grabbing her by the collar and marching her swiftly towards the farmhouse. As they stumbled towards the shabby building, his plan became clear, her captor adding:

'Let's see if *she* can loosen your tongue.'

Chapter 35

She had prepared her speech, yet was still lost for words.

Standing on the doorstep in an unfamiliar part of town, clutching a cheap bottle of red wine, Emilia suddenly felt exposed. What on earth was she going to say to this woman? How could she dress up her sudden interest in Louisa Baines so that it seemed anything other than highly suspicious? She'd never tried to contact her before, had never shown the slightest interest in any of her father's many lovers. Indeed, if she had met Louisa previously, she'd have been tempted to spit in her face, her connection to Ernesto another reminder of how little he valued his own family. And yet here she was. Curiosity had driven her to this tumbledown terraced house, a burning desire to know if her dad was telling the truth, but she regretted her decision now.

The echo of the bell ring seemed to linger, but there was no movement inside. Casting a look around the shabby, down-at-heel street, Emilia considered her options. Perhaps Louisa *was* out, contrary to her dad's insistence? Or perhaps she'd died in her sleep, lying upstairs undiscovered even now? Maybe the heavy silence within was God's way of telling Emilia to abandon this hare-brained scheme? She could still go back to her dad and say that she'd tried, but that fate hadn't been on their side this time.

But now quiet footsteps within gave the lie to her foolish fantasies. Emilia turned back to the door, pasting on her best smile, clocking the spy hole cloud over as the lady of the house surveyed the unexpected intruder. Still silence reigned, however, the owner making no move to admit her.

'Louisa? Is that you?' Emilia asked plaintively.

And now finally there was movement. First one lock, then a second and finally a third were eased open, before the reinforced door opened a crack, a pair of watchful eyes peering out over the heavy security chain.

'Thank God, you're in,' Emilia blustered, with forced good humour. 'For a minute I thought I'd come to the wrong house.'

She laughed, but it sounded as awkward as it felt. Emilia was an accomplished liar, so why was she finding this so hard? Still the eyes stared at her, appraising her, testing her.

'You are Louisa, right? Louisa Baines?'

For a moment, Emilia feared she *had* come to the wrong house, but the woman's shrewd expression suggested she knew exactly who her visitor was and, moreover, was enjoying her discomfort.

'You're Ernesto's eldest nipper, aren't you?'

'That's right,' came the quick reply.

'The famous Emilia Garanita. Made quite a name for yourself, haven't you?'

Was there an edge to her tone? Did she somehow blame Emilia for making the best of a terrible situation, of trading on her father's notoriety to forge a successful career for herself? Already Emilia felt her hackles rising – what right did this bitch have to accuse her of anything? – but she swiftly swallowed down her anger, plastering a smile across her face.

'A girl's gotta do and all that. Tell you what, if you take the chain off, I can tell you all about it. I've got wine...'

She brandished the cheap Malbec as if it was the grandest of grand crus and was pleased to see her adversary eye it with interest.

'And why would you do that?' came the terse reply. 'What have you got to say to me, or I to you? We've survived all these years without each other, so why change things now?'

There was a bitter, gloating edge to her humour, which unnerved Emilia. Was Louisa really going to send her on her way? Was she going to fall at the first hurdle?

'OK, Louisa, let's not bullshit each other,' she responded, changing tack. 'I'm not here for my benefit, I'm here for Dad.'

'Don't give me that, you hate the old bastard.'

'I've seen him twice this week, in prison. We've... we've had a bit of a reconciliation.'

'Is that right?'

'He asked me to visit, so I did. And it was good, honestly. Don't look back in anger and all that...'

Emilia felt she was making progress, Louisa seeming to relax a little, but still her dad's old flame made no move to remove the chain.

'And how is the old goat?'

'Not too good, I'm afraid. In fact, he's dying.'

This was calculated to have an effect and it clearly landed, Louisa gasping slightly, raising her hand to her mouth. Emilia had no idea how long the pair had been lovers, but the relationship had clearly meant something.

'Lung cancer. It's very sad, but he's determined to make the most of the last six months. Which is why I'm here.'

Gripping the neck of the wine bottle hard, Emilia took the plunge.

'He wanted me to come and talk to you. He wasn't sure if you'd want to see him again after all these years, but he was insistent that I came here to apologize on his behalf.'

Emilia paused, as if ambushed by emotion, before continuing, her voice quivering:

'He wanted me to let you know that he's sorry for everything. For how he treated you, how things turned out. He's just sorry really... you deserved more from him. In truth, we *all* did.'

Once more, Louisa's expression seemed to soften. There was a slight nod of her head, even as her features relaxed.

'This isn't nothing to do with your newspaper, then?' she asked, a trace of suspicion in her voice.

'No, no, nothing like that,' Emilia protested earnestly. 'This is a mercy mission, pure and simple.'

And now finally, Louisa took the bait, sliding the chain from its mooring and opening the door cautiously.

'You'd better come in then.'

Chapter 36

'Can't keep away, eh?'

PC Drayton's self-satisfied taunt was the last thing Helen needed, but right now she had no choice but to suck it up. He was the gatekeeper to Southampton Central, so she would have to deal with him, whether she liked it or not.

'Don't tell me you've been involved in *another* crime?'

Helen eye-balled him, trying to swallow down her fury.

'Or perhaps you've changed your mind and decided to come back to us? Mind you, I wouldn't expect a warm welcome, given the stitch-up job you did on us—'

'I need to talk to someone in CID,' Helen interrupted brusquely.

'Can I ask what it's regarding?' the custody sergeant enquired coldly.

'I'll discuss that with them. Is DI Brooks in?'

It still felt strange for Helen to say that, even though she didn't begrudge Charlie her promotion. It just landed oddly, as if each time she said it another piece of her own identity was erased.

'Well, she wasn't, but ...'

Following his gaze, Helen turned to see Charlie push through the doors. She was in a hurry, barely noticing Helen or Drayton, and seemed highly agitated. More alarming still, she held a wodge of bloodied cotton wool to her nose.

'Jesus, Charlie! Is everything alright?' Helen enquired, hurrying across to her.

Charlie stopped in her tracks, bewildered to see Helen in the atrium, before eventually muttering:

'Not really, but I can't talk about it right now...'

She tried to move past, but Helen took her arm, stopping her.

'Have you had that checked out? I mean I don't want to state the obvious, but it looks like your nose might be—'

'Broken, yes, I know,' Charlie fired back. 'And no, I haven't, there'll be time for that later.'

She tried to move away, but once more Helen resisted.

'Charlie, you can't possibly be thinking of carrying on working. You need to see a doctor, you need to be in A&E.'

Now Charlie paused, shooting a pained look at Helen, before diverting her gaze to PC Mark Drayton. The custody sergeant was leaning on the desk, his eyes glued to the two women. Gesturing to the corner of the lobby, Charlie ushered her former colleague out of earshot, the pair retreating behind a potted plant.

'What are you doing here, Helen?' she demanded.

Now Helen paused. She could sense her friend's anger, but also her distress, her eyes glassy and uncertain. Suddenly Helen felt foolish to have come here, as if she were a child who'd stepped into a grown-up's world.

'I... I've got some more information about that assault I was telling you about.'

She was talking quickly, keen to get the information out before she was dismissed out of hand.

'I've got the details of the van that Selima was abducted in.

In fact, I chased it for several miles around the A33, before I got pulled over. Can you believe that?'

It was an attempt to lighten the atmosphere, but it cut no ice with her former colleague. Clearly Charlie could *well* believe it.

'Anyhow, I've got the registration number, plus a link to a money transfer outlet, which the illegal workers visited. I think that could be a useful place to start.'

Charlie was looking at Helen as if she was speaking a foreign language, so she pressed on:

'I also made brief contact with one of the workers. She's Kurdish too, I think, with similar Deq tattoos. She seemed in real distress, pressed *this* into my hand as she left...'

Helen unfurled the scrunched-up note, the words 'HELP ME' crystal clear in dark black biro, before offering it to Charlie. But her former colleague simply stared at the piece of paper, dumbfounded, as if Helen had conjured up this prop to under-score her wild fantasy.

'Seriously, Helen, you want me to launch an investigation based on *this*?'

Helen was aware how foolish she looked, how pitiful her 'evidence' seemed in the cold light of day, but there was no question of giving up yet.

'Of course not, but listen to what I'm saying to you, Charlie,' she countered forcefully. 'I found the van. I saw the workers. There were at least a dozen other women, who are being held against their will, forced to do God knows wha—'

'And the woman you helped, Saskia, she was—'

'Selima.'

'Selima. She was *with* these women?'

'No, but it's the same gang, the same operation. I'm *sure* of it.'

'What do you want from me, Helen?'

Charlie's question was offered wearily, but her words were

laced with quiet fury. So much so that Helen was at a loss as to how to respond, allowing Charlie to press home her attack.

'You walk out on your team, throw us *all* under the bus, yet somehow you think you can still walk in here and call the shots?'

'Absolutely not,' Helen insisted. 'I'm *asking* for your help. I know I have no right to do so, that I don't have any sway here—'

'Are you? Are you *really*? Because it seems to me that you feel you can waltz back in here whenever you want.'

Charlie was struggling to contain her emotion now, Helen clocking the tears that pricked her eyes.

'Well, let me tell you something. You don't get to decide what happens here anymore. That's *my* job, *my* responsibility and, quite frankly, you turning up here is not helping me.'

Helen stared at her old friend, momentarily speechless. Charlie had never been so curt, so aggressive with her before, and it shook her to the core. She was tempted to push back, to remind Charlie of all the services she'd rendered *her* over the years, but the sight of other officers passing by, clearly intrigued by their discussion, stilled her tongue.

'So, please, if you have any lingering appreciation of our friendship,' Charlie continued, her voice shaking with emotion. 'Any semblance of respect for me, any sensitivity for my position, please ... just leave me alone, OK?'

And with that, she was gone, hurrying away from her old sparring partner and buzzing herself through the staff door, leaving Helen stunned. She could barely believe what she'd just witnessed, Charlie's fervent emotion and outright hostility shocking her to the core. Was Charlie really calling time on their longstanding friendship? Was this the end of the line?

Hurrying away, she ignored the smirking PC Drayton, as furious with him as she was with herself. Following her desperate pursuit this morning, she had come here with high hopes, but was leaving empty-handed. Staring down at the accusing piece of paper in her hand, Helen suddenly felt utterly at a loss. She had sacrificed a friendship, achieving absolutely nothing in the process. What was her next move? How on earth could she find the missing woman now?

And what would be her fate if she couldn't?

Chapter 37

She stood stock-still, barely daring to breathe.

Despite her pleading, Viyan had been dragged into the farmhouse, before being dumped unceremoniously in front of her lead captor. To her surprise, Leyla seemed almost amused by the situation. Viyan had expected her to rant and rave, to snarl and curse, to rain blows down on her, punishing her for rank insubordination. But instead her inquisitor sat casually on the sofa, eyeing her carefully, as she nibbled a sausage roll.

'Forgive me if I don't offer you anything...' Leyla eventually said, flicking the pastry from her chin, '...but as you can see, there's not much to go around.'

Despite herself, Viyan cast an eye over the huge quantity of food laid out in front of her. Sandwiches, pastries, crisps, cakes, even a twelve-pack of Krispy Kreme doughnuts graced the table. The sight made Viyan tremble with desire, as her stomach ached with hunger. She had been given nothing but slops to eat since she arrived in this godforsaken country. A feast like this was beyond her wildest dreams and the emaciated worker longed to fall upon it, eating until she made herself sick.

Leaning forward, Leyla perused the tray of doughnuts, before selecting one. Rising to her feet, she took one ostentatious bite of it, then threw the rest in the bin, taunting her prisoner.

'Now if you tell me what happened today,' she said, advancing on Viyan, 'I might let you try some. As long as you promise not to tell the others...'

Once more, Viyan's glance strayed to the delights on the table, but she knew this was a trick. She must say nothing, deny everything. Playing dumb was the only way to save her life. So instead, she shrugged, adding a half smile, as if she wanted to understand, but couldn't.

'Come on, Viyan,' her interrogator continued. 'You're not usually this bashful. What have you got to say for yourself?'

Her interrogator continued to smile, but there was a wicked glint in her eye, a sense of simmering anger. When Viyan had first arrived here, when she'd set eyes on this powerful, impressive woman, she'd hoped for some kinship, some sense of solidarity. How misguided and naive she'd been. Her captor seemed to possess no empathy. For Leyla any sign of vulnerability or weakness merely represented an opportunity to exploit, to persecute, to hurt. Dropping her eyes, Viyan shrugged, trying to look as confused and hapless as possible.

'No, no, don't play the ignorant Turk with me. You've worked in my house long enough for me to know that you can speak English. You're not like the rest of those worms...'

She gestured dismissively towards the yard.

'So, tell me what happened. What did you give to that woman?'

'Nothing, I give nothing...' Viyan protested.

'Bullshit. You deliberately barged into her, you must have slipped her something, said something to her...'

'No, no. It was an accident.'

'Some accident,' her captor exploded. 'Two minutes later she's on your bloody tail, chasing *my* van, chasing *my* workers. Who is she? What did you say to her?'

'Please, I tell her nothing,' Viyan bleated, trying to sound as inarticulate and terrified as possible. 'Please believe me...'

'But that's just it, Viyan. I don't believe you. I don't believe a single word that comes out of your cunning little mouth. You're trying to trick me and I don't like being tricked...'

'No, I promise. I didn't—'

But she didn't get to finish her sentence, the back of Leyla's hand connecting sharply with her cheek, rocking her head back. Before she could recover, her attacker moved in for the kill, gripping her hair with one hand, whilst snatching up the bread knife from the table with the other.

'I'm going to give you one last chance, Viyan. Tell me what you did or I will slit your throat. Do you understand?'

Wide-eyed, Viyan was frozen to the spot, unable to respond.

'I will carve you up right here,' her attacker promised darkly, pushing the serrated teeth against Viyan's neck. 'Then I'll make the rest of them clean up the mess.'

The pair stood in the centre of the room, locked together. Viyan could hear her own pulse beating fiercely in her ears, the artery on her neck seeming to bulge as the sharp metal bit into her skin.

'Well?' her attacker shrieked. 'What have you got to say to me?'

A terrible silence filled the room, only the steady tick tock of the wall clock cutting through the tension. Viyan closed her eyes, took a deep breath, then replied calmly:

'I. Did. Nothing.'

Screaming in rage, Leyla stepped away, driving her spare hand into Viyan's stomach, before tossing the knife angrily back onto the table.

'Get her out of here,' she screamed, as her accomplices hurried in to do her bidding, grasping Viyan roughly by the arms. 'Tie her to the post and beat her. Beat her within an inch of her life. And make the others watch. I want them to *feel* the price of disobedience.'

Enraged, Leyla glared at her captive for a moment, before Viyan was dragged out of the house, back into the weak sunshine of the yard. Ahead of her, she spotted the punishment post, on whose rough surface much innocent blood had been shed during the last two years. Viyan shuddered inwardly at the awful pain that awaited her, the tearing of flesh and shattering of bone that was her due, yet despite her fear, she nevertheless felt a small thrill of triumph. Yes, she would suffer, yes, she would be humiliated, but she had not given in, she had not confessed, she had not *buckled*.

She would live to fight another day.

Chapter 38

She gripped the stem of her wine glass, smiling awkwardly at her hostess. Emilia knew she had to make her move – the question was *when*.

'I never thought I'd see the pair of us sitting here like this,' Louisa said dryly, taking a generous swig of her wine. 'I was under the impression that you hated my guts.'

Emilia maintained her smile, determined to appear friendly and unthreatening, even though she knew Louisa was testing her, seeking an ulterior motive for this surprise visit. Casting an eye over the living room, a dusty space littered with cardboard boxes, a bright white rug in the centre the only available floor-space for her outstretched legs, she replied, apparently candidly:

'I did, once. But that was years ago, a bloody waterfall has passed under the bridge since then. And, besides, what's the point in holding grudges? I'm sure you suffered at his hands as much as we did.'

'That's true enough,' Louisa replied, relaxing back into her chair. 'He was no better lover than he was a father. He took what he needed and then...'

'You must have had some good times though, amongst all the bullshit?' Emilia insisted. 'I know he could be selfish and uncaring and distant at times, but he could also be generous and fun...'

'Oh, he was,' her companion responded, smiling at the memory. 'But it never lasted. He had a wife, other women on the go, it was a question of waiting your turn.'

Emilia once more forced herself to smile, but really she just wanted to scream. It was bad enough hearing about the fun times her father had had with other women, but his mistress's total lack of agency and self-respect was if anything even worse. Emilia would *never* let herself be treated that way by a man.

'That's the way it goes, I suppose,' she replied, disingenuously. 'Papa was a rolling stone...'

'That he was,' Louisa replied promptly, barking with laughter. 'Though I called him a lot worse. You wouldn't believe the rows we had. Still, the making up was always good...'

Emilia swallowed her disgust, pushing away images of her father pitching up for snatched, loveless trysts in this dusty, cluttered tomb. Keeping her counsel, Emilia let her father's ex-lover talk, dredging her memory banks for happier times, re-living her youth when an affair with a married man, and a criminal to boot, felt dangerous and exciting. Smiling and nodding, Emilia's eye now drifted to the cluttered floor, to the white fluffy rug in front of her. Making a quick calculation, she took a tiny sip of her wine, then rose quickly, interrupting her companion's flow of memories.

'Here, let me top you up, you're nearly empty,' she said, reaching for the bottle.

'No rush, my love, you've barely touched yours.'

'It's really no bother.'

Emilia took a purposeful step towards the table, loosening her fingers on the stem as she did so. The glass slipped from her grasp, causing a yelp of panic to erupt from her lips. But it was too late, the wine glass falling to the floor, catapulting its inky red contents all over the fluffy white rug.

'Oh, Jesus, I'm so sorry...' Emilia blurted, falling to her knees next to the broken glass. 'I'm such a klutz. And look, I've ruined your lovely rug...'

Horrified, Louisa was already on her feet, all thoughts of a top-up now forgotten.

'Good heavens, there's glass everywhere... ouch!'

Emilia had deliberately gripped the largest shard, a rich seam of blood now springing along the length of her index finger. She held it up to the light, as much for Louisa's benefit as her own.

'Don't go injuring yourself on top of everything else,' the flustered hostess bleated. 'Look, you get yourself cleaned up, I'll deal with this...'

She cast an anguished look towards her precious rug, then hurried out to the kitchen.

'Bathroom's in the hall, you'll find loo roll and plasters there,' she added over her shoulder as she ran to the kitchen.

Suppressing a smile, Emilia followed her out, slipping into the bathroom, just as Louisa hurried back past her towards the lounge, clutching reams of kitchen roll and a carton of salt. No sooner had her hostess swept past, however, than Emilia emerged once more, shutting the bathroom door quietly behind her. Treading lightly over the creaky boards, she then made for a door diagonally opposite, teasing it open. Dusty concrete steps led down to the basement and Emilia didn't hesitate, flicking the wall light on and closing the door quietly behind her, before disappearing from view. Hurrying down the stairs, she now found herself in a small room that was absolutely packed to the gunnels with junk. Her heart thundering in her chest, Emilia tugged her dad's instructions from her pocket. This was it. This was her moment.

But where the hell was she supposed to begin?

Chapter 39

She had to return to the scene of the crime. Stalking away from Southampton Central, Helen had been at a loss as to how to proceed. She had let the missing women slip through her fingers, failed to interest the authorities in their plight and destroyed her decade-long friendship with Charlie. The pair had fought hand in glove for years now, pulling each other up off the canvas on too many occasions to count, but now Helen had driven a wedge between them, one which might prove irreparable.

There was no question of giving up, however, so Helen did the only thing she could do, racing back to the money transfer outlet for another confrontation with the owner. She knew that a full-frontal assault would yield little – it would only serve to antagonize him, especially when he knew she had no right to demand anything of him. She could perhaps try to bribe him for information – money was something that Helen did not lack – but would he really take the bait, when he presumably stood to make far more by continuing his ongoing relationship with the people traffickers and their enslaved workers? No, she would have to appeal to his conscience, hoping that his loyalty to his country, his kinsmen, would win out, especially as these poor women were clearly being exploited by local Southampton thugs.

But as Helen parked up on the shabby street, she realized

she was too late. The metal security grille was down, the shop closed, despite the fact that it was only 3 p.m. Worse still, there was a piece of paper crudely taped to the aged aluminium shield announcing that the shop would be closed for ten days due to 'Staff Training'. Helen stared at the notice, aghast. From her experience, those sort of places *never* shut, demand for their services apparently insatiable. First thing in the morning, last thing at night, there was always someone ready and willing to do your bidding. But not today.

What the hell was going on here? How embedded was this guy with the traffickers? To willingly give up ten days business suggested either that he had a lot to gain in playing ball or that he was too scared to say no. Either way, Helen knew that the 'Staff Training' was just a ruse to stop her or the police having any further access to the owner or his staff. But what did this say about the criminals that controlled Selima and the other women? Just how powerful were they, how wide was their reach? For the first time since the attack on Selima, Helen felt a little unnerved. What exactly was she dealing with here?

Stepping back, Helen craned to look up at the shabby terraced building. On the upper floors, the curtains were drawn, despite the fact that the sun was still shining. Was the owner hiding out up there, praying that if he did nothing, kept his head down, the strange woman would go away? That normal service could resume? Outraged at his callousness, Helen strode forwards, hammering on the metal grille with her fists.

'Come down and face me,' she commanded. 'Come down and face me, you coward...'

The noise echoed down the quiet street, eliciting little but a startled look from an elderly pensioner pushing her shopping trolley along the pavement. Ignoring her dark look, Helen peered up at the building, clocking the curtains twitch on the second floor. Was that him? Looking down at her, fretting, as he assessed his options? Enraged, Helen beat on the grille once again: harder, louder, faster.

'Come down here, you ...'

Her verbal barrage petered out as she vented all of her frustration, her anger, her desperation on the quivering barrier. She was hot, she was bothered, but still she didn't relent, pounding repeatedly on the shutter as if signalling the end of days. Slowly, however, her energy deserted her, her violent efforts petering out as her body lost power, as she was overcome by another powerful wave of nausea.

Stepping away from the forbidding metal, Helen swayed slightly, suddenly seized by dizziness. For a moment she thought she was going to topple over, to fall down in a dead faint, but instead she turned sharply, bending over quickly before emptying her guts onto the pavement. Once, twice, three times she retched and then she was done, shocked and exhausted, with the sour taste of defeat in her mouth. For a moment, she remained there, bent double and reeling, before becoming aware of a looming presence next to her. Darting a wary look up, Helen saw the elderly shopper looking at her with contempt.

'Drunk at this hour? It's disgusting.'

The pensioner went on her way, muttering bitterly, full of scorn for modern life and the prevalence of drunks in the city centre. But Helen knew that drunkenness was not the problem here. No, she feared, she *knew* it was something far worse.

Chapter 40

This was madness. Sheer, unmitigated madness.

Sweating, cursing, Emilia heaved a broken coffee table out of the way, desperately trying to navigate her way to the back wall. How long had she been down in the basement? Three minutes? Four even? More? Although Emilia could still hear Louisa's urgent footsteps upstairs, hurrying back and forth from living room to kitchen, it could surely only be a matter of moments before her hostess realized something was wrong? How long did it take someone to slap a plaster on a cut after all?

This place was a nightmare, the basement a repository for all manner of junk. Tatty suitcases, boxes of files, an old medical kit, squash rackets, even an electric guitar littered the claustrophobic space, rendering progress painfully slow. How on earth could she wade through all this detritus? And was she wasting her time anyway? Pushing these unhelpful thoughts aside, Emilia re-doubled her efforts, sliding a bulky bookcase out of her way. She was making for the far-left hand corner as per her father's instructions, but her spirits sank as the removal of the bookcase revealed a large oak dresser behind. Jesus Christ, how many cats had Emilia kicked to deserve this?

Swearing viciously, she positioned her shoulder against the side of the heavy dresser. Gritting her teeth, she pushed with all her might. Slowly the dresser started to slide to the right, before coming to an abrupt halt, Emilia banging her head on the pointed corner and crying out in pain.

'Jesus, effing...'

Swallowing the rest of the expletive, she hurried round to the far corner of the oak dresser, dropping to her knees on spotting that the foot of the dresser had become caught on the uneven brick floor. Heaving with all her strength, Emilia managed to raise it an inch, dropping it back onto the lip of the obstacle, before returning to her previous position. Pressing her feet down hard on the rough tiles, she launched herself forwards once more. And now, to her immense relief, the dresser slid aside, revealing a portion of the back wall.

Collapsing to the floor, Emilia used her sleeve to wipe the perspiration from her brow. The back wall wasn't entirely visible, but there was more than enough for her to work with. Tugging the scribbled instructions from her back pocket, she counted four bricks in from the left, then four up from the bottom. Typical Dad, she thought to herself as she did so. His birthday was the fourth of April, 4/4 his signature code. Reaching inside her coat, she pulled out a chisel and then, taking her mark, tried to jam it into the mortar join between the fourth and fifth bricks. It made little impact cannoning back towards her and causing her to yelp in pain.

Annoyed, she was about to resume her efforts when she heard footsteps above. Her hostess had apparently exited the living room and made her way to the hallway, pausing now directly above her.

'Shit.'

Emilia set to work, holding the blade of the chisel to the mortar and banging desperately on it with her clenched fist.

But the mortar still refused to budge, Emilia succeeding only in bruising her hand in the process.

'Emilia, are you OK in there?'

A tentative tapping followed, Louisa knocking on the toilet door. Seething with frustration, Emilia cast around her for salvation, her eye now falling on a binoculars case nearby. Snatching it up, pushing all thoughts of damage to the contents from her mind, she rammed the case onto the end of the chisel.

And now finally she got lucky, the blade punching clean through the dusty mortar. Dropping the binoculars case, she feverishly worked the blade back and forth, slowly edging along the top of the brick as the mortar fell away. Having worked a decent fissure, she now gripped the handle of the chisel and heaved upwards with all her might. The brick resisted, the remaining mortar refusing to budge ... before finally giving up the fight, a single brick tumbling from its mooring and landing on the floor with a gentle thunk.

Still the knocking persisted upstairs, getting louder now.

'Emilia, what's going on in there?'

Ignoring her hostess's earnest enquiries, Emilia slid her hand through the hole, pulling hard at the top of the exposed brick below. This too now gave way after brief resistance and in a matter of seconds, Emilia had removed five bricks. Pulling her phone from her pocket, she shone her torch inside and there it was – a small blue sports holdall, just like her dad had promised.

'Emilia, I'm going to have to force this door open if you ... oh!'

To her horror, Emilia heard the toilet door open, her hostess discovering now that it hadn't been locked at all.

'Emilia, where *are* you?'

There was a note of suspicion in her tone, her concern ebbing away.

Reaching into the hole, Emilia pulled the bag towards her,

cursing once more as it caught on the edge of the brick. Lifting it out, she hurried across the room, in her haste losing her balance and barging into a side table. On it, an old lamp wobbled, before falling to the floor and smashing loudly. Emilia froze, swallowing another expletive, as she heard footsteps approaching the cellar door. She cast around her for some means of deliverance, or somewhere to hide, but she was too slow. Louisa had now reached the doorway to the basement, opening it cautiously, spilling light onto the gloomy interior.

'Emilia, are you down there?'

Her hostess peered down into the scruffy basement, unsettled and annoyed. Desperate, Emilia cast around her, taking in the guitar, the squash rackets ... and the medical kit.

'What's going on?'

Annoyed, Louise took a step down, but now Emilia finally stepped into view, clutching a bandage to her finger she'd culled from the medical kit.

'Couldn't find any plasters in the toilet so I thought I'd have a nose down here. And look what I found!'

She held the bandage up triumphantly, her smile winning and confident. Instantly, she saw the suspicion disappear from her unwitting hostess's face, who suddenly looked anxious.

'Oh, you can't put that old thing on a cut! I must have something better in the bathroom cabinet. Come back upstairs and I'll fix you up.'

To her immense relief, Emilia now heard Louisa hurry away down the hall, before mounting the stairs to the first floor. Emilia hared back to the hole, sliding the dresser back into position, concealing the damaged wall. Retracing her steps, she swung the holdall onto her shoulder and scrambled up the steps and out into the hallway.

'Now then, what have we got here ...?'

Emilia could hear Louisa rummaging through the cabinet upstairs, muttering distractedly to herself. Breathing a sigh of relief, she hurried to the front door, easing it open and stepping outside, closing it gently behind her. The lock clicked shut, so Emilia was swiftly on her way, racing down the steps with her prize, before hurrying away along the street. What she'd done wasn't pleasant. In fact, it was downright duplicitous and cruel, but she shed no tears for Louisa, nor berated herself too harshly for her actions. For if life had taught her one thing, it was this:

Nice guys finish last.

Chapter 41

One way or the other, she had to know.

Pushing out of the pharmacy, Helen strode back to her bike, trying to ignore the rising wave of nausea that threatened to overwhelm. On the short drive over, she had twice felt she might be sick, ripping up her visor in case of emergency, just about making it to Superdrug unscathed. Her emotions were in a riot, her mind reeling, as a flurry of troubling questions besieged her. Was it just nerves? Was she ill? Or was there a more basic, more troubling reason for her discomfort?

It had been over thirty years since she'd last bought a pregnancy test and Helen felt a fraud surveying the family planning section. This area was usually the preserve of anxious teens or hopeful thirty-somethings, not fifty-something ex-coppers who were slowly going out of their mind with worry. She felt ill at ease, a fake, and yet she had never been a coward, so after selecting two of the most expensive, most reputable, tests she hurried to the checkout. She kept her helmet on throughout, hoping that in doing so she might disguise her age, yet still detected an inkling of curiosity from the checkout girl as their eyes met.

Helen left as decisively as she'd arrived and was soon back on the roads, racing home. The familiar sights and sounds seemed to pass in a blur, driving on autopilot, barely registering her surroundings. She felt as if she was in a dream, a strange darkening fantasy which she might awake from at any minute, breathless, startled but relieved. But the minutes passed with no release and before long she was pulling into the underground car park beneath her building, bringing her Kawasaki to a halt in the usual bay.

Cursing the fact that the lift was out of order, Helen made her way to the towering stairwell. Gripped by nausea and unsteady on her feet, she nevertheless took the stairs at speed. Each second of delay now felt like agony. She wanted to do the test, find out it was negative, then spend the evening berating herself for being so foolish. Even if that wasn't the case, if she was somehow pregnant, more than anything she just wanted to know.

Eventually she crested the top-floor landing, heading fast for the front door. As she did so, her phone pinged loudly in her hand. Looking down, Helen clocked that she'd received a text from Harika Guli, the manager of the Kurdish Welfare Centre, asking if she'd made any progress in her search for Selima. Ignoring the message, she shoved the phone back into her pocket, before pushing inside the flat, slamming the door shut behind her. Helen wasted no time in heading to the bathroom. Only now did she pause, seating herself tentatively on the loo seat, her heart hammering in her chest. Did she *really* want to do this?

Summoning her courage, Helen ripped open the packet, removing the contents and took the test. To her it was as if nothing and nowhere existed apart from this small room, which even now seemed to fill with a tense, expectant hush. She barely dared to look down at the results, fearful of what she might discover, but glancing at the applicator, she saw that she had an answer.

She stared at the clear blue line, feverishly checking the box once more to ensure she wasn't mistaken, but there was no doubt. The test confirmed that she was pregnant. Tossing the applicator into the bin, she swiftly ripped open the second test, determined that this time the *correct* result would be delivered, the only result she could countenance. But moments later, her fragile hopes were dashed, the second test confirming the initial result.

Helen was carrying a child.

Chapter 42

She felt giddy with excitement, stunned at the good fortune that had just fallen into her lap.

Gripping the steering wheel tightly, Emilia drove speedily, but steadily, keen to get her hoard home as fast as possible. She was alert, focused, yet still she couldn't help stealing a gaze at the dirty holdall now wedged in the passenger footwell. As soon as she'd returned to her car, she'd locked the doors and torn open the bag. To her immense surprise, the contents were just as her father had described, two dusty, but reassuringly substantial, gold bars. Shocked, overwhelmed, Emilia had immediately closed the holdall, fearful that a passer-by might peer inside, clocking her illicit haul, but she hadn't pulled the zip totally shut and even now she could spot a tell-tale glint of gold.

Her dad had been telling the truth. Emilia still couldn't really compute this – his tale had seemed outlandish, her mission to Louisa's preposterous, and yet it was hard to argue with the evidence. Nestling next to her was a stash worth £100,000, a potentially life-changing sum. Already Emilia was scrolling forwards, imagining all the ways in which this hefty wodge of cash could transform the lives of her and her siblings, clearing their debts and opening up a brighter future, but immediately she caught herself. There were many fences to jump first, if she was to pull this off.

Fence was an apt word, for this would have to be her first port of call. Ernesto had given her the address of someone he'd used many times before – Bruce Carley, a man of questionable morals, with an extremely flexible approach to the law. Emilia was heading there now, her satnav guiding her inexorably towards the darker parts of Eastleigh. But could she trust this guy? And how would their encounter play out? She would not stumble blindly into their meet, making sure she knew her escape route and that she had her taser and pepper spray in her bag, but even if this ageing fence was benign, would he not still try to screw her on the price? She had to be ready for this, summoning her father's steel, perhaps even using the threat of press exposure or police involvement as a stick to ensure his compliance. Even if she *did* escape with the requisite cash, she would still have to be careful, taking a circuitous route home to confuse any future police investigation and wiping the address memory from her satnav. Emilia was not a seasoned criminal, but she knew caution must be her watchword.

She'd made good time so far, but now her smooth progress stalled, a line of red brake lights in front of her forcing her to come to a gentle stop. Exhaling slowly, Emilia tried to remain calm, but in truth her nerves were jangling. Already she'd missed three calls from Louisa, her hostess presumably bemused by her sudden departure. Had she sensed that the whole visit had been a ruse? Was she even now in the basement, pulling the boxes away, seeking out the damaged brickwork? Emilia had no way of knowing and it was certainly possible her father's ex-lover might divine what had gone down tonight, which meant the sooner the gold was out of Emilia's hands the better. But what would she do thereafter? How would she protect, process and disperse over a hundred thousand pounds worth of cash? There was no way she could keep it at the family home, that would be far too dangerous, but nor could she deposit it in a bank, without provoking awkward questions. Where then could she stash her haul?

Drumming her fingers impatiently on the steering wheel, Emilia craned round to try and work out what the cause of the hold-up was. She could just make out a large red van further down the street whose hazard lights were flashing. Was there some kind of problem? Had the driver broken down? Or was he just making a delivery? Emilia sincerely hoped it was the latter, but even so the delay made her nervous and she angled a glance in her rear-view mirror, contemplating a swift three-point turn. To her dismay, however, there were already several vehicles backed up behind her, ruling out any chance of retreat.

Ahead of her, the queuing motorists were now losing patience. A couple of them had emerged from their cars and, peering ahead, Emilia could make out an argument breaking out between the van driver and the aggrieved drivers. What the hell was going on? If he really had broken down, then those behind her would simply have to back up. Now the van driver was raising his voice, gesturing furiously, but still the cause of the delay remained a mystery. Cursing loudly, Emilia clicked off her seat belt and threw open the driver's door.

Emerging, she shut the door firmly, locking the car with the fob and taking a few steps forward, once more craning round the idling vehicles to see what was going on. The altercation seemed to be heating up, the van owner shoving the nearest driver. Jesus Christ, what was the issue? If he was making a delivery, he should just get on with it. If he had broken down, then the others should help him get his vehicle off the road, so they could all get moving. Angry, Emilia took another few steps forward, but now peace suddenly seemed to break out, the van driver holding up his hands in apology and shamefacedly backing away. Shaking her head, Emilia turned back, annoyed but relieved that it had all been a fuss over nothing.

Then she heard something. A high-pitched, insistent whine that set her nerves on edge. What was it? A drone? An animal in distress? A distant siren? The sound grew louder and now Emilia realized what it was – the squeal of a moped's engine. Without knowing why, Emilia suddenly felt anxious and exposed, picking up her pace as she hurried back to her Corsa. To her horror, however, she now saw that someone else had got there first, a moped with two men on it pulling up sharply next to her car.

'Hey you, get away from there . . .'

The two men were peering through the car windows, as if searching for something. Desperate, Emilia sprinted towards them, but the men had now found what they were looking for, swinging a hammer at the passenger window. The glass exploded noisily, the car alarm shrieking into life, but the thief did not hesitate, reaching down through the broken window to retrieve the holdall. Effortlessly, he pulled it free from the car, slinging it onto his shoulder. Emilia only had seconds to act now so she threw herself across the bonnet of the car, grasping at the holdall strap. The thieves, however, were just ahead of her, the driver ripping back the throttle before she could make contact. With a shrill squeal, the bike shot forwards, leaving Emilia clutching thin air.

'Hey, come back here . . .'

But already the bike was thirty feet away, driving down the narrow corridor of space next to the queuing cars.

'You bastards, come back . . .'

Emilia felt herself choke, tears pricking her eyes. All her hard work, the risks she'd taken had been for nothing, her role in this scam that of a patsy. She had believed her dad, had *trusted* her dad, but it was crystal clear that the whole scheme had been a ruse from start to finish, a carefully orchestrated trap.

One she had walked straight into.

Day Four

Chapter 43

Helen drew deeply on her cigarette, inhaling the noxious fumes. She knew she shouldn't do it, yet felt compelled to undertake this petty act of rebellion. She hadn't sought this situation, didn't want it, and desperately needed something to calm her nerves. Once she'd mainlined on pain to drive away her demons, now she favoured nicotine.

Raising her head, she blew out a long trail of smoke, her gaze drifting towards the anonymous office across the road. A year ago, the National Crime Agency had set up its elite financial tracking unit in Southampton, dozens of highly trained accountants, investigators and online experts working feverishly to track down fraudsters, gangsters and hackers, behind the tinted glass walls. Helen had never visited their office, indeed it had barely got going by the time she resigned from the Force, but she would break her duck this morning, as she had some surprising news to impart to her lover.

Finishing her cigarette, Helen drew out another, annoyed that the office had not yet opened despite the clock having hit nine o'clock. She pressed the cigarette to her lips, raising her lighter, but as she did so, she caught the eye of a young girl walking up the street with her mother, dressed smartly in her school uniform. The expression on the little girl's face was a picture, curiosity morphing swiftly to disgust, modern society's view on the evils of smoking clearly having been drilled into her. Embarrassed, Helen replaced the cigarette before concealing the offending articles in her pocket. Was she imagining it or did the little girl give a little nod of approval as she passed by, as if congratulating herself on a job well done? Either way, Helen's eyes remained glued to her, watching the youngster as she strolled away down the street, hand in hand with her mother.

It was an unremarkable sight, something you witnessed every day of the week, and yet it struck Helen forcibly this morning. The bond between mother and daughter seemed so simple, so natural, and yet it was something Helen had never experienced. Her father had beaten her, whilst her mother had neglected her, turning a blind eye to her children's suffering. Helen had never received any love or encouragement from her parents, forever the victim of their vices, rather than the beneficiary of their virtues. She didn't know what being a mother *meant*, nor what a healthy parent–child relationship felt like. Indeed, the only person who had ever looked out for her had been her sister, Marianne, and that had not ended well.

Staring at the mother and child, Helen felt mystified by their bond, or more accurately, terrified by it. How did you look after them properly? How did you teach them, guide them, chastise them? Helen had never been given the manual, let alone taught any of the rules, having little in the way of extended family. Since she was a teenager she had been isolated, abandoned, a lone rock in a swirling river. Police work had given her a sense of purpose and she had thrived in the safely of its solid, practical constraints. Yes, her chosen career had often put her in grave danger, but it had also made her, allowing her to flourish in the service of others. Now that her career was over, was she suddenly supposed to embrace a new path, finding contentment in the role of new mother?

No, it was impossible. Even putting aside the fact that she had no proper role models to emulate, nor any practical experience of parenting, she was far too old. Following through with the pregnancy could potentially put her life in danger and certainly posed serious dangers to the baby. It would be selfish to pursue the pregnancy, especially as she had never wanted to be a mother in the first place. She lived alone in a top-floor flat, was in a fledgling relationship with a man she hardly knew and had no obvious means of financially supporting herself or her family. No, it was madness to even consider it.

And yet the responsibility was not hers alone, hence her visit this morning. She had no expectation that Christopher would be overjoyed by her news, but she knew she was honour-bound to tell him. Perhaps it was his fault, perhaps he'd accidentally ripped a hole in the condom, but it was more likely hers, given her failure to take any precautions herself, wrongly assuming that she was too old to conceive. It was beholden on her now to own her mistake, deliver her bombshell and then try to work out what to do. Helen thought she knew the answer already, but part of her wanted to hear *him* say it.

Across the road, a young receptionist had opened the office door to greet a courier, so Helen took this as her cue, crossing quickly and slipping inside. The foyer was impressive, all granite surfaces and fresh cut flowers, but she didn't linger to admire the view, marching swiftly up to the front desk.

'Good morning. Is Christopher Palmer in?' Helen enquired genially.

'And your name is?' the smiling receptionist returned formally.

'DI Helen Grace.'

Instantly, the receptionist's expression changed, as recognition took hold.

'Oh, I see. Is it a professional call then, DI Grace...?'

'No, it's personal. Is he in?'

'Well, yes, but...'

'Great, I'll see myself up.'

'Hold on a minute, you can't just...'

But Helen was already on the move, swinging a leg over the barrier, before continuing on her way to the lift. Christopher had often complained to her about his poky second-floor office, so hurrying into the lift, Helen stabbed the button for that floor. The receptionist was already haring after her, but Helen's head start proved decisive, the doors kissing shut before she could intercept her. Moments later, she was striding along the corridor on the second floor, desperately scanning for Christopher's name plate. Marching towards her down the corridor was a rosy-cheeked fifty-something man in an overly tight, striped shirt.

'Christopher Palmer?' Helen enquired with a smile.

'Last office on the left. Are you a friend of his or...?'

He was clearly keen to talk, struck by the sight of an athletic woman in biking leathers, but waving her thanks, Helen continued on her way, until she came to the end of the corridor. Taking in the name plate – Christopher Palmer, Senior Analyst – she took a breath, then after a smart knock, stepped inside.

'Sorry to burst in on you like this...'

Helen petered out, disappointed to discover that the room was empty. This was not in the plan at all. Would she even get to see Christopher before she was ejected? Casting a wary eye out into the corridor, she shut the door gently behind her, retreating inside. Her lover was not here, but clearly *was* in the building, his jacket gracing his chair and a cup of coffee steaming on the desk. There was nothing to do but wait, so cracking her knuckles, she paced the room, taking in the small, but swanky office. There was clearly more money in financial scams and cybercrimes than in regular policing, the office smartly decorated and impressively appointed. A glass coffee table nestled by a smart leather three-piece suite, there were well-stocked bookcases on two walls, and a brand-new desk in front of an ultra-modern, ergonomic chair. Helen bent her steps in that direction now, taking in the large iMac computer, the vase of peonies and next to that a smart, framed photo.

Helen stared at the image, at first confused, then enraged. Christopher was his usual handsome self, beaming with happiness, in an elegant lounge suit, a white carnation in his buttonhole.

And next to him, swathed in reams of bridal lace, was his beautiful wife.

Chapter 44

'You lied to me, you piece of shit.'

Emilia glared at her father, fighting hard to swallow down her rising emotion. She refused to let this worthless toad see how upset she was, would not give him that satisfaction. What he deserved was her righteous outrage.

'This whole thing was a set-up from the start. Asking me to come here alone, to visit Louisa, it was all part of your plan to get your hands on that gold.'

'Emilia, please, not so loud,' her father protested, casting a nervous look at the loitering prison guard.

'Are you kidding me?' the journalist demanded, raising her voice. 'I want the whole world to know what you've done. You used me again, your own flesh and blood, to spring a bloody *heist.*'

'It wasn't like that.'

'It was *exactly* like that. You manipulated me, put me in danger, all because of your greed.'

'I had no choice, Emilia.'

'Oh, save it,' she hissed. 'I've heard it all before.'

'Please, believe me,' her father insisted, his expression intense. 'If I could have done this any other way, I would have done. This was the only way I could keep everyone safe.'

'Are you for real? Two men robbed me last night. One of them had a bloody hammer. What would they have done if I hadn't got out of my car? Smashed the window anyway? Attacked me?'

'I'm sorry, I'm sorry,' her father muttered, shame-faced. 'I couldn't think of another way. I owe them money. Lots of money.'

'Who?' Emilia barked.

'The guys ... the guys I used to work with.'

'The "guys" who did this to me?' Emilia fired back, aghast, gesturing to the scarring on the left side of her face.

'Yes, them,' Ernesto muttered, unable to look at his daughter. 'I've ... I've run up a few debts in here.'

'A hundred grand worth of debts? In here? Are you bloody kidding me?'

'Please, Emilia, hush now ...'

'Lobster every night, is it? Washed down with champagne? What do you take me for?'

'I got in a bit of trouble with one of the other inmates, OK?' Ernesto protested, wiping the sweat form his brow. 'He runs a book, a betting syndicate. I made some bad choices, couldn't pay him, so I borrowed money from the old crew to try and make things right ...'

'And let me guess, you bet and lost again.'

Ernesto shrugged his answer, disconsolate.

'I've never been very lucky.'

'Spare me, I forgot to bring my violin.'

Emilia, please, I'm trying to explain. The debts kept getting bigger, my associates were charging interest and they were happy to let the debts grow, thinking I'd make it back for them when I got out, but when they heard I was dying, they demanded payment.'

'You *do* actually have cancer then?' Emilia replied, witheringly.

'How can you ask me that?' her father replied, looking genuinely aggrieved. 'Do I look like a well man to you?'

Emilia shrugged, but in truth she did believe *that* part of the story. Her father seemed to be fading away in front of her very eyes.

'So why use me?' demanded furiously. 'Why not just give your associates Louisa's address?'

'I've *told* you why I couldn't do that. Do you think they would have asked her politely for the money?'

Emilia glowered at him, refusing to acknowledge that her father had a point.

'I thought if you could get it without her knowing, and they could then retrieve it from you without incident, then everything might be alright.'

'For you, you mean. But what about me? I thought you genuinely wanted to make amends for what you did to me, to us. More fool me, I guess.'

Her father once more broke off eye contact, each blow landing heavily. He actually seemed humbled, humiliated even, something Emilia had never witnessed before.

'Please, my love, if there had been any other way ...' he murmured forlornly.

'No, no, you don't get to call me "love". That is the one thing you've never given us. You have always put yourself first, *always*. I mean why did you even bother having kids if you had no interest in them?'

'I loved you all, I still do ...'

'Bullshit, we're just pawns in your game, to be used and then discarded. It means nothing to you, does it?'

'That's not true,' her father replied, colour rising in his cheeks. 'The day you were born was the happiest day of my life, my first-born, my eldest.'

'Yeah, right...'

'It's true,' Ernesto insisted, his voice shaking slightly. 'From the minute I held you in my arms, I knew what you were. A warrior. A fighter. You were so strong, so determined. I knew you would be something special even then.'

'Jesus, you're incredible,' Emilia shot back. 'Do you really think you can *charm* your way out of this? You never gave any of us a moment's thought. It was the life you loved – being a big shot, dealing drugs, throwing your money around.'

'No, no, no,' Ernesto exploded, banging the table with his fist. 'That is not true. Yes, I made mistakes, plenty of them, but I loved you all, cared for you all. You had a roof over your head, food on the table, smart clothes. Who do you think provided all that? Father Christmas?'

Emilia stared at him, wrongfooted by his anger and annoyed by this uncomfortable truth. He had provided for them, there was no question of that. But that didn't make up for the callous way he'd exploited them, endangering their own lives simply to make a buck. She hesitated, uncertain how to respond, but before she could do so, her father resumed his attack.

'I never had any of that, let me tell you. I grew up on the streets of Oporto with *nothing*.'

Emilia squirmed in her seat. She didn't really want to go there, didn't want to entertain the possibility of having any sympathy for this man.

'I never knew my father and my mother... well, she was murdered when I was eight, beaten to death by one of her "clients".'

Emilia looked away, didn't want to hear it.

'After that, it was just me, surviving by my wits, until my uncle found me, got me out of there, brought me here. He had his reasons for that too...'

Once more Emilia saw anger flare in her father's eyes, before he brusquely continued:

'I never had a family, Emilia. I never knew what that meant, what you were supposed to do. So, yes, I messed up, yes, I let you down. But I never wanted any of that, I never wanted to hurt you, I just didn't know any better. I... I did what I could do to be a decent parent. I'm... I'm just sorry it wasn't enough.'

Despite herself, Emilia felt the first stirrings of sympathy. This man had suffered in ways she would probably never know. But did this excuse his bare-faced lies, his callous treatment of them all? Emilia thought she knew the answer to that, picking up her bag and rising.

'Please, Emilia, don't go. I'm trying to explain.'

'You've said enough already.'

'Be angry with me, hate me even, but please don't abandon me.'

She stared at his entreating face, the man she had often hated, on occasion missed, perhaps sometimes even loved.

'Sorry, Dad. No one makes a mug out of me twice.'

She saw disappointment grip his features, but she wasn't done yet.

'You're a parasite, a disease. A man who has brought me nothing but trouble. So, thanks for the kind words, but it's too little too late.'

She paused briefly, before delivering her coup de grâce.

'You'll never see me again.'

Chapter 45

'What's her name?'

Christopher stood in front of Helen, ashen, silent. He was used to confronting others with their wrongdoing, but today *he* was the one in the dock.

'Well?' Helen demanded, scorn seeping from every pore.

Still he said nothing, paralyzed by shock and embarrassment. To Helen, her lover seemed to have suddenly shrunk in stature, as if the air had been let out of him, the exposure of his duplicity robbing him of his vigour, his power.

'Her name is Alice,' he eventually replied, finally meeting Helen's eye.

'And how long have you been married?' she continued, her eye zeroing in on the thick gold wedding band that now adorned his left hand.

'Please, Helen, do we really have to do this—'

'Answer the fucking question.'

Exhaling heavily, Christopher rounded his desk, running his hand along the top of his chair, studiously avoiding looking at the photo of his wife.

'We met ten years ago,' he eventually confessed. 'We've been married about six.'

'Is this the bit where you tell me that you love your wife,

but recently things have been difficult between you...?' Helen replied, caustically.

'I wouldn't waste my breath,' he replied disconsolately. 'But, yes.'

'So, what was all this? A bit of escapism? A fantasy? Executive relief?'

Pained, Christopher opened his mouth to answer, when he was suddenly distracted by a loud knocking on his door. Seconds later, a burly security guard entered.

'Everything OK in here? Reception said we had an intruder...'

He looked disparagingly at Helen, his eyes boring into her. But if he was expecting her to quail, to be intimidated by him, he was sorely mistaken. The way she was feeling right now, she would lay him out with one punch.

'It's all fine, just a misunderstanding,' Christopher blustered.

'You're sure? Because if this person is bothering—'

'It's OK, honestly,' Christopher cut in tersely. 'She's a friend.'

The guard seemed unconvinced, but there was no question of pushing it any further, so with ill grace, he retired, closing the door behind him.

'So, is that what I am? A friend?' Helen enquired, archly.

'Helen, please, I never wanted it to turn out like this,' he replied with feeling, crossing the room towards her. 'I should have been honest with you, but in truth... I bottled it. And then the longer it went on, the easier it got. You didn't seem to want a long-term relationship and neither did I, so it kind of worked.'

'Except for the fact that you were lying to your wife. And lying to me.'

'Yes, it was stupid and cowardly and selfish of me. I don't know what else to say.'

'Did you feel anything for me? Or was I just a distraction?'

'Of course I do,' he insisted earnestly. 'Which is why this is all so messed-up.'

He ran a hand through his hair, suddenly looking exhausted and deflated.

'Yes, at first, I admit I was just looking for some intimacy, some fun even...'

'There were others before me? Or maybe you've got several of us on the go?'

'No, nothing like that. I met a couple of women before you, but they were one-offs. You were something different. You're so ... so confident in yourself, so in control, so strong.'

Today Helen felt anything but yet she held her tongue.

'And I guess I was kind of beguiled by that. Alice is a very different character and, to be honest, I'm a very different character. So, in spite of myself, I did develop feelings for you. I *have* developed feelings for you.'

'How nice for you. That way you could have your cake *and* eat it.'

'No, no, none of this was intentional. And please believe me I hated myself for deceiving you. I never wanted to hurt you, Helen. You mean a lot to me...'

'I see. So maybe this is the point when you tell me you're going to leave your wife and move in with me?'

She was ready to slap him down if he even hinted at such an outcome, but his sheepish reaction rendered that unnecessary.

'Look, Helen, it's not that simple. I love Alice and the issues we've had, well, they're nobody's fault really, no one's done anything wrong—'

'That's a bit rich, coming from you.'

'Helen, please, I'm trying to be honest here.'

She raised an eyebrow at that one, but Christopher continued:

'I'm trying to *explain*. I didn't plan any of this, which is why it's all so messy, so difficult...'

'Well, it's about to get a lot more difficult. I'm pregnant.'

Her lover stared at her, stupefied, as if barely able to comprehend her words.

'Before you ask, I haven't had it confirmed by a doctor. But I did two tests last night, and two again this morning. All four were positive.'

'But... but we were careful.'

'Not careful enough.'

The colour had drained from Christopher's face, sweat creasing his brow.

'Bloody hell.'

'You don't say...'

'What... what are you going to do about it?'

'What am *I* going to do about it?' Helen replied quickly, her anger rising. 'It takes two to tango, Christopher.'

'I know that, of course I do, but you're not thinking that we...'

He stared at her beseechingly, fumbling for the right words.

'I mean this doesn't change anything, I can't just walk out on Alice.'

'Do you really think that's what this is?' Helen fired back at him. 'Do you think this is a shake down? That I'm here to trap you into a relationship with me?'

'No, no, of course not...'

'Do you really think that little of me? That I would use this to imprison you, to destroy your marriage?'

'No, no, a hundred times no. I'm just trying to be clear with you.'

'Well, you've been clear with me alright,' she rasped, her voice cracking with emotion. 'You've had your fun and now things have got complicated, you want rid of me.'

'No, it's not that at all,' her faithless lover insisted. 'Obviously I'll do whatever's required, this is my mess too.'

'Mess?'

'You know what I mean. It's just that the situation is difficult for me. I can't land this on Alice, not at the moment – it'd destroy her.'

'You should have thought of that before you started playing away.'

'Do you think I don't know that? I'm sorry, OK? I'm so sorry, I don't know what else to say...'

For a moment, Helen said nothing, the weight of her folly making itself felt properly for the first time.

'What on earth did I ever see in you?' she eventually hissed. 'You play the big shot, but actually, you're nothing, just a selfish prick who doesn't have the courage to own up to his mistakes. I should hate you, but actually I pity you.'

Shaking her head, she moved off, marching briskly towards the door.

'Helen, please don't go. We need to talk about this...'

In response, she sped up, evading his grasp.

'There's nothing to say. We're done here.'

And with that, she wrenched open the door, marching fast down the corridor with her head held high, fighting back the tears that threatened, as her life slowly imploded. What the hell had she done to deserve *this*?

Chapter 46

'I'm afraid I've got bad news to share with you all...'

Charlie took in the concerned faces of her team, trying to summon the courage to continue. She'd spent a sleepless night replaying her fractious exchange with Helen, only to be disturbed early by a phone call from the hospital. She had neither the energy nor the strength to lead her unsettled team this morning, but there was no getting around it, so taking a breath, she continued:

'Our suspect died in the early hours of this morning. The surgeons at Southants did everything they could, but in the end his injuries were too severe.'

Blank shock on the faces of her colleagues as they digested this development, many of them looking ashen. The only saving grace was that DC Shona Williams was not present, having heeded Charlie's advice to take a few days off to process yesterday's shock, but in truth this was scant consolation. The news would soon filter back to her, dragging Charlie into an emotional maelstrom she wasn't sure she had the energy to handle, but her immediate task was to keep the rest of the team on board, as their faltering investigation hit the buffers once more.

'The only good news,' she continued, trying her best to inject some optimism into her voice, 'is that we now have a name. Our suspect is … was Clint Davies, a stevedore at Southampton docks.'

Charlie pinned a photo of Davies on the board, alongside a brief rap sheet.

'Prior to that he had a number of different jobs and a handful of minor convictions – theft, handling stolen goods, possession of Cat C drugs. All fairly low-level. The deal Clint concluded yesterday is one of a long line of similar transactions he's made over the years. His partner in crime, Graeme O'Neil, is currently in custody and though I've only spoken to him briefly, he's confirmed that the pair met up every few months, to exchange cash for electrical goods.'

'And that was Davies' way of laundering the cash he received from our trafficker?' DC Malik offered, trying her best to be constructive.

'Looks like it,' Charlie replied purposefully, nodding her heartfelt thanks to her colleague. 'O'Neil has given up the dates of their last few deals and get this – they all took place shortly after the hoax phone calls Clint Davies made to Border Force.'

'So we're thinking that Davies makes the hoax calls, gets paid off, then contacts O'Neil to rinse the cash?' DC Rayson enquired, intrigued.

'Exactly. The phone Davies used to contact O'Neil was the same phone which he used to contact Border Force. Sloppy by him, helpful for us.'

Charlie was pleased to see a few heads nod, as DC Roberts took up the baton:

'So that suggests Davies is a regular contact of our traffickers. That he's used by them to throw us off the scent, to divert our attention to innocent hauliers, whilst they bring their illegal cargo in.'

'Exactly. Which is why I think the hoax phone calls might

be the key to identifying our trafficking gang,' Charlie added. 'We're all agreed that our trafficker used Clint Davies' calls to draw our attention away from the real action, right?'

The assembled team nodded, which cheered Charlie a little.

'Are we also agreed that this suggests the real trafficker would aim to slip through customs around the same time, whilst the authorities were preoccupied investigating their fake lead?'

'Probably on the same day,' DC Malik agreed. 'And preferably as close to the fake bust as possible. They can't assume we'd just up sticks and leave after one false start, so better to drive the real "cargo" through whilst we were actively involved in another search elsewhere.'

'Do you want me to pull up the details of the other European cargo trucks that came through from Rotterdam on the same day as Peeters?' DC Roberts asked perceptively, hurrying to his desk to retrieve his laptop.

'Yes, but we'll need to cross reference them with the trucks that arrived on the other days that Clint Davies made hoax calls to Border Force. If we can pick out a *specific* truck that came through on those three *specific* days, then we might have something to work with.'

Some of Charlie's colleagues looked buoyed up by this possibility, but DC Roberts looked troubled.

'Sounds feasible,' he replied cautiously. 'But I should warn you that it might be *a lot* of vehicles. You wouldn't believe the amount of cargo that passes through the port every day.'

'I'm aware of that,' Charlie replied testily. 'I've worked in Southampton a long time, DC Roberts.'

'Of course, sorry,' the junior officer replied quickly. 'I was just...'

DC Roberts petered out, applying himself to the task. He typed swiftly and purposefully, punching in locations, dates and times, before triumphantly hitting return. There was a brief pause, as the screen buffered, then the page seemed to come alive, a long list of registration numbers springing up in front of them. Shocked, Charlie moved in closer, watching on aghast as the list kept growing, dozens of vehicles piling one on top of the other.

'Are you sure you've entered the right search parameters? I only want cargo vehicles that entered Southampton from Rotterdam on those three specific days?'

'That's them. I did say that it mi—'

He declined to finish his sentence, clocking the darkening expression on Charlie's face. She'd been hoping for a break-through, revealing the human trafficker by a simple process of elimination. But the list of vehicles numbered north of fifty trucks, possibly as many as a hundred. Would they have to track them all down? Interrogate a hundred hauliers? On the face of it, there seemed little else they *could* do, and DC Roberts' pained expression said it all.

It would be like looking for a needle in a haystack.

Chapter 47

Emilia marched swiftly down the corridor, determined to put as much distance between herself and her father as possible. She had never actively contemplated murder, but any more exposure to his toxic presence might persuade her to change the habit of a lifetime. She'd had enough of him, she'd had enough of Winchester prison and now she just wanted to be away.

Retrieving her various personal security items from the front desk, she shoved them deep into her handbag, only latterly becoming aware that the custody sergeant was grinning at her, as she gave him back her pass.

'Will we be seeing you again?' he enquired, running an eye up and down her form.

'Sadly not,' Emilia replied, ignoring his leering. 'I'm done here. Others are not so lucky...'

For a moment, a frown creased his features, the prison officer seemingly uncertain as to whether she was referring to the inmates or to him. But then, shrugging off his concerns, he smiled sadly at her.

'That's a pity, because your old man has so few visitors.'

Emilia had already turned to go, but now paused, looking back at him. As she did so, her gaze settled on the well-thumbed visitors' book that sat on the desk before him. It defied belief that the systems in this place were so old fashioned, but wasn't that the criminal justice system all over?

Thinking on her feet, Emilia frowned, shaking her head as if annoyed with herself.

'You wouldn't believe it, but I've left my reading glasses in the visitors' centre. My dad wanted me to read some legal docs to him and I must have put them down.'

Her companion was already crossing his beefy arms, shaking his head in mock disappointment.

'You couldn't be a love and send someone to get them, could you? I literally can't function without them...'

She offered up her best impression of a 'pretty please' smile. It probably looked forced, but it seemed to do the trick.

'Well, seeing as you asked so nicely...'

Smiling, he bustled off into the back room. Emilia didn't hesitate. As soon as his back was turned, she started running her finger down the line of inmates' names. She swiftly found her own visit today, then pressed on. Ernesto seemed to have had no other visitors, so she kept going, flicking through the pages, running fast down the long list of names. She found herself again, two days ago now, but still no sign of any other names. It was possible of course that the threats and ultimatums had been delivered to her father via other inmates, but the duty officer had clearly suggested that he had had at least *one* other visitor in recent weeks. Perhaps one of the thugs who stole the gold from her?

In the background, she could hear the duty officer's voice, chortling at something he'd said, probably some sexist joke about her forgetfulness, but she kept her eyes glued to the page, scrolling down, down, down. And now she paused, suddenly breathless and excited. A week ago, her father *had* had a visitor. A man called Tommy Barnes. The timing would fit for sure.

Was it possible that this visit was the prompt for her dad to contact her?

Heavy footsteps made Emilia look up. Her saviour was on his way back, presumably excited to deliver the news that no glasses had been discovered. She refused to give him the satisfaction, however, turning on her heel and hurrying towards the exit. She had come here expecting nothing but rage, anguish and recrimination.

But she was leaving with a name.

Chapter 48

She paced back and forwards, a dozen confused thoughts tumbling one over the other. Having walked out on Christopher, Helen had headed straight back to the sanctuary of her flat. Usually, the serene quiet of the place, the familiar surroundings, had a calming effect on her. But today it afforded her no such relief, hence why she now found herself pacing back and forth, cursing herself.

How had she not seen through Christopher's lies? How had she allowed herself to fall into a relationship with a man who was neither committed nor honest? They had met infrequently, but always Helen now remembered mid-week, usually on a Wednesday night. Did that coincide with some regular commitment of his wife's – a book group, a gym class? Or had he invented some engagement of his own to disguise his duplicity? Staff training? Mentoring? Something operational even? The very thought sickened her, the grubby, premeditated duplicity that had facilitated their liaisons. What had once appeared fun, spontaneous and exciting, now seemed sordid and soiled.

Angrily pushing aside thoughts of her faithless lover, Helen stalked across the room to her desk. There were many questions to be answered – what to do about the baby? Whether to sever contact with Christopher completely? Whether to tell anyone else about her predicament? – but they would have to wait. There were more pressing matters demanding her attention, now that she finally had a lead as to the whereabouts of Selima and her fellow workers.

Firing up her laptop, Helen seated herself at the kitchen table. There was only one way to further her quest for the mystery van and it would take her into murky waters, with potentially damaging consequences for herself and her old friend, but Helen could see no other practical way forward. Steeling herself, she pulled up the familiar portal, the Hampshire Police logo springing to life on her screen. Technically, she should have deleted this application from her computer, making good on a promise she'd made to Rebecca Holmes in the wake of her sudden departure from the Force. But she hadn't and HR had not followed up on it, which meant she potentially still had access to the Police National Computer.

The problem of course was that her personal access had been rescinded, as she was now a civilian. Which is where Charlie came in. Her friend would go berserk if she got wind of what she was up to, but as Helen knew nobody else's access details off by heart, this was the only way. Swallowing her misgivings, Helen typed in Charlie's username and password, waiting while the screen buffered. If Charlie was already logged in, then Helen would be in trouble, denied access to the system, her digital trespass flagged. Happily, however, the screen now sprang into life, opening up its riches to her.

Breathing a sigh of relief, Helen started typing. Speed was of the essence now if she didn't want to be detected. Hammering the keys, she fed in the transit van's registration details, then punched 'Enter'. It didn't take long for the system to react, but the results were disappointing. The van was legally owned and had not been linked to any recorded crimes. It was clean.

Annoyed, Helen read on. The only notes of any interest pertaining to the van were to be found a little further on – three unpaid parking tickets accrued within the past nine months, all for the same location. Intrigued, Helen leaned in closer, drinking in the details. On three separate occasions, the van had been ticketed for parking across a hatched loading bay at South Hants hospital. More interestingly still, all the offences took place late at night – 11.05 p.m., 11.12 p.m. and 11.17 p.m. respectively. This was well after visiting hours, suggesting to Helen that the van's presence there was work-related, especially given the haphazard nature of the parking. If the van was planning on lingering, they would presumably have parked properly. Parking illegally in a loading bay suggested a brief, temporary pitstop. Were they delivering something? Picking people up? Dropping them off?

The most recent ticket was issued just ten days ago, suggesting to Helen that this line of work – whatever it was – might still be active. Scrolling further, she looked eagerly for more details on the owner of the mysterious van. Here too she was frustrated, as the van was not registered to any specific individual, but rather to a company. This did, however, give her a steer as to the nature of the van's business at the hospital and provided Helen with a solid lead, her next port of call.

The van was registered to Regus Cleaning Limited.

Chapter 49

Pulling the flimsy mask up over her mouth and nose, Viyan stumbled onwards, trying to ignore the pain that gripped every inch of her battered body. She could scarcely credit that she was once more shuffling along the familiar corridors of the drug rehabilitation centre, put to work despite her grievous injuries, yet here she was.

As she'd clung to that awful pole last night, as the heavy chain had fallen on her time and again, Viyan had prayed first for deliverance, then for immolation, but neither had come. Instead, her attacker had eventually tired of his assault, leaving Viyan a bloodied, broken mess on the ground. Unable to move, Viyan had 'hoped' that she'd be dragged back to the dormitory, there to cry out her agony and despair. To her horror, however, after lying in the yard for over an hour, her co-workers walking around her as they executed their duties, she'd had to crawl back to bed by herself, losing consciousness three times as her agony consumed her. Worse was to follow, Viyan allowed only a few hours 'rest', before she was roughly hauled from her bed to begin another day's work. She was clearly unfit to do anything, could barely walk in fact, but her minders paid no heed to her protests. Once her injuries were concealed beneath a face mask and tracksuit, she was good to go, her captors half-marching, half-dragging her to the awaiting vehicle.

Thrown around in the back of the van as they sped into the city, Viyan's bitterness had steadily grown. None of her co-workers spoke to her, or even looked at her, not one of them reaching out to her in her hour of need. It was a miracle she was alive, her back mutilated, her ribs cracked, her breathing short, yet still no one was prepared to comfort her. Her captors were worse still, abusing her, manhandling her, hurting her as they pulled her from the van, forcing her to limp down the quiet corridors, only relenting when a staff member came into view. She was here to do a job and they would ensure that there was no shirking, despite her obvious discomfort.

'No dawdling. Get on with it...'

As Naz's harsh voice rang out, a firm hand slapped Viyan's buttocks, propelling her forward. Smarting, she refused to acknowledge the slight, instead limping into the waste disposal area and making for the large metal bin, levering the heavy lid open. Immediately, her heart sank. A bulging yellow waste bag lay at the bottom, supposedly safe and sealed, but Viyan immediately clocked the two syringes that had punctured the thick plastic, pointing up at her accusingly.

She shuddered, unease stealing over her. She understood why these places existed, a safe space where drug users could wean themselves off their addictions, but dealing with their detritus was something else. She had no idea who these people were, what diseases or germs they might be carrying. She didn't want to judge anyone, but still it angered her that her own well being was of such scant interest to those who worked here, those who professed to be doing good. The work done in this particular establishment was shoddy and reckless, placing Viyan and her co-workers in real danger. Yet what thought was given to them?

What thought for their future? None, people seemingly happy to turn a blind eye to their predicament, as long as the used needles disappeared promptly every day.

Reaching into the bin, Viyan grasped the bag firmly, lifting it from the metal container. Catching on the rim, the yellow bag swung precariously for a moment, one of the syringe ends darting towards Viyan's exposed arm, but raising her elbow, she deftly avoided the danger. She had no intention of getting sick, of dying even, thanks to her own carelessness. Her minder, who had stuck closely to her throughout the morning, reacted immediately, backing away sharply. Retreating to the doorway, he took up position there, a safe distance away, but with his eyes still glued to his charge, determined not to cut her any slack. Sighing wearily, her ribs pulsing with pain as she reached into her pocket to pull out another heavy-duty liner, Viyan double-bagged the dangerous contents, before securing it firmly.

'Right, let's get that shit out to the van. Walk five metres ahead, but no more, OK? I'll be watching you ...'

Eyeballing her, Naz let his hand come to rest on the butt of his gun, carefully concealed beneath his leather jacket. Viyan knew she had no choice but to comply, so gripping the bag, she exited, making her way slowly down the corridor, her shadow close behind. Each step was pure agony, Viyan once more cursing herself for sleepwalking into this horrific ordeal. If she'd had any inkling that this is what her life would become – harvesting human tissue, stained bandages and dirty syringes fourteen hours a day – she would have taken her chances in the refugee camp. The whole enterprise was disgusting, immoral and cynical, a stain on everyone involved. But it was those who had to load up the putrid bags, pushing down on them with their dirty Crocs to ensure no space remained in the shipping container, who had the worst of it. Often the bags would bulge ominously, the taut plastic threatening to split. When they did eventually erupt, the results were horrific, nauseating and often downright dangerous. During her two years of anguish, Viyan had witnessed numerous injuries caused by blood-caked scalpels or used syringes. Indeed, she was sure that three of her co-workers had succumbed to illnesses related to such injuries, though there was no way of knowing for sure, nor any point in complaining. Their job was to handle the human tissue, dirty bandages and soiled utensils swiftly, efficiently and with good grace, whilst those who profited remained at a safe distance.

Even as this bitter reflection landed, a thought occurred to Viyan, one which suddenly filled her with excitement, even hope. The task she and the others were asked to perform was disgusting. They recoiled from it, just as their minders and guards recoiled from *them*. This had always enraged Viyan, the way they were made to feel like lepers because of the work they were *forced* to do, but this morning it occurred to her that she might be able to use this to her advantage. Their minders' disgust was born of fear – fear of infection, contamination or injury. So why not make use of this? Why not exploit this weak spot, this vulnerability, to help her escape? If one of these heavy bags, with their viscous contents, were 'accidentally' to split open one day, soiling her captor whilst also creating a major hygiene incident, would this buy her the precious few seconds she needed to escape? Could the very worst aspect of her existence actually hold the key to freeing her from this life of servitude?

It was an intoxicating idea, one which sent adrenaline flooding through her ailing body. Which is why, even as she stumbled breathlessly towards the exit, labouring under her heavy load, Viyan felt a lightness in her step. Had she accidentally stumbled upon a route out of her never-ending nightmare?

Chapter 50

Rachel Firth lived in a penthouse flat atop a luxury new development in Ocean Village. Walking along the quayside, feasting her eyes on the sparkling white yachts, listening to the gentle thrumming of the rigging, Helen couldn't help but be impressed. Life in this part of town was opulent, pristine, expensive, the towering apartment block peering imperiously out over the marina, the boats and the lapping water, confident in its luxury, status and authority. Helen had had little idea that industrial cleaning and waste disposal paid so well, but the boss of Regus certainly appeared to have landed on her feet.

It was a sunny Saturday lunch time and the quayside was crawling with pleasure seekers and holidaymakers. Sidestepping them, Helen walked quickly to the entrance of the towering apartment block, pushing inside and gliding across the central lobby. This impressive development was more hotel than flats, right down to the smartly dressed receptionist on the front desk, carefully positioned to keep ordinary mortals at bay.

'Good morning, madam,' the smartly dressed young man said, almost managing to bury his Eastern European accent.

'Rachel Firth, please.'

'Is Ms Firth expecting you?' he enquired politely.

'Not exactly, but I'm sure she'll see me. It's Detective Inspector Helen Grace.'

The words tripped off her tongue effortlessly, but Helen felt an odd pang offering them up. Was this because of the gross dishonesty in trading on her former glories? A fear of being found out? Or just a stab of regret for the loss of her old self? The receptionist barely noticed, however, pressing a button to connect his phone to the top-floor apartment. A short period of theatrical whispering followed, before he turned back to Helen once more.

'Ms Firth is curious to know what it is regarding?' he asked, striving to sound more English than the English.

'It's about the illegal immigrants she employs to clean South Hants hospital,' Helen replied, loud enough for Firth to hear.

There was a moment's shock, a brief whispered conversation, then he responded:

'Ms Firth will see you now. Eighth floor.'

'I'm afraid I can't chat for long, as I'm meeting friends for lunch. Hopefully we can sort out this confusion quickly and be on our way.'

Rachel Firth cut a striking figure, matching her opulent sur-roundings. Immaculately dressed in Boxfresh jeans and a sharp bolero jacket, her short blonde hair framing her perfectly oval face, she seemed the epitome of the elegant modern profes-sional, dressing down expensively for the weekend. She had a confidence and attitude to match, casually attaching drop earrings with one hand, whilst tossing her keys and purse into her handbag with the other. She seemed unperturbed by Helen's surprise visit, suggesting she was either entirely innocent or a very good actor.

'I won't keep you then,' Helen said politely. 'We're looking for a van which we believe is being used to transfer illegal immigrants to and from their place of work at South Hants hospital. The van is registered to your company.'

Helen knew that with no warrant card in her possession, no legitimate reason for being here, she had to start on the front foot, praying her confidence would carry the day. Fortunately, her hostess seemed unconcerned with formalities and unruffled by her accusation.

'I hardly think that's likely,' Firth responded easily. 'All our workers are carefully selected and assiduously assessed, applying all the official protocols and procedures. I can assure you, Inspector, that not a single member of our significant workforce is in this country illegally. They are all bona-fide workers with verified employment histories. What's more they enjoy good pay and excellent benefits. There is no question of any form of exploitation.'

'Yet the fact remains that this van was seen transporting a dozen young women, women who were clearly being held against their will...'

Firth looked up from her handbag, a puzzled frown on her face.

'What's more, when we tried to intercept the van, the driver took off at high speed, disappearing somewhere to the east of the city.'

'And you've got evidence of this? Footage of this alleged "chase"?' Firth enquired, her tone one of pure mystification.

'We have eyewitnesses,' Helen responded quickly, ducking the question.

'But I thought all police vehicles had dash cams these days?'

'Not in this instance,' Helen covered. 'But we have a concrete

ID on the van registration, plus a detailed description of the driver.'

Helen was reaching here, but kept up the attack, refusing to show any indecision.

'I'm happy to share these with you, if you felt they would be helpful in identifying—'

'Well, of course I'm happy to help,' Firth interrupted. 'But I'm not sure it'd do any good. Regus is a company with wide-ranging interests in many different sectors, the vast majority of which are sub-contracted to smaller firms. The disposal of medical waste at South Hants hospital is one such contract. Recruitment isn't handled directly by me, or indeed any of my leadership team, even though we insist on the very highest of standards. I'm afraid I probably wouldn't recognize one of our individual service providers if they walked past me in the street.'

Helen had to suppress a smile. This young executive was typical of the modern management class, spouting meaningless jargon, in which cleaners were 'service providers', seemingly ever ready to distance themselves from any semblance of account-ability. Who cared where the workers came from? Who cared what they endured, as long as the profits rolled in and the share price continued to rise? It was a problem endemic in the water industry, the hospitality industry and, it appeared, the waste disposal industry too.

'And these sub-contractors who handle these contracts for you, they use your vans?' Helen enquired.

'Sometimes they lease them from us. In other instances, we've been known to sell the vans to them, if it's going to be a long-term, rolling contract. I suppose it's possible that one of our sub-contractors lent a van to someone or sold it without formally changing the registration. That would obviously be very foolish, not to mention illegal, but that *might* explain what's happened here ...'

It was offered helpfully, earnestly even, but Helen knew this was a concerted attempt to end the conversation. Ignoring her, Helen persisted:

'As I said, I'm specifically interested in the sub-contractor who handles the disposal of medical waste at South Hants hospital. Who runs that contract for you?'

And now Rachel Firth paused, her smile fading slightly as she replied cautiously:

'Look, Inspector Grace, I really *do* have to go. As I say, I'm happy to help, but I would need to have your request in writing first, just to keep the lawyers happy, you know?'

It was offered cheerily, but was a concerted pushback, nevertheless. Did Firth suspect Helen was on shaky ground? Or was she covering herself in case there *was* a serious problem with her contractor at South Hants hospital? It was hard to tell, though it was clear that her cooperation was at an end, their interview over. As if underlining this, Firth now escorted Helen to the lift bank, shaking her hand warmly, before bidding her farewell.

'Thanks for your visit, DI Grace. It's been a real pleasure.'

Descending to ground level, Helen pondered their conversation. The young executive had appeared cool, calm and collected, keeping Helen at a safe distance throughout. Was her subtle probing of Helen's case, the evidence, necessary circumspection or evidence of a guilty conscience? Helen heavily suspected the latter, but at this stage it was impossible to prove either way. She was still pondering this as she stepped out into the cavernous lobby, her phone pinging in her pocket. Tugging her mobile out, she flicked opened her messages, to find a text from Christopher.

'Can we meet? I *need* to talk to you.'

A moment's hesitation, then Helen responded in the affirmative. There was nothing to be gained by snubbing her lover and, having had a few hours to calm down, she was rather looking forward to calling him to account.

Rachel Firth was not the only liar she'd be confronting today.

Chapter 51

'I don't really know where to start...except to say that I'm sorry.'

Christopher sat across from her, looking uncomfortable and embarrassed.

'It was such a shock to see you in the office,' he continued, 'and then your news...'

Helen frowned, angered by the euphemism, but her ex-lover appeared oblivious.

'It was hard to process it all, but that's no excuse. I handled it badly and I'm really sorry, Helen. You deserved better.'

'Agreed.'

'It must...must have been as surprising, as difficult, for you as it was for me, more so I imagine...'

He was fishing, trying to probe Helen's feelings about her unexpected pregnancy, but she remained silent. She wasn't going to give him any steers. She wanted him to say his piece, to show his mettle, so she knew what she was dealing with.

'I mean it seems crazy to say it, given everything, but we don't really know each other that well. Is this...is this something you've considered? Something you want?'

It was such a direct question, such a searching question, that Helen was momentarily taken aback. She had never talked about this sort of stuff with anyone and instinctively she now shied away from sharing her innermost feelings with a man she barely knew and certainly couldn't trust.

'It's never been an option,' she replied carefully. 'My job was too all-consuming and, frankly, too dangerous, so ...'

Christopher nodded thoughtfully, trying his hardest to be sympathetic and respectful.

'And now? I mean obviously your situation has changed ...'

Helen's immediate reaction was to tell him to sling his hook. What right did he have to quiz her about anything?

'You think that would be a good next step, do you?' she replied coolly. 'A woman of my advanced years spending her days at baby music classes with all those yummy mummies?'

'It doesn't have to be like that, Helen. There are other ways of doing these things.'

He was trying to be encouraging, supportive even, but Helen just stared at him with incredulity.

'Sorry, are you actually trying to persuade me to *keep* the baby?' she demanded. 'A child that was conceived accidentally, through subterfuge and infidelity. You think I should roll with the punches, become a single mum, take all this on by myself?'

A couple of customers in the café looked up now, intrigued by the volume and venom of Helen's response. Lowering her voice, she continued:

'I mean, what planet are you on? You get to swan back to lovely Alice, whilst I push a buggy around by myself, exhausted, lonely and angry? Is that what you're suggesting? Because if so, you've had a wasted journey.'

'No, no, no, that's not what I was suggesting at all,' Christopher rushed to reassure her. 'I just wanted to ask you what you felt about it and whether it was something you would ever consider, that's all. It's not my position to assume anything.'

'So, if I decided to keep the baby, you'd what? Provide for its upbringing, pop round at the weekends, if you could persuade Alice to let you, of course ...?'

'Do you really think I'm that shabby, Helen?' Christopher demanded, suddenly looking angry.

'Well, I'm a copper by instinct, Christopher. I can only go on the evidence.'

He took that one on the chin, nodding in agreement, his brow furrowed, his expression anxious.

'Look, I know any explanation I can give will seem insufficient and self-serving,' he continued eventually, choosing his words carefully, 'but things have been very difficult between Alice and me for a year or two now. I do love her, but we have drifted, no question. The way things have worked out ... well, there's a distance between us now, a lack of intimacy, and honestly I'm not sure we're going to make it.'

Helen stared at him, surprised. They had never had a far-reaching emotional discussion before, had never been really candid with each other, and in spite of her natural inclinations, she believed him.

'I think this is why I was looking for something else. Some warmth, some fun, some affection. My relationship with Alice now is awkward, difficult for both of us.'

'So why haven't you spoken to her, rather than pursuing other women?' Helen asked, a hard edge to her voice. 'Why couldn't you just be honest with her, instead of betraying her, humiliating her? Why couldn't you do the courageous thing? The *right* thing?'

Again, her ex-lover offered no defence, accepting the charge. Exhaling slowly, he puffed out his cheeks, clearly finding this difficult. Helen was surprised to see that he looked oddly emotional, even conflicted.

'Look, the truth is that we've been trying for a baby for years now,' he said quickly, as if keen to get it out in the open. 'We tried the usual route, then when that didn't work, IVF. We've done four rounds – which has been bloody awful if I'm honest – and I think we... I think we both probably feel that it's not going to happen now.'

And now Helen saw a sadness, even a grief, in his eyes that she hadn't been expecting.

'It's devastated Alice. It's all she's ever wanted and of course she blames herself, when obviously it's not her fault. And it's upset me too. I'm the youngest of four, always wanted a big family myself, and this thing... this whole process... the emotion of it, the indignity of it, the endless hopes raised then dashed, well, it's really knocked us both, affected our marriage in ways we could never have anticipated...'

Helen said nothing, struck forcibly by the dark irony of the situation. Here was a couple who had tried everything to get pregnant without success, whilst she had managed it accidentally and, if she was honest, unwillingly. What a sorry mess it all was. As if reading her mind, Christopher now responded:

'Look, I know this is a really awful situation and I can only apologize again for not being straight with you. I suspect you'd have told me to take a running jump if I had—'

'Dead right I would.'

'...but I didn't do it to deliberately to mislead you, or take advantage of you, please believe me. I like you, Helen, I care about you. It kills me to think that I've sacrificed your good opinion of me through my own stupidity and cowardice, because I'm not a bad guy, I'm really not and I do have feelings for you...'

He was beseeching her, in deadly earnest, but Helen felt only a rising anger inside her.

'Sorry, are you making a play for me?' she countered, shocked.

'Are you saying you want to make a go of this? To raise this baby together?'

Her tone couldn't have been more withering, but it seemed to have no effect, Christopher maintaining his earnest expression.

'Is that something you'd ever consider? I mean I know we've got off to the shakiest of starts, but we should at least think about...'

'But you're married, for God's sake. You're married to Alice, who you swore to be faithful to, who you wanted to have a baby with and now...'

Helen almost couldn't bring herself to say it.

'And now you want to switch horses? Without a thought for your wife? For what she's been through?'

'No, of course not. I know it won't be easy, I know this is diffic—'

But Helen was already on her feet, determined not to listen to another word.

'Jesus, what kind of man are you? After this morning, I didn't think I could think any less of you, but... Do you really care about anyone, or anything, other than yourself?'

Shocked, Christopher opened his mouth to defend himself, but Helen was already on the move. There was no way she could listen to another word. He was a deadbeat, pure and simple, unreliable, faithless and selfish. It beggared belief that she'd ever been attracted to him, but all that was over now, the scales having fallen from her eyes. Like it or lump it, she was on her own now.

Chapter 52

Pulling her hoodie up round her face, Emilia walked briskly along the street. She was on her own, in a dubious part of town and keen to keep a low profile. The scarring on the left side of her face made her an easily identifiable figure and it wouldn't do for her to be recognized around here. Not when she was walking directly into harm's way.

It hadn't taken her long to track down Tommy Barnes. Driving back to Southampton from Winchester prison, she'd put in a call to the office, seeking out Elaine Martin on the news desk, who was able to give Emilia a speedy rundown of the dealer's chequered career. Tommy Barnes wasn't anyone particularly high up in the drugs world, but he was a persistent offender, having been picked up numerous times for minor offences. The authorities had never been able to make a supplying charge stick though it was clear that this *was* his line of work. According to Elaine's sources at Southampton Central, his role was on the distribution side, more dependable mule than drugs baron, and he'd always been a bit part player in all honesty.

Had this been the end of his misbehaviour, he would perhaps have not registered with her colleagues at the *Southampton Evening News*, but Barnes had a more notable sideline in casual violence. A frequent user of alcohol and drugs, he had often got himself into scrapes at raves, nightclubs, city centre pubs and most recently in a street in St Denys. According to a small column in the paper, a fight had broken out between Barnes and an irate neighbour, who had the temerity to complain about the drill music blasting out of the former's open window at 3 a.m. Predictably, things had not ended well for the complainant. Once again, however, the criminal justice system seemed to have let the injured party down, meaning Barnes was still at liberty, whilst his neighbour was presumably busy consulting local estate agents.

The street in question was Leighton Avenue, a shabby, neglected residential enclave that seemed oddly peaceful this afternoon. Padding along the uneven pavement, Emilia kept her head down, but her eyes open, taking in the street scene, alive to possible problems or threats. But the street was deserted, with no sign of stand-up rows, blaring music or indeed dealing today. This should have reassured Emilia, but actually the opposite was true. The silence had a brooding quality, as if it was the quiet before the storm, and the lack of activity meant her arrival was much more noticeable. And that was the one thing she didn't want today.

Number fifty-two was coming up fast on the other side of the street, so Emilia now slowed her pace, pulling her phone from her pocket and checking it carefully, as if reading a message. In reality, her eyes strayed to survey the terraced house opposite. It certainly didn't seem very welcoming, with rubbish discarded in the small front garden and a peeling front door, but perhaps that was the point. It was not a house that religious zealots, political activists or charity muggers would approach with enthusiasm. Emilia, however, was very interested in it, her attention seized by the battered black moped half concealed amidst overgrown foliage out front. During last night's smash and grab, she hadn't had the presence of mind to note any number plate, but she had registered that it was a black Vespa with a brown leather saddle, exactly like the one now parked outside Barnes' house.

Realizing she'd slowed almost to a halt, Emilia picked up her pace again, passing the shabby terraced house without a second glance. Inside, her heart was soaring, however, convinced now that the same man who'd strong-armed her father into betraying his family was also the low-life who'd snatched the gold from her. A double shot at revenge now presented itself.

But was Tommy Barnes at home? It was late in the afternoon, which might suggest he was out, his daily routine presumably starting around lunchtime and progressing late into the night. Would she have to come back tomorrow morning, surprising the minor criminal when he was still slumbering? Or was there a chance she would catch up with him tonight?

Footsteps now made her look up sharply, a young man hurrying directly towards her. Alarmed, Emilia moved quickly to her right, her hand reaching into her handbag for her pepper spray. But the young guy hurried past as if he hadn't seen her, his eyes wide and unfocused. Pale, skinny and determined, he had the look of an addict and it was no surprise to her when, dropping her gaze to the reflection in a car's side mirror, she saw the young man enter Barnes' front yard. Seconds later, she heard the muffled report of the doorbell.

Immediately, Emilia was on the move, darting into another resident's front garden, taking cover behind an unruly hedge. She had no right to be here, of course, but her vantage point gave her an unobstructed view of Barnes' house. She was hoping to spot her quarry, assuming the young addict had come here by appointment, but to her annoyance, the front door now buzzed loudly and the visitor let himself in. Irked, Emilia let her eyes drift to the first floor and now finally she got a break.

The curtains in the front bedroom hung loosely apart, with a clear gap down the middle. Already Emilia could make out figures within, a tall, thin man now joined by another, presumably his customer. Screwing up her eyes, Emilia peered intently at the pair, watching as the deal was done in plain sight, cash being taken in return for a small package. It was blatant, a testament to Barnes' feeling of invulnerability, given that he was currently still on probation here. But was it definitely him? There could, after all, be other low-lifes residing in this dump. Seconds later, Emilia had her answer, Barnes moving forwards to send the addict on his way, stepping into the gap between the curtains. Emilia took in the shaven head, the tattoos on his neck, the broad shoulders. A quick check of the mug shot Elaine had sent her confirmed it – this was Tommy Barnes alright. She had found her mark.

Now it was time to take her revenge.

Chapter 53

Charlie stared at the screen in shock, scarcely able to believe her eyes.

'I'm resigning with immediate effect. Given recent events, I feel unable to execute my duties as a member of the MIT team. My union representative will be in touch shortly to complete the formalities.'

Short, but far from sweet, DC Shona Williams' resignation email had taken Charlie completely by surprise. She'd spoken briefly to her new recruit earlier in the day and, though under-standably sombre and quiet, the young DC had seemed stable enough, promising to engage with HR later in the day to discuss a measured route back to work. Clearly something had happened in the interim to change her mind, however, her email a brutal full stop to her brief career at Southampton Central. It beggared belief that Shona's upward trajectory, her whole future, could have been derailed so quickly and so catastrophically, but the evidence was there on the screen in black and white.

What should she do now? Charlie knew Shona's unexpected departure would reflect badly on her leadership of the MIT team and her first instinct was to pick up the phone and beg the young DC to reconsider. But Williams' email had made it clear that she wanted no more contact with anyone at Southampton

Central, her despair total, her decision irrevocable. Charlie's heart bled for her, remembering full well how tough she herself had found her early days as a DC, but she was also concerned for what it might mean for team morale and her own position at the station. Not for the first time in the last six months, Charlie found herself wondering what Helen would have done in this situation. Holed up in her predecessor's office, it felt impossible to shrug off Helen's mantle – to stop herself wondering what *better* decisions she might have made – however much Charlie tried to distance herself from her former mentor. Sitting behind Helen's desk, on Helen's chair, Charlie had often questioned whether she was woman enough to fill Helen's shoes. Today she thought she had her answer.

Frustrated, unsettled, Charlie rose from her seat, heading out into the incident room, determined not to give into morbid introspection. The team were hard at work, unaware they'd just lost one of their team, but concrete results were proving elusive. DC Roberts was directing a small group of them, who continued to pore over freight immigration records, so instead Charlie bent her footsteps to DC Malik, with whom she'd tasked tracking Clint Davies' movements over the last few months, hoping that she might offer some cause for optimism.

'How're you getting on?' Charlie enquired cheerfully.

The junior officer smiled wearily, before replying:

'I've spent the last few hours checking and re-checking Clint Davies' movements, seeing if triangulation can cast any light on his activities and I have made some progress, but I'm not sure it gets us any further on really...'

'Go on,' Charlie encouraged, happy to take whatever slender piece of good news her colleague had to offer.

'So we know Davies lives in St Denys with his girlfriend,' DC

Malik replied, gesturing to the map on her screen, 'and that each day he takes the bus down to the docks.'

'Correct.'

'Well, other than that, he doesn't do much, he's not the most social of animals. But when he does go elsewhere, he heads here.'

The junior officer gestured towards a series of red flags super-imposed on a digital map of Southampton.

'Where is that?' Charlie said, leaning in closer.

'Highfield,' DC Malik responded. 'Close to the uni campus.'

'Good place to go for a cheap beer.'

'Plus, there's lot of clubs and bars. Discount stores too, selling anything from 5K TVs to dusters. It's possible he goes there to offload some of his goods. Or maybe he just goes there for a night out.'

'No links in his socials to any students? Anyone who might live in that area?'

'Not that we've found so far.'

'But it does seem to be an area of specific interest for him,' Charlie said, intrigued. 'Have we checked out what these indi-vidual establishments are?'

She gestured at the red flags.

'I was about to do that now,' DC Malik responded. 'And once I've got a comprehensive list, I was going to give them a buzz in the morning. See if any of them know Davies, professionally or personally.'

'Do you think that's where he might have met his paymaster?'

'Possibly,' DC Malik responded. 'He was definitely in the area when he made the call that we traced. And obviously he had a stash of cash on him when he was . . . apprehended.'

She might have said 'run over', but avoided rubbing salt in the wound.

'But he was on the move when we traced him and, as he

visited a number of different places in the area that morning, it's not entirely clear to me yet where he'd been.'

Charlie nodded, wanting to appear encouraging and supportive, but as her eye fell on the screen once more, her heart sank. The Highfield area was dotted with red flags, so which ones should they prioritize? Where should they concentrate their efforts?

And would any of them hold the key to cracking this baffling case?

Chapter 54

It was getting late and already the hospital car park was starting to thin out. Parking up her bike, Helen scanned the bleak vista in front of her, but was unsurprised to find no trace of the battered white van. It was too early for that. She suspected it would only surface once the majority of ordinary folk had departed. Certainly that was what the timings on the parking tickets suggested, meaning she had time to kill.

Crossing the car park, she made her way to the Londis on the other side of the road. There was a fancy new M&S in the hospital foyer, but caution won out, as Helen couldn't be sure there weren't spotters in the vicinity, keeping an eye out for any suspicious activity or police presence before the arrival of the enslaved workers. Helen was a striking figure, well known to many local criminals, and it wouldn't do to advertise her presence here, so she moved away from the entrance, stepping inside the convenience store. As she did so, her stomach growled angrily. Helen realized that she hadn't eaten a thing all day, distracted by her distressing confrontations with Christopher and her ongoing hunt for Selima. Grabbing a packet of salt and vinegar crisps from the shelf, she moved on to the refrigerated section in search of a sandwich. Over the years, she'd toyed with various eating regimens, in an attempt to be healthier or more principled, but was quite traditional when it came to her choice of sandwich, usually opting for a BLT, tuna mayo or a chicken tikka wrap.

Staring at the rows of colourfully packaged offerings, however, Helen suddenly realized that she couldn't face any of those, the mere thought of them making her feel sick. This unnerved her. Was this her mind playing tricks on her or was her pregnancy once more making its presence felt? Pushing these thoughts away, she selected the blandest cheese and pickle she could find and marched to the till.

Heading back out onto the street, Helen made her way down the left-hand edge of the car park, keeping a wary eye out for any loitering figures. Her helmet remained on, in a deliberate attempt to conceal her identity, but in truth this was overkill, as the entrance to the hospital seemed deserted. Still, it wouldn't do to linger, so she hurried on her way, ducking under a barrier to continue down the western boundary of the hospital building. The van's parking tickets were for violations at the rear, where staff and tradespeople accessed the hospital. This made perfect sense as the workers presumably had a job to do and would be out of sight behind the main building, an arrangement that no doubt suited their handlers.

Keeping her pace high and purposeful, Helen walked fast down the towering open-air walkwaysbetween the main hospital buildings, before eventually emerging into a small courtyard to the rear. Immediately, she found what she was looking for, the yellow hatched area close to the rear entrance in which the van had been photographed by the enforcement officer. They were unlucky to have been ticketed so late at night, leading her to wonder if the authorities had been tipped off. Was it standard practice for the van to park up in a loading bay, ignoring the no-parking signs, provoking the ire of hospital staff? Was it a staff member who'd lost patience and called the traffic enforcement unit? If so, Helen suspected it made little difference, the van only needing to be in position for a few minutes to drop off and pick up the workers. Better to swallow the odd parking fine than loiter in plain sight on the street or by the front entrance, where CCTV cameras were plentiful.

Slowing, Helen cast an eye over the loading bay, then down the alleyway ahead which connected the rear of the hospital to Marshall Street. This was presumably the access point for the van, so she would have to set up camp here, if she was to smoke them out. Casting around her, her eye alighted on a scruffy portacabin twenty feet or so away, used by those engaged in onsite construction, the builder's logo displayed next to a scattered selection of concrete mixers and breeze blocks. Making her way over, Helen was not surprised to find the cabin locked, but was pleased nevertheless to see how easily the door rattled in her hand, how flimsy the lock actually was. Applying her shoulder to the door, she leaned on it, testing its resistance, then taking a brief step back, launched her shoulder at it. The door instantly flung open, the lock surrendering easily, and she stepped quickly inside, closing it behind her and securing it shut with the help of a fire extinguisher.

Moving to the window, she teased the blind open, wary lest a passing porter or nurse had spotted her trespass, but the yard remained deserted and quiet. Pulling a battered plastic chair over to the window, Helen removed her helmet and took up her surveillance post as she had countless times before. There would be no sign of the van for a while yet, so now all she could do was wait.

In times gone by, Helen would have had a colleague with her to discuss the case and distract her from her thoughts. Tonight, however, she had no one to divert her, her mind constantly turning on her predicament. Would Christopher give up his pursuit of her or was he committed to jumping ship? Helen didn't want any part of that, not merely because she would be happy now if she never saw Christopher again, but more because she didn't want to become the third party in an acrimonious marital break-up. She hadn't signed up to be 'the other woman' – Helen didn't even know she was Christopher's lover – and couldn't face his wife's righteous anger, however justified it might be.

Rising, Helen stretched her legs, trying to shake off these thoughts, to force her mind onto happier topics. But even as one hour passed, then another, she kept coming back to the bind she now found herself in. She had no appetite to see her body grow, alter and stretch, the poor baby coming to life inside her, yet how easy would it really be to pick up the phone and make an appointment at the abortion clinic? Even entertaining the thought made her feel cruel and heartless, yet what choice did she have? Even if the baby did make it into the world unscathed, Helen knew she would be a terrible mother, hopelessly ill-equipped to deal with this ultimate responsibility. She had such a cynical view of the world, was so jaundiced by past experience, how could she possibly avoid infecting a new baby with her own peculiar brand of darkness? It wasn't a kind thing to do, it wasn't even fair. Wasn't history always destined to repeat itself, her own emotional and psychological damage running down through the years? Would it really be wise to bring another 'Helen' into the world?

Sighing bitterly, Helen walked back to the creaky chair, throwing herself disconsolately down into it. She put her feet up on the wall, expecting another long bout of anguished tedium, but as she did so, she heard something. The low growl of an engine. Straightening up, she peered through the blind. At first, she saw nothing, only then to pick out twin beams of light growing stronger as a vehicle approached. Helen held her breath as the sound grew louder and now a battered white van pulled up in the parking bay, Helen's eyes fastening on to the registration plate. To her dismay, the registration plate was different to the one she'd clocked during her desperate pursuit, but now her eye was drawn to the brake lights, only one of which worked. Running her eye over the shattered left brake light, the battered bodywork, Helen felt sure this *was* the same van. The criminals who used it had taken basic precautions to disguise its provenance, but she was certain that this *was* them.

Exhilarated, Helen moved closer to the glass, determined not to miss a beat. The driver's door flew open and a muscular man jumped out, his face briefly illuminated by the street lighting. Helen's heart skipped a beat as she took in his ravaged features, her gaze fixing on the heavy scarring and unmoving eye. Casting warily around him, the man moved to the rear of the vehicle, flinging the doors open. Sliding along the window, Helen changed her angle, keen to see what was happening. And now she saw them, a line of silent, downtrodden women in tatty tracksuits, plastic aprons and white face masks filing silently out of the back of the van. Was the woman who bumped into her at the money exchange present? It was hard to tell, but Helen earnestly hoped so, her desperation, her anguish still fresh in her mind.

So what now? Part of Helen was tempted to call the police, to have them swoop down on the thuggish guards and cowed workers, setting the latter free from their misery. But another part of Helen, the wiser part, urged caution. For her, there was no question that this unfortunate group of broken women were just a small part of a much bigger picture, one of the many posses of illegal workers sent out every night in Southampton. If her instinct was right, they were part of a sophisticated and wide-ranging operation, a criminal enterprise that was worth hundreds of thousands, possibly millions of pounds each year. So, desperate as she was to intervene, to save these women, Helen knew that she had to remain concealed for now. She needed to find the source of these women's misery, the gang bosses and paymasters who controlled them.

She needed to find out where they were being held.

Chapter 55

She kept her eyes glued to the back of the house, searching for any signs of movement. Straining to hear, Emilia could just make out the sound of sirens now, faint but slowly getting louder. Had Tommy Barnes heard them too? If so, how would he react? The success or failure of Emilia's plan depended on his decision-making in the next five minutes.

Having deliberated for twenty minutes or more on the best way forward, Emilia had made her decision. Ideally, she would have liked to have seen inside the house first, to ensure that the stash of gold *was* still there, but there was no question of sneaking in as Tommy Barnes was obviously up and active, nor did she fancy a face-to-face confrontation, even though she felt sure she could have handled herself. She had no idea who else might be in the house with Barnes, providing extra security or potential obstacles, and even now that remained a complicating factor, which is why Emilia felt agitated and tense.

In the end, she had opted for a bit of subterfuge. Assuming the anguished tone of a terrified homeowner, Emilia had dialled 999, tearfully whispering that a man was breaking into her house, as she cowered in the bathroom. Predictably local patrol cars had been scrambled immediately – who can resist a damsel in distress? – and they were now beating a path to the address she'd given, which just happened to be Tommy Barnes' residence.

Assuming the patrol cars would screech to a halt outside Barnes' front door, Emilia had retreated to the rear, parking her patched-up Corsa on an adjacent road, which afforded her a clear view of the upper stories of the building. The shabby terraced house was divided into flats and, as she'd clocked Barnes in the first-floor flat, she guessed that he had no easy access to the garden. This, of course, was all supposition. Whether she was right or not only time would tell, but the success of her plan depended on her having gambled correctly.

Still, the scream of the sirens grew louder. Barnes must have heard them by now and surely his first instinct would be sheer alarm, given his track record of arrest and the fact that he was actively dealing, despite being on probation. Was it possible he'd make a break for it out front? Try and get to his moped? If so, he would be disappointed, Emilia already having let the air out of the tyres, but if he did opt for that method of escape, it would not serve the journalist's purpose at all. No, she needed him to be smart, if she was to benefit.

Right on cue, she saw movement. The curtains in the rear bedroom were pulled apart, then the sash window yanked open. A head emerged, shaven and pale, swinging erratically left and right, as if scanning the scene for signs of danger. Barnes was clearly agitated, the dealer visibly reacting now to the sound of police cars screeching to a halt in the street outside. Moments later, there was a heavy pounding on the door and loud shouting as the police officers identified themselves. This seemed to decide Barnes, who disappeared inside for a moment, before re-emerging clutching a dark blue holdall, stepping carefully out onto the roof of the tired, single-storey extension.

Amused, Emilia watched as he crept across the flat roof, his white sports socks clearly visible. The terrified crook hadn't even had time to put his shoes on, so desperate was he to escape arrest – no surprise perhaps given the hugely valuable stash of gold he had in his possession. Reaching the edge of the roof, Barnes paused now, picking his spot carefully before dropping the bag into the garden below. As he did so, Emilia heard the unmistakable sound of the front door caving in as the attending officers finally breached the property. Barnes still had the lead on them, however, and took full advantage, sliding down the drainpipe, before disappearing from view. The rear wall of the property now obscured the fugitive, prompting Emilia to brace herself for action. It was time.

Hurrying back to her car, she zapped it open. As she did so, she heard footsteps pounding towards the rear gate, before it was roughly wrenched open. Though she now had her back to Barnes, Emilia could see him in the reflection of the driver's window. What would he do now? Take a chance on foot? Seek out public transport? Or would the urgency of his plight prompt more desperate measures? Emilia tugged the car door open, pulling out her keys before deliberately dropping them to the ground in a jangling pantomime of incompetence. Clocking her, Barnes made his decision. As Emilia scooped up the errant keys and opened the driver's door fully, she heard the desperate dealer pounding towards her. Seconds later, he was upon her, grasping her by the shoulder and spinning her round.

'Right, bitch, give me your keys or—'

He didn't get any further, Emilia raising her pepper spray and shooting a jet of vile liquid directly into the startled thug's eyes. For a moment, Barnes stumbled backwards in shock, before the screaming started, the injured man falling to the ground, his hands clamped to his eyes. It was an arresting sight and in days gone by Emilia might have whipped out her camera, but this evening, she simply reached down to pick up the discarded holdall, tossing it into the passenger footwell, before climbing inside and slamming the car door shut.

Firing up the engine, she was soon on her way. It wouldn't do for her to get pulled into the unfolding police drama, so she drove quickly to the end of the street. Only once she'd reached the junction a hundred feet or more away, did she take her foot off the gas, pausing to look in the rear-view mirror. Barnes was still rolling on the ground, stricken, but now to her immense satisfaction, she spotted a couple of uniformed police officers running down the back alley towards the injured fugitive. Smiling happily to herself, Emilia slipped her Corsa into gear and eased around the corner, disappearing from view.

Chapter 56

Should she make her move now?

A thin film of perspirations clung to Viyan's brow as she yanked open the bin, peering down at the contents. It was not the exertion, nor even the impact of her injuries that was making her sweat, it was *tension*. More by accident than design, she had stumbled upon a possible route out of her misery and suddenly it was all she could think of. Should she seize the moment now, act before her courage failed her? It was sorely tempting, the prospect of liberation dizzying to comprehend. Her mind was suddenly full of possibilities, her body fizzing with energy. Why not cover her captor in rotting tissue and run? Why not seize the day?

'What the hell are you doing? This isn't a rest break...'

Viyan snapped out of it, realizing that she had frozen with the bag half-out of the bin. Hurrying to comply, she grasped the heavy receptacle, but her hands were shaking and the liner slid from her grasp, crashing back into the dirty metal bin.

'For God's sake, what's wrong with you? Get on with it...'

Her minder was eyeing her keenly, his exasperation clear. But was there something else in his expression? Curiosity? Suspicion? Had he clocked the change in her demeanour? Earlier she had been bitter and angry, scowling at both her captors and fellow captives. Now she appeared skittish, distracted, tense. Had he picked up on this? Could he sense that something was up?

'Sorry, sorry...' Viyan muttered, reaching back down into the bin.

As she did so, her eyes strayed to the window. She knew Southampton's main hospital well, as they visited it every night. She was confident she could navigate her way to the main entrance, but what then? Should she throw herself on the mercy of the doctors and nurses? Or should she run? The first option sounded more appealing, but would they believe her story? Or would her minders convince the authorities that Viyan was lying, confused or even mentally unstable? They certainly wouldn't let her out of their clutches without a fight. Should she take her chances in the outside world then? Stay under the radar until she'd worked out a plan? Her gaze now picked out the railway line that ran past the hospital. She'd often seen large passenger trains lumbering along the tracks, starting their journey northward. Could she stow away on one of those? Or failing that, simply follow the train line until she was clear of the city? If she kept at it, she would one day reach London or another big city that she could lay low in.

To most people, hiding out on the streets, begging to survive, would have seemed like a nightmare, but to Viyan it felt like a wonderful dream. Hauling the heavy bag from the bin, she took a breath. This was it then. This was the moment when she threw off the shackles, stood up to her tormentors and brought two years of misery and degradation to an end. Gripping the top of the bag, she took a breath and prepared to yank it open. Counting down in her head, she willed herself to be strong. Five, four, three, two—

'We're going.'

Viyan froze, poleaxed by the sound of Naz's voice. Casting

a cautious look over her shoulder, she saw that he'd joined his fellow minder in the doorway, the former glaring at her with his single, beady eye. Immediately, Viyan felt her courage fail her, the prospect of forcing her way past two burly men robbing her of all conviction.

Desperate, disappointed, she knotted the bag tightly and hauled it across the floor towards them. Liberation was what she craved, it was what she was *owed*, but she would not be rid of their hateful presence tonight.

Chapter 57

They emerged as silently, as mysteriously, as they had arrived. Exactly one hour after they'd been dropped off, the line of browbeaten workers slipped unobtrusively from the hospital building, walking robotically back towards the van. This was clearly a slick, well-practised operation, designed to allow the workers minimal time in the real world. This would always be the point of greatest danger, when a curious hospital doctor might stumble upon them, or a desperate worker might make a break for it, but there seemed little chance of that tonight. The loading bay was deserted and their minders seemed on high alert, force-marching their charges to the vehicle, insisting on speed, efficiency and obedience.

The whole enterprise had been characterized by caution and circumspection. Two minders had gone into the hospital with the women, another had loitered by the back door, whilst another drove the van away, perhaps worried about being bothered again by the local parking enforcement officer. The burly one who remained guarding the back door, a murderous-looking villain with pitted skin and unruly curls, presented a problem, as he was only twenty feet away from her, meaning it would be impossible for Helen to move from her hidey-hole without being spotted. His proximity did allow her, however, to take several good clean shots of him with her phone, which she was sure would come in useful later.

Fortune was on her side today it seemed, as eventually the minder turned away from her, talking urgently on his phone, whilst drawing on a cigarette. This had been Helen's cue to act, snatching up her helmet and hurrying from the portacabin. She did this with some regret as she would lose her perfect vantage point, but she knew she had to be ready to move when the van departed, and there would be no way of emerging from her hiding place without being spotted once all the minders were back on the scene. Padding quietly away, sticking to the shadows, she hurried to the end of the access road, taking cover behind a parked ambulance. From here she could see both the van in the loading bay and her Kawasaki out front. And although she was nowhere near as close to the action as she had been, she was still close enough, zooming in on her screen to snap the silent workers as they emerged at the end of their shift. The women looked indistinguishable. All wore tired tracksuits and all carried tightly knotted, heavy-duty refuse bags, decorated with warning signs of danger and toxicity. The last one had now emerged, the automatic doors at the rear of the hospital kissing shut behind her. This was Helen's cue to move again, the former police officer stepping out of her hiding place and stealing away down the side alley. Once out of view, she didn't hesitate, jogging fast towards the car park. Moments later, she was on her bike, the engine purring. She had to be ready, she had to be on her mettle tonight – if she lost sight of the van now, all her efforts would have been for nothing.

Easing away from the curb, she skirted the front of the hospital, stationing herself behind a pay station, which gave her a good view of the main road, onto which the van would have to emerge. Sure enough, the beaten-up transit came into view, indicating left, before pulling out and driving off down the road. How smooth an operation it was, the enforced workers in and out of the hospital in an hour, without once exciting any interest. Was this how it was every night, these poor women utterly invisible as they were forced to do the grimmest of jobs without adequate protection or any concern for their well-being? It was gruesome, inhumane, a prison sentence in all but name.

Had they finished for the night? Or did they have more arduous work ahead? If they were to move on to other jobs, this might prove useful, helping Helen to piece together the jigsaw of complicity and exploitation, seemingly bona-fide institutions happy to turn a blind eye to this illegal practice, but in truth Helen hoped their work was complete. Not only for their sakes, but her own, Helen was curious to find out where these poor women were housed, where the beating heart of this evil operation was to be found.

Happily, the van seemed to be heading away from the city centre, raising her hopes that the workers' shift was done. Given the late hour, traffic was scarce, so Helen kept a safe distance, the best part of a hundred yards behind the van, using the few other vehicles that presented themselves as cover.

They were heading south, moving fast now through St Mary's. Ignoring signs for the Saints stadium, the van pressed on, speeding up slightly now in its haste to be out of the city. Helen matched its pace, keeping a beady eye on the approaching traffic lights. A sudden change from green to amber might necessitate a burst of speed, which could prove disastrous. Following the chase the other day, she felt sure that the thugs in charge would be keeping a beady eye out for interfering bikers, even if they must have suspected that her interest in them was not 'official'. Happily, however, the driver of the van seemed unconcerned tonight, driving briskly and steadily ever southward.

Now, however, he changed course, indicating diligently, before swinging left onto the Itchen Toll Bridge. The way was clear and the van sped on, Helen clocking that it had almost reached the far end, when she too mounted the bridge. Concerned, she tugged back on her throttle, her tyres gripping the tarmac, powering her forward. The van was speeding towards Woolston, apparently gaining pace, despite the punitively low speed limits round here. Was this simply natural excitement at finally escaping the CCTV-rich environs of the city centre? Or had she been spotted? Immediately, Helen dropped her speed, allowing the van to turn the bend and disappear briefly from view, before raising her pace once more. Careful pursuits such as these were always about balance – press too hard and you'd be spotted, be too cautious and you'd lose your mark. Scared of the latter, Helen took the bend fast, leaning into the turn, thrilled by the exhilarating turn of speed. To her surprise, however, on mastering the bend, she realized the van was now nearly two hundred yards ahead and in grave danger of disappearing alto-gether. Once they were through Woolston and Newtown, the countryside really opened up and there would be all manner of turn offs, discrete woodland spots or remote farms to disappear into. Tense, anxious, Helen raised her speed. Better now to risk detection than to lose sight of her quarry.

Her speedometer was tickling seventy miles per hour now, far too fast for these city streets. The van must have been doing similar, for it maintained a healthy lead, even though Helen was slowly closing the gap. Gripping the handlebars tightly, she sped on, avoiding a gaping pothole at the very last moment, as she maintained her pursuit. With each passing minute, she was gaining on the van. She felt instinctively that the driver hadn't spotted her, as he wasn't making any evasive moves, but she wondered where he was heading so fast? To some hideout deep in the countryside? Another town entirely? And why the urgency? Was there somewhere he needed to be? Or was he just keen to get his charges back home as swiftly as possible?

Helen roared on, loving the feeling of the powerful bike beneath her, the low growl of its engine sending shivers of excitement pulsing through her. This was when she was happiest, when she felt truly free, the added edge of the pursuit heightening her pleasure. She felt sure that tonight she would finally make some progress, throwing light on the fate of poor Selima, exposing the dark cancer at the heart of her hometown. Still, however, the van maintained its lead, a good sixty yards ahead, and now Helen spotted a problem.

They were right on the edge of the city, the border of town and country. One of the natural boundaries to the east of Southampton was the train line that cut south through Newtown and Netley, before veering off again, hugging the coast all the way to Portsmouth. Driving east out of the city involved passing through the occasional and one now came into view. Normally this would have presented no obstacle, but tonight the warning lights were flashing, beacons in the night sky, signalling that the barriers were about to descend, a train due imminently. Would the van slow, forcing Helen to come to a halt behind them? Or would they try to get across before the barriers fell?

Immediately, Helen had her answer, the van powering forwards, racing towards the crossing. Instinctively, Helen responded, ripping back her throttle and speeding after the fugitives. They were one hundred yards from the crossing, now fifty, the pair locked together in a furious race. To Helen's horror the barriers now started to descend, lumbering slowly downwards. The van barrelled on heedless, a collision seemingly inevitable, but to her surprise the speeding vehicle made it across, bumping over the trainlines and missing the descending barriers by a whisker.

The lights were flashing vigorously now, the alarms going crazy, but Helen refused to relent, raising her speed still further. The barriers were down now, there was no question of going around them, meaning she had only one option. She waited until the last second, before tugging on the brakes and wrenching the handlebars sideways. The wheels slid out from beneath her, allowing the bike to slide sideways, her helmet skimming the first barrier as she glided underneath. Holding her breath, she released the brakes and tugged hard on the throttle, the tyres biting the road and propelling her into an upright position. Speed was of the essence now. She had only seconds in which to beat the approaching train, seconds in which to maintain her desperate pursuit. Ratcheting up her speed, she roared forward, the train's horn blaring in her ears. But then, at the very last moment, she jammed on the brakes. The bike bucked violently, Helen nearly catapulted up and over the handlebars, before her Kawasaki came back down to earth with a crunch. Horn blaring, the train roared past in front of her, buffeting Helen with its tail wind. Her heart thumping, sweat sliding down her cheeks, Helen sat totally still, in shock. She was *sure* she could have made it ... and yet at the last second she had chosen not to, for the first time opting for caution over risk. Why? The answer was simple and crushing.

Because she had too much to lose.

Chapter 58

'What the hell's going on?'

Rachel Firth tried hard to keep her voice down as she clamped the phone to her ear, aware that her friends were enjoying their cocktails just a few feet away, but her anxiety, her fury, was making this extremely difficult. The young company director had spent most of the day trying to contact Leyla, outraged at being accused of breaking the law. She was intent on letting her contractor feel the weight of her displeasure.

'I'm sure it's just a misunderstanding,' Leyla replied calmly.

'Well, she seemed pretty convinced,' Firth rasped, flicking a strand of blonde hair from her face irritably. 'She told me in no uncertain terms that I was employing illegal workers at South Hants hospital and that they were being transported there regularly in one of Regus' vans. She had the registration number, a description of the driver...'

There was a brief silence whilst this landed, but when her associate responded, her tone was the same as it always was – reassuring, condescending, even a little maternal.

'Look, try not to worry, Rachel. I'm sure this can all be smoothed over. No need for it to impact you, or us for that matter. It's all under control.'

'It doesn't feel like that from where I'm sitting,' Firth barked back. 'She was in my apartment, for God's sake. Bad enough that she aired her accusations in front of the lobby guy, but what if I'd had friends or family with me? She wouldn't have held back, I can assure you, which would have put me in a very awkward position. I care about my reputation. I've spent years fostering it with the local council, business leaders, politicians – I can't have my good name questioned, my business tarnished. I cannot and I will not.'

'You're making that abundantly clear,' came the reply, a hint of irritation creeping into Leyla's tone. 'But, like I said, I'll deal with it.'

'Is she right? Are we ... are *you* employing illegal workers at the hospital?'

There was a brief pause, then:

'Well, it's fair to say that not all of them have the official ID and work accreditation one might ideally hope for—'

'Jesus Christ, that was *never* part of the deal!' Firth exploded. 'You explicitly told me that everything would be above board.'

'And in an ideal world it *would* be. But you know how hard it is to get British workers to do these kinds of jobs and with legal migration restricted, now you have to be creative if you want to survive.'

'Creative? Is that what you're calling it?'

'It really doesn't matter how you dress it up. It's the reality. I don't like it any more than you do.'

'Like hell you don't! How much are you skimming off? How much *actually* makes its way to your workforce? You're taking us for a ride, a bloody ride. Well, I won't have it. I won't be scammed.'

What had she been expecting? A retreat? An apology? Leyla's response when it came was acerbic and withering.

'Oh, wake up, Rachel. What do you think this is? How on

earth do you think we can charge you fifty per cent less than our rivals? How do you think you get these specialist services so cheap?'

Rachel Firth said nothing, stunned by the ferocity of the attack. She was supposed to be the boss, the one in charge, but it didn't feel that way.

'Don't pretend you didn't know that we'd have to cut corners, that we'd have to find inventive ways of fulfilling the brief. You knew, and what's more, you were happy about it. I didn't see you complaining when your profits soared on the back of the hard graft and ingenuity of entrepreneurs like me. You're only in that fancy apartment because you were happy to turn a blind eye to what we do on your behalf. You'd do well to remember that.'

Now the contractor's tone had a distinctly menacing edge, one which Firth found distinctly unnerving.

'Alright, alright, there's no need to fly off the handle,' she backtracked quickly. 'But we do need to remedy the situation fast. Get rid of the van and sort out your workforce. We can't have illegals working at the hospital.'

'No can do, I'm afraid.'

'I'm not asking, I'm *telling*,' Firth continued. 'I don't want them at the hospital.'

'Then the job won't get done. And you'll have to explain to the council, to the hospital management, why you're reneging on your contract. Won't do much for your precious reputation, especially if the local press were to pick up on your difficulties.'

The threat was clear as day this time, leaving her boxed into a corner.

'Well, what would you suggest then?' she demanded. 'I can't have this copper sniffing around me or Regus.'

'I'd suggest you let *me* deal with this,' came the cool response. 'My own way.'

The executive hesitated. She didn't like the sound of that at all, but what choice did she have?

'What was the copper's name?' Leyla demanded, her voice laced with menace.

Once more, Firth hesitated, fearful of what she was getting herself into, before reluctantly replying:

'Detective Inspector Helen Grace.'

Chapter 59

She stared out at the raging sea, her emotions in riot.

Even before the freight train cleared the crossing, Helen had known that the chase was over, the van having vanished into the night. Abandoning the hunt, her body still shaking with the shock of her near miss, Helen had sped from the scene, racing back towards the city. Her first instinct had been to head home, but somehow she couldn't face the crushing silence of her flat tonight, where she would be assaulted by her own thoughts and fears. Eschewing that idea, she instead considered plunging into the bars and clubs in the centre, losing herself in the noise, energy and vibrancy of the late-night scene. In times gone by this would have been appealing, but the thought of all that alcohol-fuelled happiness sickened her, so instead she headed south, skirting the edge of the New Forest as she raced towards Calshot.

She had been down this lonely road before, sometimes in a professional capacity, sometimes as a speed-loving biker, bursting free of the city's confines. Some of her visits here had been shocking and traumatic, others exhilarating and liberating, but it was neither agony nor ecstasy that she was seeking tonight. Instead, she wanted to free herself from her confines, to try and banish the insistent, nagging fears that threatened to assail her and, as she marched away from her bike across the shingle, battered by the howling wind, whipped by the vicious sea spray, she did for a moment feel part of something bigger than herself. Standing on the beach on this remote spit of land, she was able to fool herself that her issues, her problems, were trivial, insignificant next to the sheer majesty of nature. Framed by the huge sky and the vast, churning body of water, Helen seemed a tiny figure, a dot on the landscape, a curiosity. How she needed that feeling of space, of insignificance, now.

Yet try as she might to banish her woes, the same thought kept intruding. She had saved herself, she had saved her baby, rather than risking all in the pursuit of justice. Perhaps for the first time in her life, she had done the sensible thing, caution winning out. The mere thought of this hit her like the charging freight train that she had just avoided. She was physically shaking, finding it hard to breathe, the very basis of her existence seemingly under threat tonight. Dozens of times before she had encountered danger of far greater significance and not blinked. Her mind rocketed back to varied scenes of crisis – strangling her murderous assailant in a burning house, crashing through the shadowy New Forest in pursuit of a madman, plunging from the deck of a cargo ship towards inky black waters – shocked now at how little she'd cared for her own safety, how little she valued her life. Was this because of the strength of her calling? Or a marker of how little she thought of herself? Maybe it was both of these things, but either way she had never hesitated to put her body on the line to bring the guilty to justice. Now she found she could not, that suddenly there was something more important in her life. Was this the birth of maternal feelings? Was this the night when Helen discovered what it truly meant to be a mother?

It was impossible, an over-exaggeration, Helen scolding herself for reading too much into a single incident. Maybe relenting had been the right thing to do. Perhaps if she hadn't stopped she would have been seriously injured or even killed. And yet in her heart Helen knew this was post-rationalization, that there had been no forethought to her actions. She had acted purely on instinct, partly to save herself, but more to save the innocent child growing in her belly who had never asked to be put in danger, who'd never asked for *any* of this.

This then was being a parent, a sudden and irrevocable shift in priorities, where the self had to surrender primacy to the greater good. Perhaps this shouldn't feel unnatural or uncomfortable for Helen – she had, after all, always put others first, going beyond the call of duty to protect the innocent, the weak and the vulnerable. But it did and there was no disguising the deep disquiet she felt tonight. Rather than being the making of her, her pregnancy felt like it might be her undoing, unbalancing, confusing her, skewing a moral compass which had always been so clear. Was this it for her now? Would she spend the next nine months walking on eggshells, terrified to damage the growing child inside her? Would she retreat from the world now, retire from the fight, to nest alone until the baby came? Obviously this was a nonsense, yet what was the alternative, when she knew instinctively that she couldn't casually, recklessly, endanger the baby's life?

Part of Helen longed to share her burden, to appeal for help. She was sorely tempted to call Charlie, to feed off her experience of motherhood, to take advantage of their long-standing friendship to appeal for help and guidance. But how could she do that after their last conversation? Moreover, how could she admit the truth of her pregnancy to Charlie, when she couldn't truly admit it to herself?

Staring out at the crashing waves, at the brooding swell of

the sea, Helen knew she would have to face this alone, grapple with this burgeoning crisis by herself, as she had so many times before in her difficult and unpredictable life. Usually she met these challenges head-on, fighting fire with fire, praying that she could live with the outcome. But not this time. This was a challenge the like of which Helen had never faced before and although she would attempt to rise to it once more, in truth she had never felt so helpless, so lonely and so *scared* as she did tonight.

Day Five

Chapter 60

'What have you done, you stupid bitch?'

Her father hissed the words at her, fury oozing from every pore.

'Do you *want* me dead?'

Emilia said nothing, gathering herself. She had expected her heist to have implications, but she hadn't expected it to be so swift or so brutal. Her father's face was a mess of cuts and bruises, his left cheek a deep purple colour. And though this man deserved no pity, no sympathy from her, she couldn't deny that she was upset that he had suffered so badly because of her.

'What the hell happened?' she demanded.

'It doesn't matter what happened,' he snapped, casting a fearful eye around the room. 'All that matters is that you do the right thing and *fast*.'

'Give the gold back you mean?' Emilia asked, incredulous.

'Unless you want to see me on the mortuary slab, yes.'

He glared at her, sweaty and hostile, but his fear was palpable. Ernesto obviously believed he might not see out the day, unless she rectified matters. Once the idea might have given Emilia a dark thrill, but not now.

'Where is it?' he hissed, keeping his voice low.

Emilia's mind rocketed back to the lock-up where she had

stored both her car and the gold, a carpenter friend's dumping ground for timber offcuts, but said nothing. Once bitten, twice shy.

'It's best I keep that information to myself for now,' she responded coolly, aware that they'd reached crunch point, the real reason for her visit today.

'Have you lost your mind?'

Ernesto slammed the table, making Emilia jump and causing a number of other visitors to turn their heads.

'I'm sitting here, telling you I have hours to live,' her father continued in a fierce whisper. 'And you want to play games?'

His outrage was intense, his desperation clear.

'You think this is funny?'

'I'm not laughing,' Emilia responded calmly. 'In fact, I'm deadly serious. I will help you out, I've no desire to see you suffer, but I'm not just going to roll over. I took that gold for a reason.'

Now her father faltered, unnerved by this unexpected turn in the conversation.

'What reason? I thought you wanted it for yourself...'

'Not at all. I've no interest in your dirty money, in fact I don't propose to keep a single penny.'

Ernesto stared at her in astonishment, as if he couldn't understand how – why – anyone would turn their nose up at such a fortune.

'In fact, I plan to give it back to your associates, to clear your debts.'

'Then why... why did you take it?' her father stuttered, struggling to keep up. 'Tommy Barnes would have given it to the right guy in time. You got in the way of that.'

'True, but I don't like being hoodwinked. And I don't like being dictated to. So now I'm going to be the one calling the shots.'

'Be careful, Emilia,' Ernesto warned. 'You don't know who you're dealing with.'

'On the contrary,' she fired back angrily, gesturing to her face. 'I know exactly who – what – I'm dealing with.'

For a moment, Ernesto said nothing, his gaze dropping to his feet. Happily for him a coughing fit now took hold, allowing him to turn his face from his daughter, whilst he gathered himself.

'Here's what I propose,' Emilia eventually continued, trying to keep a lid on her emotions. 'I will give them back the gold, I will get you off the hook, but I will only hand it back to *him*.'

There was a long, heavy silence, before a startled Ernesto found his voice.

'You can't be serious?'

Emilia's stern look told him that she was.

'He's a dangerous guy, Emilia. An *experienced* guy. You try and negotiate with him and he'll take your head off.'

'Well, he can certainly try,' she replied, forcefully.

'I mean it. Think of your siblings, think of yourself. Please don't do this.'

'I *have* to do this. I have to look him in the eye, see what manner of man could do this to a child...' she gestured to the side of her face once more '...and still sleep soundly at night. And I want him to ask politely for his gold back.'

'Emilia, this is completely crazy. You don't tell this guy what to do. You don't ask him to grovel.'

'That's the deal. Take it or leave it. I trust you can get a message to him?'

'Well, yes, I can, but...'

And now he paused, a dark suspicion stealing over him.

'Is this some kind of trap? Are the police involved?'

He was looking at her shrewdly, as if concerned she was wearing a wire.

'Of course not,' she replied, waving her hand dismissively. 'I'm as deeply involved in this as everyone else. I stole the gold from Louisa, attacked Tommy Barnes, lied to the police. I've got no interest in coughing up to any of this.'

She paused, gathering herself before she continued:

'What does interest me is meeting the man who tried to destroy me. Who shattered my kneecaps, who melted my face. I will meet him, I will tell him what I think of him. Then he will politely ask for his haul and I will hand it over to him. That's it. So, you tell him. You tell him what I propose. If he's amenable, he can text me and I will set the time and place. Is that clear?'

Ernesto nodded, still dumbfounded by the boldness of her play. Smiling, Emilia rose to her feet, casting a triumphant eye over the grim surroundings.

'Good, because we're done here.'

Chapter 61

'And you're sure you've thought this through?'

Helen nodded soberly, not trusting herself to speak.

'The emotional and psychological impact of a termination can be significant,' the doctor cautioned, her tight ponytail swinging gently back and forth as she spoke. 'Women sometimes feel guilty, ashamed, angry and, in some cases, suffer from depression. I'm not saying that you would experience any of these reactions, nor am I saying that a termination isn't the right choice for you, I just don't want you to rush into anything.'

'I understand that and I'm grateful for your concern,' Helen replied, feeling all those things.

'So, you first discovered you were pregnant two days ago?'

'That's right,' Helen replied, maintaining eye contact, trying not to sound sheepish.

'And what was your reaction?'

'Shock, disbelief.'

Doctor Moorhouse nodded sympathetically, but didn't respond.

'It's never been on my agenda really, because of my job, because of my relationship history. It's never been a priority, put it that way.'

Privately, Helen cringed. Every word that came out of her

mouth made her sound clinical and cold, when in reality she was none of these things. She just wanted this sudden crisis to be over, which is why she'd contacted the clinic this morning, despite the doubts and reservations that plagued her.

'I take it the father isn't on the scene?'

'No.'

'But you *have* talked to him about this? About the prospect of a termination?'

'Well, not yet, but he's married, so it's complicated, you know?'

She didn't mean to sound chippy, but she clearly did. Doctor Moorhouse nodded cautiously, wanting above all else not to appear judgemental.

'I see. Well, it's your body, your choice, but I would suggest that to avoid any issues in the future, you try to have an open dialogue with him about it.'

Helen shrugged uneasily, but didn't refuse.

'I'd also suggest that you don't hurry into this. We'll do the usual tests, find out exactly how far along you are ... but you're clearly still processing things, Helen, so I'd advocate a brief period of reflection, before you make any hard and fast decisions. You've plenty of time to work out what's best and, as I say, if you decide that a termination is right for you, we will obviously be here to support you every step of the way.'

Helen suppressed a shudder, the sudden thought of having to go through with the procedure making her feel uneasy. The reality of the situation was making itself felt, the enormity and significance of her decision punching hard, yet what choice did she have? She had not asked for this, so why should she be left to carry the can?

'Look, I'm happy not to rush it, but I want the tests done ASAP and I want to put a date in the diary now. I ... I appreciate all that you're saying, but I really don't think I'm going to change my mind, so I don't want to drag this out unnecessarily.'

'As is your right, Helen,' Doctor Moorhouse replied kindly. 'But please do bear in mind what I've said. There are *no* easy choices.'

Unsettled, Helen left the office, clutching a stack of reading material, none of which she had the courage to face right now. Coming to the clinic had been an instinctive thing, Helen racing over before she changed her mind, and now her strong instinct was to get away. Away from the sober posters on the wall, the kindly staff and the sea of anxious faces in the waiting room. She was out of place here, too old, too determined, too steely, so hurrying to the exit, she pushed out into the fresh air, keen to make her escape.

As she walked briskly back towards her bike, her phone started buzzing. Intrigued, she dug it out her pocket, only for her face to fall when she took in the caller ID.

Christopher.

Her finger hovered over 'Accept'. Should she talk to him as Doctor Moorhouse advised? Should she include him in this decision? If so, to what end? She wanted nothing to do with him, and certainly didn't want to raise his child, so what then? Was she going to have the baby and hand over care of it to him, this duplicitous, self-serving man of straw? No, there was nothing more to be said, so sliding her finger over, Helen stabbed reject.

The truth was that she had made up her mind. Getting into a long debate with her former lover would cause unnecessary upset, confusion and delay, none of which she could countenance that morning.

She had somewhere she needed to be.

Chapter 62

The incident room was deserted, somehow encapsulating the lack of energy and belief the team were currently feeling. Yet even amidst the lifeless hush, there was *some* life, the tiniest semblance of a dull, repetitive noise disturbing the peace. Scanning the room, Charlie was not surprised to find DC Malik back at her workstation, bulky, noise-cancelling headphones attached to her head.

'Anything good?' she enquired as she approached, nodding at the headphones.

'Pardon?' her colleague returned politely, tugging them off.

'What are you listening to? Don't tell me you're a Swiftie...'

'Nothing like that,' DC Malik laughed. 'I was just going over the hoax calls that Clint Davies made to the Border Force hotline.'

'Because?'

'Well, I got in early, just wanted to go back over what he'd said and...'

She hesitated as if uncertain whether to continue then, but taking courage, she pressed on.

'...well, I think that the sound we can hear in the background on a couple of them, the repetitive, mechanical sound... I think it's music.'

'Really?'

'Have a listen, see what you think.'

She handed Charlie the headphones, who promptly put them on. As DC Malik pressed 'Play', Charlie closed her eyes, focusing all her attention on the recording. Immediately, Clint Davies' voice filled her ears, a ghoulish reminder of the man who'd sacrificed his life in his desperation to escape, but Charlie blocked him out, zeroing in on the dull chugging sound in the background. DC Malik might be onto something; it did have a certain rhythm to it, but it was hard to know for sure.

'Have we got another clip?' Charlie asked, lowering her voice on realizing that she'd shouted her request at her startled colleague.

Laughing, DC Malik gave her the thumbs-up, deftly manipulating the mouse to pull up another clip. Charlie listened once more, taking in the repetitive grind, her sense of conviction growing all the time. It *did* appear to be music of some kind and in this recording, there was a brief pause, a lull in the sound for maybe a few seconds, before the noise started up again, this time slightly faster and more intense. Had this been the gap when one track had finished and another started?

Tugging off the headphones, she removed the jack from the laptop.

'Let's both listen to that one again,' Charlie suggested, DC Malik immediately hitting 'Play' once more.

'It sounds quite full-on, quite heavy. Is it industrial dance? Some offshoot of grime?'

Charlie strained to take in the beat, this time fastening on the furious, urgent rhythm.

'Or is it metal of some kind? Sounds like it might be ...'

Leaning in, DC Malik closed her eyes, screwing up her face in

271

concentration. Then suddenly and unexpectedly, she straightened up, a broad smile spreading across her face.

'Yeah, I think you're right,' she confirmed. 'It's thrash metal.'

'How can you be sure?' Charlie queried, surprised.

'I can't, but for me it fits, the way the accent always falls on the last beat, plus the sheer speed of it.'

'I didn't have you down as a metaller?' Charlie responded, smiling.

'Angry phase in my teens. We all had shit to deal with back then, right?'

To her surprise, Charlie found herself laughing, catching herself in the process. It seemed like ages since she'd had anything to smile about.

'So maybe he's in a bar or a club or something when he makes the call?' she continued, gathering herself. 'Can you pull up his movements?'

DC Malik obliged, the forest of red flags filling her screen once more.

'So that's his main area of interest, isn't it?' Charlie said, indicating a circular shape on the screen. 'Highfield. Are there any metal bars there?'

'What about this place?'

Already Malik was zooming in.

'Exodus. It's bang in the middle of his area of operations. Specializes in metal of all kinds, but with a heavy accent on thrash. We busted a couple of guys for peddling amphetamines there a month or so back.'

'Was Davies in that area when he made the latest hoax call?'

'Absolutely.'

'And what about on the day we tried to lift him?'

DC Malik checked her screen once more.

'Yes, his movements were pretty identical. He certainly could have been in Exodus on both days.'

Charlie broke into a smile, the prospect of a concrete lead sending a shiver of excitement through her.

'Then why don't we go and pay them a little visit?'

Chapter 63

'Someone to see you, Emilia.'

The words were a godsend. For the past hour, she had been staring at her screen, willing the prose to come together, aware that she was already three days late filing her piece. She had promised her editor a double-page spread on county lines, to break open the predictable and depressing story of exploitation and coercion, but this morning the words wouldn't come. She was exhausted, distracted and tense, having heard nothing yet from her nemesis. She had primed the trap, laid the bait, so why hadn't he contacted her? Did he not *want* the gold?

Looking up from her computer, she turned to her junior colleague Daisy, who had her phone clamped to her ear.

'Who is it?' Emilia enquired.

'Helen Grace,' her colleague returned, raising an eyebrow. 'Says she hasn't got an appointment or anything, but she's very keen to talk to you about a potential story.'

'Well, a change is as good as a rest, so ask them to send her up, will you?' Emilia said, rising and hurrying towards the meeting room, snatching up her notepad as she departed.

'We really must stop meeting like this, Helen. People will begin to think that we're friends.'

The former police officer smiled, but in truth she looked pale and drawn today. Emilia had been surprised by her visit, her old adversary having been in the building only a couple of times in the last ten years, but she was even more disconcerted by her demeanour. Normally so powerful, so commanding, the ex-inspector looked restless and uneasy, bereft of her usual certainty and vigour. She was putting a brave face on it, however, responding to Emilia's enquiry briskly and soberly.

'I've got something for you, a story that I think might become a major local issue.'

'What are we talking?'

'Corruption, exploitation, human slavery. Seemingly blue chip, bona-fide local companies using slave labour to cut costs and boost profits.'

Emilia nodded, noting the parallel with the story she was supposed to be writing. What had gone wrong with the modern world? Why were people so swift to exploit the most vulnerable members of society these days?

'I don't know how wide it goes,' Helen continued. 'But I can give you a company name and that of its chief executive. I think exposing their illegal practices will create a lot of local interest. It could really put your paper front and centre in the fight against modern slavery.'

'And might benefit you too?'

It was said as a tease, but Helen shrugged it off.

'What are you up to, Helen? Don't tell me you've got your badge back?'

'No, no, nothing like that. I'm just a concerned citizen.'

Now it was Emilia's turn to smile. She was clearly nothing of the sort, but the journalist was happy to let it go.

'So, who is it?' she asked, picking up her pen.

'Rachel Firth, CEO of—'

'Regus Cleaning,' Emilia overlapped. 'I know her. Young, pretty, cocky with it. Have you spoken to her?'

'Yeah, we had a chat at her flat in Ocean Village. Nice place. Pity it's bought off the back of other people's misery.'

'Specifics?'

'Whoever she's sub-contracting her big council gigs to is using illegal workers to collect hazardous medical waste. It's an international "workforce", but the majority of them appear to hail from central Asia. I can send you pictures that I took late last night at South Hants hospital. These women are clearly working under duress in the most appalling conditions.'

'Did you put this to Firth?'

'Sure. She obviously wasn't having any of it, but the van used to transport these women was registered to her company, so ...'

'You've photos of the van too?'

'Oh, yes,' the former police officer returned, with uncharacteristic relish.

'And, what, you want to turn up the heat up on her, smoke her out ...?'

'I want to rattle some cages and I can't think of anyone better qualified to do that than you, Emilia.'

'You're very kind.'

The journalist placed her hand on her chest with faux humility.

'Well, it looks we have a deal, Helen.'

'How quickly can you get on to it?'

'If you send me everything you've got now, I can get it up on the website tonight, with a full-page spread in tomorrow's edition.'

Nodding her gratitude, Helen rose, departing swiftly. As the journalist watched the former officer go, she reflected on the strange state of their relationship. For so long arch-enemies, were they now becoming allies? Shaking her head, Emilia returned to her desk, all thoughts of county lines a distant memory. She had bigger fish to fry now.

But as she sat down, her phone buzzed violently in her pocket. Extracting it, she felt a shiver of excitement as she spotted a text from an unfamiliar number. The message was short and sweet:

'Where and when?'

Smiling, Emilia leaned back in her chair, a broad grin spreading over her face.

Chapter 64

Helen hurried away from the *Southampton Evening News* offices, marching fast down the road. Later today, Emilia's allegations would hit the headlines, the paper's digital feed disseminating news of Regus' criminal behaviour onto phones, tablets and computers all over Hampshire. Helen wanted to be ready to strike when the bomb dropped.

She was deep in thought, her mind already scrolling forward to future confrontations, when she suddenly became aware of a noise behind her. The harsh, rhythmic slap of boot on concrete, growing ever louder. Suddenly tense, she strained to hear, now detecting two sets of footsteps coming up fast. Darting a glance at the front window of a nearby house, she caught sight of two burly forms in the reflection, closing in fast. Their body language, the speed of their approach, suggested that they meant business. Had they been waiting for her outside the newspaper's offices? If so, how did they know she was there? Had they been following her all morning, trailing her to the clinic, then here? The thought made Helen uneasy and she instinctively pressed a protective hand to her midriff.

Increasing her pace, Helen strode on, casting surreptitious glances into the windscreens of the parked cars to her right. And now her heart skipped a beat, as she caught a clearer glimpse of her pursuers. Both had shaven heads, both wore dark leather jackets and jeans, but it was the sight of the leader's heavily scarred face and immobile eye that sent shivers down her spine. This was no chance encounter. This was an ambush.

The two men were nearly on top of her, so what to do? Now a civilian, she was not armed in any way. She had no baton, no spray, nothing with which to defend herself. Scanning the streetscape, she searched eagerly for a construction site or builder's skip, somewhere she might find an offcut of discarded pipe. But there was nothing, nor was there any obvious escape route, the street flanked on either side by residential houses, their interiors gloomy and lifeless. There was a nursery towards the end of the street, but she hardly dared lead her assailants there, then a branch of H. Samuel's. Beyond that, Helen thought that there was a Tesco Metro around the corner, but she wasn't totally sure and, besides, what chance did she have of making it there when they were nearly upon her?

Striding forward, Helen picked up her pace yet again. There was no question now that they were following her and they appeared to have chosen their spot well, the quiet street all but deserted this morning. Helen's brain was firing, seeking solutions, opportunities to escape, but with each passing second the window was narrowing. What did they intend to do? Threaten her? Abduct her? Kill her? Helen suddenly felt hopelessly exposed, cursing herself for not having parked closer to the newspaper's offices, for not having anticipated this attack.

Passing the nursery, she spotted an alleyway up ahead that ran off the street to the rear of the jewellery store. The faint echo of a memory flitted across her mind and with a sudden burst, Helen ran to the mouth of the cut-through, taking her pursuers by surprise. Behind her, she heard angry curses as the men took to their heels, thundering towards her. Bursting into the alleyway, Helen hurdled a discarded packing case, landing deftly. Dropping her shoulder, she prepared to sprint away, but before she could do so, a meaty hand grasped her trailing arm, tugging her violently backwards. Her momentum arrested, Helen staggered sideways, off-balance. Now another hand gripped her neck, prompting an immediate response from Helen, kicking out violently behind her. Her thrusts met thin air, however, and now she felt herself spin, her attacker flipping her round before slamming her back into the alley wall. Helen connected sharply with the rough brickwork, the air punched from her lungs, as she came face to face with her heavily scarred assailant. Enraged, sweating, he looked like a man who'd known a lot of pain in his life, who'd doled out plenty of the same himself. He was hungry for violence, fizzing with a dark energy, one eye eagerly seeking out his victim's startled gaze, even as his other eye stared straight ahead.

'You can run, but you can't hide, Helen...'

He pushed his face into hers as he spoke, his breath rank and bitter. Clearly, he was expecting the use of her name to freak her out, but Helen refused to give him the satisfaction. Instead, she looked him up and down, before shooting a look down the alleyway, seeking a way out of her desperate situation.

'Don't think of trying anything,' her captor breathed angrily. 'You wouldn't stand a chance.'

'Is that right?' she fired back.

'You can't fight your way out of this and you can't arrest us, can you?'

Helen glared defiantly at her attacker, refusing to be intimidated.

'I take it *she* sent you?'

'It doesn't matter who sent us,' he spat back. 'All that matters is the message.'

He pressed his elbow onto her throat, pinning her hard against the wall.

'Forget what you saw, forget what you *think* you know and walk away.'

'Or what?'

Quick as a flash, the gun was in her face, her assailant taking great pleasure in running its snub nose down her cheek, before ramming it into her throat.

'Or I'll splatter your brains all over this wall.'

His grim smile revealed an array of stained teeth, his excitement, his lust for violence, palpable.

'Trust me, I'd enjoy doing it.'

He eased back the hammer, his gun now primed and ready to fire.

'Well, that sounds charming,' Helen gasped in response, struggling to breathe. 'But before you do so, you might want to know that you're being watched.'

Despite his vice-like grip, she nodded towards the end of the alleyway. Confused, her captor shot a look back towards the street. Helen clocked his confusion – there was no one in the mouth of the cut-through – then his sudden realization as he noticed the CCTV camera high on the wall, pointing directly down at them.

'The jewellery shop has been broken into three times in the last two years, hence why they've put up extra security back here. Safety first and all that...'

Helen had hoped this might give her attacker pause, might even convince him to turn tail and flee, but to her surprise, he now threw his head back and laughed.

'You think *that* will stop me?' he replied, incredulous.

'You're really going to murder someone live on camera?' Helen challenged, sounding far more confident than she felt. 'You think you can do something like that and *get away* with it?'

'I *know* I can,' he replied, grinning. 'Don't you get it, Helen? The police don't run this city anymore. We do. Which means we can do whatever the fuck we want.'

His finger tightened on the trigger, ready to fire.

'I could shoot you right now and nobody would lift a finger to stop me. Is that how you want to die, Helen? Alone, with us, in this dirty alleyway?'

He squeezed the trigger, blood lust consuming him. Instinctively, Helen turned away, closing her eyes, but the image of her brains coating the wall, her lifeless body slumping to the ground, forced its way into her mind. Was this how it was going to end for her? For her child?

Then suddenly, unexpectedly, the pressure was released, her assailant stepping back smartly, removing his arm from her neck, as he slid the gun back into his jacket. Breathless, unsteady, Helen stared at him, shocked.

'Last warning, Helen, or it's …'

He ran a finger across his ravaged neck, before turning and heading away, his accomplice trotting dutifully behind. Reaching the end of the alleyway, he paused to look directly into the CCTV camera, blowing a kiss at the lens, before rounding the corner, chuckling darkly to himself. Helen watched him go, her hand once more clamped to her belly, her body pressed tight to the dusty brickwork. She was fighting hard to regain her composure, to shrug off this distressing encounter, but in truth she was deeply unsettled by it. She was enraged. She was relieved.

But most of all, she was scared.

Chapter 65

Her heart was thundering in her chest, her breath short, but there was no question of backing out now.

Hanging the wet cloth over the tap to dry, Viyan cast another wary look out of the kitchen window. To her relief, Leyla was still deep in conversation with her Dutch accomplice, the latter appearing to be unsettled and unhappy about something. Leyla was working hard to reassure her partner in crime, reasoning earnestly with him, even laying a comforting hand on his arm, which suited Viyan just fine. The more distracted Leyla was, the better.

The young mother had waited all morning for her opportunity. It had been hard to concentrate on her chores, her mind full of what today might bring, but she'd tried hard to appear as docile, broken and listless as usual. She avoided Leyla's eye at all times, terrified her vengeful captor might sniff out her treachery, even when she was reeling off the extra chores she expected Viyan to complete. Nodding obediently, Viyan had complied, despite the agony which still racked her body, silently praying that Leyla would leave the farmhouse soon. But her captor seemed to linger longer than usual today, finding things to do, never straying far from her charge. As the minutes slowly passed, Viyan began to despair of ever being left alone, but then happily, the Dutch haulier intervened, summoning Leyla outside for a private conversation. Something was clearly up, but Viyan had no interest in the little drama playing out in the yard: she had a job to do.

Hobbling from the kitchen, she made for the staircase. There was no way that Leyla could hear her from here, but still she trod lightly on the stairs as she hauled herself up, the aged floorboards emitting the gentlest protest as she rose. Cresting the landing, Viyan made straight for the master bedroom. There were a number of small rooms on the first floor, but Leyla knew which one to target. She had never been allowed up here, her duties strictly reserved for the ground floor, but she knew from experience that Leyla conducted all her important business in the main bedroom, away from prying eyes. Many times Viyan had stood in the kitchen, hearing the boards creaking above, earnestly wondering what was playing about between Leyla and her accomplices.

Now there was no such time for speculation and Viyan hobbled into the master bedroom, closing the door behind her. It seemed profoundly odd, and dangerous, to be stepping into her captor's inner sanctum, but if she wanted to make good her escape, if she wanted to see her family again, Viyan knew she had to hold her nerve.

The room was simply furnished, a large double bed, a desk and a fitted wardrobe providing the only decoration. Bending her steps to the desk, Viyan tugged the top drawer open. It was full of make-up and jewellery, so, closing it, she moved on to the next drawer. This was more promising, stacked full of papers, but rifling through them, Viyan could find nothing of any interest. The bottom drawer was the same, so abandoning her search, she crossed to the bed. Dropping to her knees, cursing at the pain, she peered underneath.

This was immediately more promising, a heavy trunk catching her eye. Grasping the handle, she pulled it out from under the bed, exhaling with the effort. Eagerly, her thumbs sought out the padlock, but it was locked and there was little chance of her guessing the code. Angry and frustrated, she was about to replace the trunk when her gaze landed on a pair of shoeboxes, which had been secreted behind the bulky obstacle. Ignoring the dust that danced around her as she burrowed under the bed, Viyan grabbed both, sliding them towards her. Straightening up, she pulled the lid off the first one and gasped.

It was stacked to the brim with passports, the box a collage of burgundy, blue and black covers. The contents of the second box was similar and Viyan now set to work, rifling through the little books, searching desperately for the familiar burgundy of her Turkish passport. She found one, two, three, four documents belonging to her compatriots, but it was on the fifth go that she discovered what she was looking for.

Viyan Bashur. Her eyes drank in the detail of her name, her date of birth, her hometown, before alighting on the photo. Instinctively, she let out a sob, saddened beyond measure by the elegant, handsome, hopeful young woman in the photo. She looked so different now, drawn, thin, her raven hair thinning and flecked with grey, but here was a powerful reminder of who she had once been, who she could be again. This was the real Viyan, not the helpless wraith that haunted this awful camp. This document, this testament to her identity, her essence, was not only a tonic and an inspiration, it was also her ticket out of this country. With her passport in hand, she would beg, steal, borrow, do whatever she had to do to raise the money for an airfare. And once she was home, she would walk all the way from Istanbul to the Syrian border if she had to to be reunited with her children, to hear them call her 'Mama'.

'Viyan.'

She froze, her body suddenly rigid with tension, as Leyla's cry drifted up from the ground floor. Viyan had been so intent on her task that she had not heard her mistress return.

'Where the hell are you?'

She could hear her tormentor stomping around downstairs, angrily searching for her servant. It would only be seconds at most before she discovered Viyan was missing and headed upstairs, so stuffing the passport into her hoodie, she replaced the lids on top of the shoeboxes and slid them back under the bed. With a hefty tug, she replaced the trunk too, before gingerly rising to her feet, terrified of giving her presence away.

'Where are you, you stupid bitch?'

Now she heard her accuser stalk back into the hallway. A moment's hesitation, then Leyla began to mount the stairs, the boards creaking ominously as she stomped up, up, up. Terrified, Viyan scanned the room, realizing she was now only seconds from disaster. She had two options, the wardrobe or the bed. She took a tentative step towards the former, but immediately the floor squealed in protest, so retreating, she dropped to the ground. Outside, she heard Leyla crest the landing, so scrabbling over the dusty floorboards, she slid underneath the bed, pulling her feet in just in time.

The door swung open, cannoning off the wall, as Leyla burst in.

'Viyan? Viyan?'

Her angry cry echoed off the walls.

'You'd better not be up here...'

Leyla took a step closer to the bed, then another. Viyan stilled her breathing, knowing that she would not survive discovery, that she would pay a terrible price for her trespass. Still Leyla came, eventually halting right next to the bed. Viyan could hear her mistress's breathing, could almost smell her anger, but she dared not make a sound herself. Dust continued to dance around her, creeping up her nose, a sneeze surely only moments away. Was this it then? Was she going to fall at the final hurdle?

'I haven't got time for this bullshit...'

To her enormous relief, she now heard Leyla move away, the coat hangers in the wardrobe jangling wildly as she roughly extracted some item of clothing, before heading from the room and away down the stairs. Only when she heard the front door slam did Viyan dare to relax, the tension flooding from her body as she greedily sucked in oxygen. Sliding from her hiding place, she limped from the room, stumbling down the stairs, before making for the back door. She would have to invent some story about finishing her chores early, make her peace with Leyla and take whatever punishment was coming to her, but it mattered little. Her plan had worked. She had the means, the resolve and the opportunity to make her escape from this blighted country.

Now she just needed to seize it.

Chapter 66

There was no question about it. She was living on borrowed time.

Quickening her pace, Charlie tried to ignore her vibrating phone, knowing full well who was calling. Chief Superintendent Holmes had been messaging, emailing and calling her all morning, impatient for an update, for some signs of progress. As yet, Charlie had none to give her, so was grateful when the call now rang out. Before the tell-tale voicemail alert could ping, raising her stress levels even further, Charlie plucked her phone from her pocket, switching it off. Seconds later, DC Malik's phone started ringing, but a swift shake of the head was sufficient steer for her colleague to ignore the summons.

They had raced to Highfield and were now marching along Rochester Road, taking in the beleaguered assortment of pound shops, convenience stores and takeaways that decorated the shabby street. Thirty yards ahead of them, the Exodus pub, once a working man's boozer, now a metal hangout, stood out loud and proud, a large black monolith at once depressing and intimidating. Hastening to the front door, Charlie tugged her warrant card from her jacket, determined and purposeful.

'Ready?' she queried.

'You bet,' DC Malik replied, gamely.

'Then let's do this.'

Taking a breath, Charlie hauled open the door and stepped inside. The interior was gloomy, but familiar, the long wooden bar and wrought iron fixtures reminiscent of Victorian pubs up and down the land. The smell also struck a chord, a mixture of stale beer and citrus bleach, as did the sticky floor, smoothed by a thousand footfalls and marinated by numerous spillages over the years. There, however, the familiarity ended, most of the tables having been cleared to make space for dancing in front of a wide stage, the walls festooned with posters for bands Charlie had never heard of, bands whose names had aggressive, violent, often Satanic themes. It all seemed so childish to Charlie, but she wasn't here to quibble about the music: she had a job to do.

Walking up to the bar, she slammed her bag on the counter, causing the manager to look up. He had barely responded to their arrival, seemingly engrossed in his rota, but now ambled over. He was not your usual management material, a huge barrel of a man with a thick beard, unruly hair and a healthy beer gut only partly concealed by a threadbare Metallica t-shirt.

'Help you?' he drawled, suggesting he wanted to do anything but.

'Southampton Central CID,' Charlie responded with a smile, proffering her warrant card.

The burly manager looked at her photo, then up at Charlie's badly bruised face, but said nothing.

'I'm sure you're busy,' Charlie continued, 'so I'll cut to the chase. Do you recognize this man?'

She held up a copy of Clint Davies' work photo.

'Not sure,' he shrugged. 'Get a lot of dockers in here.'

'His name's Clint Davies, we think he might be a regular of yours.'

'And?'

'Well, we're not after him for anything, if that's what you're worried about. He's dead actually, died two days ago.'

The manager looked shocked, so Charlie was swift to follow up her advantage.

'We're trying to trace his last movements. We think he might have met someone here on the morning of Friday 16th. Were you on shift then?'

The curtest of nods.

'So ... did you see him?' DC Malik now offered encouragingly.

'Can't say I did. Get all sorts drifting through here and he hardly has a memorable face, does he? Kind of bloke you walk past on the street every day of the week.'

Charlie regarded him curiously, intrigued as to why he was so determined to impede their enquiry.

'So if we look through your till roll, your accounts, we won't find any payments from Davies?' DC Malik persisted.

'You're welcome to look,' the manager replied, smiling. 'Most folk pay in cash, though, so I wouldn't fancy your chances.'

'What else do they buy in here with cash?' Charlie said, an edge to her voice now.

'Excuse me?'

'Well, it's not just the beer and music people come for, is it? There's a good trade in amphetamines too, right? Speed, MDMA, ketamine ...'

'Now, hold on a minute, you've got no proof of that.'

'Come off it, mate, we busted two of your pals less than a month ago for doing exactly that,' Charlie retorted angrily. 'Now I guess you get a cut for turning a blind eye, or maybe it's just loyalty to the low-rent crooks who frequent this place that's making you so reluctant to assist us, but let me be clear. Clint Davies was in this establishment two days ago and I want to know who he met. My colleague and I are prepared to stay all day if necessary, chatting to your punters, talking about the current state of our investigation, explaining our policing priorities. I've got nothing on tonight, so we could stay all evening. I'm sure *someone* would be able to help us.'

Her adversary started at her blankly, suddenly looking deeply uncomfortable.

'Not sure it's really my kind of music, but a change is as good as a rest, right?' Charlie continued brightly. 'Or you can cut the crap, tell us what we need to know and we'll be on our way. The choice is yours.'

There was no choice of course, the prospect of the two police officers clearing the bar by their presence an intolerable imposition.

'OK, he was here on Friday morning, but only briefly...'

'Who did he meet?' DC Malik demanded.

'Middle-aged guy, tanned, muscular. Don't know him, though he sounded foreign.'

'Catch any of what they said to each other?'

'No, they kept themselves to themselves. I can give you a full description of the guy though, if you'd like...'

He was looking at Charlie earnestly, desperately trying to be helpful now, but her attention had drifted to the blinking camera high up on the wall.

'Or you could just give me your CCTV footage from that day?'

The manager looked nervously up at the camera, suddenly reluctant, but the battle was lost and he knew it.

'We'll wait here while you get it for us, shall we?'

Chapter 67

She strode along the corridor, deep in thought. The last few hours had been some of the most stressful of Rachel Firth's life. First the phone call from that bloody journalist, then the damning headlines on the *Evening News* digital feed, then the endless emails from the shareholders. Firth had worked hard to dampen the fires, claiming to some that it was simply a mistake, to others that it would not come back on Regus, but the damage was done, the company she'd spent fifteen years building from scratch now tainted, appearing grubby, heartless and grasping in the public's imagination. Her rear-guard action had been hard-fought, determined, but ultimately fruitless, the major shareholder groups demanding an Emergency General Meeting.

She had less than an hour to prepare for it and made her way swiftly to the boardroom, which would shortly be the scene of argument, accusation and recrimination. Firth knew her position as CEO was in jeopardy, perhaps even her shareholding too, if the others united to force her out of the company that had been her creation, her baby. She understood that there would be no place for sentiment in their discussions, the investors simply wanting to protect both the share price and the bottom line. If the cost of that was her expulsion, so be it. No, the only way she could survive this was to bat back the accusation, challenging the so-called evidence and distancing the company from her sub-contractors in a concerted show of strength. A bold, public move, such as the instigation of legal proceedings against Emilia Garanita and her newspaper would also help, alongside a very strongly worded statement lambasting lazy journalism and baseless innuendo. Rachel Firth had already summoned the lawyers, but she knew time was tight if they were to get all their pawns in place by the time of the EGM this afternoon.

Stepping into the boardroom, she was surprised to see that one of the lawyers had already arrived, taking a moment to enjoy the commanding views of Southampton offered by the floor-to-ceiling windows. Firth's relief at seeing the cavalry palled, however, as the statuesque figure turned to face her.

'What the hell are you doing here?' she demanded, her face blanching as she stared at Helen Grace. 'This is a private company. You can't just waltz in here when you want to.'

Furious, Firth marched to the phone, snatching up the handset.

'No need to get excited,' her adversary responded harshly. 'I just wanted a quick word.'

Helen's angry assurance sent a shiver down her spine, Firth's voice shaking as she summoned security, alerting them to the presence of a trespasser, before slamming the phone down.

'Well, I haven't got time. And, besides, I've got nothing to say to you. You tricked your way into my apartment, claiming that you were a police officer, when actually you're nothing of the sort.'

Firth had hoped this would land, but to her annoyance, the former police officer seemed unmoved.

'A necessary subterfuge,' she replied coldly. 'Especially when the odds are so weighted in your favour.'

'That's a bloody joke,' Firth hissed back. 'Fifteen years I've spent building up this company, fifteen years without a single peep of complaint from anyone. And yet one phone call to your pal Garanita and suddenly I'm the crook?'

'If the cap fits...'

'Don't you dare,' Firth responded fiercely, jabbing a finger in Grace's face. 'I'm not the law-breaker here, *you* are. Impersonating a police officer, trespass, libel. I'm going to make sure they throw the bloody book at you.'

'Be my guest. I've got plenty of good stuff to share with them, about your operations, about your workforce...'

'No, no, not another word. I've done nothing wrong, *we* have done nothing wrong, and the evidence will prove that. I don't know why you've got a particular vendetta against me, against my company, but time will show that your disgusting allegations are utterly baseless.'

'So how do you explain this?'

To her surprise, Helen Grace now stepped forward, shoving her phone into the executive's hand. Part of her was tempted to tell the ex-copper where to go, but the other part had to see. Peering at the footage that now played on her accuser's phone, she saw Helen being pushed roughly up against a brick wall, a brutish, shaven-headed man shoving a gun in her face. Firth stared at it, aghast, the victim now providing a running commentary.

'That was earlier today. I was followed to the newspaper's offices and afterwards these two thugs jumped me. This is from H. Samuel's own feed, logged at ten fifteen this morning.'

'So you got mugged,' Firth blustered, trying to muster a response. 'I'm obviously sorry about that, but I don't see what that has to do with me.'

'These are the same thugs I saw loading your workers into the van outside the hospital last night. The same guys...'

Firth felt sweat prickle on her neck, her heart racing now.

'They're not my workers, I've already told you that...' she insisted weakly, shocked at how swiftly things were spiralling.

'Don't think that contractual niceties and legal loopholes will get you of this, Rachel. These people ultimately work for Regus, they are your responsibility. Besides, if you're so innocent, why was I targeted this morning? I take it *you* sent them?'

'Of course not,' Firth replied, panicked, her mind racing. 'I would never do something like that. It's an outrageous suggestion.'

'But you must have spoken to your sub-contractor, right? Must have warned them that I was onto you?'

'No, no, I never called anyone,' Firth insisted, hesitating just too long to earn a bitter smile from her accuser.

'So, if I was to look at your phone log, I wouldn't find any numbers connecting you to whoever employs these thugs?'

'Of course not.'

'Give me your phone then. Show me.'

For a moment, caught in the tractor beam of Helen's fierce determination, Firth was about to comply, before she came to her senses.

'No, no, you have no right to demand anything of me. You are an ordinary citizen with no authority to ask me for a goddamn thing...'

Right on cue, the door opened and two towering security guards entered, their expressions earnest and intimidating.

'You took your bloody time,' she fired angrily at them. 'Get her out of here.'

Annoyed, her adversary scowled as one of the guards grabbed her by the arm.

'This isn't over, Rachel.'

'Get out. Just get out!' Firth screamed.

Helen allowed herself to be frog-marched to the door, pausing briefly before she departed to add:

'Good luck with the EGM, by the way.'

Then she was gone, hauled down the corridor and away. Biting her lip, Rachel Firth felt tears threatening. How had things gone so wrong so quickly? And how on earth was she supposed to remedy the situation? She'd had no idea she was getting into bed with such violent crooks, but who would believe her now? The connection between her initial conversation with the former police officer and this thuggish attack was an easy one to make. It made her look like some kind of criminal gang leader, protecting her empire at all costs. Why hadn't she taken better care of this? Why hadn't she asked more questions of the people she employed?

She knew the answer, of course. Money. The cash had poured in, confidence in her, in her company, growing year on year, so what was to be gained by rocking the boat? If she'd had doubts, she'd suppressed them in the interests of her opulent lifestyle. But now all that was threatened, her ruin imminent. Looking down onto the street below, she saw Helen Grace being led to an awaiting police car, but neither the look of weary resignation on her face, nor the embarrassment of the former officer being led to her old stomping ground in cuffs, afforded Firth any satisfaction today.

It was she who was staring down the barrel this morning.

Chapter 68

She fidgeted nervously, tugging insistently at a stray tress of hair, the tension now almost unbearable. Emilia Garanita had been at the Westquay for well over an hour now, checking out the entrances and exits, scanning the concourses for signs of suspicious activity or concealed thugs, before eventually taking her place in the third-floor café. With each passing minute, her nerves had increased, her shirt sticking to her back, as her anxiety slowly peaked. She had planned for this meeting, had fantasized about it many times, but now that it was here she felt utterly out of her depth. She had faced down many threats before, but this guy was a hardened, sadistic criminal who thought nothing of taking a hammer to a young woman's knees, of tossing sulphuric acid in her face. What's more, he was seriously pissed off.

A noise startled Emilia, making her look up sharply. But it was just an old man, scraping his chair back as he struggled on his way. Nervously, Emilia wound her fingers round the strap of the holdall, nestled between her feet, as if fearing someone might tear towards her, knocking her to the floor and seizing the booty. But the café seemed sleepy, its few customers utterly unaware of the drama playing out beneath their noses. Privately, Emilia urged herself to be strong, to be calm. She had thought this through carefully, had chosen her spot well. She was at the highest point of the shopping centre, her sight lines to the escalator, to the lifts, unimpeded, so there was no way anyone could surprise her. If her nemesis was smart, he would obey her instructions, play by the rules, retrieve his haul. Yet how could she assume that he'd do so? She didn't know him, would have walked past him in the street and, besides, hadn't he made a career out of breaking the rules?

Trying to calm her breathing, Emilia glanced over the café once more, surveying the quiet scene. And now she spotted something, a tall, tanned man in his early forties cresting the escalator and stepping out onto the third floor. He was athletic and muscular, with a lived-in, slightly pitted face and wary, shifting eyes. Dressed in jeans and a dark blue blouson jacket, he looked like a casual shopper, but his behavoiur gave him away, his body language tense, his gaze wary. Scanning the café, he spotted her. A fierce energy seemed to pulse from him, projecting itself towards the journalist, but Emilia maintained eye contact, refusing to buckle. A moment's silent communication ensued, Emilia inclining her head in a gentle nod, then he was on the move, making his way directly towards her.

Emilia straightened up, determined to appear confident, powerful. Without a word, the man who'd haunted her dreams for years seated himself opposite her. At first, he didn't look at her, his eyes taking in the perimeter of the café, before straying over its occupants, searching for hidden threats.

'There's no need to worry,' Emilia said calmly. 'I haven't brought you here to trap you.'

Slowly, he brought his gaze to rest on her. Unzipping his coat, he leaned back in his chair, the hilt of a knife visible just above his belt, but he never took his eyes off his adversary as he replied:

'Why *have* you brought me here, Emilia?'

Instantly, she reacted, unnerved by the way he lingered on

her name, but more startled still by his strong Dutch accent. Gathering herself, she replied:

'Because I wanted to see you. I wanted to look the beast in the eye.'

He snorted, raising a contemptuous eyebrow, half amused, half annoyed by the insult.

'But we've already met. So why the need for all this...?'

He gestured airily at the café.

'Well, you'll forgive me, but you didn't give me much warning last time we met, just stepped out of the shadows and bam!'

Once more, her nemesis shrugged, as if it was obvious that he'd had no choice.

'Plus, I was writhing in agony, trying to keep the acid from my eyes, so the whole thing's a bit of a blur. I guess it must have been different for you. You seemed very focused, taking advantage of my agony, pinning me down, taking a hammer to my kneecaps...'

Now his expression hardened, her derision annoying him.

'Tell me, what was that like?' Emilia continued, warming to her theme. 'What did it feel like, brutalizing an innocent girl?'

'You weren't so innocent,' he countered dismissively. 'You were a drug dealer, like your father.'

'I was a drug mule,' Emilia spat back. 'Who was acting under duress. Forced to swallow condoms of cocaine, to risk our lives, just so you could peddle drugs to your continental friends.'

'I know, I know,' he said, looking amused, rather than ashamed. 'It was embarrassingly... how do you say it? ...small fry, but everyone has to start somewhere.'

'And you started with us. With children, for God's sake. Putting their futures in jeopardy so you could make a buck.'

'You could have shared in that, Emilia. We asked you to carry on, we *wanted* you to carry on, you said no.'

'And this was my reward.'

She gestured to the scarring on her left cheek.

'My prize for having some fucking morals, for doing the right thing.'

'If you say so.'

'I do, which is why I want to know what it felt like, what went through your mind during your attack on me. Did you feel excited? Exhilarated?'

'Are you serious?' he countered, aggravated.

'You must have got off on it, right? You must have enjoyed it. All that pain, all that power.'

'Do you really want to do this?'

'I've spent years trying to work out what possessed you to do this to me. I could have been blinded, I could have died. Yet you don't seem bothered at all. Looking at you now, I can't see a single shred of remorse. Tell me I'm wrong.'

She was glaring at him, emotional, but her attacker just shrugged, as if bored by the whole conversation.

'You ask me what I felt,' he eventually answered, his eyes glued to her ravaged skin. 'I felt ... nothing. Nothing at all.'

Emilia felt like she'd been slapped. His indifference, his boredom, was beyond evil.

'I did what I had to do,' he continued coldly. 'It was just ... business.'

His eyes locked onto hers, boring into her. And though tears of indignation, of outrage, pricked her eyes, she refused to blink.

'Talking of which, where is it?'

For a moment, Emilia couldn't speak, so inflamed were her emotions, but eventually she found the words.

'It's underneath the table,' she replied calmly, releasing her grip on the holdall and pushing it towards him with her foot.

'You can take it now and walk right out of here.'

Once more, the Dutchman hesitated, his eyes flicking around the café as if sensing danger. Satisfied that undercover police officers weren't about to spring out, he looked down, unzipping the bag quickly to check the contents.

'It's all there, payment in full,' Emilia intoned dryly.

'I'm glad to hear it, as I really do have to go.'

Rising abruptly, he pulled the holdall onto his shoulder. A quick check that his route to the escalator was clear, then he turned back to Emilia:

'Well, what can I say? It's been nice doing business with you, Emilia.'

He smiled contemptuously at her as she rose, but Emilia now surprised him, lurching across the table, grabbing him by his collar and pulling him in close.

'This isn't over,' she hissed, her nose touching his. 'This will never be over.'

Startled, angry, he pulled back sharply, batting her hand away.

'Yes it is, you mad bitch. You will never see me again.'

Turning on his heel, he hurried away. Emilia watched him go, ignoring the startled looks of the other customers, her heart pounding in her chest. Though breathless and exhausted, she was nevertheless elated. She had handled herself well, had said what she needed to say, and the whole thing had gone completely to plan. Her Dutch tormentor was wrong. They would meet again. And sooner than he imagined.

Judgement Day was at hand.

Chapter 69

'This is it then. The moment of truth.'

Charlie breathed the words, cutting the tension in the room like a knife. DC Roberts nodded earnestly, as did DC Malik, so without further ado, Charlie pressed 'Play'. The CCTV feed jumped into life, the high angle of the camera making the interior of the Exodus look strangely striking and atmospheric, like a movie set before the big fight scene. The manager, all beard and gut, could be seen idling behind the bar, but the attention of the police officers was drawn to the stocky figure of Clint Davies hurrying over towards a table at the rear. They watched him in silence, all struck by the weirdness of what they were witnessing, the sprightly docker going about his business utterly unaware that he was just hours away from disaster.

Seating himself, Davies looked restless, anxious even, twirling his phone around and around on the table, before moving on to toy with the beer mats. Now, however, he looked up sharply, as another man approached the table. They were clearly on friendly terms, Davies rising and shaking his hand, as the pair exchanged a few words. Then his companion headed to the bar before returning to seat himself opposite the docker.

'Bugger...' Charlie exclaimed. 'He's got his bloody back to us.'

The other officers shared her frustration, craning towards the screen, as if they could somehow peer round the muscular man's imposing shoulders to take in his face. Davies and his associate already seemed deep in conversation, chatting together like two old friends, the latter removing his jacket.

'Is this him, do we think?' DC Roberts asked urgently. 'Is this our trafficker?'

'I think we're about to find out,' Charlie replied.

On screen, Davies' companion shot a quick look towards the bar, before heading briskly in that direction, ordering himself a whisky. Frustratingly, his face was still turned away, his gaze down, and soon he was back at the table. Now he returned his attention to the docker, as he removed something from his jacket, passing it underneath the table. Davies received it, checked the contents, then slid the envelope into his jacket.

'That's it,' DC Malik said triumphantly. 'That's the payment.'

'Agreed. So this *is* our guy,' Charlie concurred.

Now DC Roberts took up the baton.

'So, what can we make out? He's about six foot, maybe slightly more. Athletic, muscular, jeans, dark blue jacket and a t-shirt, I'm guessing it's white from the glare. What's that on his arm? Is it some kind of tattoo?'

'Looks that way,' Charlie added. 'But hard to make out what it is from here.'

On screen, their suspect now rose, pumping Davies' hand once more.

'They clearly like each other,' DC Roberts said, raising an eyebrow.

'Partners in crime,' DC Malik mused, a wry smile on her face.

Charlie's focus remained glued to the screen, however, slowing the footage down as the man hurried to the doorway. Her finger tensed on the mouse, then just as the man raised his head, preparing to push out of the main door, she clicked sharply, freezing the image.

'There we are, that's it. That's as good as we're going to get.'

She was breathless, excited, staring directly at the man's face. It wasn't a perfect image by any means, but they could see the narrow shape of his face, his mottled skin, the cut of his hairline, his dark black curls, the Nike logo on his t-shirt, the tattoos on his arms, one of which appeared to be a name, the other some kind of crest. This was it. This was what they been searching for.

The first sighting of the mysterious trafficker.

Chapter 70

'Well, this is a sight I never expected to see.'

Recognizing the condescending tone, Helen looked up sharply to see Chief Superintendent Rebecca Holmes standing in the doorway of the holding cell.

'Helen Grace locked up in her own nick.'

Helen's former boss could barely conceal her amusement at her predicament, a smile tugging at her lips.

'Yeah, it's a surprise to me too, but the law's an ass, right?'

Helen was staring meaningfully at Holmes when she said this, pleased to see her smile curdle at the jibe. The pair had fallen out spectacularly when Helen quit the Force six months ago, her very public criticism of Southampton Central's leadership team going down very badly. She did not regret her actions for a minute, but it put her in a tricky spot now, Holmes clearly delighted at her misfortune.

'As soon as I heard you'd been arrested,' Holmes continued, recapturing her swagger, 'I just had to come straight down. Are they looking after you, Helen? Do you have everything you need?'

Holmes already knew the answer, hence the question. Helen had been roundly ignored by the custody officers since she arrived, shoved into the tiniest cell without a word of explanation, a bottle of water, a blanket or any of the basic comforts usually afforded to the vilest of offenders. She was still persona non grata in this place, her former colleagues determined to show their continuing anger and disappointment at her disloyalty.

'Well, I've had better service, but then again this place has really gone to the dogs, hasn't it, Rebecca?'

Another reaction from Holmes, Helen enjoying the freedom her civilian status afforded her. Previously she would have had to call Holmes 'Chief Super' or 'Ma'am'. Now she could call her what she liked – a very tempting prospect.

'I understand you were picked up for trespassing,' Holmes responded, changing the subject. 'Is that true?'

'Well, obviously I'm not going to say anything that might incriminate me, especially as I haven't been offered a lawyer, contrary to both law and precedent,' Helen shot back. 'All I will say is that I was doing some research which I hope will soon bear fruit, to the embarrassment of both Regus Cleaning Limited and the authorities who *should* have been investigating them.'

'And do they plan to press charges? Can we expect to see *more* of you, Helen?' Holmes gloated.

'I very much doubt it. In fact, I rather think Rachel Firth might be about to get the chop.'

Holmes narrowed her eyes, the thought of anyone prominent and high-profile being sacked clearly unsettling for her.

'Given that, I think it might be best for everyone if I'm bailed and on my way.'

'Well, of course that would be the sensible thing to do,' Holmes responded swiftly. 'And personally I would like nothing better than to see you out of this tiny, malodorous box...'

Holmes cast an eye over the faded yellow brickwork, which

was almost obliterated by graffiti, her nose wrinkling as she continued:

'But we do have rather a backlog at the custody desk at the moment, some kind of fight in the city centre, I believe. Lots of arrests, lots of paperwork...'

Helen didn't believe a word – the custody area had been *dead* when she was brought in – but she said nothing, determined not to give her former boss the satisfaction.

'So I suspect you'll just have to sit tight for the moment. Do *try* and make yourself comfortable.'

She offered a warm, maternal smile, which wasn't returned. Amused by Helen's cold stare, her patent hostility, Holmes turned to leave, pausing only once she'd reached the doorway. Looking back, she added:

'I must say, Helen, I am impressed by your ingenuity. The things you do to get back inside Southampton Central...'

And with that, she was gone, slamming the iron door shut behind her.

Chapter 71

Emilia hurried away from the Westquay, marching fast towards her battered Corsa. After the Dutchman had left their meeting, she'd remained in position for a full twenty minutes, checking out the other occupants of the café, keeping a beady eye out for hired thugs blocking her route to the lift or escalator, but the scene in front of her seemed utterly unremarkable. Nattering friends, boisterous families and the odd pensioner eking out a pot of tea. Peaceful, workaday and completely unthreatening.

Still, Emilia had kept her wits about her as she hurried down the escalator and along the concourse, using the tall shop windows to check for any signs of pursuit. Reaching the main entrance, she'd finally reduced her pace, casting one searching look back along the main concourse. Satisfied she wasn't being followed, she rose and departed.

There was no logical reason why she should be in danger – her nemesis had his gold – and yet Emilia was determined to take no chances. Could you apply logic to vicious thugs who threw acid in young girls' faces? Would her power over him have aggravated the seasoned Dutch smuggler? Would he have raged internally as a woman quizzed him over his actions, his morals, his soul?

On the flip side, if he was only interested in money, Emilia wanted to give him plenty of time to get well clear of the Westquay. She had no idea of the provenance of that gold and if for any reason her nemesis was stopped by security guards or a passing police officer, curious to know what was inside the tatty holdall, she wanted to be well clear of the whole thing. She was done with the gold and, in truth, she was done with her dad too.

The same could not be said of her Dutch friend. She had meant every word when she warned him that their story wasn't over, which is why she needed to exercise extreme caution now. If he sensed that he'd been tricked, then the consequences for her could be dire, which is why she kept a close eye on those around her as she scurried down the street. She avoided passing vans or trucks, anything she might be bundled into, and crossed the road to avoid a couple of shaven-headed louts who approached at speed. Happily, they sailed by and speeding up, Emilia swiftly made it to her Corsa. Only once she was inside, with the doors safely locked, did she breathe a sigh of relief.

Her body was still tense, however, as the moment of truth was now upon her. Plucking her phone from her pocket, she swiped swiftly to her tracking App. Her nemesis was no fool and would presumably have transferred the gold to another bag as soon as possible, the holdall being the most obvious place for Emilia to conceal a tracking device. Which is why she had decided on a bolder strategy. Grabbing the Dutchman by the lapels had been fun for the shock factor alone, his face a picture of surprise and anger, but her actions had concealed a darker purpose. Grasping his jacket, she had taken the opportunity to attach a tiny tracking pin to the underside of his collar, only releasing the surprised trafficker once she was sure it was firmly attached. But was it transmitting? Had her wild plan actually *worked*?

The app now provided the answer, the flashing blue circle on her screen moving steadily east, as her enemy raced from the city. Emilia let out a bark of triumph, her body pulsing with adrenaline. Letting his love of money override the need for caution, he had walked into the trap and swallowed the bait.

Hook, line and sinker.

Chapter 72

The door flew open, flooding the cramped cell with light. Alarmed, Helen looked up, expecting more aggravation – a sarcastic custody officer, the gloating Holmes again – but was surprised to see Charlie filling the doorway.

'I wondered when the cavalry was going to arrive,' Helen said, rising slowly.

'You're bloody lucky I'm here at all. We should be throwing the book at you.'

Helen stared at her old friend, surprised by her tone. She knew things were difficult between them, yet surely she was the one who should be aggrieved, given her treatment?

'For what?' Helen demanded.

'For trespass. For harassment.'

'Rachel Firth and her cronies deserve everything they get. I explained all this to the custody sergeant, showed him the footage of me being threatened, not that he took a blind bit of interest.'

'And how did you get onto Regus in the first place?' Charlie countered. 'How did you trace your mystery van back to her in particular?'

Now Charlie had her and Helen knew it. Clearly Helen's

illicit use of Charlie's log-in details to access the PNC had not gone unnoticed.

'Yes, HR told me about that,' Charlie continued, aggrieved. 'Traced the breach to a city centre flat, didn't even need to check the electoral roll – everybody in the station knows your address.'

'Yeah, that was a mistake. I should have been more careful about where I accessed it from,' Helen replied briskly.

'It's not where you logged in that's important,' Charlie fired back. 'It's the fact that you did it all. You must have known that it would come back on me. How do you think Holmes will take this? It makes it look as though I'm assisting you, as though I'm encouraging your strange obsessions, facilitating your law-breaking, when in reality I'm trying to make a name for myself, to prove to everyone in this station that I can stand on my own two feet.'

Helen immediate reaction was to hit back, hurt by Charlie's continued insistence on pushing her away, but realizing the pressure her former colleague was under, she chose a more conciliatory approach.

'You don't need to prove yourself to anyone, Charlie. You're too good, have too much experience—'

'Well, that's easy for you to say,' Charlie interrupted. 'But my head's on the block here. We've been up against it from the start, clutching at straws, but *finally* we've got a tangible lead. Which is why it's not bloody ideal to have to come down here to bail you out.'

Charlie stared at Helen, defiant and emotional. Realizing the gravity of the situation, Helen suddenly felt chastened. She had thought too much of herself these past few days, not enough about her old friend.

'Look, I'm sorry. I shouldn't have done it, you're totally right.

And I apologize sincerely for that. I wasn't aware how tough things were for you.'

Charlie said nothing, but Helen could see that the apology had landed.

'If you need me to straighten things out with Holmes, I will do so, of course. I never meant to cause you any trouble and I know what she can be like. She was in here not half an hour ago, crowing at my misfortune, revelling in my discomfort.'

Now it was Charlie's turn to look regretful.

'I'm sorry about that,' she responded sheepishly. 'If I'd known you'd been picked up, I would have come down here earlier.'

'Well, I would have called you, but I wasn't allowed a phone call. Or any water, or access to a toilet, which I could really bloody do with ...'

And now Charlie's expression seemed to alter, concern dissipating her evident annoyance.

'Are you OK, Helen? You *do* look really pale ...'

Never had her friend's words been truer. Helen looked like death and felt little better. Taking a breath, she chose her words carefully:

'Well, let's just say that your joke was on the money.'

For a moment, Charlie stared at Helen in mystification, then the memory of her parting shot in the pub slowly took hold.

'Oh, my God, Helen, you're ...?'

Her eyes dropped to Helen's belly.

'Looks that way. Going to congratulate me?'

Helen's tone was dry as a bone, but Charlie seemed not to notice.

'Well of course, I'm thrilled for you, if this is what you want ... but I'm more concerned with *you*. You shouldn't be getting into fights, getting arrested, when you're pregnant. Jesus, Helen, you should be taking fewer risks, not *more*. You need to look after yourself.'

Normally, Helen would have bridled at being lectured, but in truth, Charlie's concern nearly undid her, acts of kindness, of simple fellow feeling, having been scarce of late.

'Yeah, well I've never been very good at that,' Helen conceded, swallowing her emotion. 'Things keep getting in the way.'

'Well, first things first,' Charlie replied, 'let's get you out of here.'

The pair marched along the corridor, as they had countless times before. This time the dynamic was very different, Helen no longer leading her deputy in the hunt for justice. Now they were simply two old friends, muddling along in very difficult circumstances.

'Look, I may be a distinctly average DI,' Charlie said eventually, 'and a neglectful mother to boot...'

'That's not true,' Helen protested. 'None of it.'

'But I can at least be a decent friend,' Charlie insisted, guiding her towards the exit. 'Which is why I'm ordering you to go home and put your feet up. I'll call you later, OK?, and when I've got a spare second, I'll pop round, so we can have a proper chat.'

Helen paused on the threshold, ignoring the custody sergeant's curiosity, staring at Charlie with real emotion. She'd hated this feeling of distance between them, the sense that she had angered and disappointed her by the stance she'd made, somehow sacrificing the only real friend she'd ever had in the process. She longed for reconciliation and now, for the first time in ages, she saw a softening in her old friend's expression, hints of the former warmth they'd shared. Relieved, she leaned in for a hug, pulling her colleague to her.

'You are a good pal,' Helen whispered fiercely. 'I do know that and I'm sorry.'

'Nothing to be sorry for,' Charlie responded, slowly dis-engaging. 'Now, you get yourself straight home, right? I'll deal with the paperwork.'

She gave Helen a mock stern look, earning a smile. Turning, Helen patted her on the arm once more, heading out of the building and down the steps towards the car park, adrenaline and sheer relief driving her forward. Her arresting officers had at least allowed her the courtesy of driving herself to the station, once she'd promised to comply with all their instructions, and she made her way to her Kawasaki now. Mounting it, she fired up the ignition and pulled smartly away, keen to put her embar-rassment behind her.

Cruising through the city centre, Helen's mind pulsed with contradictory thoughts, her heart with competing instincts. Charlie was right of course, she was foolhardy to put herself in danger, for her own sake as much as for the baby she was carrying. But the logical extension of this line of thought was that Helen would soon be pottering around at home, taking care of herself and her offspring, whilst outside the world continued to turn with its predictable parade of selfishness, wrongdoing and criminality. Could Helen just sit back and pretend that none of that existed? That the suffering she'd glimpsed first-hand in the last few days was some kind of illusion? She already knew the answer to that.

It was late now, the city lights sparkling in the darkness, so Helen made swift progress through the quiet streets, arriving at South Hants hospital in under ten minutes. Parking up, she padded down the western fringe of the main building, making her way to her hiding place behind the parked ambulances. Her plan was a simple one, possibly a forlorn hope, but it was her only play now. She had done as much as she could with Rachel Firth, who would no doubt be scrupulous now to keep any connection to the illegal workers concealed. Business was business, however, and contracts had to be honoured. Medical waste still had to be bagged up and spirited away, hence why she'd returned to the hospital tonight.

Minutes became hours and still there was no sign of the van, then suddenly two beams of white light illuminated her hiding place. Ducking behind the parked vehicles, Helen clung to the shadows, watching as the dented white van pulled up in the hatched loading bay. Moments later, the back doors were flung open and the disenfranchised workers piled out, the masked women trooping into the hospital through the staff entrance. One of the workers was markedly slower than the others, hobbling towards the hospital as though barely able to stand. Taking a step forward, Helen ran her eye over the poor woman. Was it her imagination or was this the same woman who'd thrust the note into Helen's hand? She looked about the same height, had the same build and similar shoulder-length hair. Was this her? If so, what on *earth* had happened to her?

Consumed by anger, Helen watched the woman disappear inside, waiting patiently for the remaining minder to wander off, phone clamped to his ear. Then, spying a porter approaching the rear doors, Helen made her move, waiting until he'd buzzed the doors open, before slipping inside the building behind him. Up until now, she'd sat back, been circumspect, but the time for caution was over. These women were clearly in grave danger and she was no longer prepared to sit back and ignore their plight.

It was time to act.

Chapter 73

The moment of truth was approaching, but still Viyan wondered if she would have the nerve to go through with it. Following Leyla's bitter denunciation of her indolence and disobedience earlier, her minder had been told to stick to Viyan like glue, an order he was clearly determined to fulfil. The heartless thug followed his orders to the letter, whispering dire threats whenever a hospital porter or nurse came into view, reminding Viyan that, if necessary, her life could be snuffed out in an instant. How she loathed him and his accomplices, how she despised the Dutch low-life who'd brought her here, how she hated Leyla, the malevolent, beating heart of this awful nightmare. They seemed to enjoy her humiliation, her pain, and would no doubt continue to do so until her beleaguered body finally gave up the ghost. She was resolved, however, not to give them the chance.

Quiet determination was one thing, however, taking action quite another. She knew this was her moment, but her whole body was shaking, her nerves jangling wildly. Approaching the surgery block, Viyan felt in her hoodie pocket for her latex gloves, trying her best to act as if it was business as usual. Retrieving them, she tried to put the gloves on, but the latex stuck to her fingers and she found it impossible to tease them open.

'Come on, come on,' her minder breathed angrily. 'We haven't got all day.'

Viyan could feel his eyes upon her, struggling desperately to conceal her anxiety, the tension which gripped her body.

'I'm trying,' she whispered fiercely.

'Well, try harder. Because I ain't going to do this shit for you.'

Irked, he gestured at the bins, which contained the detritus of a day's surgical work. Stained swabs, discarded clips, blood, bone, tissue and mucus, the contents always turned Viyan's stomach and it was no different today, the young woman swaying slightly as she approached the forbidding containers. Liberation was close at hand, but she suddenly felt faint and breathless.

'I said get on with it, bitch.'

A fist connected with her spine, sending her stumbling into the bins, her hip connecting sharply with the metal edge.

'We've got two more jobs after this one, so get a move on...'

Angry, hurting, Viyan tugged on the gloves and opened the nearest bin, heaving the bulging sack out of the container and laying it carefully on the floor. This one was even heavier than usual, Viyan unsure whether she'd be able to carry it in her current state and she paused to gather her breath, energy leaching from her delicate frame.

'Don't you dare dawdle, because I will hurt you...' her minder breathed.

Wasn't that the truth? Hadn't he and his fellow thugs been hurting her every day since she first stumbled out of the shipping container? As her captor advanced upon her, Viyan felt a righteous fury rise in her heart, suddenly overcome by the desire to throw his anger, his disgust, his vitriol back in his face. He was nearly upon her now, so channelling her fury, Viyan tugged at the adhesive strip that sealed the top of the bag, ripping furiously at the heavy plastic.

'What the hell are you doing?' her minder cried out, alarmed.

But it was too late. With a roar of pure rage, Viyan tore the heavy bag open, its gory contents erupting onto the floor, splashing up off the tired lino and cascading onto her tormentor's shoes.

'Oh God,' he howled, gagging. 'What the hell have you done?'

Desperately, he extricated his feet and searched for something to get the offending waste off his clothes, wrenching open a nearby cupboard. For a moment, all thoughts of his charge were forgotten, his attention consumed by his dripping trousers and sodden shoes. And in that instant, Viyan made her move.

Dropping the filthy bag, she turned on her heel and started to run.

Chapter 74

Helen tore along the corridor, desperately scanning for the masked figures who had suddenly vanished into thin air. She had only been a minute or two behind them, yet incredibly none of the dozen workers were now visible, every one of them having vanished into the bowels of the labyrinthine hospital.

Hurrying on down the main corridor, she spotted a young doctor emerge from a side room, making his way fast towards the cafeteria.

'Hey, excuse me...'

The doctor turned, clearly surprised to see a biker in full leathers bearing down on him.

'Which way for the surgical block, please?'

'Two floors up and all the way to the north end, but it's closed for the night now, and you can't just...'

Helen didn't hear the rest, eating up the yards to the stairs. Pushing through the doors, she took them three at a time, emerging two floors up in a matter of seconds. Turning left, she hurried down the long corridor, following the arrows pointing towards the surgical block. She felt sure that if she was to find the bedraggled workers anywhere it would be here, executing their unpleasant duties. Helen expected to find them labouring in silence, broken in spirit if not in body, but to her surprise, she now heard angry shouting ahead. Moments later, a figure burst around the corner, running directly towards her. She was dressed in mask and tracksuit, her feet clad in bloodstained Crocs, the soles of which squeaked noisily on the plastic flooring. The young woman was clearly struggling, breathless and agonized, moaning pitifully as she ran for her life. Now Helen clocked the cause of her desperation, a burly figure clad in jeans and a bomber jacket skidding around the corner in pursuit. To her surprise, his feet also seemed to be coated in blood, a fact which appeared to enrage him, his vicious face purple with fury.

The pair raced down the corridor, giving Helen only a split second to react. Dropping her helmet, she hurried towards them, holding out her free hand to the fleeing woman. The latter slowed now, confused and concerned, but then recognition took hold, the desperate fugitive hurling herself towards her. As she did so, however, the young woman appeared to lose her balance, crashing heavily onto the floor, skidding to a halt by Helen's feet. Helen stooped down to help her, instantly realizing her mistake. Her pursuer was nearly upon them, primed to launch himself at them both. She could hear his low growl, sense his eagerness for violence, knew she was only seconds from impact.

Straightening up quickly, she cast desperately around, her eye falling on a metal catering trolley, laden with dirty plates and mugs, lying abandoned to her side. Seizing it, she swung the heavy trolley round, before propelling it directly towards the approaching thug. He had no time to react, the obstacle connecting sharply with his gut, arresting his progress and sending him sprawling onto the dirty plates, several of which crashed noisily to the floor. Winded, shocked, he tried to right himself to attack, but once more he was too slow, Helen's fist connecting sharply with his throat. Gasping, clutching his Adam's apple, the figure stumbled backwards, collapsing into the side wall.

Helen didn't waste any more time on him – that fight was won – turning instead to the young woman who looked up at her with wide, frightened eyes.

'Come with me,' Helen said, picking up her helmet, as she hauled the startled worker to her feet.

Within seconds, they had disappeared from the corridor, throwing themselves down two flights of stairs, Helen clutching her helmet in one hand and her companion's hand in the other. Pushing out into the main corridor, Helen paused for a second to get her bearings, then clocking the sign for the main exit, dragged the young worker in that direction. On they ran, dodging staff cleaners and bemused nurses, charging on as if their lives depended upon it. Up ahead, Helen spotted the automatic doors that led out onto the main concourse and the car park beyond. Scenting deliverance, she upped the pace, ushering the limping woman towards the exit. They were so close now, a couple of hundred feet more and then they would be safe.

The doors parted and Helen propelled them out into the cold night air. The drop in temperature was a tonic, suffusing Helen and her companion with energy, but now at the point of deliverance, danger reared its head once more, another bomber-jacketed thug looming up in front of them, intent on cutting off their escape. Had he got wind of their escape attempt? Had his mate called ahead to warn him of the danger? Helen took a bold step forward and swung out with her helmet. Her assailant had not been expecting this and reacted too late to stop the heavy mass of fibreglass crashing into his temple. He hit the ground hard, but Helen didn't look back, skirting her fallen assailant and sprinting to her bike.

'Get on,' Helen demanded urgently, installing herself on the front of the saddle, as her companion painfully manoeuvred her leg over. 'And hold on tight.'

Helen felt the woman grip her fiercely and, tearing back the throttle, they tore off into the night, racing through the car park and out onto the city streets. Streaking through an amber light, Helen sped on, steadily increasing her speed, as she looked nervously in her side mirrors. But there was no need to worry, the hospital, their attackers, the van just a receding speck in the distance now.

They had escaped.

Chapter 75

It was as if a great weight had been lifted from her shoulders. Speeding through the city streets, Emilia felt stronger, happier, younger even, as if facing her nemesis, confronting her trauma, had rejuvenated her. Only now did she realize how the events of the past, her rage, her bitterness, her sense of injustice, had coloured every aspect of her life, making her cynical, defensive and wary. It seemed incredible to her now that she hadn't realized this before, her past mistakes all too evidently a product of childhood trauma. Now, however, it felt as if all that pain, that heartache, had just slipped away, as if it had never even existed. A professional scribe, Emilia worked hard to avoid cliché, but today really *did* feel like the first day of the rest of her life.

And the fun wasn't over yet. In fact, the best was yet to come. Gripping the wheel, she kept one eye glued to her phone, relieved to see that the little blue dot was still stationary. As it had been thirty minutes ago and thirty minutes before that. She had lost count of the number of times she'd checked it since she left the Westquay, but the result remained the same. Unless Emilia was badly off beam, unless the tracking device had fallen off or been discovered, the progress of her nemesis was clear. Having left their meeting, he had headed east, out of the city, making his way to Dearham Farm, a nondescript place which used to grow arable crops, but now seemed to be some kind of recycling centre or waste disposal facility. She could think of nicer places in the Hampshire countryside to spend the night, but as long as the Dutchman stayed put, Emilia wasn't complaining.

Pushing down hard on the accelerator, she sped on. Initially, she'd been tempted to call the police, the safest course of action given her attacker's track record, but in the end her journalistic instincts had won out, hence her mission to seek out the farm now. She wanted more – she wanted to know what he was up to now, who he was working with and in what manner of inventive ways she might ruin his life. He thought he'd won, he thought he'd forced her hand, but she was determined to have the last laugh. Only when she was sure what she was dealing with, how best to ensure his total downfall, would she consider calling in the authorities. She had no desire to confront him herself, but she would make sure she was on hand to witness his arrest, her faithful Nikon poised to capture the magic moment.

She was making good progress, using her local knowledge to avoid the predictable bottlenecks. Soon, she was crossing the Itchen Toll Bridge, her nervous energy rising as she hastened to the inevitable showdown. Had her whole adult life been leading to this moment? Emilia couldn't answer that for sure, but it certainly *felt* that way. Suppressing her anxiety, she drove on, rehearsing in her head what she would say to her tormentor when he was dragged off, what sweet morsels of abuse she might muster. But she had barely completed her first mental denunciation when her phone started ringing, the announcement of an Unknown Number suddenly impeding her view of the tracking app. Angry, she rejected the call, relieved to see the little blue dot re-appear. Moments later, however, her phone rang again: the same, persistent Unknown Caller.

'Bloody hell...' Emilia muttered, as she stabbed Accept. 'Emilia Garantia. How can I help?'

She was keen to be rid of them, her tone harsh and imperious, prompting the caller to hesitate.

'Well?' she demanded impatiently.

'Ms Garanita, it's Sarah Fuller here. I'm the governor at HMP Winchester.'

Taken aback, Emilia slowed the car, suddenly confused and concerned. Her mystification was short-lived, however, the governor adding in a solemn tone:

'I'm very sorry to have to tell you that your father passed away this afternoon.'

Chapter 76

'How could you let this happen?'

Leyla had never seen her Dutch accomplice so angry, so assertive, before. It unnerved her, but she knew she needed to talk him round, if this crisis was not to burgeon into a full-blown disaster.

'Your men are supposed to control these people. Instead, they let her walk straight out of the hospital.'

'It wasn't like that,' Leyla protested. 'That bitch Viyan tricked him.'

'Tricked him? She could barely walk after what you did to her…'

He glared at her, his fury clear, but she thought she detected something else there too? Suspicion? Unease? Was he *doubting* her?

'How could she out-fight your man?' Visser persisted. 'Outrun your man? It doesn't make any sense.'

'Look, she was smart, OK? She split one of the waste bags, there was blood, tissue, used swabs everywhere. He was worried about infection.'

'I don't give a shit. It was his job to keep her in line.'

'Plus, she had help,' Leyla insisted, talking over him. 'She would never have got away without someone else's intervention.'

'That's supposed to make me feel better?' her accomplice erupted. 'The fact that she's now hidden away somewhere, spilling her guts to her guardian angel. She knows all about the operation, she knows my nationality, what I look like. She can spoil everything, for you as well as me.'

Visser didn't need to spell that out. As soon as she'd heard about the calamity at South Hants hospital, Leyla's mind had been turning on the implications. The Dutch haulier was right – it could spell the end for *all* of them.

'Who was it? Who helped her?' Visser demanded angrily.

'Just some local busybody. Her name is Helen Grace and—'

'Who is she? A doctor? A social worker?'

Leyla hesitated, weighing up how honest to be with him, and then decided there was no point lying – he would smell her deception.

'She's a former police officer.'

Visser stared at her, lost for words, running his hand through his thick curls in anguish, as if trying to pluck a solution from his addled brain.

'It's not as bad as it sounds,' she insisted, prompting a snort of derision. 'Grace is estranged from her colleagues. She has no sway with them anymore.'

'It doesn't matter!' Visser exploded. 'She has evidence. Living, breathing evidence. A woman who can tell her the route we took to the UK, how far out of Southampton your camp is, who her co-workers were, who imprisoned her. She can put us all behind bars for a very long time.'

'Look, there's no need to fly off the handle, OK? It's my problem, our mistake, and we will deal with it. There's absolutely no reason why any of this should come back on us. She doesn't really know where the farm is or what our real names are. She's running blind. Trust me, I can contain this. I know I can...'

'Well, I'm not waiting around to find out. I'm heading back to Holland as soon as possible.'

'But the container's not full yet,' Leyla protested.

'Do I look like I give a fuck?'

The Dutchman glared at her, his eyes bulging. Leyla could scarcely believe it – her accomplice had always been so amenable, happy to take her money and run the risk. But something had changed today.

'Keep calm and think of the money. I'm happy to raise your fee if you'll just be patien—'

'To hell with the money,' Visser interrupted. 'I'll be on the first available ferry tomorrow,' he declared. 'And you can be sure this will be my *last* visit.'

'But we had a deal, Visser. We *have* a deal,' she countered, shocked.

'Not any more we don't. I can't take the risk of working with amateurs. We're through.'

Now finally Leyla lost her temper. Nobody got to call her an 'amateur'.

'You're actually serious? You're going to throw away everything we've built, this whole operation, because of *one* setback?'

'Setback?' he laughed. 'Don't you see? It's over, finished.'

He turned to leave, but she moved forward quickly, grasping him by the sleeve.

'No, we're not done yet, I'm not done you—'

She didn't get any further, the back of Visser's hand connecting sharply with her right cheek. Surprised, wrong-footed, Leyla stumbled backwards, before righting herself, ready to spring on her attacker, to tear his eyes out. But Visser had already reached the doorway, casting one last look back, as he concluded:

'I'm sorry it had to end this way, Leyla. But I'm getting out. And if you have any brains, you'll do the same.'

Turning, Visser marched away, the front door slamming shut behind him. Leyla stared after him, her cheek throbbing, her lip bleeding, consumed by rage. She had liked Visser, had come to rely on him, but the reality was that he was just as selfish and gutless as the rest. Like many others before him, he doubted her resolve, her strength. But she would show him, she would show them all. She'd achieved too much, come too far to give up at the first sign of trouble. No, she would fight tooth and nail to defend herself, to survive, to *win*.

This wasn't over yet.

Chapter 77

She stumbled up the stairs in a daze, allowing herself to be led. Her saviour had tried to explain who she was and why she'd intervened, but Viyan had been unable to take much of it in. The events of the last few hours had been insane, bewildering, unbelievable. Was she dreaming? Or was it real? Had she really just driven off into the night on the back of a motorbike? Was she finally *free*?

Even now, Viyan pushed that thought away. She had been a prisoner for too long to believe that her liberty could be so easily won. And yet the powerful, athletic woman who was now half-helping, half-carrying her up the stairs *seemed* kind and solicitous, gently supporting her, whilst whispering encouragement.

'Come on, you're almost there. You can do it.'

Viyan wanted to believe her, to prove that her spirit had not been broken by the endless cycle of exploitation and abuse, but every part of her body throbbed with pain. Her ribs ached, her breathing was short and shallow, her legs constantly threatening to buckle, Viyan stumbling now as they continued their journey up, up, up. Their progress here had been a blur, the liberated worker pressing her face into the firm leather of her rescuer's jacket as they sped away, keeping her eyes to the floor as her saviour chatted quietly with the manager of the women's refuge, focusing on putting one hesitant foot in front of the other as they climbed the stairs to the top of the building. Small clusters of women gathered on the landings, falling silent as the strange pair limped past, but Viyan didn't begrudge them their curiosity. She didn't care who looked, didn't care where she was, as long as she was away from *them*.

Cresting the top-floor landing, Viyan allowed herself to be led to a heavy-duty door. It looked more like the entrance to a prison cell than a bedroom door and Viyan hesitated, suddenly wary. Sensing her disquiet, the woman – Hannah? Helen? – released her grip, stepping away to give her some space.

'It's OK, you're perfectly safe. This is a women's refuge that I've used many times before. It's very discreet, very secure. No one can get to you here.'

She smiled warmly at her, before adding:

'But if you want to go, you are free to. Or if you want me to call the police straight away, I'll happily do so. I know you've been through so much...'

The kindness in her voice, the warmth of her tone, almost undid Viyan. Emotion burned in her chest, but maintaining her composure, she simply shook her head.

'It's OK...' she whispered.

'Good, then let's get you inside.'

Bending, her guardian angel fiddled with the lock, before swinging open the door. Moments later, they were inside, the door secured behind them, standing in the small, well-appointed bedroom. Once again, Viyan struggled to take in what was happening – mere hours ago she had been bloodied, broken and betrayed, now she was standing in this tastefully decorated bedroom, gazing at the ensuite bathroom. How on earth had she ended up here?

'Come on, sit down, you must be exhausted,' the woman urged.

Together they staggered forward, Viyan collapsing onto the bed. She seemed to melt into it, startled that such softness could exist, her battle-hardened body accustomed now to rough, wooden boards. It was almost too much for her to process, a great gulp of sadness, of regret, of anguish erupting from her. Only now was reality making itself felt. She had escaped her ordeal. There was no need to suffer anymore. No need to be scared. Suddenly she couldn't stop herself, her relief, her sadness, her exhaustion consuming her, as the tears flowed freely. Her whole body was shaking, she was making strange, unnatural noises, her composure deserting her. She wanted to sob her heart out, to weep for a thousand years, finally releasing all the pain and despair she had swallowed down during the last two years. Distraught, wild, even unhinged, she half expected her host to back away, to summon a doctor, to run a mile from this wailing dervish, but when she looked up through tear-filled eyes, she found the woman next to her, her expression suffused with generosity and kindness.

'I know you've seen some terrible things, I know you've been through hell, but you're going to be OK.'

Viyan half-nodded, but she continued to quiver, months of trauma making themselves felt.

'It's over, finished. They can't get to you anymore.'

She gestured towards the window through which could be glimpsed the twinkling lights of the city. Instinctively, Viyan shot a nervous glance in that direction as if fearing a face might suddenly appear at the glass, a phantom sent to drag her back to that terrible nightmare. Sensing her alarm, her rescuer crouched down next to her, gently seeking out her hands, her sparkling eyes meeting Viyan's, as she added:

'You're perfectly safe here.'

And, to her astonishment, Viyan believed her.

Day Six

Chapter 78

'Are you sure you're ready for this?'

Helen was sitting on the bed with Viyan, regarding the young mother with real concern. The rescued worker had hardly slept last night, riven with pain, consumed by nightmares, Helen often having to hurry from her spot on the hard floor to tend to her traumatized companion. Having spent over two years in captivity, the young mother was clearly finding liberty hard to handle – unable to rest, unable to get comfortable, unable to relax.

Both rose at the crack of dawn and, over coffee and rolls, the root cause of Viyan's anxiety became clear. Helen had struggled to get much out of her guest the previous night, but now in stumbling, broken English, Viyan revealed the full extent of her trauma. Her arduous journey to the UK, her imprisonment on a remote farm, the backbreaking labour and, most shockingly, the inhumane violence. Helen was devastated to learn of Selima's gruesome murder, but oddly it was not this, nor the violence meted out to her, which troubled Viyan the most. It was thoughts of those left behind that consumed her. Helen now learned that Viyan had left her family in Turkey – her mother tending to Viyan's young children, Salman, Defne and Aasmah. When she'd left them to come to the UK, they'd been living in a dangerous, unsanitary refugee camp, relying on aid handouts to survive, running the gauntlet of local hostility and the overt prejudice of government officials. It was a desperate situation, the thought of which obviously tortured Viyan. She'd had no contact with them since she left Turkey two years ago, no idea whether they were still living, still together, still safe. She'd been allowed no phone at the farm, no method of communication whatsoever, so first thing this morning she'd asked to borrow Helen's phone, promising to pay her back for the call when – if – she could.

Helen dismissed that idea out of hand, taking time to help Viyan navigate her unfamiliar device. Viyan knew her mother's number off by heart and was desperate to FaceTime her, desperate to find out if her children were alive and well. This was pain of a different kind, worse even than the broken bones and heavy bruising she'd sustained, her uncertainty, her frustration, but above all, her *hope* causing her real anguish.

As she dialled, Helen offered up a silent prayer that all would be well, fearing how Viyan would react if the worst had come to pass. Helen suddenly realized how invested she was in the happiness of Viyan and her family, how she wanted more than anything for them to be reunited again. For their story to have a happy ending.

The phone continued to moan in her hands, desperately seeking a connection. Then suddenly it went quiet, as if the call had been cut off, before unexpectedly bursting into life, the suspicious face of an aged woman filling the screen.

'Mama?' Viyan gasped, holding her hand to her mouth in shock, as tears filled her eyes. 'Mama?'

Viyan could barely speak and now Helen saw the elderly woman react, her expression transforming from concern to shock and then to tearful elation.

'Viyan,' she moaned, lifting her eyes to the heavens in thanks. 'Viyan, Viyan...'

Helen watched on transfixed, as mother and daughter stared at each other, overcome by emotion, their relief, their love plain to see. Conversation was stuttering and largely impenetrable to Helen as she spoke no Turkish and both women seemed to be finding it hard to make themselves understood, thanks to the bad connection and flowing tears. And yet, even though the words made little sense to Helen, she could read these women, watching on in delight as Viyan insisted that she was alive, she was safe, she was still in the UK. Her aged mother, who was not in great shape herself, was clearly horrified by the bruising on her daughter's face, gesturing with agitation towards the screen, but Viyan waved her concern away, smiling and laughing even, to Helen's enormous relief.

Now some more familiar words cut through. Salman, Defne, Aasmah, Viyan appealing for news about her children. Once more, Helen held her breath, but moments later she heard cries of delight, as Viyan's mother urged her grandchildren to join her. Once more, Viyan fell silent, her hand clasped to her mouth, as the three children jostled to appear on screen.

'Defne, Aasmah, Salman...'

The words tumbled from her mouth, Viyan's cheeks now stained with tears. She had clearly dreamed of this moment, had perhaps thought it would never happen, yet here she was, staring at her beautiful children. Defne was tall and dark, like her mother, wearing a pretty yellow polo shirt, whilst Aasmah was shorter, more diffident, but with a winning smile. And then there was Salman, just a baby when Viyan had left her homeland, but now a confident toddler, sporting a well-worn Nike t-shirt emblazoned with Kylian Mbappés face, something he seemed inordinately proud of.

M.J. ARLIDGE

Viyan threw words at them, terms of endearment, affection, of happiness and relief, before the well ran dry, the overjoyed mother turning to Helen, speechless, tearful but totally content. It was a sight to melt any heart and Helen beamed back at her, her own eyes brimming with tears. For a moment, the two women stared at each other, sharing their relief, this unexpected triumph, then once more the onslaught began, the emotional children peppering their mother with questions, chief amongst them, Helen presumed, when she might be coming home.

At this point, Helen withdrew, keen to give Viyan and her family the privacy they needed. Tiptoeing out onto the landing, she nevertheless paused in the doorway to look back, drinking in the scene one last time. Viyan was oblivious to her presence, utterly absorbed in an impassioned conversation with her children. Her features had come alive, her eyes sparkling, her cheeks full of colour, staring longingly at her offspring. It was an image of total devotion and unquestioning love. It was a sight which moved Helen deeply, but also troubled her. If she had *her* baby, would she too feel such overwhelming love, such joy? If so, the thought of willingly sacrificing such an opportunity seemed utterly crazy. Who wouldn't want that? Who wouldn't want something that lifts your heart and defines your mission beyond question every single day? Helen didn't feel ready for it, had no clue what to do, but surely it couldn't be beyond her?

Maybe it was the emotion of the morning, maybe it was fatigue, but for the first time in her adult life, Helen found herself wondering if perhaps she *was* ready to be a mother.

Chapter 79

Ernesto Garanita lay on the metal trolley, the sheet pulled up to his chin. It was less than twenty-four hours since he'd passed away, so a modicum of colour remained in his puffy cheek, which flanked his pride and joy, the luxuriant moustache that he'd sported since before Emilia was born. He still looked like her father, some vestige of life clinging to his rigid features, and yet there was a serenity in his expression which his eldest child had never seen before.

Emilia stared down at the corpse, trying to make sense of her emotions. She had come alone, uncertain how to break the news to her siblings, but now regretted her decision. She felt overwhelmed with regret, with sadness, but also anger and bitterness too. What was she supposed to say to this man, who had brought her into this world, raised her to be strong, defiant and rebellious, only then to torment, exploit and abandon her? How was she supposed to deal with his sudden death? How was she supposed to *feel*?

She now became aware of a presence behind her, the mortuary attendant hovering. Gathering herself, she turned to him, addressing him briskly:

'Did he suffer?'

'He died of natural causes, if that's what you're asking,' the mortician responded kindly. 'And no, he wouldn't have felt any pain. He passed quietly whilst taking a nap, which is probably the best any of us can hope for.'

This was designed to comfort her. And in some ways it did. Despite the rage she'd often felt towards this man, she hadn't wanted him to suffer and was glad that his end had been peaceful. And yet the thought of him dying alone, in the isolation cell that he'd been moved to for his own protection, cut her to the quick. Was he scared at the end? Did he cry out? She would never know and it was pointless to conjecture, but Emilia sensed it would haunt her thoughts for a good while. After all, which of us wants to die alone?

Thanking the mortuary assistant, Emilia turned back to her father, tentatively laying a hand on his chest. This was it, this was her moment, her chance to say goodbye. Soon her siblings would be summoned, then the whole circus of a traditional Catholic burial would crank into action. This was probably the last time she would be alone with him, father and daughter, sharing a private moment. Gazing at him once more, she felt her heart swell with warring emotions, the desire to lambast, the desire to forgive, the need to continue their battle, the need to call a final truce. Whispering her last goodbye, Emilia padded away from her father, torn, uncomfortable but resolved. She had much to do now, taking care of his affairs and her siblings' grief, whilst also dealing with the man who had tried to destroy her all those years ago. Those tasks must take priority now – she would have plenty of time to navigate her conflicted feelings in the weeks ahead. Even so, as Emilia left the viewing area, walking quietly down the corridor, a part of her felt she already knew where the road would take her, how she would make her peace with her difficult inheritance. The man she'd once adored, then loathed, was gone, his life, and her feelings towards him, now a simple question of arithmetic, an equation that must include all the good and the bad. There was no easy answer, no clean solution, Emilia feeling more keenly today than ever that love and hate were after all just opposite sides of the same coin.

Chapter 80

Charlie stared at Helen in disbelief. Things were moving at lightning speed this morning and she was struggling to keep up.

'You're sure she was brought to this country by a Dutch trafficker?'

'Yes,' Helen insisted, impatiently. 'She got to know this guy pretty well on their journey to the UK. He's about six foot one, dark curly hair, muscular build, early forties. She even knows what kind of cigars he smokes – Royal Dutch in case you're interested...'

Charlie was swimming in the detail, Helen's urgency prompting her to offer up all her information in one seemingly never-ending stream. Gathering herself, she flipped open her file, pulling out a copy of the grainy CCTV still.

'Could this be him?' Charlie asked eagerly, showing it to her former colleague.

'Possibly,' Helen said cautiously, studying the image. 'She says he *definitely* has tattoos on his right arm, one for a football team of some kind, the other with a woman's name on it, Suzanne, I think she said.'

Charlie felt the hairs on the back of her neck stand up, that familiar prickle of excitement which always accompanies a major breakthrough.

'Viyan will be able to tell you more when I bring her in later. I've asked Harika Guli from the Kurdish Centre to join us, as Viyan's English is pretty basic.'

'But according to Viyan, he's still in the country?' Charlie asked urgently.

'I can't say for certain, but he was still on site when Viyan left for the hospital last night, the container still being filled, so it's a fair bet he's here.'

'We can check last night's records for Southampton, well, for all the major ports…' Charlie responded, her mind whirring. 'And it's definitely medical waste he's transporting?'

Helen nodded.

'That's the way this thing works. He brings illegals in, takes hazardous waste out. I'm guessing whoever's behind all this charges a healthy fee for disposing of the medical waste, given its dangerous nature…'

'And then he probably dumps it as fast as he can when he gets back to Holland.'

Helen raised an eyebrow in weary agreement.

'Odds on they're paying their workers a pittance too, so they must be making thousands,' Charlie added, her mood dark.

'It's the backbone of the local economy,' Helen replied. 'They do all the jobs that no one else wants to do, and the gangs get fat off the profits.'

'Well, hopefully we can take one of them down today. Did Viyan have any idea where she was being held?'

Helen shook her head.

'Somewhere east of the city. A remote site deep in the countryside with significant waste disposal capacity. I'd set half the team to run the rule over rural properties in that area, and the other half to finding this guy.'

Helen stabbed the picture of the Dutch trafficker.

'You're looking for a Scania truck, registration plate R 945 DX. My guess is he might try to leave today, given Viyan's escape last night. If you're quick, if you get Border Force on side, then I think you've got a chance of bringing him in today.'

Charlie couldn't help but smile. It was a throwback to times past, Helen running with a case once more, exhilarated, hot on the scent.

'Can't stop yourself, can you?'

'Sorry?' Helen replied, momentarily confused.

'I mean, look at you. You're supposed to be an ordinary civilian, doing ordinary civilian things. Instead, you're stalking the bad guys, gathering evidence, pulling off daring rescues, constantly putting yourself on the line, despite my explicit advice to take it easy ...'

Helen waved this notion away, clearly not wanting to go there, but Charlie wasn't prepared to let it go.

'Why don't you just admit it, Helen? You miss this place, you miss the thrill of the hunt.'

'I miss you,' Helen agreed. 'The rest I can take or leave.'

'Rubbish, it's in your blood, always will be.'

Now Helen seemed to falter, as if uncertain how to respond, so Charlie pressed home her advantage.

'Why don't you come back?'

'Charlie, please ...'

'I mean it, Helen. I'm trying here, God knows I'm trying. But I'm not a natural leader, I can't fill your shoes. Honestly, I'm not sure anyone *could.*'

'That's nonsense. Don't let Holmes grind you down,' Helen interrupted sternly. 'You're ten times the police officer, ten times the leader she'll ever be. Your instincts are good, you've experience and you care, Charlie, you really care. That will always be your greatest asset.'

'Maybe,' Charlie replied dolefully. 'I'm just not sure I'll ever be what they want me to be, what they *need*. Whereas you ... you're a natural, this is what you were born to be.'

'No.'

Helen's tone was firm, decisive. Taken aback, Charlie stared at her old friend, surprised to see real steel in her expression.

'I'm done here, Charlie, I've made up my mind about that. But you have years ahead of you, during which you will blossom into an officer who will eclipse me and everything I've done. I believe that with all my heart, but you need to believe it too.'

'And you?' Charlie asked, evidently disappointed by her robust response.

And now once more, Helen seemed to hesitate.

'Well, I ... I've got other priorities now.'

'You mean ...?' Charlie responded, nodding at Helen's stomach.

'Something like that. I mean, I don't really know what I think, but maybe ... maybe it is the right thing for me. The right time. God knows, there's probably never going to be another chance, so ...'

'Well, if that's how you feel, then I'm very pleased for you.'

Stepping forward, Charlie folded Helen into a hug, pulling her close. For a moment, it was as if the distance, the difficulties, evaporated as swiftly as if they'd never been there at all. Her eyes brimming with tears, Charlie held Helen to her, adding:

'You deserve a bit of happiness.'

Chapter 81

It was like she was dreaming. Despite all the agony, all the despair of the last two years, here she was. She was alive, she was happy, she'd *survived*. Viyan felt as if she'd stumbled out of some subterranean cave into the light, suddenly blinded by its power, its life-affirming warmth. Things that would be entirely normal to anyone else – a warm bed, a decent breakfast, privacy, safety – seemed utterly fantastical to her. Yet here she was, revelling in these simple pleasures.

Once more, Viyan felt her chest burn, joy wrestling with sadness, hope with regret. It had been the greatest experience of her life to see Defne, Aasmah and Salman staring down the shaking camera at her, giggling, tearful, excited, but it also underlined for her how much she'd missed. Not just them growing up into spirited young children, but also the missed opportunities to hold them, to comfort them, to urge them to be strong. There must have been endless challenges, numerous dark moments over the last couple of years, when they had longed for their mother's presence. Someone to kiss them, cuddle them and assure them that everything was going to be OK. The mere thought of this made Viyan feel sick with guilt. When she'd made the fateful decision to travel to England, she thought she'd had no alternative, so grave was their situation. She was desperate, convinced her family would slowly starve to death if she didn't do something. How wrong she'd been. It would have been better – a thousand times better – to have stayed in Turkey, fighting to survive amidst the aftermath of the earthquake, rather than willingly walking into the hands of her abusers.

Still, that was behind her now. Although she'd refused all thoughts of charity, her rescuer was insisting on paying for her flight home, even offering to accompany her on the journey. Viyan had no words to express her gratitude, simply sobbing out her joy on her hostess's shoulder, but she knew she would accept her offer, the pull of seeing her beloved family too strong.

Before she did so, however, there was something she needed to do. Despite her good fortune, Viyan had not forgotten her co-workers, indeed she shuddered at the thought of what her escape might mean for them. Had they been punished for her boldness? Had security been stepped up, their meagre comforts taken away? She didn't want them to suffer, nor would she turn her back on any of them. Whilst she was still here, she would do everything in her power to free them and bring their abusers to justice. Helen Grace was at the police station now, hopefully convincing them to take action, but whilst she waited she intended to use her time wisely.

Helen had managed to source her a pad and pencil from Eloise, the manageress of the refuge. So, seated on the bed, Viyan began to draw, neatly sketching out the layout of the farm, highlighting the various different buildings, the loading bays, the washing facilities, even the hateful incinerator. Viyan had always enjoyed drawing and was soon lost in her task, utterly absorbed in bringing to life the nightmare she'd been through. Oddly, the experience was not troubling for her. Wielding her pencil over the smooth white paper she suddenly felt as if she was in charge, as if she could use a rubber to wipe out her trauma, to

349

erase faces, buildings, as if she was playing God. If only things had been that easy during her lengthy captivity.

She was so lost in her task that it took a few seconds for the shriek of the alarm to jolt her out of her reverie. Putting her pad down, Viyan rose sharply, suddenly very concerned. Moving swiftly towards the door, she listened intently, trying to hear through the wailing siren, trying to work out what the hell was going on. And now she smelt it – the unmistakable aroma of burning.

Panicked, Viyan pressed her eye to the spyhole. Now she could see it too, wisps of dark smoke weaving their way towards the landing ceiling, dancing around the wailing smoke alarms. Suddenly her heart was in her mouth. Had she escaped Hell simply to be plunged into burning fire? The smoke seemed to be getting thicker, the situation more urgent. Peering through the spyhole, Viyan saw the woman from the room opposite hurrying onto the landing, looking breathless and scared. She seemed utterly bewildered, before heading quickly for the stairs, desperate not to be stuck at the top of a tall building during a fire.

Terrified, Viyan pulled away from her vantage point. What should she do? She had promised not to open the door under any circumstances, but Helen could not have foreseen this. Viyan had no mobile phone with which to summon her guardian angel, so what should she do? Hurrying to the window, she looked down onto the street below, hoping to see Helen racing homeward. But instead she clocked a growing body of women emerging from the building, gathering in concerned huddles in the street. In the distance, Viyan could hear sirens. A fire engine heading their way perhaps?

Turning, Viyan was alarmed to see a thin veil of smoke clinging to the ceiling of her bedroom now, the air pregnant with a nasty, acrid stench. Summoning her courage, she raced back to the door. There was no point letting her idle fears cost her her life, not after everything she'd been through. So, checking once more that the landing was clear, she unlocked the door, tugging it open. Liberated, she stepped forward, then immediately froze, shrieking with terror.

Naz, the man who'd tortured and humiliated her relentlessly for the last two years, had stepped out of the shadows, blocking her path.

'Hello again, Viyan,' he grinned wickedly.

Then he drove a fist into her stomach.

Chapter 82

Helen roared through the city streets, weaving in and out of the traffic. Having been nervous and uncomfortable on arrival at Southampton Central, she'd left feeling exhilarated and energized. After the distance and arguments of recent days, she had re-connected with Charlie, which Helen suspected was a profound relief to them both. Just as importantly, Charlie was now running with the information she and Viyan had provided. DC McAndrew was talking to Interpol to see if they could identify the mysterious Dutchman, whilst one of the new DCs was marshalling efforts to unearth the farm where the trafficked migrants were being held. Charlie, meanwhile, was bringing Holmes up to speed, prepping the interview suite for Viyan's arrival. Although it would be an ordeal for her, the key thing now was for Charlie and Holmes to hear Viyan's story first-hand. It would not be easy, it would not be quick, but getting her evidence recorded and logged was critical. Currently all the team had to go on, all the CPS had to interrogate, was Helen's tall tale.

For the first time in weeks, Helen felt she had the wind at her back, powering through the streets towards the refuge. For so long, she had been belittled, disbelieved, but now finally people were taking her seriously. This sense of purpose, this sense of mission thrilled her, the way ahead now clear. She would help Viyan through this process, ensure the bad guys were brought to book, then she would help reunite the young mother with her family. And then what? Was it possible Helen could find a way to contribute *and* be a mother? Was there a job in law enforcement that would allow her to make a difference without constantly putting her neck on the line? Or would the role of motherhood be so all-consuming, so enjoyable, that she wouldn't want to do anything else? Helen didn't have enough money to retire yet, but would it be so bad to kick back for a bit and enjoy her unsolicited good fortune? Suddenly the future seemed alive with possibilities, the permutations endless, the opportunities dizzying.

Spotting traffic up ahead, Helen took a late decision. She could obviously sail past the stationary traffic, but you could never be sure some idiot wouldn't suddenly pull out, chancing an illegal stunt to reduce the delay, and there was no point taking any unnecessary risks. So, instead, she used her local knowledge to cut down one back street, then another, then a third, eventually emerging within five hundred yards of the refuge where she'd secreted Viyan.

To her alarm, the quiet residential street was now a hive of activity. Dozens of women milled in the street, some in their dressing gowns, whilst others walked back and forth, phones clamped to their ears. And now Helen realized why. Beyond the throng, a fire engine was bullying its way towards the tall building, out of which dark smoke was billowing.

Helen's blood ran cold. Her bike slowed to a crawl. Desperately, she scanned the crowd for Viyan, but there was no sign of her. Was she still in the building? Had she heeded Helen's instructions to stay put? If so, she might be trapped or passed out. But what if she wasn't? What if this unexpected fire was just a ruse

353

to smoke her out? Helen tried to dismiss this unsettling notion, yet the timing of the fire was unquestionably suspicious. Was it *possible* they had traced Viyan here?

On cue, the manageress emerged from the throng of women, looking frantic and scared, as she hurried over to Helen.

'It's not my fault,' Eloise breathed, tears pricking her eyes.

'What do you mean? What's happened?' Helen demanded.

'They must have broken into the basement, set a fire. I did try to stop them, but they pushed a gun in my face...'

'Who? Who did this?'

'Two shaven-headed guys,' she gasped. 'One of them had awful scars on his—'

'Where are they?' Helen interrupted tersely. 'Where did they take Viyan?'

'Out the back. There's a small car park there...'

Helen didn't linger for the details, ripping back the throttle and roaring away down the side of the building. Abandoned boxes and bulky bin bags littered the narrow side passage, but Helen sped down it, bursting out into the small car park beyond. Immediately, she spotted her charge. Viyan was once again in grave danger, Helen's heavily scarred adversary from yesterday forcing the distraught woman into the back of a van with the aid of an accomplice. Spotting Helen, Viyan screamed out in terror, but her appeal was brutally cut short, her abductors hurling her into the vehicle. Her cry seemed to alert her assailants to the danger, the battle-scarred leader now clocking Helen's arrival. Making a split-second decision, he grabbed his accomplice and leapt into the back of the van himself, slamming the doors shut behind him.

The driver reacted immediately, spinning the van around and driving directly towards Helen. She had only a moment to react, yanking the handlebars to the left to avoid a sickening collision.

She almost made it, leaping clear of the onrushing vehicle, only for the speeding van to clip her rear wheel at the last moment, catapulting the bike around. Instantly Helen lost her grip, the force of the impact too hot to handle, and she felt herself flying through the air, before connecting sharply with the ground, skidding to a halt on the tarmac.

Surprised, but unharmed, Helen clambered to her feet. She expected to see the van driving free and clear, but the contact with her bike had flummoxed the driver, the vehicle suddenly changing course, sliding sideways towards a parked car. Tyres shrieked and a loud bang rang out, the right side of the van dented badly by the collision. Spotting her opportunity, Helen sprinted towards the van, determined to get there before it moved off again. She powered across the concrete, zeroing in on her prey, but at the last moment the van moved off once more. Acting on instinct, Helen threw herself forwards, her fingers reaching out towards the departing vehicle.

This time her luck was in and she felt her right hand grip the van's rear handle, fastening her gloved fingers around it. She held on for dear life, even as the tips of her biking boots ripped across the tarmac, throwing her legs up and down in the air. The van was moving fast now, speeding out of the car park and out onto the street. Helen was being buffeted from all sides, but held on grimly, determined not to desert Viyan. Reaching the corner of the street, the van swung sharply right to avoid the growing crowds. Helen felt her world turn as her body swung dizzyingly to the left, her legs connecting painfully with the side of a parked car. Still she didn't let go, putting her left hand on top of her right, anchoring her to the van, as she tried to drag her legs upwards. If she could mount the bumper, put a foot on the protruding tow bar, then she might save herself, riding the vehicle until it was forced to slow for traffic.

Suddenly, however, the world seemed to stop. Helen had only a split second to process that the van had braked violently, before she was catapulted into the back door, her helmet smashing into the sheet metal. Her left hand came free and as the van now roared off again and she felt her right-hand loosening, as she bounced along the road, her body slammed up and down on the rough tarmac. Screaming, she tried to hang on, using every ounce of strength she could muster. But the battle was lost, the buffeting too severe, and with a cry of defeat, Helen finally let go, her helmet striking the ground hard as she plummeted downwards. Bouncing off the road, she managed to scramble to her feet, but the van was already some distance away. Now her legs seemed to give way, as the world slowly span around her, and she slumped back down on to her knees.

Breathless, defeated, Helen stared after the retreating van. And it was as she was kneeling there, distraught, desperate, that she felt it. A hot stickiness on her left thigh, as the blood crept down her leg. And in that moment she *knew*.

Throwing back her head, ripping open her mouth, Helen let out a howl of pure agony.

Chapter 83

Viyan lay on the floor of the van, sobbing as her abductors stared down at her. Each jolt, each bump in the road seemed to go right through her, but Viyan barely registered the blows, still in a state of shock. How could this have happened? How could things have gone so disastrously *wrong*? She had been set fair, she had been *free*... but now she was heading back to Hell.

The journey passed in a blur of tears and anguish and to her horror, Viyan soon recognized the familiar lurching of the van, as it negotiated the rutted dirt track that led up to the camp. Soon they were barrelling across the yard, before the speeding vehicle came to an abrupt halt. As the engine died, Viyan's fevered mind scrolled forwards to what lay ahead. The reckoning was at hand and she would not have to wait long for her punishment, her captors flinging open the doors and hauling her out. Crashing to the ground, Viyan tried to raise herself, but before she could do so, a familiar voice rang out:

'Well, well, well... Look what the cat dragged in.'

Looking up, Viyan saw Leyla standing above her, her eyes ablaze.

'Thought you'd got away from me, did you? Turns out it's not that easy.'

Viyan looked away, unable to stomach her tormentor's triumphant smile, but she could hear the joy in Leyla's voice. The truth was that she *had* broken free, she *had* escaped, only to blunder back into captivity through her own stupidity. Viyan had suspected it was a trap, so why hadn't she heeded Helen's advice? Why hadn't she just stayed put?

'What's the matter? Cat got your tongue?'

Viyan kept her mouth firmly shut, refusing to respond.

'Oh, I know I won't get an apology,' Leyla continued bitterly. 'But you are going to tell me what you told that bitch, Grace, and I mean *everything*…'

Viyan's thoughts rocketed back to her rescuer. She'd seen her race towards the van, had shuddered when she'd heard the vehicle clip her bike, had marvelled when she realized that Helen was clinging onto the back of the van. For a moment, panic had reigned, her abductors terrified that Helen would manage to open the doors and climb inside. Viyan had no idea what kind of police officer Helen Grace had been, but clearly she had a formidable reputation. Her hopes of liberation, however, were no sooner raised than dashed. The van braked sharply, there was a loud bang, then silence, the vehicle continuing on unencumbered. What had happened to Helen? Was she injured? Killed even? It beggared belief, after all she'd done for Viyan, the bravery, kindness and determination she'd shown. Had it all been for nothing?

'I know you can hear me,' Leyla continued aggressively. 'And you will talk.'

Viyan now heard the familiar, repetitive whooshing noise as the bicycle chain gained speed, arcing round and round in her tormentor's hand. Bracing herself, Viyan heard her attacker let fly, the first blow striking her on the shoulder and neck, rocking her sideways. Straightening up, she felt it bite again, this time on the side of her head. She fell to her left, before righting herself, aware now of a terrible ringing in her right ear. The third blow landed heavily on her back, her assailant circling her now, forcing Viyan's face into the dirt. As she raised herself up once more, the battered worker felt blood pooling in her mouth, tasting its coppery bitterness, as she turned to take in her captor.

'I am not going to tell you *anything*,' she hissed fiercely.

Leyla looked outraged, bending down over her to strike once more, but Viyan beat her to it. Turning to confront her, she looked Leyla squarely in the eye before spitting a mouthful of blood straight into her startled face.

Silence filled the yard, the handful of workers present stunned by this shocking act of defiance. For a moment, Leyla did nothing, simply staring at Viyan, bug-eyed with rage, as the sticky blood crept down her cheeks. Tensing, Viyan waited for the inevitable explosion, for the barrage of blows, but to her surprise Leyla tossed aside the chain, reaching down to grip her arm instead.

'Have it your way.'

Hauling Viyan up off the ground, her captor marched her fast across the yard.

'No one disrespects me, least of all you,' Leyla hissed.

Surprise now turning to alarm, Viyan looked up, horrified to see that they were heading directly for the incinerator.

'Please, no ...' she cried, digging her heels into the dirt.

Leyla's knee crushed into the small of Viyan's back, robbing her of breath, causing her to stumble forwards. Her assailant half-dragged, half-carried her the rest of the way, before dumping her in a heap by the locked metal door. Laughing darkly, Leyla lifted the lever lock, throwing it open to reveal the ash-strewn floor.

'I'm begging you ...' Viyan pleaded.

Leaning down, Leyla hauled Viyan to her feet, propelling her bodily into the tall metal cylinder. Stumbling, Viyan landed in a heap, sending a thin cloud of ash into the air. Triumphant, Leyla stood in the doorway, glaring down at her.

'I always suspected that you and Selima were close. Well, guess what? Now you're going to see each other again...'

Viyan cried out in terror, but it was too late, her tormentor slamming the heavy door shut, plunging her into darkness.

Chapter 84

Helen sat alone in the sterile room, staring at the ceiling, wishing she was anywhere but here. She was still trying to process the events of the morning, stunned that a day that had started so brightly could have suddenly pitched into such abject misery.

To her, it still felt as if all this was happening to someone else. The passer-by helping her to her feet, the earnest enquiry of the attending paramedics, the concerned look on their faces – Helen seemed to experience all this at a remove, barely taking in the details. Perhaps she was still in shock, perhaps it was just deep denial, but she found it hard to believe that any of this was real. Even when the emergency gynaecologist had hurried into the examination room, gently asking her to remove her trousers and underwear, still none of it felt believable. It was like a bad dream.

Helen had suffered throughout her life, never more so than during her time in Southampton, when she had put body and soul on the line time and again to protect the weak and vulnerable. Past injuries, past traumas, had been breathless, agonizing, occasionally exhilarating affairs, wounds she had willingly endured to serve the greater good. How ironic that the cruellest blow should land in an atmosphere of austere calm, in near-total silence, the only sound in the hushed examination room the monotonous ticking of the clock, which Helen had noted was running ten minutes slow, her eyes glued to it throughout.

She felt empty and dizzy, her memory of the morning fragmentary at best. She remembered her chat with Charlie, her feelings of optimism as she sped away from Southampton Central and then *this* – a grim parade of anguish, violence, injury and failure. Was a miscarriage always likely, given her age? Or was this tragedy *her* fault, the result of her wilfully placing herself in danger? She suspected the latter, cursing herself for her recklessness and stupidity. In trying to play the hero, she had thrown away her only chance of motherhood, a stark fact that she knew would haunt her for the rest of her life. This defeat was hers to own and hers alone.

For the first time in her life, Helen felt utterly rudderless. She had not intended to fall pregnant, had not wanted to accept that she *had* initially, but there was no denying that she had slowly embraced the idea, a whole new future mapped out for her. Birth, child-rearing, pre-school and more, she would have thrown herself into motherhood, blundering her way to some kind of happiness. It had given her life a real sense of meaning, a definitive future. In a stroke that future had been ripped away from her, the reality impossible to ignore. She was going to have a baby, but now she was not.

A sharp knock on the door made Helen look up. A nurse, smiling a sad smile, poked her head round the door.

'So sorry to disturb you, my love, but we're going to need to move you. If I had my way, we'd let you stay just where you are—'

'But you need the room,' Helen said bleakly.

'Something like that. Now I've got a change of clothes for you and some disposable underwear, I'll just pop them here for you ...'

She stepped inside the room, placing the small pile on a chair.

'Is there anyone I can call for you? Someone who could come and pick you up?'

Unbidden, an image of Christopher flashed through her mind, but she dismissed this out of hand. He was the last person she wanted to see right now. Charlie then? She was the obvious choice and had been trying to contact Helen for the past two hours. Yet, Helen hesitated, partly because she knew Charlie was under real pressure herself, and partly because Helen knew instinctively that she wouldn't have the strength to rehearse all that had happened to her with someone else, however sympathetic and supportive her old friend might be. For reasons Helen couldn't fully explain she wanted to keep her grief close for now. Which is why she now found herself saying:

'No, you're alright. But I could do with a cab?'

Half an hour later, Helen was back outside the refuge. Still a few women lingered in the street, talking to reporters about the incident, but Helen ignored them, walking gingerly past in the direction of the alleyway. All she wanted to do now was retrieve her bike, return to her flat and try and make sense of the morning's shocking events. But once again, she was to be denied any respite, Eloise's voice ringing out:

'Helen, is that you?'

Slowing, she turned to see the refuge manageress, hurrying over.

'Dear God, Helen, are you alright?'

Helen dropped her gaze to the floor, unable to find the words.

'I saw what happened. You could have been killed...'

Still Helen maintained her silence. She knew Eloise meant well, but every word was torture.

'I told the police all about it. Hopefully they'll catch the bastards. They've already been and gone actually... so I wasn't sure what you wanted to do with these?'

Now, finally, Helen raised her head, the effort making her feel faint. Eloise was holding out Viyan's meagre possessions. Staring at them, Helen suddenly felt overwhelmed with sadness and regret. What on earth had happened? How had those thugs found Viyan? Helen had one dark, nagging suspicion, but surely that was too far-fetched to be true? Pushing these thoughts away, she accepted the passport and sketching pad, nodding briefly at the concerned manager, before heading on her way without a word.

Half an hour later, she was back in the underground car park at her apartment block, cursing once more that the lift was not working, as she shuffled towards the towering stairwell. Her legs felt weak, her head light and it was an effort to keep going, all energy, all resolve, having deserted her. She kept her head down, her eyes fixed ahead, but the stairs seemed to spiral ever upwards. As hard as she worked, she never seemed to be getting any closer to her flat. Eventually, however, she reached the familiar landing, crossing it breathlessly, before teasing open the door.

Gripping the wall, Helen propelled herself forward. Moving slowly, she made her way through the kitchen, tossing Viyan's passport and pad onto the table. As she did so, the pad flipped open, revealing some sketches inside. Surprised, Helen seated herself carefully, leafing through its contents, amazed by what she was seeing. Viyan had clearly been busy before the fire, making copious notes regarding her time in captivity. There were names of the main players, names of her fellow workers, but also illustrations. Helen pored over her sketch of the farm where she'd been held, lost in the intricate details, before turning the page. Now she stopped in her tracks. For on this page, Viyan had drawn a picture of 'Leyla', the overseer of the horrific prison camp, the woman who'd made her life a living Hell for over two years. In an instant, everything fell into place, Helen's dark suspicions all too prescient.

For this was a woman she recognized. A woman Helen had *met*.

Chapter 85

'Stop what you're doing and gather round.'

Leyla's command echoed across the dusty yard, startling several workers. They visibly jumped, before swiftly abandoning their duties to hurry over, which brought a smile to Leyla's blood-smeared face. Despite Viyan's wicked behaviour, her blatant challenge to Leyla's authority, her co-workers seemed as obedient and pliant as ever. If the treacherous Viyan had hoped to start a rebellion, she had surely failed.

'Faster, faster, this is not an excuse for a break…'

Those closest to Leyla stepped up their pace, whilst beyond them, others emerged from the farmhouse, the accommodation block, driven in her direction by the angry shouts of Leyla's associates. The workers were clearly alarmed by this unexpected summons, fearful that it might presage some unforeseen punishment or misfortune, looking at their mistress with trepidation. How pitiful they were – their spirits broken, their resolve crushed. They were little more than automatons, with no sense of agency, courage or self-respect.

How did people get like this? The answer was obvious. Weakness. Leyla had always despised those who couldn't stand up for themselves, who let themselves be broken by life's vicissitudes. Her parents had been weak, allowing themselves to be driven from their homeland by the brutality of the Turkish authorities, only then to be exploited and abused in their adopted country, forced to clean toilets, sweep the streets, working for pennies whilst their employers grew rich. Growing up in Southampton, Leyla had watched them work themselves into an early grave, leaving her in loco parentis to her three younger brothers. That had been *another* sign of her parents' weakness, a gross betrayal of their own flesh and blood, but as ever they'd blamed others for their misfortune, citing prejudice as the root cause of their misfortune. Her father had often said that their community was persecuted the world over and Leyla had taken that to heart, but not as an excuse for failure, more as an opportunity for *gain*. Having been born in the UK, Leyla knew how the system worked, how it functioned by perennially exploiting the weak and vulnerable. Using this knowledge and her ties to the Kurdish community back in Turkey, she'd grown strong, rich, powerful. She would not go meekly to an early grave as her parents had done and she would call no one master. Thanks to her ingenuity, cunning and ruthlessness, *she* was the one in control.

The workers were now forming a circle around her. In other circumstances, this might have alarmed Leyla, but they would be no trouble today, the assembled drones kept in line by the iron bars and snub-nosed revolvers that her brothers used to instil fear. No, they would stand there, passive and blank, as Leyla showed them the price of disobedience. They would say nothing as one of their own was reduced to ashes, her tortured screams the only sound in this isolated yard. This was true weakness and Leyla despised them for it.

She, by contrast, would not waver. In normal circumstances, she would never let one of her workers be harmed, but this was different. Viyan's gross disrespect, her attempt to destroy her highly successful enterprise, could not go unpunished. Leyla had offered Viyan the hand of friendship, the chance of a new life in a new country, but the ungrateful bitch had spat in her face. She'd turned on the one person who'd tried to lift her out of poverty and disgrace and now she would pay for it. In this camp, in Leyla's universe, the price of ingratitude was death.

Chapter 86

'Are you out of your mind, Helen?'

It certainly felt that way, but there was no way she was going to let Christopher fob her off like that, so Helen pressed on:

'I know it's unorthodox, but there's no other way.'

'Unorthodox?' Christopher stammered. 'It's *illegal*. I can't possibly action a search without the proper paperwork. You don't even have a warrant.'

Her ex-lover had looked shocked when she'd turned up unannounced at his office, then aghast when she'd made her request. It had been an impulsive decision to come here, but Helen felt in her bones that there was only one way to reveal who Harika Guli really was. She had to follow the money.

'I'm convinced that this supposed charity worker is *actually* a human trafficker. God alone knows how many poor souls she's smuggled into this country. They are being kept in the most inhuman conditions, forced to work for a pittance—'

'I get all that,' Christopher interrupted firmly. 'And I *believe* you, Helen. But I can't do anything unless the police or the NCA ask me to.'

'That'll take days, when we have hours at the most.'

Even as she said the words, Helen's heart sank, horrified by the thought of the retribution Viyan would face at the hands of her cruel mistress. She would be tortured, perhaps even killed like her poor friend Selima, which is why Helen knew she had to fight, despite lacking either the strength or energy to do so.

'If you do it now, if you do it quickly, I can be out of here before anyone notices.'

'I'm sorry, Helen, but it's out of the question. It's more than my job's worth.'

'It'll take five minutes. I just need to know who pays the rent, the bills, for the Kurdish Welfare Centre on Roehampton Road. My hunch is that it's actually a front company, set up purely to facilitate human trafficking.'

Christopher ran his hand through his hair in exasperation, staring at Helen as if she was speaking a foreign language. It was a look she was getting used to.

'I don't know what to say to you, Helen. I just can't do it. I understand that you're concerned about Viyan, but you know full well that I can't do what you're asking, so unless you're here to make my life difficult for me, to punish me in some way—'

'This isn't about you, you prick,' Helen interrupted. 'It's about saving lives. It's about doing what's right.'

'Well, I'm sorry, but I've said all I'm going to on the matter. The answer's no.'

Helen stared at him, exhaustion battling with her anger, her strength leeching from her and, with it, her resolve. It would be so easy to give up, to throw in the towel, but when had she ever done that?

'Then you leave me no choice,' she breathed, steadying herself on the corner of his desk. 'Which is your boss's office?'

'I'm sorry?!'

'I think he might be interested to know that you've been having an affair, sharing off-the-record stories and insider gossip with someone outside the department.'

'For God's sake, Helen,' Christopher spluttered, the blood draining from his face.

'Or maybe I should just contact Alice.'

Stepping forward, Helen picked up his wedding photo, running her eye over it.

'Tell her who her husband *really* is. How does that sound?'

Her former lover was staring at her, his shock and anger rising by the second. It was clear he was about to explode, so Helen cut in:

'Look, I can see you're cross, but can we skip the misogynistic rant and just cut to the chase? I'm on a schedule here.'

She was glaring at him, daring Christopher to defy her. It was clear he would like nothing more than to rant and rave, but she also knew that he would prefer deception to disgrace. Which is why she wasn't surprised when he crumpled, huffily collapsing into his chair and starting to type.

'See, you can be a good boy when you want to be.'

Ignoring her, he worked fast and five minutes later, she had her answer.

'You're right,' he said brusquely. 'The general donations that the centre receives don't remotely cover its costs. It only stays afloat because of regular payments from a Leyla Rashidi, a British national, born and raised in Southampton.'

Now he had Helen's interest. Perhaps there *was* hope after all.

'Where does she live?'

'Her registered address is Dearham Farm, which is out near Swanwick. I think it's some kind of waste disposal facility.'

Helen couldn't suppress a smile as Christopher scribbled down the details, handing it to her. Finally, she'd found the camp where Viyan and the others were being held. Scanning the address, she walked swiftly to the door.

'Helen, wait. Before you go ...'

Helen paused, turning back to look at her flustered ex-lover.

'When all this is over, can we talk? I want us to find a way through this ...'

'There is no "us", Christopher. Turns out there never was.'

And with that, she left, shutting the door firmly behind her. All thoughts of Christoper's betrayal, of her own suffering, would have to wait. Finally, she had a location. Finally, she knew where she was heading. The only question now was whether she would be too late.

Chapter 87

The end could not be far away now. In truth, Viyan was surprised she wasn't dead already, such was Leyla's anger as she tossed her captive into the incinerator. Viyan had expected her tormentor to slam the door shut, stab the controls, then stand back to enjoy her immolation. But nothing had happened, an anomaly that fostered a fragile flame of hope in Viyan's heart. Was there some kind of problem? A fault with the machine? Or had Helen somehow traced Viyan here? Were the police even now descending on the remote farm, intent on freeing *all* the captives? Such a happy outcome seemed far-fetched and sure enough, Viyan soon divined the reason for the delay, Leyla's harsh voice commanding her fellow workers to gather round. As with poor Selima, Viyan's death was not going to be a private act of punishment, rather a public act of retribution.

Her fear spiking, Viyan clambered to her feet, stumbling blindly forwards, her outstretched hands eventually finding solid metal. She was surprised to discover how warm the surface was, momentarily alarmed that Leyla had in fact started the machine, but now sense prevailed. The machine was quiet and lifeless, its exterior simply warmed by the spring sunshine. It made the atmosphere cloying and uncomfortable here, the air thin and dusty, prompting Viyan to re-double her efforts, despite the sweat that already crawled down her back and clung to her brow, despite the lightheadedness that seemed to come and go in disorienting waves. If she was to have any chance of escaping this fetid tomb, she had to act now.

Guiding herself by touch, the young mother made her way round the cylinder, until she eventually located the door frame. Pausing, she found the handle, yanking at it with all her might. Predictably it refused to budge, so moving her fingers down the frame, she teased the seal, searching for any small gaps, any signs of weakness, something she might work with. Finding little, she moved up and over the lintel, down the other side, but her meticulous ferreting revealed nothing. She was trapped.

Cursing, Viyan leaned on the warm metal wall, sweaty, uncomfortable and dispirited. The reality was that she'd been trapped ever since she had met Leyla. How she rued ever listening to her enticing promises, her vision of England as a land of hope and opportunity. When Viyan had first encountered Leyla, handing out bottles of water in the refugee camp on the Syrian border, she'd appeared like a guardian angel, dispensing water, food and smiles. The pair had quickly become fast friends, Leyla discreetly slipping Viyan little extras for the children, candy from Europe and sweetmeats from Istanbul. Viyan had come to cherish her presence, putting their family's survival down to her kindness. So when Leyla suggested a route out of their poverty and degradation, a way to earn good money to send back to her family, Viyan had demanded to know more. She had no reason to smell a rat at that point, why would she? Up until that point, Leyla's motives had seemed pure and honourable.

It was true that Viyan had not accepted Leyla's proposition straight away, nervous about abandoning her children to the care of her elderly mother. But the worsening situation in the camp had forced her hand, Leyla insisting that she could be in the UK and earning good money in less than a fortnight. Viyan was sorely tempted, Leyla convincing her that the operation was both well-established and legitimate, with a committed and spirited welcome party awaiting her on her arrival in England, care of the good-hearted volunteers at the Kurdish Welfare Centre in Southampton.

The reality had been very different. Viyan had never seen the Welfare Centre, nor did she meet Leyla again, until she dismounted from the filthy cargo container into the bewildering surrounds of the farm. The traffickers, far from being sympathetic to the desperate migrants, were brutal and heartless, barely feeding their charges as they were transported in blacked-out vans across shadowy border crossings in Bulgaria, Serbia, Slovenia and more, before eventually arriving in a refugee hostel in Holland. Perhaps the place was genuine, perhaps there *were* genuine asylum seekers there, but Viyan never got to find out, bundled into the Dutchman's container truck, with only the shortest of breaks to use the bathroom and beg a slice of bread. A day or two later, she had found herself at this hideous farm, imprisoned by her desperation, her vulnerability, her gullibility.

How she cursed herself now for her naivety. For believing Leyla's wicked lies. And yet, what reason did she have to question this kindly woman's motives? She was of Kurdish heritage, she was a charity worker, she even claimed to be a mother, mentioning a trio of beloved children whom Viyan now knew didn't exist. Leyla had preyed on Viyan's maternal love, playing on her fears for the welfare of her children. She had assured Viyan that if she accepted her proposal that her family would prosper, that they would grow up happy, healthy, even wealthy, that it was her duty as a mother to put them first. She had sealed the deal by invoking their shared heritage, citing the duty of every Kurd to look out for each other in the face of relentless suspicion, hostility and persecution. And it was that, her gross misuse of this sacred bond, amongst a plethora of other lies, obfuscations and half-truths, that had been the greatest betrayal of all.

Chapter 88

Helen was heading east, gliding over the Itchen Toll bridge, speeding fast out into the countryside. The M27 came and went, then the village of Swanwick, Helen pushing deeper into the remote agricultural land that bordered the east of the city. Seldom visited and little explored, it was the perfect spot for a criminal enterprise that needed to remain below the radar.

How well Leyla Rashidi had fooled them all, keeping her operation, her success, her very existence totally under wraps. She was a devious criminal who for years had operated in the shadows, presenting to the outside world as Harika Guli, loving mother and protector of her community, whilst in reality operating a sophisticated and successful trafficking operation. Helen's mind was still reeling from all that Viyan had told her, marvelling at the audacity, duplicity and cruelty of this mysterious woman. She was obviously greedy, ruthless and sadistic, delighting in tormenting her charges when they behaved, eliminating them in the vilest way possible when they didn't. Helen had been devastated to learn of Selima's terrible end, her fellow worker's fractured description of her agonized screaming utterly sickening. It was yet another death on Helen's conscience, the very last thing she needed today.

Would Viyan perish in the same agonizing way? If so, would

Helen be able to live with herself? It was *she* who'd asked 'Harika' to come to Southampton Central to help translate for Viyan. It was *she* who'd unwittingly given away Viyan's hiding place at the refuge, handing the young mother over to her captors on a plate. Helen raged against herself for her stupidity, yet in her heart of hearts she knew it was Leyla Rashidi who was to blame, the pitiless gangmaster to whom killing was as natural as breathing.

How convincing she'd seemed when Helen had been quizzing her only a few days ago, concerned, committed and eager to help. At the time, Helen had no doubts as to her sincerity, nor she assumed did her fellow volunteers, who appeared to hang on her every word. Loath though she was to admit it, Leyla's diabolical scheme had a touch of genius to it, using her charitable work in the UK to justify numerous trips to the remote villages, slums and, on occasion, disaster zones of Turkey. No one, not Interpol, not the UK police, nor the refugee charities, would have any cause to question her activities or motives, giving her total freedom to recruit desperate new migrants. With that kind expression, those big brown eyes, that winning smile, who wouldn't be convinced? Preying on fellow Kurds, exploiting their difficult situation for her own gain, she'd ensured a steady supply of illegal workers, topping up the numbers with other refugees from central Asia who'd managed to make it to the asylum centre in Rotterdam. Was that organization in on it too? Or were they innocent dupes? Time would tell.

Time, however, was the one commodity Helen didn't have. Cranking up her speed, she raced on down the deserted country lanes. Her satnav was leading her ever deeper into the unknown, indicating that she should turn right onto a dirt track which led away into woodland. Skidding onto it, Helen bumped down the rutted path, each impact shooting right through her weakened body. Despite this, she was heedless of caution, determined to locate the camp, taking the next bend as fast as she could, before suddenly coming to an abrupt halt, sending up a cloud of dust. Her prize was just a hundred feet in front of her, access barred by a pair of tall, metal gates. This then was Dearham Farm, surrounded on all sides by a chain-link fence which was topped with razor wire. Killing the ignition, Helen dismounted swiftly, tugging off her helmet and wheeling her Kawasaki off the road.

Leaving her bike concealed, Helen crept back to the roadside. As she did so, the towering metal gates suddenly opened. Intrigued, she hung back, wondering what this sudden movement might mean. The sharp toot of a horn explained all, an articulated lorry leaving the farm and heading away fast down the dirt track. Surprised, Helen stepped back into the shadows, watching with interest as the Dutch lorry thundered past.

A smile spread across her face as she watched it go, another piece of the puzzle falling into place. Fired up, Helen pulled her phone from her pocket, then quickly dialled Charlie's number.

Chapter 89

'Where the hell have you been, Helen? I've been going out of my mind here.'

Charlie's overriding feeling was one of relief, but her enquiry was nevertheless tinged with anger. She'd spent the last few hours trying to placate an irate Holmes, but more than that had been genuinely worried about her old friend. News had reached her of the arson attack at the women's refuge and the subsequent discovery of an injured woman lying in the street, but her enquiries at the local hospitals had yielded nothing, Helen having apparently discharged herself a couple of hours ago.

'Look, I'm sorry about that and I'll explain later,' Helen replied, her voice catching. 'All you need to know right now is that they've got Viyan. It's my belief that she's being held at Dearham Farm, which is just on the outskirts of Swanwick. I'm there now. Also, your man is on the move. A Dutch registered Scania truck just left the farm at speed. I think he's making a break for it, trying to get home before the shit hits the fan.'

'Did you catch the registration plate?' Charlie enquired urgently.

'R 945 DX, so it's definitely our guy,' Helen replied quickly.

'If he's heading to the docks, he should be there in under an hour. Anyway, that's all, I've gotta go. See you on the other side.'

She rang off, leaving Charlie hanging.

'Bye then…' Charlie said to the dead line, shaking her head at her old friend's unfailing ability to surprise her.

'Good news?'

Charlie spun round to find DC Malik staring at her curiously.

'Very good news,' Charlie replied, raising her voice as she continued. 'Right, listen up everyone. We have a confirmed sighting of our man. He's just left a remote farm in Swanwick and, we presume, is heading for the docks. DC Malik, can you liaise with the port authorities? I want a name for whoever's booked a crossing today for a Scania truck, registration number R 945 DX.'

'I will alert Traffic and Border Force and I want us all on the road in five minutes. Our top priority now is to intercept him with the minimum drama, bringing him into custody safely and securely.'

For a moment, the assorted team members did nothing, staring in astonishment at this sudden change in their fortunes.

'Well, what are you waiting for? This is our chance to show what we're made of.'

Now there was a flurry of activity, as phones, jackets, batons and more were scooped up, the team keen to respond to her call to arms. It was a sight that stirred Charlie's heart, sending pulses of adrenaline coursing through her. After months of dead ends, embarrassments and failures, this was her chance to make amends. To show Holmes she was worthy of her rank. To convince the team that she was fit to lead.

To prove to herself that she *could* do the job.

Chapter 90

Emilia drummed her fingers on the wheel, frustrated and anxious. She had been camped out at the petrol station for four hours now and still there was no sign of him. Curious as to why the tracking signal had hardly moved since last night, she'd driven straight to Dearham Farm from the mortuary, only to be deterred by the high chain-link fences and perimeter guards. Executing a swift U-turn, she'd retreated to the nearby Shell station to ponder her next move. Would her plan still work or had something already gone wrong? She had terrible visions of the Dutchman's jacket lying discarded in the dirt as he crept away via some secret route, but now to her immeasurable relief, he appeared to be on the move again. The little dot was gliding fast away from the vast swathe of green on the digital map, heading down Swanwick Lane towards the heart of the village.

'Come on, come on...'

She craned left and right, peering through her windscreen. Suddenly Emilia was desperate to lay her eyes on her assailant again, to convince herself that he was still unaware of her subterfuge. The flashing dot was almost on top of her now, so exhaling slowly, she turned the key in the ignition, sliding the gears into first.

And then, suddenly, there he was. A loud roar presaged his

arrival, then the Scania truck swept past the Shell garage, his dark, angular profile visible in the driver's seat. Offering up a silent prayer, Emilia eased off the handbrake, speeding across the empty forecourt and onto the road. Fifty yards ahead the truck lumbered on its way, its driver utterly oblivious to the fact that he now had a tail, one that would stick like glue to him until his inevitable downfall and disgrace. Things had not gone totally to plan for Emilia – she had hoped to investigate Dearham Farm herself, before calling in the police, but the high-level security had put paid to that. Still, it was better to adapt to a changing situation than mess things up in the pursuit of perfection. Life was never straightforward and you had to take your victories where you could find them.

And what a victory it would be. This moment had been fifteen years in the making and Emilia intended to enjoy herself, her eyes straying to the Nikon camera nestling in the passenger seat. How sweet it would be to capture the moment of realization, when the man who'd tried to crush her all those years ago discovered that he had been outwitted by the woman he failed to destroy. If it was a good photo, Emilia might even frame it, a permanent testament to her cunning, persistence and nerve. Revenge, redemption, rebirth was now only a matter of minutes away, the unwitting trafficker enjoying what would prove to be his last few moments of freedom. Smiling to herself, Emilia leaned towards the phone cradle, keeping her eyes firmly on the truck as she punched in three digits – 999.

It was time to set the trap.

Chapter 91

She reacted instinctively, turning away sharply from the blinding light. Viyan had been lying in the dirt, forlorn and despairing. Then suddenly the metal door had burst open, her betrayer stepping into echoing cylinder. Shocked, Viyan tried to rouse herself, but she was too slow, a heavy boot pushing down on her cheek, grinding her into the dust.

'Are you ready, Viyan? Any last words?'

Viyan said nothing, merely groaning, her lips coated in filth.

'No? How disappointing. I was hoping you'd at least beg, especially as you've got a captive audience...'

Her tormentor laughed as she gestured to the gloomy faces watching through the open door. Returning her attention to her captive, she leaned forward, increasing the pressure. Viyan could feel the rubber ridges of her abuser's sole pressing down hard on her, threatening to crack her cheekbone at any moment. Was this how it was going to end? Crushed by a woman who'd promised to save her? Viyan would take that, at least it would be quick, but predictably her tormentor now raised her boot, determined to deny her prisoner any respite, any clemency.

'I really did do my best for you, Viyan,' she continued, shaking her head in disappointment. 'I raised you up out of the dirt, gave you a job, a roof over your head, a purpose in life and how did you repay me? By plotting and planning and conniving. Poor, deluded Viyan. Did you ever think you could succeed? That you could outwit *me*?'

Viyan refused to look at her, wanting no part of her sick games.

'When will you understand that I can't be beaten, I can't be stopped? In this place, I am *everything*.'

Viyan clamped her hands over her ears, couldn't bear to hear any more of this delusional bullshit, but Leyla's voice cut through.

'I am the dispenser of charity, I am the bringer of retribution. I can give life ... but I can also take it away. You should have thought of that, before you dared to betray me.'

Raising her boot, Leyla turned away. Released from her vice-like grip, Viyan struggled to her feet, but her captor was already in the doorway, casting one last, gloating look back.

'What a shame your family will never see you again. I'll make sure to send them your regards ...'

Stepping out of the incinerator, Leyla slammed the door shut. The heavy lock lever now fell, then to her horror Viyan heard footsteps pounding the perimeter to the control box. For a second, there was a terrible, pregnant silence, then with an ominous creaking sound, the machine came to life. The roar of a flame, the clanking of heating metal, the sound of death.

Scrabbling up onto her knees, Viyan clamped her hands together and began to pray.

Chapter 92

The fence was high and forbidding, razor wire curled maliciously around the top. Helen had spent ten minutes stalking the perimeter, looking for holes, but there was nothing. It was clear that Leyla Rashidi and her cronies were determined to keep Dearham Farm free of prying eyes, numerous signs on the fence warning of dire consequences for trespassers. But Helen had no choice – if she wanted to rescue Viyan, she had to get over that fence.

Tugging off her jacket, she took a deep breath, then wearily launched the heavy leather garment high into the air. Wary of tossing it up and over the fence, she put too little energy into it and it fell back onto her. Annoyed, she tried again and this time she judged the trajectory correctly, the flapping jacket landing on top of the razor wire. She did this with a heavy heart, concerned that her favourite jacket would pay a high price, but there was no other way. The razor wire glinted wickedly in the sunlight, promising to lacerate fingers and arms, a thought which made Helen shudder. She would need all her limbs, all her strength for what lay ahead.

Gripping the wire, Helen took a deep breath. She had never felt so hollow, so lethargic as she did today. Part of her doubted she would even be able to make it to the top of the fence, let alone effect Viyan's rescue, but the imprisoned woman's needs were more pressing than her own, so gritting her teeth, she put one boot on the fence and started to climb. Weaving one hand over the other, she clambered clumsily up, her determination propelling her towards the top. In less than five seconds she was there, clinging to the edge of the chain-link fence, as it swayed back and forth under her assault. Gathering herself, she raised one foot onto the top of the fence, levering herself upwards, arching her body up and over the razor wire. She was straining every sinew not to touch her jacket, not to expose herself to danger, but this came at a cost, the effort suddenly making her feel dizzy and unstable. For a minute, she thought she might collapse onto the deadly blades, but closing her eyes, she managed to regain her composure, sliding one leg over and raising her torso over the top. Her foot now made contact with the other side of the fence, her toe desperately, digging in. Now she hauled the rest of herself over, confident she had defeated this deadly obstacle.

But now disaster struck. Her leading foot suddenly slipped from its mooring, throwing her off balance. Now she was falling, tugging at her jacket in desperation to arrest her fall. With a savage ripping sound it came clean away, exposing the cruel wire. Pushing away from the fence she tried to jump clear of it, but her trailing hand ripped over the wire, tearing flesh and belching blood.

She landed with a crash on the ground, her hip jarring nastily on a rock, the impact rippling through her. For a moment, Helen lay there, shocked and breathless, before slowly pulling herself up onto her knees. Looking down, she saw a long, deep gash on her left hand, which oozed crimson. The sight made her world spin and for a moment she thought she was going to faint, the trees seeming to dance around her. Helen clamped her eyes shut, willing herself to be strong, but as she knelt amidst the foliage, she heard a noise that froze her blood. Footsteps coming fast towards her, pounding through the woods.

Her eyes snapped open. Two muscular thugs were tramping along the perimeter, their gaze alert and suspicious. Desperate, Helen scrabbled forward, forcing her narrow frame into a thick gorse bush. Immediately, she was set upon, a thousand tiny thorns tearing at her skin. The footsteps were getting louder now, so gritting her teeth, she crawled in deeper, completely consumed by the foliage. Holding her breath, she kept a careful watch eye on the sentries as they passed by unawares, laughing and joking with each other. Only once they were well clear did she emerge from her hiding place, rising to her knees and stumbling on into the woodland.

Progress was slow and faltering, tree roots and rabbit holes conspiring to trip her at every stage. Helen did not relent, however, convinced that every second counted now. And before long, the forest started to thin out, revealing a sprawling farm littered with tumbledown buildings. At the heart of the site was a large, two-storey farmhouse, its interior gloomy and lifeless. The yard, by contrast, was alive with people. A handful were at work, emptying sacks into battered industrial bins. The vast majority of the workers were gathered towards the rear of the yard. Helen marvelled at the numbers, there must have been at least fifty immigrants here, all dressed shabbily, their body language listless and defeated. Creeping forward to the fringes of the undergrowth, she scanned the terrain, looking for the spider at the heart of this tangled web.

Leyla Rashidi was standing at the back of the site next to a giant, cylindrical structure, hectoring her charges, who surrounded her in an uneven circle. To her dismay, Helen now realized the horror of the situation. Something – or someone – was in the deadly incinerator. There could be no other explanation for Leyla's strange behaviour, the enraged gangmasters shouting abuse at the machine, occasionally turning to admonish the knot of workers, who surrounded it, some looking sheepish, others sickened. Desperately, Helen scanned the yard, searching for Viyan, but there was no sign of her. Helen could draw only one conclusion – the young mother of three was about to be burned to death.

Helen took a step forward, straining to see what was going on, then froze in her tracks. Out of the corner of her eye, she glimpsed something, turning to see a tiny electronic device hidden in the trunk of a tree, flashing red at her accusingly. Cursing, Helen realized her presence had been detected, the hidden sensor reacting to her movement. There was nothing for it, she would have to move fast now, throwing caution to the wind. She hadn't planned it this way, but there was no point prevaricating. Reaching down, she scoured the ground for a weapon, seizing upon a fallen branch.

'Hello again.'

Straightening up, Helen saw the heavily scarred thug approaching, flanked by his sidekick from yesterday's ambush. Helen's eyes narrowed, this was the third time she had faced off with this vicious bully and she was determined to make it their last. Gripping the branch firmly, she stepped forward to confront him, only for her intended victim to raise his gun, levelling it directly at her.

'So, Helen, shall we finish what we started?' he drawled, flashing a set of stained teeth. 'Or are you going to come quietly?'

Helen glared at him. The distance between them was only a few feet, but there was no way she could cover the ground before he got a shot off. What then was the alternative? Surrender? Whilst Viyan was burned alive?

The smiling thug cocked the hammer, offering Helen a final warning. She knew she should relent, but a towering rage was growing inside her. These sadistic bastards were responsible for Selima's death, for Viyan's imminent immolation, for the loss of her own child, denying Helen the motherhood she suddenly found she craved. Was she going to let them get away with these outrages? Was she going to let them *win*?

Bowing her head as if conceding defeat, Helen took a step forward, then hurled the branch at her captor with all her might. Surprised, her assailant moved fast to deflect the branch, but in so doing was forced to lower his gun. Summoning her last vestiges of energy, Helen ran forwards, arriving just in time to bat the gun from his hand as he tried to raise it once more. Now she didn't hesitate, driving her fist into his stomach, before following up with a vicious upper cut. Her victim had recovered from his initial shock, however, jerking his head back just in time to avoid the blow. Helen's fist sailed clean past, leaving her hopelessly exposed. Her enemy took full advantage, his clenched fist exploding into her right cheek. Defenceless, off balance, Helen flew backwards, colliding heavily with the ground. The breath was punched from her, her head hit an exposed rock, then suddenly everything went black.

Chapter 93

He only had one overriding priority now. He had to escape.

Keeping his eyes fixed on the road, Visser pressed hard on the accelerator, the heavy articulated truck thundering forward. He was comfortably over the limit, but felt speed was now more important than caution, his instinct telling him that he was in danger. He had no idea what the escaped illegal had told her rescuer, or indeed the police, during her brief interlude of freedom, but he knew this horrific lapse in security meant only bad things – for him, for Leyla, for their whole operation. The illegal had seen him face on, had no doubt already provided the police with a physical description, his nationality, details about the Rotterdam hostel and possibly more besides. Should he lie low then, wait for the heat to die down, then attempt to leave the UK? His gut told him no. Viyan had been recaptured fairly quickly, her rescuer injured in attempting to save her and, with both of them out of the game, there was a chance, a window to exploit. If they hadn't yet made contact with the police, or if the authorities were slow to connect the dots, then he might still be able to slip out of the country with his stash of gold before the shit hit the fan.

Racing past a thirty sign at well north of fifty miles an hour, Visser now took his foot off the accelerator, bringing the truck down to a more acceptable speed. He was now only a few miles from the docks. If luck was on his side, if fate smiled upon him, he would be on a crossing tonight, back to his beloved Holland. He enjoyed his visits to England, had made good money here, but he never felt comfortable until he was back amongst his own countrymen, able to blend into the background. Here he always felt like a curiosity, the locals taking great pleasure in his accent for reasons which were beyond him. The sooner he was back in Rotterdam, his hometown, the better.

Even as he thought this, his eyes strayed to his faded Feyenoord scarf, a good luck charm he always took with him on foreign trips. It had not let him down yet and he longed to be wearing it once more in its proper setting, the majestic De Kuip stadium in the south of the city. The thought made his heart ache, picturing himself amidst the throng, enjoying the roar of the crowd, the crisp bite of cheap beer, the tang of his post-match smoke. Simple pleasures, but he had learned to treasure them, so unpredictable, dangerous and fraught had his day-to-day life become. Maybe he should give it all up, embrace a quieter life now that he had a golden retirement pot, acknowledge that he had had a good run. That might help persuade Suzanne to finally take him back, but was it realistic? Was there not a part of him that enjoyed the tension, revelled in the drama? Was he really cut out to be *ordinary*?

Checking his mirrors, Visser realized there was a queue forming behind him. Uncomfortable with a long line of cars sitting on his bumper, he wound down his window, gesturing for them to pass. The way ahead was clear and the first car in line needed no second invitation, the souped-up Mazda roaring past and racing away into the distance. After a small delay, a second car also followed, a Land Rover Discovery turning on the burners, the attractive driver looking up at him as she sped past. The third car, a red hatchback, remained where it was, however, keeping a safe distance between them. Surprised, Visser stuck his arm out again, gesturing once more for the Corsa to pass, reluctant to have anyone sitting on his bumper. But once more the driver made no move to respond, despite the open road ahead.

And now a disturbing thought stole over Visser. Was it possible he was being followed? That someone was on to him? Raising his speed slightly, he was alarmed to see the red Corsa respond, matching his pace. Frowning, Visser stabbed the brake quickly. This seemed to take the hatchback by surprise, suddenly drawing it close to his truck. Now he had a clearer view of the driver and what he saw shocked him to the core.

It was Emilia Garanita. He would recognize that face anywhere. She was following him. She was stalking him, intent on gaining her revenge. Keeping his speed steady, determined not to reveal that he'd spotted her, Visser thundered on towards the docks, his mind reeling. How on earth had she found him? Had she already called the cops? Were they lying in wait for him? If so, with only a mile or so until the port, was it too late to do anything about it?

Had he finally run out of road?

Chapter 94

'Where is he?'

Charlie's tone was urgent and tense, demanding a response.

'He's about half a mile away,' DC Roberts responded briskly, checking the tracking app that Emilia had told them to download. 'He's making steady progress, doesn't seem to be much in the way of traffic today, so my guess is that he should be here imminently.'

'Alright, tell everybody to stand by,' Charlie replied. 'Our top priority is to stop him safely and without incident. Timing is going to be crucial though – remind everyone to hold back until I say so, I don't want him getting spooked and diverting before he's boxed in, OK?'

Nodding, DC Roberts pulled his radio from his belt and began relaying the order to the other teams. The whole of the MIT had been deployed to Southampton docks, just as they had been four days ago, but this time Charlie was hoping for a very different outcome. That outing had ended in humiliation, their real target slipping through unscathed, whilst they mistakenly persecuted an innocent Belgian haulier. Back then they had no idea who they were dealing with, nor how sly his operation was, but now the boot was on the other foot. Thanks to Helen's intervention they not only knew the lorry's registration number, they also knew the name of the driver – Matthijs Vissser, a Dutch national. And thanks to Emilia's tip-off, they were able to track the driver's progress via the journalist's surveillance app. If Charlie felt a slight twinge of guilt that the majority of the detective work had been done by an ex-police officer and a journalist, she pushed it away. It didn't matter who'd done the leg work, all that mattered now was the result.

How would the trafficker react? Would he abandon his vehicle and flee? Would he try to fight his way out? Whatever lay in store, the key thing now was to take him by surprise. If he clocked the heavy police presence before he reached the heart of the port, then he might turn right around and head back onto the ring road, a disastrous prospect given the potential for casualties on that perennially busy road. No, they had to let him enter the ferry terminal, make him feel that the sea-bound traffic was proceeding as normal, before they made their move. Border Force could manipulate the traffic flow, ensuring there was a decent gap between him and the preceding vehicle, but after that it would all come down to them. Timing would be crucial, it being vital that the stingers were laid front and back, the roadblock erected, before he had a chance to react. Once he was on the main thoroughfare to the departure point, he would be hemmed in, with no side roads to escape down, so if the team did their job right, if they timed their intervention wisely, then surely there would be no escape?

Exhaling slowly, Charlie tried to clamp down her nerves. The last few months had been fraught, the past week borderline traumatic, but finally she had the sense that things were coming to a head. This man had mocked them for too long, presumably taking great pleasure from his subterfuge, consistently hoodwinking the authorities who searched fruitlessly for him. But now his luck had run out, his cover was blown and at long last, Charlie felt certain that victory was at hand.

Chapter 95

Her eyes were filled with dust, her head was spinning, but still Helen could make out her attacker's enraged face as he squeezed the life out of her. Helen had hit the ground hard, the back of her head connecting sharply with an exposed rock, leaving her confused and disoriented. Her attacker had capitalized on her misfortune, pinning down her arms with his knees and sliding his hands around her exposed neck.

Through the dancing dirt, Helen tried to fix her attention on her attacker. His face swam in and out of focus, but his intention was clear: he meant to crush the life out of her. This was a man who thrived on violence, on control, who enjoyed forcing himself on those less powerful than himself. Twisting and turning on the dirty ground, Helen laboured to free herself from his hold, desperate to shake him off, to wipe that gruesome smile from his face. But her assailant's blood was up, the furious thug hell-bent on destroying the woman who'd become a major thorn in their side.

With each passing second, the pressure increased. Helen's vision was dimming, her last remaining vestiges of energy ebbing away, and she could sense that the end was near. Was this how it was supposed to go? Was this darkest of days always destined to be her last? It made sense perhaps, one fight too many at the culmination of a troubled and often painful life.

Helen had only seconds left, but could do nothing whilst pinned down and helpless. Frantically, she twisted and tugged, desperate to free her arms from beneath his bulky knees. And now finally she caught a break, her left hand slithering free. Her attacker barely noticed, thrilled by the sight of her bulging eyes and flushed face, excited by the prospect of the kill. Unable to see clearly, gasping for breath, Helen's outstretched fingers now alighted on the rock she'd hit her head on. Gripping it firmly, she summoned her last shred of resolve, then smashed the rock into the back of his skull. Caught off guard, her assailant cried out, immediately loosening his grip. Released from his hold, Helen was quick to follow up her initial assault, swinging the rock round with all her might. Reeling, her enemy did not see it coming, the pointed end of the stone hitting him hard in the temple. Groaning, he rolled off, then lay still in the dust.

Helen's throat was on fire, her chest burning, her legs as shaky as a newborn lamb's, but somehow she managed to clamber to her feet. Swaying like a boxer on the ropes, she still had to deal with her attacker's companion, who had snatched up the discarded gun and now pointed it directly at her. There was little chance of her giving up now, however, especially as she could make out shouting elsewhere in the yard, screams of shock and confusion as people became aware of the vicious confrontation taking place. Without hesitation, she spun on her heel, hurling the rock directly at the thug. Her aim was true, the rock hitting him squarely between the eyes. Stunned, the man staggered backwards, clutching his face. This moment of hesitation was all Helen needed and, stepping forward, she swung her heavy boot up between his legs. The burly man virtually leapt into the air, spilling the gun from his grasp. As he came back down to earth, shocked and gasping, Helen took another purposeful step forward, driving her fist into the middle of his face. With satisfaction, she felt his nose snap before he too hit the ground, out cold.

Snatching up the gun, Helen limped across the yard, breathing heavily as she cut a faltering path towards the clanking incinerator. Terrified workers scattered in her wake, Helen scrambled on, on, on, until suddenly she found herself directly in front of Leyla, who turned to greet her, eyes ablaze.

Outraged at this unexpected intrusion, the gangmaster tugged a bicycle chain from her pocket and began to advance. Helen knew she had no energy left, no resolve for another confrontation, so swallowing her scruples she raised the gun, aiming it at her assailant's legs.

'Not another step or I *will* fire,' Helen barked.

But still the trafficker kept coming.

'I mean it, Leyla...'

Her assailant was now only ten feet away, so gritting her teeth, Helen squeezed the trigger, determined to subdue her opponent.

Click.

To Helen's horror, the chamber was empty. Shocked, she pulled the trigger again. Then a third time. But the result was always the same, the hammer clicking pointlessly on the empty chambers. Looking up, she was surprised to see that her antagonist was smiling.

'Oh, they're never loaded on site. Can't risk damaging the merchandise, can we?' Leyla gloated, chuckling darkly at Helen's surprise.

Alarmed, Helen raised the butt of the gun to strike, but she was too slow, the chain slamming into her cheek. Reeling, she staggered backwards, but a second blow to her neck felled her and she collapsed to the ground. Her attacker took full advantage, pinning Helen down with a heavy boot, whilst whirling the chain above her head. She now had Helen completely at her mercy.

And this time her nemesis planned to finish the job.

Chapter 96

Viyan hammered at her metal prison, each blow robbing her of energy and resolve. The temperature inside the incinerator was intense now, wave after wave of searing hot air ripping over her. Terrified, desperate, she maintained her assault, but slowly, inexorably, she was running out of power. Sweat poured from her brow now, stinging her eyes, the salt bitter on her lips. Her clothes clung to her as if she'd been for a swim, cloying and uncomfortable, impeding her movement, dragging at her arms and pressing down on her chest. Had she imagined hearing shouting outside? The sound of someone thundering towards the incinerator? It seemed so for now all she could hear was the triumphant clanking of the deadly machine as it pushed the temperature remorselessly up, up, up.

Her eyes were burning now and Viyan clamped them shut, desperate to find some relief from the assault on her failing body. It was getting hard to breathe in here and she exhaled heavily, but the air she expelled was hot and unpleasant. Finally, her resolve deserted her, her desperate hammering petering out in the face of total failure. Now she simply clawed at the burning metal, her fingertips stinging violently as her skin was seared off, and pulling her hands away, she collapsed to the floor in a cloud of ash.

For a moment, Viyan was transported back to her wedding

day, the particles of dirt reminding her of the rose petals that had been thrown over her as she stood with her husband, smiling nervously at him. Those had been happy times, as had the miraculous joy of giving birth to Salman, Aasmah and Defne, her greatest achievements and perhaps all she would have to show for her short, difficult life. It seemed incredible, impossible that she should end her days in such an appalling fashion, but Viyan knew in her heart now that there would be no escape. Even down here on the floor the temperature in the giant metal can was beyond endurance and there was nothing the young mother could do now, but whisper her children's names and pray for a swift death.

Chapter 97

There would be no escape now.

Emilia gripped the steering wheel as she watched the Scania truck indicate left before executing a long, lazy turn into the freight lane at Southampton docks. Her prey was in the port system and once he'd passed the initial barriers, there would be no way out. He would have police and border officials in front of him and behind him dozens of carefully concealed officers fanning out to cut off his retreat. He would be caught like a rat in a trap.

Slowing her Corsa, Emilia dawdled at the entrance, aware that a hatchback turning into the freight channel would inevitably attract attention. She was not concerned for herself, she could deal with the immigration staff, but she *was* worried about alerting her nemesis to her presence, before he'd passed the threshold into the port proper. She was a little concerned that he might already have clocked her, the covering traffic accelerating past his truck on an open patch of road a mile or so before the docks. The sudden braking of his lorry had almost propelled her into the back of him, Emilia half-convinced that she'd clocked her quarry's concerned face in one of the side mirrors. Panicked, she'd eased off on the gas, her mind frantically role-playing alternative endgames if the Dutchman changed course. Mercifully, progress thereafter had been smooth and uneventful,

Emilia hanging back before happily merging with passenger and freight traffic as they approached the docks.

Now the chase was nearly over. Crawling past the entry to the freight terminal, Emilia was pleased to see the man she now knew to be Matthijs Visser chatting amiably with the Border Force official, who wore a broad smile as he confirmed the haulier's passage and checked his passport. Emilia took in the scene, savouring the moment. For years, she'd wondered who her nemesis was and now, following her phone call with the police, she had her answer. Whether Matthijs Visser was his real name or not, Emilia couldn't be sure, but it felt good to have something to call her attacker, a label which made him feel real, tangible, fallible. The man himself seemed supremely relaxed today, smiling broadly as the port official waved him through. And then he was gone, the lorry picking up speed as it roared away from the booth. So much the better, Emilia thought to herself, he'll be in handcuffs quicker that way.

It had been a long journey to this point for her, physically, emotionally, psychologically, but it was nearly at an end. Soon he would be behind bars where he belonged, receiving the same pitiless treatment he'd meted out to her father. He would rage, he would protest, but most of all he would *suffer*, his liberty taken from him, his future snuffed out. How Emilia would enjoy that, how she would revel in her triumph. He had won the early rounds, causing her enormous pain and hardship, but she had landed the final blow. And how did the saying go?

She who laughs last, laughs longest.

Chapter 98

This was it then. The moment of truth.

Charlie watched on, tense and expectant, as the truck moved purposefully towards them. Visser was stuck in the main freight thoroughfare now, queuing lorries on either side of him forming a channel from which he could not escape, his vehicle hemmed in on all sides. So far the seasoned trafficker seemed unaware of the danger, hurrying towards them as if eager to be on the ferry and heading home. But Visser would be going nowhere today, the assembled officers from MIT and Border Force would make sure of that.

'Team A, stand by, please, over.'

'Standing by, over,' came the crackled response.

Turning to her own unit, who were concealed nearby, poised with stingers and a mobile roadblock, she raised the radio to her lips once more.

'Team B, stand by, over.'

'Ready when you are, boss,' came DC McAndrews' excited reply.

Finally, she cast an eye towards the pair of patrol cars concealed behind the dock buildings, their engines humming, radioing the drivers quickly to ensure they were ready for action. Satisfied, Charlie turned her attention back to the lorry, which was maintaining its healthy speed. She and her team were ready to receive Visser, the important thing now was to cut off any chance of a retreat. Such a course of action seemed highly unlikely, as he would have to reverse some two hundred yards up a very narrow corridor, but it wouldn't do to take any chances. There was too much riding on this.

'Team A, it's a go. Repeat, it's a go . . .'

A combined team of MIT and Border Force officers sprang into action, appearing at the entrance to the corridor, some fifty feet behind the advancing lorry, laying down stingers before sliding the heavy mobile roadblock into place, a weighty and effective insurance policy. Curious, Charlie returned her attention to the speeding truck, keen to see if Visser had spotted this first move by his pursuers. But the sun was strong today, glinting wickedly off the windscreen, rendering it impossible to clock Visser's response. There seemed to be no marked reaction to the sudden burst of police activity, the lorry maintaining its brisk pace as it swept towards them. Surely he would have to slow soon to avoid having to brake sharply at the last minute, a manoeuvre which might send him skidding dangerously into the embarkation zone. He was certainly driving punchily, even recklessly. Just how keen was this guy to get away?

And now Charlie felt her first shiver of alarm. He was going to stop, wasn't he? Initially, she'd put his concerted speed down to a desire to flee Southampton. Now she wasn't so sure. The lorry thundered on towards them, seemingly oblivious to the stop sign at the end of the lane, veering slightly off course now as it did so. Had Visser lost control of the steering? His truck had drifted ever so slightly to the right, moving perilously close to the neighbouring line of vehicles. Charlie held her breath as it got closer and closer to the idling lorries, before a shriek of metal announced that his truck had clipped one of them. Glancing off it, the lorry righted itself, before drifting to the left, nudging off another lorry, this time taking the wing mirror clean off.

What the hell was happening? Was he panicking? Drunk? Was it possible even that he'd passed out? Whatever the reason for his erratic driving, he was now bearing down on the end of the narrow lane, seemingly with no intention of stopping.

'Team B, go, go go...' Charlie shouted into the radio, suddenly alarmed beyond measure.

Emerging from their hiding places, DC McAndrew and her colleagues threw out the stingers, even as their Border Force colleagues wheeled out the temporary roadblock. Behind them the two patrol cars pulled up sharply, completing the barrier. There was no way out for Visser now and turning back to the vehicle, Charlie expected, hoped, to see a reaction, but still the massive articulated lorry hurtled towards them.

'Back, back, back. Everybody *back*...' Charlie screamed.

What the hell was Visser thinking? If their intel was correct, he had a huge shipment of hazardous waste on board. Did he think that that would somehow buy him passage, that the threat of a collision would force them to retreat? Surely not, it was madness. Was he trying to go out in a blaze of glory then? That also seemed unlikely – Visser was experienced, canny, a survivor. What then was going on? What was his game plan here? Had he somehow not seen them?

Taking a snap decision, Charlie stepped out into the lane, warrant card raised in one hand, gesturing frantically with her free hand for him to stop. But still he came, cannoning off another vehicle as the heavy truck bore down on her. Shouting in frustration, Charlie leapt out the way just in time, buffeted savagely by the sidewind as the vehicle tore past her. Stumbling backwards, she nevertheless managed to stay upright, craning round to follow the vehicle's progress. The lorry roared over the stinger, its tyres hissing as the air was punched from them, before slamming into the roadblock. The heavy metal obstacle crunched into the front of the cab, dramatically slowing its progress, as the lorry reared up in the air. Such was its velocity and power that the truck now crested the barrier, smashing down heavily on the other side, before crashing to a stop into the awaiting patrol cars, bending metal and shattering glass.

Her heart in her mouth, Charlie raced towards the savage collision, relieved to see that the startled occupants were already emerging from the patrol cars, shaken but clearly unhurt. Hurdling the mangled roadblock, Charlie raced to the stationary lorry, fizzing with anger. How dare Visser put innocent lives at stake in his desperate attempt to escape? How far gone was he? Pulling out her baton, she jumped up onto the cab, seized the passenger door and threw it open.

'Right, you piece of sh—'

The words died in her mouth. Incredibly, the cab was empty. Stunned, Charlie tried to process what she was seeing. A football scarf had been tied to the steering wheel, the other end secured to the headrest of the empty driver's seat. Beneath this, a long steering lock had been jammed up against the accelerator, ensuring the gas remained pressed firmly down. Visser was not blind to the threat posed by Charlie and her officers, nor was he minded to go out in a suicidal blaze of glory. Quite the opposite, in fact.

He intended to escape.

Chapter 99

There was no let-up, no reprieve, no escape from the savage blows which rained down on her. Disoriented, desperate, Helen writhed in the dirt, twisting and turning to try and avoid the relentless assault, but each time the chain seemed to evade her defences. A wicked blow to the small of her back made her buck, rearing up in pain, opening up new angles of attack. The wicked chain now slammed into the side of her head, causing Helen to cry out. Breathless, reeling, she scuttled backwards, her hand held up in a futile attempt to defend herself. But in the confusion, she had lost her bearings, jarring her shoulder harshly now as she collided with the unyielding bulk of the metal incinerator.

'There's nowhere to run, Helen,' her assailant crowed, whirling the chain viciously. 'Nowhere to go. This is it for you…'

'Go to Hell,' Helen fired back, spitting blood onto the floor, even as she tried to raise herself once more.

'Oh, it's not me that'll be going to Hell…' her attacker laughed, delivering another savage blow.

Helen slumped to the ground, the world seeming to spin round her now. All thoughts of rescue, of victory, were fast ebbing away as she realized now that she stood on the brink of disaster. Viyan was probably already dead and she would shortly follow her, her defences shattered, her resistance broken. The only question was how long Leyla would make her suffer first.

'You shouldn't have stuck your nose in, Helen. I did *try* to warn you...'

Once more the chain descended, slamming into Helen's stomach, punching the breath from her.

'But you wouldn't be told...'

The chain landed again, ripping into Helen's cheek, shredding skin and muscle. Howling, Helen turned away, but only succeeded in pressing her other cheek into the burning metal behind her, causing her to cry out in pain.

Cackling, her tormentor swung the chain high over her head, spinning it faster and faster, intent on inflicting maximum damage. A couple more blows and it would surely be over, her victory complete. Desperately, Helen threw up a hand as the chain descended, the weapon connecting sharply with her palm, before wrapping itself around her traumatized knuckles. Despite the pain that ripped up her arm, Helen felt a momentary spasm of relief. The longer the chain was caught around her fingers, the longer she'd be spared from further attack. Instinctively, she clenched her fist, holding on fast to the chain.

'Get your dirty fingers off that,' her attacker roared, prompting Helen to tighten her grip.

Leyla tugged violently at the chain, but Helen refused to budge, pulling back with equal force. In her heart she knew that if she let go of the chain again, it would all be over. She had to hang on at all costs. Her assailant seemed to sense this, pulling on the metal links with all her might, wrenching Helen's arm upwards sharply. Helen felt something pop in her shoulder and cried out once more, but the chain remained locked firmly in her fist. Summoning all her energy, she yanked it towards her, unbalancing her attacker, and another sharp tug saw Leyla tumbling forwards, crashing down onto her victim. Helen's tormentor was not done yet, however, grabbing the trailing tail of the chain with both hands and pressing it firmly against her bruised throat. Surprised, Helen gasped and choked, what little breath she had left now squeezed from her. An intolerable pressure on her throat was now matched by a burning sensation on the back of her head. Assaulted on all sides, Helen felt the fight going out of her, as an enraged Leyla pressed down ever harder.

'I said you were going to Hell...' she hissed, her eyes glinting wickedly.

She leaned into Helen as she spoke, her eyes riven with violence. She was on the cusp of victory, of squeezing the life out of her adversary, and was clearly enjoying it. Helen could smell burning now, her skin singed and cracked, even as she felt her windpipe protest under the intolerable pressure. Desperately, she tugged at the chain, but could get no purchase, the links biting into her skin. Panicked, she flailed wildly, her damaged fingers connecting harmlessly with her attacker's face, then her long, black hair. In a last, desperate act of defiance now, Helen wrapped her fingers round one of Leyla's tresses, yanking it towards her. Enraged, in pain, her assailant tried to tug herself free, but Helen pulled harder, moving her attacker's face ever closer to the wall of the incinerator. At first, Leyla seemed confused, then realizing what Helen intended, tried desperately to pull away. But the momentum was with Helen now, pressing her attacker's exposed cheek against the burning hot metal. Immediately, she felt the chain go slack, but still Helen didn't relent, pressing her attacker's face harder still into the searing flank of the incinerator. Leyla was howling now, the skin seared from her cheek, but Helen kept up the pressure for five seconds, ten seconds, twenty seconds before suddenly releasing her grip. The traumatized trafficker peeled away, staggering backwards, her hand clamped to her melting face, Helen clambering to her feet and sweeping out her assailant's legs with one graceful kick.

Surprised, Leyla crashed to the ground, sending up a cloud of dirt. Helen was quickly upon her, snatching up the discarded chain and delivering one, two, three savage blows. Her blood was up, all the agony and anguish of the past few days pouring out of her as she rained down blow after blow. As she raised the chain once more, however, her eyes fell on the woman's blistered cheek, and instantly all thoughts of revenge evaporated, Helen dropping the chain like a hot coal. Turning, she raced back to the incinerator, and hauling the heavy lock lever up, threw open the door.

Instantly a wave of heat erupted out of its gaping jaws, sending Helen staggering backwards as she tried to penetrate the gloom within. Was it all over? Had all this been for nothing?

Was she too late?

Chapter 100

She sprinted across the tarmac, racing towards the docks. Behind her, Emilia could hear the angry shouts of the Border Force officials, but she ignored them, confident that she had enough of a head start to evade them. Having confused the immigration officials by jogging up to the freight terminal without a vehicle, she'd startled them still further by ducking under the barrier and making a run for it. She'd no doubt have to answer for her trespass at some point, but right now her sole focus was getting to the scene of the crash.

What on earth had happened? Was her nemesis even still alive? Or had Emilia been robbed of her sweet moment of revenge at the eleventh hour? She'd parked up at the entry to the freight terminal and was waiting impatiently for news from Charlie when she heard it. A cacophonous eruption of shrieking metal and shattering glass. Instantly she knew it was Visser. That there had been an almighty collision. The only question now was with what? Or perhaps with whom? Alarmed, Emilia had abandoned her vehicle and taken to her heels. Now all thoughts of waiting evaporated, she had to know if anyone had been hurt, or God forbid, killed. She had to know what had gone *wrong*.

Racing past the parked lorries, Emilia searched desperately for the site of the collision. Already, surprised hauliers were emerging from their vehicles, concerned no doubt for the people involved in the crash, but also perhaps for the impact on their departure time. As a group they seemed to be descending on the main embarkation point, so bursting past them, Emilia sprinted in that direction. What on earth would she find when she got there? When she'd spoken to Charlie earlier, everything had seemed so simple, so straightforward. And when she'd watched Visser pull into the docks, chatting amiably with the immigration officials, everything had appeared settled in their favour. He had walked into the trap and would shortly be in police custody, destined to answer for his many crimes.

But as Emilia rounded the final lorry in the long snake of freight traffic, she saw instantly that this would not be the case. The mangled remains of the truck's cab was pressed up against two badly damaged police cars, the lorry's dangerous cargo jacknifed behind, the connecting axel having warped on impact. It was an impressive, yet deeply worrying sight, several tons of reinforced metal crumpled and destroyed, not to mention two police cars damaged beyond repair. As she tore towards the scene of devastation, Emilia's feet crunched on endless shards of broken glass, her fears rising with each passing step. Surely Visser couldn't have survived such a savage impact? Had the mad bastard chosen death before dishonour?

But even as this unpleasant thought landed, it was instantly dispelled. The breathless journalist had expected to see police officers and Border Force officials climbing all over the vehicle, trying to extract Visser, attempting to make the lorry safe. But to her surprise, she now saw that the assembled law enforcement officers were fanning out, some charging up the empty corridor between the parked lorries, others sprinting off in the direction of the docks, radios clamped to their lips, as they cast about them desperately. It couldn't be, could it? The fleeing Dutchman couldn't have escaped after such a violent impact. It seemed impossible and yet, as Emilia's eyes met Charlie's, she knew that she was right. Somehow the trafficker had wriggled out of the trap that had been laid for him and now looked set to evade justice once more. Emilia burned with anger and frustration, her plan in tatters. How had he escaped? How had he slipped through their fingers?

And where the hell was he now?

Chapter *101*

'I need an answer. And I need it *now*.'

Visser hissed the words at the startled seaman, who stared blankly at him, shocked by both his sudden appearance and his surprising proposal.

'You do speak English, right?' Visser persisted, moving a step closer.

'Yes, of course,' the young man managed in response.

'So, do we have a deal or not? This is a one-time offer, believe me, and you need to give me an answer right now.'

'You want passage on our ship?' the Polish seaman asked, gesturing to the vast container ship that loomed behind them in the docks beyond.

'I want to get to the Continent,' Visser repeated, keeping his voice low. 'No questions asked. No passenger logs, no immigration checks, no issues of any kind. If you can do that for me, I will pay you well, trust me...'

A sudden noise behind them made them both look up sharply, a stevedore roaring past on a forklift truck. Alarmed, Visser took the seaman by the arm, ushering him out of sight behind a packing crate.

'Well?' he demanded impatiently. 'What do you say?'

The young man looked at him, wary, uncertain. For the first

time, Visser felt a shiver of alarm. Had he picked the wrong guy? Had he unwittingly managed to find the one honest seaman in the whole of Southampton?

'How much?' the young man asked, scrutinizing the trafficker's face.

'Two thousand pounds now, two thousand when I'm free and clear on the other side.'

'Five,' came the instant response, putting paid to the notion that the young sailor might have qualms about breaking the law. 'Five now, five on arrival.'

Visser glared at him, well aware that the boyish seaman was rinsing him, taking full advantage of his precarious situation.

'OK then,' he muttered angrily. 'You tell me where and when and I'll be there.'

'Money first. You have it on you?'

Now for the first time, Visser hesitated. What if this young man simply intended to rob him, leaving him high and dry, without any resources to attempt an escape? And yet what choice did he have? Even now Visser could hear shouting from the docks, as dozens of law enforcement officers swept the warehouses and docksides looking for him. So far his plan had worked well, jumping from his speeding lorry as it raced down the corridor of trucks towards certain ambush, buying him precious seconds to make good his escape. But how long could his luck hold out? How long before they descended on him, hauling him away in cuffs? He needed to get away from here *fast*.

'Have it your way,' he grumbled, turning away. Deftly, he unbuttoned his shirt to reveal the money belt strapped to his torso. Then running a finger down the bulky stash of £50 notes, he extracted a large bundle, counting them out rapidly, before zipping up his hoard once more. Re-buttoning his shirt, he pivoted, thrusting the notes into his accomplice's hand.

Surprised, an amused smile playing over his face, the young Pole methodically checked his haul, before looking up at Visser, holding out a meaty hand.

'Departure in thirty minutes.'

Pocketing the money, the sailor walked off whistling to himself, his happiness shared by his new accomplice. Against all the odds, Visser now had a chance to evade his pursuers. And he planned to make the most of it.

Chapter 102

'Come on, Viyan, *please*...'

Helen crouched over the injured woman, desperately searching for signs of life. But her appeal fell on deaf ears, the young mother remaining lifeless and still. Leaning down, Helen parted Viyan's lips, cupping her ash-smeared face as she blew blasts of oxygen into her damaged lungs. But her kiss of life had no effect at all.

She had got to her too late. The time wasted besting Leyla's thugs, then the gangmaster herself, had cost both Helen and Viyan dear. Having been blown off her feet by the eruption of heat, Helen had scrambled back up, racing round to smash the prominent red button on the control panel, killing all power to the machine. Limping back to the open doorway, Helen had bravely stepped inside, shielding her eyes, her face, holding up her arm to deflect the savage blasts of heat that ripped over her. It was impossibly hot inside, Helen's skin prickling in agony, every instinct in her body urging her to turn and flee the inferno, but pressing on, she collided with Viyan, lying face down in the dirt.

Grasping her arm, she felt the skin shift beneath her fingers as if it might slide clean off, but forcing down her unease, she dragged the unconscious mother to the door, lifting her over

419

the treacherous lip and out into the fresh air. The temperature change rocked Helen once more. Dizzy, she sank to her knees, turning her attention to the badly burnt worker. To her dismay, the change in temperature had not stirred Viyan, who remained motionless, her blank face turned up to the sky. Most of the exposed parts of the poor young woman were cracked and blistered, but fortunately her face had not been so badly damaged, perhaps because it had been pressed down into a thick layer of ash. Seizing on this, Helen had set to work once more, desperately trying to revive her, but to no effect, all her efforts falling short. How she cursed herself now for not getting here sooner. If she had, then things might have been different. But her tardiness had proved fatal, the incinerator putting paid to another life.

Agonized, Helen laid Viyan's body gently onto the ground, before turning to advance on her killer, determined to vent her burning rage on the floored trafficker. To her surprise, however, Helen realized that she was too late. The yard was now a writhing sea of violence, a pitched battle taking place between the oppressed workers and their minders. For months the threat of a bullet between the eyes had kept the masses in check, but having realized they had been duped, that the guns were not loaded on site, they had thrown themselves at their captors, sensing that liberation was finally at hand. Leyla's arrogance, her cocksureness, had come back to haunt her, her own words releasing the workers from her thrall. Some of the guards were trying to hold their own, others had already fled, realizing the game was up. Which meant that Leyla no longer had anyone to protect her.

The gangmaster lay on the ground, ten yards away from Helen, clutching her face and groaning loudly, but already the vultures were circling, a couple of the desperate workers standing directly over her. Having suffered under her pitiless yoke for so long, they now had the upper hand and planned to exact their revenge.

'No, no, no...'

Helen was already on the move, urging the pair not to give into their growing bloodlust. But one of the assailants now struck Leyla, stamping violently on her floored adversary.

'Please don't...' Helen cried out. 'Let me handle this.'

Others had now realized what was happening, joining the attack in growing numbers. And though some also called for caution, mercy even, trying to pull the aggressors away, they were in the minority. There was a murderous fire in the eyes of the growing mob. They wanted justice. They wanted revenge.

Still Helen pushed through the crowd, grasping desperately at the trailing arm of a young woman, who'd just picked up a rock. She wanted to still her violence, make her see reason, but Helen now felt herself being dragged back, before being thrown roughly to the ground, her way to Leyla blocked off by the encircling group of workers.

Terrified, Leyla made a desperate attempt to free herself from the clutches of her attackers, but catching hold of her, they threw her to the ground with a roar of anger. Lying on her back in the dust, breathless and immobile, Helen caught sight of the gangmaster as a trio of irate workers descended upon her. Leyla tried to cry out, to raise an arm to defend herself, but it was hopeless, the women falling on her, hammering her with fist and foot. Their violence was immediate and extreme, Leyla shrieking out in terror and pain, before suddenly falling silent. Was she already dead? Helen hoped so, because the frenzied group now fell upon her, tugging at her hair, tearing at her ears, determined to rip her limb from limb. Sickened, Helen turned away, unwilling to witness this brutal end. Perhaps Leyla deserved an agonizing death, but this wasn't justice, this was vengeance, and she wanted no part of it.

Turning away, Helen crawled back to Viyan's body, her sense of defeat total. Even as she did so, she heard one last blood-curdling scream that seemed to echo around the farmstead, as if the unfortunate Leyla was dying a dozen gruesome deaths. And it was as this piercing noise was slowly dying away that Helen noticed something. Viyan's right hand had started to twitch. Stunned, Helen scrabbled over to her, cupping the young woman's head in her hands.

'Viyan, Viyan. It's me, Helen. Can you hear me?'

Helen scanned her face, hoping against hope that this beautiful woman might live, might somehow survive this awful nightmare. There was no response. Helen couldn't believe it. Had her mind tricked her? Then slowly, almost reluctantly, opened her eyes.

Chapter 103

'Has anyone got eyes on him?'

Charlie had dispensed with the protocol of addressing each team individually, such was her desperation. But her general appeal yielded nothing.

'No sightings currently,' DC McAndrew announced, her desolation clear.

'Same here,' DC Roberts concurred, his voice crackly but distinct. 'He's vanished into thin air.'

Cursing, Charlie lowered her radio, scanning the dockside urgently for any sign of their quarry. But the scene in front of her seemed entirely normal and workaday, dockers and stevedores going about their business largely unconcerned. If Charlie had her way she'd demand that they all down tools immediately and join the search, in fact if she had any power here she'd close the whole bloody port down until Visser was found. But the port authorities had already made it plain that *that* was not going to happen, meaning Charlie and her team were now engaged in a desperate race against time.

There were over a dozen ships due to set sail today, some of them in the next few hours. If he was smart, Visser would try to board one of these vessels, either sneaking directly onto the ship itself or hiding out in a container lorry queuing to board.

She had already dispatched officers to the ships that were due to leave imminently, paying particular attention to one bound for Amsterdam, but who was to say he would target that boat? Maybe he'd head to France first, or Belgium, before making his way home? Or perhaps he'd head further afield to Spain or Scandinavia to really throw them off the scent? That was assuming he was still on site, of course, that he hadn't found a weak point in the port's perimeter to slip back into the city.

Chiding herself for her defeatism, Charlie pushed away this last notion. Visser knew that the game was up, that Viyan's intervention would prove crucial in the dismantling of this horrific trafficking operation. He had no associates, no cronies here, his network was back in his hometown of Rotterdam. Surely he would have to head there as soon as possible, especially as there was now an international warrant out for his arrest? His best chance of escape lay here, amidst the hustle and bustle of the busy port complex. But which ship would he target and how would he make good his escape?

Striding along the quayside, Charlie frantically scanned the workers before her, seeking Visser's now familiar form. But already she felt like she was looking for a needle in a haystack. The port covered three hundred and seventy-five acres of land and employed thousands of people daily. With only a dozen of her officers combing the site, how on earth were they supposed to cover all bases? To cut off all escape routes? In her mind's eye, Charlie could already picture Visser sneaking up the boarding ramp or secreting himself in a lifeboat, privately congratulating himself on his wit and ingenuity. The thought made her blood boil. Surely they couldn't let him just slip away after all the blood, sweat and tears they'd exhausted in identifying and locating him? Was all that hard work, all that pain, really going to be for nothing?

Upping her pace, she hurried along the quayside, her eyes crawling over a large container ship bound for Denmark. This ship was due to leave within the hour, its walkways and ramps alive with sun-kissed sailors who called out to each other in Polish, laughing and joking, buoyed by thoughts of their departure. None of her officers had yet made it here, so Charlie paused, her eyes raking over every inch of the battered vessel, searching for some anomaly, something out of the ordinary, that might direct her attention to a trespasser on board. But there was nothing that seemed remotely out of place and cursing, she turned away.

Moving on, she pushed into the huge warehouse that bordered the dockside. This would be a fantastic place to hide out, endless rows of crates and containers waiting to be dispatched, a makeshift maze of assorted goods from around the world. Suddenly, Charlie felt very small, very insignificant, framed by the huge expanse of cargo, the cavernous warehouse seeming to grow in front of her eyes, mocking her with its vastness. Robbed of all energy, she stood stock-still, defeated and despondent, letting the sights, the sounds, the smells of the huge space wash over her, her failure all too obvious. They had had Visser in their clutches, but he had vanished into the ether, perhaps never to be seen again.

And yet it was as she was standing there, forlorn and helpless, that she noticed something. Or, more accurately, smelt something. There were a host of competing aromas in the atmospheric warehouse, from the aged timber of the crates to the salty tang of the sea air, but this smell was different. Pungent, rich, aromatic. The memory of something Helen had said to her now stirred in Charlie and she held her nose to the air, trying to work out from which direction the aroma was coming. Padding slowly forward, she seemed to lose the scent almost immediately, pausing to change direction before picking it up again as she moved to the right-hand wall of the warehouse. Convinced she was on the right track, she picked up the pace now, but even as she did so, her radio crackled into life. Shocked, she reached down to turn it off, managing to kill it before it revealed her presence. Slowing her breathing, she crept on, padding as quietly as she could, the rich smell of tobacco smoke growing stronger with each passing second. She was making her way to the far back corner, into the darkest recesses of the warehouse, her heart thumping now as she proceeded cautiously, but purposefully, forwards. She was sure she wasn't imagining the smell, that her mind wasn't playing tricks on her, Viyan's reported testimony that Visser smoked Dutch cigars now fresh in her mind. Was it possible that he was really here? That she might yet snatch victory from the jaws of defeat?

The smell was strong now. Creeping up to the edge of a crate close by the rear corner of the warehouse, slowly, cautiously, she peered round the edge, fervently praying that the gods were on her side today.

And, to her immense surprise, there he was. It was Visser, no doubt about it, casually smoking the thin cigar as if he had not a care in the world. Oddly the sight filled Charlie with anger – what right did he have to be so relaxed, so insouciant when her officers were frantically searching high and low for him? When he had conspired to abuse, exploit and degrade so many innocent people? Gritting her teeth, she crept forwards, inching her way towards him. She was only twenty feet away from him, the trafficker's face turned to the wall as he blew plumes of smoke into the air, contemplating the way they danced and dissipated above him. Visser seemed utterly transfixed, revelling in his own invulnerability, totally unaware of the danger he was in.

Taking great care with each step, Charlie continued to move

towards him. The floor was rough and dirty, splinters of wood and bits of gravel decorating the surface, but tiptoeing between them, Charlie continued to make good progress. Her heart was pounding, her fingers slippery with sweat as she now eased the handcuffs from her belt. She was now only five feet from her quarry, but he remained oblivious, his hand resting on his belt as he drew the cigar to his lips, drawing in deeply. Did she spot a slight shift in his head position? A sidewise glance in her direction? Either way, she didn't hesitate, stepping forward boldly as she declared:

'Matthijs Visser, you are under arrest for—'

But she didn't get any further, the desperate fugitive spinning on his heel and driving a knife into her chest.

Chapter 104

They were battered, they were bruised, but they had *won*.

All was chaos in the dusty farmyard as the liberated workers embraced their freedom. High on blood lust, ecstatic, they tore through the farmhouse, gorging themselves on the delights of the kitchen, pulling clothes from the wardrobes, revelling in the piping hot water, but Helen ignored this gruesome carnival, doggedly placing one foot in front of the other as she made her way to the main gates. The ambulance was on its way and all that mattered now was getting Viyan to safety. Despite her rapidly fading strength, Helen cradled the young mother in her arms, determined to deliver her personally into the care of the paramedics.

Despite the meagre weight of the emaciated worker, Helen found the going incredibly hard. She had been burned, beaten and strangled, her aching, beleaguered body already a riot of bruising, and she swayed back and forth as she staggered towards the road. This had been one of the darkest, most difficult days of her life and it was hard to summon the resolve to keep going, her buckling legs threatening to give out at any point. Despite this, she kept moving, her mission, her purpose clear. Viyan, a young mother of three, needed help and Helen was going to ensure she got it. If Viyan survived this, if she managed to recover, to embrace her life again, then perhaps some good could be culled from the wreckage.

This is what propelled Helen on now, the image of Viyan reunited with her children once more. Their joyous, youthful faces had been such a tonic first thing this morning and she clung to their exuberance now, imagining the overwhelming happiness and relief Viyan and her family would feel when reunited. Although she had a long road to travel, Viyan's cruel nightmare was over and with a bit of luck and a lot of determination, a better future awaited her. Helen had money and though she knew instinctively that Viyan would not want charity, there was nothing to stop her getting the young mother and her family back on their feet. A terrible natural disaster had driven Viyan into the hands of the worst of humanity. It was Helen's job now to show that in the end goodness, love and compassion always prevailed.

Sweat creasing her filthy brow, Helen battled on. To her immense relief, however, she now saw blue lights up ahead, an ambulance bumping down the dirt track towards them, a police car close behind. Now finally, she admitted defeat, dropping to one knee to rest, as she continued to cradle the injured woman. Moments later, the ambulance pulled up alongside them, the doors flying open as the paramedics hurried over.

'Twenty-seven-year-old female, with severe burns and possible damage to lungs. Her name's Viyan and she's from Turkey. She has no family here, so for now I'm your point of contact. My name is—'

'We know who you are, DI Grace,' the paramedic replied, smiling warmly. 'Right, Viyan, let's get you to hospital ASAP, shall we?'

Stepping forward the young paramedic and his colleague gently hoisted Viyan from Helen's arm, transferring her swiftly to the back of the ambulance. Rising to her feet and dusting herself off, Helen felt an uncharacteristic surge of pride, pleased that the paramedics had recognized her, that her service and dedication to the people of Southampton had not been entirely forgotten. She was still the woman she'd always been, capable of doing good, of protecting the weak and the vulnerable, of making a difference.

The ambulance was already on its way, blues and twos blaring, a curious PC now making his way over from his patrol car towards her. Helen had a long, strange tale to tell him, but as she prepared to recount her recent adventures, her phone started buzzing urgently in her pocket. Tugging it out, she was surprised to see that it was DC McAndrew calling.

'Hello Ellie,' Helen said brightly, as she answered the call. 'Have you got your Dutchman in cuffs yet?'

There was a long, pregnant silence, DC McAndrew's short, gasping breathing the only sound.

'Ellie, are you OK? What's wrong?' Helen demanded, suddenly on edge.

'I'm fine,' she gasped, her voice riven with anguish. 'It's Charlie.'

Helen froze, a sickening, terrifying fear stealing over her. Her voice shaking, she demanded:

'What do you mean? What's happened to her?'

Helen waited breathlessly for a response, her heart pounding in her chest. But DC McAndrew didn't respond, couldn't respond, simply bursting into tears instead.

Chapter 105

'Don't you die on me. Don't you *dare* die on me.'

Emilia hissed the words at Charlie, her desperation rendering her pleas harsh and urgent. If she could command the fallen officer to survive by sheer force of will alone, she would do so, but Charlie was slipping away and she knew it.

Emilia was hunched over the new head of the MIT, who lay on the dockside outside a cavernous warehouse, in a pool of her own blood. The sticky, crimson trail from within the building told of her erratic progress, the injured police officer just about making it out of the storage area before collapsing in a heap on the ground. Still Charlie's life force seemed to flow from a nasty wound in her chest, so Emilia redoubled her efforts, increasing the pressure on the wound, rich, dark blood seeping through her fingers. Cursing, panicking, she tugged off her jumper and held it tight to the wound, the rich, luxuriant wool greedily sucking up the viscous liquid. If she just kept the pressure on, if she kept her conscious until the ambulance arrived, there was a chance, wasn't there?

'How long until the ambulance gets here?' Emilia barked, but when she looked up, she saw only anguish on DC Roberts' face.

'Five minutes, maybe a touch more,' he replied, stricken.

'That's too long, that's too bloody long.'

The fresh-faced DC stared back at her, helpless and forlorn, agonized by his powerlessness. Behind him, DC McAndrew appeared equally poleaxed, weeping copiously as she spoke urgently into her phone. In truth, Emilia felt much the same way, still desperately trying to process what was happening. She had been the first to spot Charlie, as she raced along the dockside, desperately searching for the missing fugitive. Confused at first by the MIT chief's odd gait and jerky movements, she had been shocked to see her collapse to the ground. As she tore over the rough concrete towards her, she prayed that she'd simply fainted or at worse been struck by Visser. For a moment, she was tempted to continue into the warehouse in pursuit of him, but the sight of the blood pooling around the fallen officer had stopped the journalist in her tracks. Horrified, Emilia had immediately gone to Charlie's aid, waving the approaching DCs into the warehouse. Visser had vanished, however. Only his grim handiwork remained, coughing and gasping in Emilia's arms.

'Come on, Charlie, stay with me ...'

Emilia's tone was stern, urgent, but it elicited no reaction, as Charlie slid into unconsciousness. The journalist had had her run-ins with the new DI in the past, but had never disliked her, finding her always fair, committed and honest. She also knew that Charlie had a partner and two daughters, who stood on the brink of catastrophe. Pressing down hard on the wound, Emilia felt more determined than ever to save this young woman, to ensure that her death wasn't Visser's final insult. It was she who had summoned Charlie and her team here, she who had followed him into their carefully laid trap, she who would be responsible if anything happened to Charlie.

'Come on, Charlie, I know you can do this ...'

Once more she glanced up at the growing crowd of by-standers, who looked as distraught and desperate as she was, then beyond them to the port entrance. There was plenty of activity there, but still no sign of an ambulance. Where the hell were they? Didn't they realize how urgent the situation was?

Returning her attention to Charlie, Emilia was alarmed to see that the fallen officer had gone slack in her arms, her head lolling backwards. Panicked, Emilia removed her right hand, shoving two blood-stained fingers onto the side of her throat, desperately searching for signs of life. For a moment, time seemed to stand still, all present falling silent, until finally DC McAndrew's voice cut through, tentative and fearful:

'What's happening? Is she going to make it?'

Devastated, Emilia turned to face her. No words were required, her stricken expression giving the clearest of answers. There was no pulse.

Chapter 106

Visser threw back his head and roared with laughter. He had done it. He had escaped.

His body was suddenly convulsed with mirth, all the tension and agony of the past few hours pouring from him, as he revelled in his triumph. Even though he was hidden away in the bowels of the ship, concealed behind endless boxes of cleaning equipment in a tiny, cramped store cupboard, with no window or access to air, there was no question that they *were* moving. A celebratory blast of the foghorn had signalled their departure, yet still Visser waited impatiently for signs of momentum, of speed, of action. It was subtle at first, the ship taking a while to reach its cruising speed as it exited cautiously from the docks, but now there was no doubt about it. They were on their way to Denmark.

It was a profound relief, after the worst couple of days of his life. His meeting with Emilia Garanita had been horrendous, not simply because of the unconscionable insults she rained down on him, but more because of his overriding feeling that he was missing something, that unbeknownst to him she had played some trick on him, a feeling that had only grown when he later discovered that she was tailing him. How else could she have found him unless she was tracking him in some way? Paranoid, anxious, he had taken the precaution of dumping his clothes in favour of sailor's overalls, remembering also to toss his knife into the murky waters of the harbour as he slipped onto the ship. It had served its purpose and there was no point holding on to anything incriminating now.

Emilia's close attention had been bad enough, but things had really gone south when that Turkish whore escaped from the hospital. The desperate act had provoked an avalanche of unfortunate consequences, not least the severing of his relationship with Leyla and the collapse of their profitable joint venture. Thereafter, pretty much everything had gone wrong. He'd lost his truck, the gold, his beloved Feyernoord scarf and been chased halfway round Southampton docks. He'd nearly been caught, only the tiny squeak of gravel on concrete alerting him to the approaching police officer at the last second. Fortunately, his mind had been clear, and his hand true, allowing him to step over the fallen officer and be on his way to the departing ship, before anyone could apprehend him. For a moment, his mind flitted back to the sprawled woman, her face ashen, her chest oozing blood, wondering what had happened to her. But then he realized he neither knew nor cared, so pushed the image from his mind.

She was the price of his freedom and that was all there was to it. He had no idea what he would do once he got to Copenhagen, how he might slip off the vessel unseen, how he would make his way back to his native Rotterdam undetected. He had a yearning now to be back amongst his own people, in the city's boisterous bars, enjoying a glass of bockbier and a smoke. That was where he belonged, where he was safe, it was there that he needed to be right now. Leaning back against the humming wall of the storeroom, Visser toyed with his last remaining cigar, imagining the joy it would bring him as he set foot on dry land once more, lighting it up in triumph. It would be a fitting celebration following his lucky escape and he intended to enjoy it to the full.

Unlike the fallen officer on the dockside, he would live to fight another day.

Epilogue

Chapter 107

Would they be scared? Would they cry out in terror? Or would they simply turn away in disgust? With the help of the wonderful nurses in the burns unit, Viyan had tried her best to make herself presentable, but she still feared how her children would react to seeing their mother like this, swathed in bandages, hooked up to machines, unable to lift her arms to wave hello. Salman, Defne and Aasmah were familiar with trauma and suffering, sadly, but still Viyan worried about the effect her injuries would have on them. Having seen her three days ago, looking tired, thin, but defiant, how would they react when they saw her now, lying in a hospital bed, brutalized and bandaged?

Swallowing down her fears, Viyan chided herself for her foolishness. Yes, she had suffered grievously, only cheating death at the last minute. Yes, she was in agony, with severe burns to forty per cent of her body. But the fact was that she was lucky to be here at all. Unlike poor Selima, she had *escaped* the diabolical incinerator, dragged from the darkness into the light. What's more, her face was largely unharmed, the ashen remains of those who had gone before her shielding Viyan's delicate features from the worst ravages of the heat. This was not only a huge relief in terms of her sense of self, her identity, it would also markedly improve the speed of her recovery and rehabilitation, as she could eat normally and communicate freely. Given the extremity and desperation of her situation during her final hours on Dearham Farm, this was a major saving grace, a huge positive to pull from her terrible ordeal. And never had words been more apt – she had been saved by Helen Grace. It was thanks to her and her alone that she could embrace her future, heal her wounds and be reunited with her family again.

Unable to move her head, Viyan blinked at Peter, the kindly Kenyan nurse, who pressed 'Connect' on the phone that Helen had given her. Immediately, Viyan's heart started to pound in her chest. She knew she should be feeling an enormous sense of relief, of triumph even, but instead she felt anxious and tense. Her nemesis was dead and the farm shut down, her fellow captives freed from their living nightmare, yet the shadow of Viyan's experiences there lingered, leaving her unsettled, mistrustful and fearful. Though she was now free, she was finding it hard to embrace her good fortune, even though preparations were in hand to transfer her to a specialist hospital in Turkey. Helen had said she would pay for all her expenses and Viyan believed her, but still she expected the twist in the tail. Could it really be *true* that her nightmare was over?

In front of her, the screen now sprang into life, revealing a joyful, chaotic scene. Viyan's mother could be glimpsed in the background, holding the phone up in her wobbling hand, but in front of her the smiling trio of Aasmah, Defne and Salman jostled for position. Instinctively, Viyan returned the compliment, breaking into a heartfelt smile, only to wince as pain arrowed down the side of her face into her neck. It was pure agony, but she didn't relent, determined that her children should see that she was happy, safe and well. Her subterfuge was not entirely successful, however, the trio pausing as they took in her sterile surroundings, her bandages, her pale face.

Salman in particular looked troubled, his bottom lip beginning to quiver, but sensing the danger, Aasmah took over, placing an arm around her little brother, reassuring him that Mama was fine and would be coming home soon. For a moment, Salman seemed to hesitate, uncertain whether to believe his sister, but a gentle prod from Defne brought him to his senses. Snapping into action, he bent down out of sight, reappearing clutching a posy of wild flowers, offering the explosion of colour up to the camera, as if he could pass them through the lens to his mother.

Now tears flowed, running down Viyan's features and sliding off her chin. She cried freely, generously, joyfully. Though separated for now, her family would soon be together again, united, happy, optimistic for the future. The forces of darkness had tried to destroy Viyan, life had tried to break her, but both had failed. She had withstood the onslaught, weathered the storm, taken her punishment.

She had *survived*.

Chapter 108

Death. Pain. Suffering. Emilia had been surrounded by these dark forces for as long as she could remember, but never had she felt their presence so keenly as she did today.

For the first time in her life, Emilia genuinely felt that she might not be able to cope. She had endured all manner of injuries and insults over the years, emerging victorious and defiant each time, but the avalanche of misfortune that had cascaded over her in the past three days beggared belief. First had come Ernesto's unexpected death, then the botched operation at the dockside culminating in Visser's shocking escape. And finally, worst of all, there'd been the brutal stabbing of Charlie Brooks, the fallen officer now fighting for her life in ICU. Though Emilia had never been close to her, this last outrage cut deepest. This brave and resourceful officer had simply been doing her duty, yet Visser had seen fit to thrust a knife into her chest in his desperation to evade capture. Emilia's heart broke for Charlie, and she raged against Visser, her eyes filling with angry tears as memories of that awful, blood-soaked scene on the quayside pushed their way back into her thoughts.

Wiping her eyes, Emilia stalked along the hospital corridor, her trainers squeaking noisily. She'd wanted to visit before now, but she'd barely had time to catch her breath since the disaster at the docks. First, she'd had to endure lengthy questioning at Southampton Central, as Charlie's colleagues tried to make sense of what had happened. Though exhausted and upset, Emilia had not complained during the many hours of discussion and repetition, determined to do her duty. For their part, Rebecca Holmes and her colleagues in CID had been unfailingly polite and responsive, Emilia detecting a marked change in their attitude towards her, their gratitude for her heroic efforts on the quayside plain to see. Following her departure from Southampton Central, Emilia had had to run the gauntlet of the press, who swarmed around her, desperate for the inside story. She'd been a journalist for many years, but only now realised what it truly felt like to be in the eye of the storm.

Thereafter, Emilia had been sucked back into family life, trying to make sense of recent events for her shocked siblings, whilst simultaneously trying to plan for her father's funeral. There was so much to do, so much to process, not least how to say goodbye to a man she had often hated. Emilia's head was already swimming with details of all the things she needed to organize, all the people she needed to contact, and was relieved to tear herself away from the preparations for a while in order to check on Charlie's condition.

A noise ahead made Emilia look up and she now spotted Helen Grace walking away from the ICU, her expression set, her face solemn. Immediately, Emilia felt another rush of emotion, fear, horror, grief wrestling for supremacy. Was she too late? Had Charlie lost the fight? Helen continued to march towards her, clocking the journalist but barely reacting, as if her mind was elsewhere. Nevertheless, her former sparring partner slowed as the two women approached each other, Helen's sad nod speaking volumes. Emilia was almost too afraid to ask, but found herself muttering:

'How is she?'

Helen's expression was grave and her words, when they came, were measured.

'She ... she's fighting.'

She was trying to be positive, but to Emilia it sounded like it was a fight Helen expected Charlie to lose.

'The surgeon said the knife missed her heart by a millimetre, hence why she's still alive. But she lost an *awful* lot of blood and is still in a coma.'

Helen's voice shook, Emilia shocked to see her naked emotion. In all the years that they'd locked horns together, the former DI had never shown any vulnerability in front of her. But now there was no hiding it – Helen looked desperate, anguished, grief tinging her every word.

'Honestly, Emilia, it's not looking good, but every second she clings on is a plus. If she can hang in there, if she can stay strong, then ...'

Emilia nodded vigorously, willing the fallen police officer to find the strength to survive.

'Am I OK to ...?' Emilia asked, gesturing towards the ICU.

'Sure. You can't see much, but it would be good for someone to be there with her.'

For a minute, Emilia was tempted to ask Helen where she was going, baffled as to why she was leaving her old friend's side, but instead she simply nodded again. For once, it was not her place to pry.

'Of course,' Emilia replied reassuringly. 'I'll obviously let you know straight away if anything ...'

Her sentence petered out, neither woman wanting to contemplate a sudden change in Charlie's condition. Helen offered her thanks with a tight smile, patting Emilia briefly on the arm, before heading off. This friendliness, this strange rapprochement, was just another bizarre detail in Emilia's increasingly surreal existence, very little of which seemed to make sense anymore. But shaking off her disorientation, Emilia walked on, heading swiftly towards the ICU. She had come here to do a job and there was no point putting it off, however unnerved and unsettled she might be feeling.

Soon she was in the small viewing area opposite the ICU, exchanging brief, sympathetic nods with the other hospital visitors, who huddled in the small room, tense and fearful. Turning away from them, Emilia peered through the glass, just able to make out Charlie Brooks in the far-left hand corner. It was a sight that pierced Emilia's heart, the officer's lustrous hair now flat on her scalp, her huge, expressive eyes taped shut, her mouth straddled by a bulky breathing tube. This vibrant woman, usually such a ball of energy and emotion, was perfectly still, the only sign of life now the dancing line on her heart monitor. It was an image of quiet desolation that struck Emilia forcefully. This was what this diligent, spirited officer had been reduced to by one vicious thrust of the knife. This is what Visser had done to a healthy, happy mother of two.

And now amidst Emilia's sorrow and grief, the embers of her anger started to flare. The same man who'd tried to destroy *her* had tried to kill Charlie Brooks. Once more Visser had shown himself to be a man without scruples, without conscience, without pity. He was a monster, devoid of humanity or emotion. A fiend who remained at large to inflict yet more damage and ruin more lives. This was why Emilia knew it wasn't over yet. Whatever happened to Charlie, wherever Visser might have fled to, the journalist knew she could not let this lie. This ghastly narrative could not end in his triumph. Such an idea was outrageous, appalling, and Emilia would not sanction it. This man, who had haunted her dreams for so long, must be made to pay for his crime. Shockingly, unjustifiably, Visser had escaped justice *twice* now.

Emilia would make sure he did not do so a third time.

Chapter 109

She strode across the floor, her heavy footsteps echoing around the lobby. Startled, PC Mark Drayton looked up sharply, surprised to see Helen back at Southampton Central yet again. For once, however, there was no caustic comment, the impact of the last few days making themselves felt, the custody officer sombre and respectful today.

'Good morning. How can I help you?' Drayton asked, his voice shaking slightly.

'You can buzz me through,' Helen answered curtly, without breaking stride, her eyes locked on the staff entrance.

Without hesitation, Drayton reached under the desk and punched the button. Nodding her thanks, Helen heaved open the door, briefly clocking the relief on Drayton's face, before pushing inside.

Moments later, the lift doors slid open on the tenth floor. Helen was quick to emerge, her boots sliding over the lush carpet that smoothed the passage of the top brass in this lofty outpost. Heading fast along the corridor, she made her way to Holmes' office, the Chief Superintendent's long-suffering PA, Susan, rising from her desk on Helen's approach, her expression a mixture of surprise and alarm.

'Helen, how nice to see you. Do you have an appointment or ...?'

Holmes' gatekeeper clearly knew the answer to this, but Helen ignored her intervention, striding past her.

'You can't go in there, Helen. The Chief Super's on a call...'

But Helen barely heard her, stepping purposefully into Holmes' office and shutting the door firmly behind her.

'It's completely out of the question.'

Holmes' tone was defiant, but Helen could see the uncertainty and alarm in her eyes. It had been a difficult few days for the station chief, but she had not been expecting *this*.

'I know you're deeply upset by what's happened to Charlie, we *all* are, but it changes nothing,' the station chief continued quickly.

'On the contrary,' Helen shot back, 'it changes *everything*. Visser stabbed your best officer, my oldest friend. I will not be shut out of the hunt for this bastard. I've known Charlie too long, owe her too much, to let this go.'

'No one's letting this go,' Holmes countered vigorously. 'Visser *will* be found, he *will* be arrested, he *will* be brought to justice. We are working night and day to root him out, liaising with the NCA, Interpol, as well as with the Dutch police in Rotterdam. Our strong suspicion is that he will return to his hometown and, when he does so, the authorities will be waiting for him.'

'Who are you dealing with out there?' Helen demanded. 'Who is your point of contact in Rotterdam CID?'

'I can't tell you that,' Holmes replied sharply, shaking her head.

'So who's running it this end then?'

For a moment, Holmes appeared lost for words, stunned by the relentlessness of Helen's interrogation.

'You?' Helen continued.

'Of course not,' Holmes stammered. 'It has to be CID-led, you know that...'

'Who then?'

'Well, we're still deciding. Not that it's any of your business, but my intention was to speak first to DC McAnd—'

'It has to be me,' Helen interrupted forcefully. 'Ellie's not experienced enough, she doesn't have sufficient pull and she's never handled an international investigation.'

'Absolutely not, Helen. There's no way that—'

'I've have broken up more smuggling rings than you've had hot dinners. I've worked successfully with the Dutch police before and, let me tell you, no one will work harder to bring that piece of shit to justice.'

'Helen, can you even hear yourself?' Holmes protested indignantly. 'You're not a police officer anymore. You walked away from here. You can't just pick up the baton again when you feel like it.'

'That was then. This is now,' Helen replied, glowering at her old boss.

'No, no. It doesn't work like that. You resigned, you washed your hands of us, you don't get to call the shots. But please be under no illusion, we will pursue Visser to the ends of the earth if necessary. We will bring him to book, you have my word on that.'

'Well, apologies if I don't break into applause, but I know what your word is worth.'

Rebecca Holmes looked like she was about to explode, but Helen continued assertively:

'Empty words, empty promises. And that won't wash here. This man must be caught, he must be made to answer for his crimes and I will see that he does so. The MIT is *my* team,

Charlie's well-being is *my* responsibility, this investigation is *my* investigation.'

Helen fixed the station chief with a steely glare, as she concluded:

'I want back in.'

Credits

M.J. Alridge and Orion Fiction would like to thank everyone at Orion who worked on the publication of *Into the Fire*.

Agent
Hellie Ogden

Editorial
Emad Akhtar
Leodora Darlington
Millie Prestidge

Copyeditor
Patrick McConnell

Proofreader
Jane Donovan

Editorial Management
Jane Hughes
Charlie Panayiotou
Lucy Bilton
Patrice Nelson

Audio
Paul Stark
Louise Richardson
Georgina Cutler-Ross

Contracts
Rachel Monte
Ellie Bowker
Tabitha Gresty

Design
Tomás Almeida
Nick Shah
Deborah Francois
Helen Ewing

Photo Shoots & Image Research
Natalie Dawkins

Finance
Nick Gibson
Jasdip Nandra
Sue Baker
Tom Costello

Production
Paul Hussey
Katie Horrocks

Operations
Group Sales Operations team

Marketing
Hennah Sandhu

Publicity
Leanne Oliver
Ellen Turner

Inventory
Jo Jacobs
Dan Stevens

Sales
Dave Murphy
Victoria Laws
Esther Waters
Group Sales teams across
    Digital, Field, International
    and Non-Trade